CRY SPY

Also by William Hood

Mole
Spy Wednesday

CRY SPY

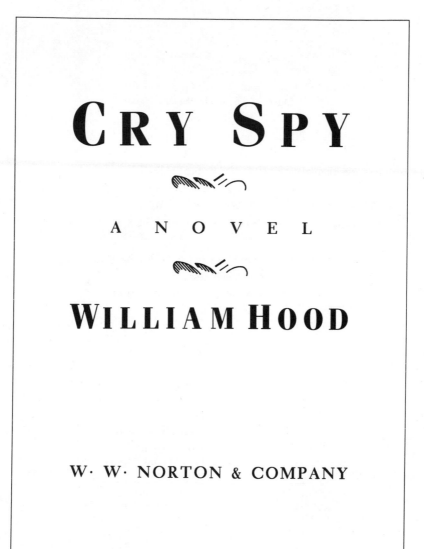

A NOVEL

WILLIAM HOOD

W· W· NORTON & COMPANY

New York   London

Library of Congress Cataloging-in-Publication Data
Hood, William, 1920–
Cry spy: a novel/by William Hood.—1st ed.
p. cm.
I. Title.
PS3558.0545C79 1990
813'54—dc20   89–8576

ISBN 0-393-02639-6

W. W. Norton & Company, Inc.
500 Fifth Avenue, New York, N. Y. 10110
W. W. Norton & Company Ltd.
37 Great Russell Street, London WC1B 3NU

For Jack Fieldhouse

"It was like the night Lester left town . . ."

ACKNOWLEDGMENTS

AT W. W. Norton, Starling Lawrence has again proved that he is the most perceptive and patient of editors. Mary Seton has been helpful throughout. Roy Doliner, a generous and gifted teacher, offered much needed encouragement. Edward and Ilse Grainger generously provided background information, as did Cameron and Linda LaClair.

"Cry spy, and sound alarum . . ."

CRY SPY

1

SMILOVICHI, NEAR MINSK
1 9 4 3

"BY the time I got there, they'd hanged the girl," Tolya said. "The body was still strung up." He shook his head. "She couldn't have been more than sixteen."

Oberleutnant Dieter Fuerst, *Frontaufklaerungstelle IV, Gruppe Walli,* detached to SS *Sonderkommando VII,* tossed a sheaf of papers onto his field desk. He knew the SS rarely bothered to hang partisans properly. They threw a length of rope over a beam, knotted a noose, and hoisted the prisoner off the ground. Death came by strangulation, and the corpse remained hanging until the SS troops left the area. "What about the others?" Fuerst asked.

"The older man was wounded when they were flushed out. The *Sturmfuehrer* said he was too far gone to bother with. They finished him off and left the body. I've got the young one outside."

"What were they carrying?"

"No radio, no equipment of any kind. They were on a scouting mission."

"That's not possible," Fuerst said abruptly. "Reconnaissance agents—observers—always travel alone."

Tolya started to protest.

Fuerst brushed him aside. "Every time we've picked up two crossers, one has been a courier who knew the area, the other a Moscow-trained agent."

"Then why were there three of them?" Tolya asked irritably.

"That's something you might have uncovered," Fuerst said. "What about documents and letters?" Colonel Gehlen, chief of *Fremde Heere Ost,* the German military intelligence staff on the Eastern Front, was almost as keen on captured personal letters as he was on Red Army documents. Even the *Landsers* in the line outfits recognized documents as important but, unless regularly reminded, few of the enlisted men remembered to take mail from prisoners. Gehlen's enthusiasm for the letters was so intense that Fuerst suspected the written comments from the home front provided the best unvarnished intelligence available on conditions in the U.S.S.R. Not that Gehlen would have admitted it to his superiors on the General Staff in Berlin.

"I said they weren't carrying *anything*," Tolya said. He turned his hands palm upward as if to show he had nothing to conceal. "What could I do in a barnyard with those *Sonderkommando* apes kicking the prisoner around?"

"Did *you* check the bodies?" The older man had probably been landed in the partisan area by light plane. But if he had parachuted in, there would be bruises on his shoulders and crotch from the harness. Along with his other faults, Tolya was lazy.

"The *Sturmfuehrer* said he had searched all three thoroughly. By the look of the girl, he had made a good job of it—she was nude." Tolya laughed appreciatively.

Tolya was a *Hilfi*, one of the *Hilfsfreiwillige*, the indigenous collaborators with the Nazi forces in Russia. His German was fluent, and he served the Wehrmacht as a Russian interpreter. Fuerst despised him.

"The three of them crossed last night," Tolya said. "They holed up at daylight in a hut, four kilometers west of the guard point on the Minsk road. The *Sonderkommando* patrol got them just after dawn. The *Sturmfuehrer* said he searched the hut for equipment, and left the body where it was. He brought the girl and *der Junge* back to the command post. When he finished playing around with the girl, he hanged her." Tolya looked expectantly at Fuerst.

But Fuerst had given Tolya too many insights into his opinion of the SS.

"That was when the gallant *Sturmfuehrer* remembered that the other prisoner might be of interest to us," Tolya said. "By the time the officer got to me, it was dark. I'm not foolish enough to give some half-crazy SS lieutenant the idea I don't think he did his job right, and I'm not going out at night to look for one stinking corpse—you know what will happen if the partisans lay hands on me."

"What about the one you got?" Fuerst asked.

"He told me he's a peasant, from a *kolkhoz* south of Borisov. He says the partisans are forcing the peasants to join them. He didn't want any part of the war and had got all the way down here when he bumped into the guy and the girl. They said they knew the area, and he decided it would be easier to go along with them." Tolya swung his arms up and mimed a gypsy playing a violin. "It's a sorry legend—his hands are soft, like a surgeon, and he can't even *imitate* peasant dialect. He's a partisan all right."

"Stop calling them partisans," Fuerst barked.

"Bandits," Tolya said with a smirk. He fixed an imaginary mono-cle in his right eye. "Special Instruction, August 23, 1942. For psychological reasons the term 'partisan' is not to be used. By order of *Oberkommando des Heeres.*" It was a reasonable imitation of the tone affected by the German General Staff officers, and Fuerst would have laughed if anyone but Tolya had done it.

Tolya peeled off his Wehrmacht greatcoat. "That was a year ago, and now there are more shitting bandits than ever." He rum-maged in the deep pockets of the greatcoat. "The bandits are pretty well equipped for bandits—the Little Father in Moscow is even flying artillery pieces into their goddamned bandit area."

He pulled a bottle of vodka from the gray coat and put it on the desk in front of Fuerst. "The spoils of battle—you want a drink?"

Fuerst shook his head. Fuerst had been on the East Front long enough to know it was bad luck to take anything but weapons from the dead.

Tolya spilled the dregs of a coffee cup onto the dirt floor of the hut and filled the cup with vodka.

"He's tough for a seventeen-year-old, I'll give him that," Tolya said. "When the patrol tossed an incendiary grenade into the shack where they were holed up, young Ivan got a pretty good burn. The skin is hanging off his arm and wrist. But aside from that ridiculous story, he hasn't said a word. He's probably behaving the way some shit NKVD commissar told him to." Tolya poured more vodka into the cup. "He does it better than most I've seen. Maybe he's too quiet."

He's wondering why he is still alive, Fuerst thought. And that's the sort of question that might keep even a Polish renegade like Tolya quiet. "Get him a dish of something hot, and have a *Sanit-aeter* check his burn. I want him back here in half an hour."

"Zu Befehl, Herr Leutnant," Tolya barked, his voice insolent with irony.

Tolya never knew when he had gone far enough.

"Ask him if he would rather be hanged as a spy or a terrorist."

The Russian stood at attention, the prescribed five feet from the field desk. He was taller than most Russian enlisted men, and beneath his ragged canvas jacket, bone-thin. The deep circles under his dark eyes threw his delicate features into sharp relief. His lips were chapped and cracked. Across his forehead, above the line left by his knit cap, his white skin was blotched with a red rash. His hair was cropped so close that Fuerst could see the splotches on his scalp. The Russian did not look at Fuerst. He kept his glance fixed on the desk.

Tolya stood behind the prisoner and to one side. He repeated Fuerst's question in Russian.

The prisoner made no sound.

Tolya repeated the question.

The Russian remained silent.

Tolya tightened his light leather gloves, shifted his weight, and swung a looping right-hand punch that caught the Russian behind the ear. He pitched sideways, falling flat as he shielded his left arm from the dirt floor of the wood-framed hut.

Tolya flexed his fingers and glanced at his pigskin glove. It had split across the knuckles. *"Scheisse,"* he said. He kicked at the Russian's shoulder. The stiff canvas jacket made a crackling sound. "Get up," Tolya screamed. "You're not lucky enough to be dead yet."

The prisoner rolled over and struggled to his feet. Beneath the charred sleeve of the jacket, Fuerst could see that the burn-blackened flesh had torn open. The Russian's forearm looked like an underdone pork roast.

"Did someone look at the burns?" Fuerst asked quietly in German.

"He wouldn't eat, so I decided not to bother."

The Russian stood, weaving slightly.

"Tell him I have many questions and very little time," Fuerst said softly.

Tolya translated.

The Russian remained silent.

"Tell him he has one more chance to answer."

The Russian cradled his burned arm. He turned to Tolya. "I must ask the officer's permission to sit."

Tolya translated.

"Get that stool," Fuerst said with relief. "We can start now." As soon as a prisoner began to talk—about anything—Fuerst knew it would be only a matter of time before he broke.

Tolya kicked the stool toward the Russian.

The Russian slumped onto the stool. Hunched over, he began to rock slightly and to hold his burned arm against his chest.

"Your name and your mission, right now," Fuerst said. He spoke softly, as if reluctant to use Russian.

"*Now,* the officer said," Tolya shouted. He jabbed at the burned sleeve. The Russian retched and began to mumble.

It wasn't much of a cover story.

Ivan Ivanovich Ivanov was, he said, the son of a schoolteacher in Leningrad. When the German troops rolled across the Soviet border he was visiting his mother's parents in Minsk. He had lingered in Minsk until the city was overrun. Months later, and afraid of being drafted as a forced laborer, he had fled to the partisan area north of Smilovichi. He tried to avoid combat, and worked as a clerk at the brigade headquarters. He had only been on two raids against the Nazi communications lines when he was ordered to guide the Moscow parachutist through the German lines to the road to Minsk. The girl, a native of Minsk, was to lead the parachutist to a safe house in the city. That was all young Ivan Ivanovich knew. He had no idea what the parachutist's mission might have been, nor where in Minsk the girl was to take him.

Ivan Ivanov spoke rapidly when he added that he had misjudged the partisans. The officers were mostly NKVD men, even worse than the Party people in Leningrad. Because he was desperate to escape from the partisan camp, he had welcomed the assignment. Once free of the older man, he planned to volunteer for labor with the German liberation forces.

Tolya was right. Fuerst knew it wasn't much of a cover story, but it would serve to set the stage for the second phase of the interrogation.

"I HAVE a proposition for you," Fuerst said. He had wrung as much routine information from the prisoner as he thought it likely he could get.

Tolya translated rapidly.

"An exchange," Fuerst said. "Your life for a little more information."

"I've told you everything," the Russian said. "There's nothing more."

"Look at the officer when you speak," Tolya shouted.

The Russian looked up at Fuerst.

"If you agree, we will pass you safely back to your own area. Once you are in bandit territory, you will have forty-eight hours to get the answers to a few questions and cross back to us." There were no fixed lines this far behind the front. The Nazi forces held the towns and villages and the main lines of communication. The partisans used the woods and swamps as base areas from which to harass the roads and railway.

In the dim light of the flickering oil lamps, Fuerst caught a hint of surprise or perhaps hope in the Russian's eyes.

"There will be little risk to you—you know the area well enough to avoid anyone who might recognize you. If your information is good, we might ask you to make another trip. Perhaps more than one. If you get the information I want, we will see that you are evacuated to Germany."

Tolya turned to Fuerst and began an angry protest. Fuerst waved him aside and told him to continue to translate. Even if the prisoner could not understand any German, the acting was broad enough to get the message across. It was a primitive technique—the correct German officer versus the savage *Hilfi*, with the prisoner's life in the bargain—but it worked.

"You will be given a job in Germany, and a chance for a new life." Fuerst wondered how even the most desperate prisoner could believe such transparent nonsense. "We will guarantee this treatment." Fuerst could not bring himself to say, "*I* will guarantee . . ."

He watched the Russian as Tolya translated.

Recruiting low-ranking prisoners as spies and sending them back across the Soviet lines was the simplest form of espionage operation. Of those who made it safely back into the partisan area, not one in ten ever returned to his German controller. Those who did come back had usually turned themselves in, or been uncovered by the NKVD officers, and redoubled against the Germans. Only a handful of the surviving line-crossers provided enough information to justify the effort. But, as in most intelligence operations, there was always the possibility that the *next* agent might provide worthwhile information.

In his frustration, Fuerst had improved on the operational doctrine he had learned at the *Abwehr* training school near Brandenburg. He had discovered that once a prisoner accepted the idea that the Germans would actually send him back across the lines to his own forces, the Russian considered the desperate game over, and that by some miracle he had won a kind of victory over his tormentors. The prospect of returning made the prisoner subconsciously grateful to his interrogator, and seemed to sap his resistance. Fuerst had learned to intensify his questioning at this point, and it was in these final sessions that he and Tolya elicited the data that had won praise from Colonel Gehlen himself.

When this second interrogation was finished, Fuerst would decide if the prisoner was alert and intelligent enough to bother sending back across the line. If he was dispatched and returned successfully, the prisoner would have no choice but to continue until the game ended, on one side of the line or the other. If he refused, and was sent to a prison cage, he would starve to death.

"I'M taking a risk in sending you back," Fuerst said. "If you do not return, I will be in trouble."

Again Tolya slipped into his act, remonstrating vigorously.

"I'll come back," the Russian said. "If I turn myself in the NKVD will know you would not have sent me back unless I gave you information. They will shoot me. I have no choice."

"There's something else," Fuerst said quietly. "Before you leave, I want one more piece of information."

The Russian glanced from Fuerst to Tolya.

"Leave us for a moment," Fuerst said to Tolya. With a shrugged protest, Tolya stepped outside.

"To protect myself, I must have some assurance you will come back," Fuerst said. His Russian was slow and heavily accented, but the prisoner nodded his understanding.

Fuerst pulled a photomosaic and small-scale map of the partisan territory from his desk. The heavily wooded area was thirty kilometers deep.

"Show me the exact position of your brigade headquarters."

The Russian's eyes opened wide and his mouth moved as if he were struggling to keep from responding.

This was the breaking point. Fuerst had no intention of letting the prisoner linger on it.

"Before you speak," Fuerst said deliberately, "it is only fair to tell you that this is a test." He paused, wondering how any prisoner could think that fairness played a part in interrogation. "If you lie, we will know about it within twenty-four hours, and you will go straight back to the SS." Fuerst began to speak even more slowly, ostensibly struggling to phrase each sentence carefully. "You have *one* chance—if you are right, I will assume that I have your loyalty."

Ivan Ivanovich Ivanov bent forward, cradling his arm. A thin, keening sound came from his cracked lips. He looked up, about to speak. But Fuerst cut him off. "There is one more consideration," he said.

The Russian was motionless.

"Before we pass you back through our lines, we will attack the headquarters," Fuerst said quietly. "If we fail, I will know that you deliberately misled us."

Ivanov remained silent and motionless until, with a sudden movement, he seized the photomap with his good hand. Peering closely at the mosaic, he twisted the map, and began to orient himself.

THE radio transmission was weak and choked with static. SS *Standartenfuehrer* Zeiss slammed his hand on the desk. *"Der schoene* Mueller has done it," he roared. "It was brigade headquarters. He has six prisoners, the radios, and all their damned documents." The SS colonel clapped Fuerst lightly on the shoulder. "If you want the truth, I thought you were talking the usual intelligence piffle. But you can tell your red-stripe Colonel Gehlen that this is a coup. A real stroke against them."

THROUGH the clumsy night glasses he considered all but useless, Sergeant Pieck strained to keep the prisoner in view as the Russian picked his way across the rough field toward the woods, three hundred meters to the northeast. Now, in the half-light, with the Russian almost out of sight, Pieck thought he saw the prisoner veer to the west, away from the slight fold in the terrain that Pieck had carefully pointed out. Shit, he thought, if he's too dumb to follow that track, it's his ass. The way he's headed, he'll be back on the

Minsk road in three hours. Pieck closed his eyes and lowered the glasses. He kept his eyes closed for the prescribed eight seconds and raised the glasses again. He scanned the area from west to east. When he was finally satisfied there was no movement, he turned, and crept silently back through the brush-choked gully.

Pieck was a veteran reconnaissance man, but he had no patience with complicated reports. He had delivered the Russian to the jumping-off point, and he had observed his movement for at least three hundred meters. Under the circumstances, it did not seem worth mentioning the possibility that the Russian might not have returned to his own lines.

"For a seventeen-year-old, he was a smart one," Tolya said. "Even his phony name, Ivan, son of Ivan Ivanov . . ."

If Fuerst had liked Tolya he would have told him about the photomosaic. Except for officers, young Ivan Ivanov was the only Russian prisoner Fuerst had ever interrogated who could read a photomap as casually as if it were a copy of *Red Star.* Fuerst had little doubt that he was a trained agent, on a special mission and dispatched from Moscow to the partisan area. But Fuerst was tired of the war and sick of killing. One brave young agent would not make any difference.

"Christ, it's already getting cold," Tolya said. He kicked at the wood stove in the corner of the hut. A shower of sparks spilled onto the dirt floor. "At least he was smart enough to save his life—for a few days anyway."

"He swapped their headquarters for something he thought was more important," Fuerst said quietly. "Maybe it *was* his life. Maybe it was something else."

Tolya laughed. "Whatever it was, it isn't anything he can ever explain—the commissars won't think much of his protecting his secret at their expense." He slumped back in his chair. "What do you think, are we ever going to see him again?"

Fuerst reached for the brandy. It was French cognac. Only the best for the men at the front.

———

ON September 23rd, *Reichskommissar* Wilhelm Kube, the most notorious of the Nazi officials appointed by Hitler to administer the conquered territories in the U.S.S.R., was blown to pieces in the bedroom of his sumptuous quarters in Minsk. His eighteen-year-old mistress, Olga Petrovna, who planted the bomb beneath the bed, died with Kube.

An urgent message from Colonel Gehlen informed all intelligence and security forces on the East Front that, by order of the Fuehrer, information leading to the arrest of the assassins was a first priority. Gehlen was particularly interested in learning how the explosives got to Minsk.

First Lieutenant Dieter Fuerst sniffed. "No matter what Marshall Timoshenko is planning, we're supposed to drop all intelligence collection and play policeman looking for the murderers of that fat swine in Minsk."

Before Fuerst could transmit a negative report to Gehlen, a second urgent message was received. In view of the increased bandit activity along the Minsk highway, and the heavy buildup of Soviet forces in the sector, Lieutenant Fuerst was to move west with *Sonderkommando VII.*

2

LONDON

1 9 8 6

PETER GANDY slipped into his trench coat, squinted briefly at the notices board, and stepped out of the Special Forces Club.

The invitation from Paul and Betsy Wilder was for drinks. December the tenth. Six to eight. Regrets only. No one would be there at six, and if he arrived by 6:30 he would still be among the first. That would be all right. Aside from the Wilders, and perhaps Alan and Emily Trosper, he would not know anyone. He could stay long enough for three, maybe four, stiff whiskeys and still catch the 8:30 train to Gerrards Cross. He would be home before ten. By that time most of the whiskey would have worn off, not that Placide would say anything anyway.

As he paused on the marble and brick steps to hitch at the collar of his coat, Gandy turned slightly. Just enough to give him a glimpse along the gentle curve of Hans Crescent.

Stupid, damned anachronistic reflexes, he told himself. Two years out of the racket and still checking for Indians. He wondered how many of the old lags leaving the club took a look along the street.

It was raining, a chilling London rain, made colder by the gusting December winds.

But there *was* a man leaning against the iron railing around Hans Place Garden, across the street, and a hundred yards from the club. And now that he thought about it, there certainly *had* been someone, just enough out of place with the bicycle to have caught his eye, at Gerrards Cross on Monday a week ago. He could not have imagined two separate incidents.

Gandy bent against the blowing rain and hurried along to Sloane

Street. He glanced at the rush of traffic and continued down Sloane to Pont Street, near the entrance to the Cadogan Hotel. As he waited for the light to change, he remembered that it was at the Cadogan that Oscar Wilde was arrested. He sniffed, and glanced along Sloane Street toward Knightsbridge. Except for a solitary, rain-soaked figure, sheltering under a metal awning, there was no one behind him. Gandy corrected himself. He could not see anyone behind him.

It would not be more than a five-minute walk from Pont Street to the Wilders' flat in Wilton Crescent. Which meant there was still time for a quick whiskey at the Turk's Head. As soon as he could get away from the traffic crowding along Sloane Street it would be darker, and whoever might be behind him would have to move closer. If he did a spin near the pub, he might even catch a glimpse of the tail.

But he had had three drinks at the club. If he stopped at the pub, he would have had four whiskeys before he even got to the Wilders' flat. This would mean holding himself to two drinks there and remembering to tuck into the hors d'oeuvres. The Wilders lived high off the right end of the hog, and Gandy knew there would be smoked salmon and pâté from Fortnum's. There was nothing like expensive food to blot up a tot too much whiskey.

He walked thirty paces past the Turk's Head and then, whirling abruptly, retraced his steps. It was a proper spin. Gandy chuckled and ducked into the saloon bar.

Pulling off his dripping tweed hat, he eased his way to the bar. "A large Bells, soda and a bit of ice," he said. The barmaid pushed the siphon and ice bucket toward him on the bar and turned to the bottles mounted in the dispenser rack.

There was at least one thing to be said for December in London. The odds were twenty to one against there being a fly in the ice. A sprinkling of cigarette ash was something else—at best that would be an even-money bet.

Gandy picked up his drink, glanced around the crowded room, and slowly made his way to the fireplace where he could watch the door.

He took a sip of his drink. It could not have been his imagination. He hadn't been out of the racket that long. As he had completed his spin, and retraced his steps, he had caught *two* men just at the edge of his line of sight. If they were professionals, they were damned well walking too slowly to be convincing on a night as wet as this.

But it made no sense. The Brits knew he had retired. Duff Whyte had seen to that. A few weeks after he was named Controller, Whyte had sent a letter to the Limeys' new head man. It was part of Whyte's tidying up after replacing Bates as head of the Firm. Later, on a trip to London, Whyte had shown Gandy a copy of the letter. This wasn't just courtesy to an old colleague. It was Whyte's way of reminding Gandy that the Firm had vouched for him and that he was to keep his nose clean in the U.K.

Since everything had been done according to protocol, the bloody Brits should damned well know that he was out of it, once and forever. And after his more than twenty-five years in the racket, they had a good enough book on him to know that he was not likely to piss in his own mess kit by free-lancing in the U.K. Besides, for all their posturing, the faithful cousins didn't have the resources to waste two more or less competent Indians on the tail of someone they knew as well as Peter Gandy. If the Limeys wanted something, all they had to do was telephone and ask him to stop by for a chat.

The hell with it. He pushed his way back to the bar and ordered another large whiskey. The hell with being retired. And the hell with trying to stop drinking.

It was like Paul Wilder, Gandy mused, to have spent most of his career as a goddamned owl, to take early retirement, and then to land a job with a public relations outfit. It was a case man's dream—a job that came with a posh, rent-free flat on the edge of Belgravia, and spank on the London gold coast.

But for all Wilder's pretenses, he was okay. It was decent of him to have sent the invitation to "Mr. and Mrs. Peter Gandy." Wilder knew that Placide had never accepted a drinks invitation, and he damned well knew there was nothing that Gandy, almost two years into retirement, could do for him.

Now he was late. Gandy took a final swig of whiskey, balanced the empty glass on the narrow shelf beside the fireplace, and pulled on his tweed hat. He eased his way to the door.

The rain had thickened. He hurried along Kinnerton Street and slanted for Belgrave Mews. If he had the geography straight, he could nip through the mews and come out a hundred yards from the Wilders' front door.

But he had it wrong. The mews was a dead end. Gandy slowed his pace. Now he would have no choice but to turn and possibly confront . . .

The rain-soaked hat cushioned the blow which caught him behind the right ear. As Gandy's knees buckled, the man behind yoked his forearm under Gandy's chin, choking off his scream for help. The thick lining of Gandy's trench coat absorbed some of a savage punch to his kidneys.

Gandy kicked backwards, but his shoe slipped on the rain-slick cobblestones. Half-conscious, he tore at the arm across his throat.

A second man, his cap pulled far down on his forehead, stepped in front of Gandy, and set himself as deliberately as if he were working out on a heavy training bag. He threw short left- and right-hand punches that landed inches below the cinched belt of Gandy's coat. Then, lifting his gloved hands, he ripped the coat open and clawed for the wallet in Gandy's breast pocket.

Gandy lashed out, trying to hit the man with the back of his wrist. The man blocked the stroke and set himself to throw another punch. Gandy twisted to avoid the blow and kicked backwards again at the unseen assailant's shins. He heard a hoarse curse as the half-moon cleat on his leather heel dug into the man's shins, and he felt a sharp burning along the back of his neck. The bastard behind had a knife, maybe an ice pick. Warm blood ran from the cut.

Gandy lifted both feet from the cobblestones and tried once more to kick backwards. Sour vomit sprayed from his mouth as the man behind yanked his arm from Gandy's throat and pitched him forward onto the cobbled pavement. He felt his watch being torn from his left wrist and could see the man pull bank notes and credit cards from the wallet before tossing it onto the pavement.

If they are going to kill me, it will be now—kicks to the head if they are muggers, or two shots from a silenced .22 if they are professionals.

He wondered, and not for the first time in his life, if this was the end. What a silly-ass way to go out.

The wet cobblestone was cold against his cheek. He closed his eyes.

In the distance he heard a woman scream. There was the sound of running footsteps in the narrow mews. A man shouted.

Maybe it wasn't all over. Gandy decided to rest a little longer before trying to get up.

LATER he would remember that the man who hit him wore a belted, single-breasted mackinaw. He did not even get a glimpse of the second man, the one behind who had cut his neck.

3

LONDON

"This was supposed to be a quiet service," Alan Trosper muttered as he guided Emily to a pew in the cold church. "I can see the headlines now—'Spy Establishment Honors Byron "Bunty" Myles.'"

"Stop grumbling," Emily said. "The *Times* will be more discreet. 'Myles Memorial Service, Lieutenant General Sir Thomas Bandury Reads Eulogy,' will be lively enough for its readers." She looked slowly around the rapidly filling church. "Do you recognize many of these people?"

"Some of them," Trosper said. "They're mostly people who worked with Myles. The old man had an absolute genius for inspiring loyalty." He nodded toward the front of the church. "The fellow beside Lady Myles is Leslie Barking-Jones. He recently took over a shop modeled very much on my old outfit."

"And the handsome young devil beside him?"

"The guy in the black suit and old-boy tie?"

Emily nodded. "Old Harrovian, I think."

"He's probably an aide, maybe a bodyguard. Although I don't see how he could wear a gun under a suit that fits as if it had been cut a thread at a time."

A score of veterans, most of whom dated back to the wartime organization, were scattered among the senior military and naval officers in uniform in the front pews. The chief of the security service and his wife were seated close to Lady Myles, and Trosper could see a number of old security hands among the guests.

The local station chief, who could scarcely ever have met Bunty Myles, represented the Agency. At a discreet distance, Charlie Pottle, chief of the Firm's London office, sat with his wife, a vacuous California blond with the iron smile of a cheerleader.

In stiff dark suits and black ties, a handful of pensioned Eastern European émigrés, survivors of the cold war, had slipped into widely separated places at the side. Their weathered Slavic features were conspicuous among the Anglo gentry.

"Who are the others," Emily persisted.

"Some of the older women might have been beavers," Trosper said. "During the war your people called the women who ran the file rooms and did the research 'beavers.' "

"Who else?"

In for a penny, Trosper thought, and said, "I think I can see a couple of waffle-bottoms."

"You're making this up . . ."

"Not at all, waffle-bottom was OSS slang for communications people. I wouldn't be surprised if it was still used."

"Who else?"

Trosper laughed. "The most attractive women may have been cipherenes . . ."

"Uh-huh . . ."

"I mean it," Trosper said. "About the time Hitler moved into Poland and the British declared war, Myles is supposed to have recruited a bunch of well-born young women as code clerks. It was National Service and probably more exciting than driving a staff car or emptying bedpans." He laughed again. "From what I've heard some of those who served abroad married very well, what with their bosses being so far from home and all."

Toward the rear of the group, Trosper recognized a cluster of younger case men, none of whom had brought their wives.

When the service ended, Barking-Jones spoke briefly to Lady Myles and then hurried out the massive front door. Trosper waited until the family had left and then followed the émigrés and case men to the exit at the side of the church, away from the handful of photographers and spectators clustered on the steps.

As Trosper and Emily threaded their way through the group at the side of the church, he noticed two or three of the older case men greet the émigrés and exchange a few words—offering promises, he guessed, of a lunch or dinner that would never happen. Remembering the scrupulous loyalty that Myles showed everyone he worked with, Trosper wondered if the old man might not have wished that someone from his service had thought to see that each of the pensioned agents was greeted and taken to lunch. It would have been a decent and professional gesture.

"Who is the tiny woman tugging at the arm of that fellow in the bowler?" Emily asked as they stepped into the street at the side of the church.

Trosper peered toward the group at the front of the church and said, "It looks like Peter Gandy's wife. It's odd, but I haven't spotted Peter here." He could see Paul Wilder turn from Mrs. Gandy and begin to pump Barking-Jones's hand. When Wilder moved to speak to Charlie Pottle, he glimpsed Trosper in the distance and, signaling vigorously, beckoned him to join the group on the steps.

Trosper waved a greeting and hustled Emily into a taxi.

EMILY BEAUFORT TROSPER wrote with an old-fashioned fountain pen and dark blue ink. Her bold, clearly formed script with its boarding school cachet was quite different from the usual, crabbed English scrawl that Alan Trosper could never be sure he had deciphered correctly.

"Back in time for tea my darling," her note read. "Your chum 'Mr. Paul Wilder' telephoned twice—*please* call him." And then in a P.S., she asked, "Why *do* you Americans announce yourselves as 'Mister' on the telephone? Isn't Paul Wilder good enough?"

Trosper hung his coat on the hall rack and picked up the mail. Not the least of the advantages in being out of the racket was the blessed freedom from the telephone. It had been almost four years since he had been leashed to a telephone beeper twenty-four hours a day. Somerset Maugham, he recalled, had observed that when someone leaves a message instructing you to call at once, it is certain that the matter in question is of more importance to him than it is to you, and it is equally sure that he will soon telephone again.

He was in no rush to call Wilder. Emily would be home soon and he looked forward to tea. It was still a matter of some wonder for Trosper to realize how much he liked being married to Emily and how warmly he embraced the developing rituals of their marriage.

"WAS he at the memorial service, the fellow in the bowler?" Emily asked.

"Paul Wilder," Trosper said. "Bowler, brolly, and Betsy. After eighteen years, he still calls Betsy his 'bride.' "

"It's probably chauvinism," Emily said, "but I think Americans look funny in bowlers."

"We used to say that when an American buys a bowler he's gone bloke, and that it's past time for him to leave the U.K."

She poured the tea. "He seemed to know everybody . . ."

"He does give that impression."

"Who is he exactly?" Emily asked. "I don't recall you ever mentioning his name."

"Wilder was an owl," Trosper said. "When he wasn't coordinating papers in Washington, his job was to sit in committee meetings."

"I can't believe you."

Trosper shook his head. "A few months after the Firm was established, Darcy Odlum realized how much time he was spending in committee meetings where things were supposed to be coordinated. He picked a couple of presentable fellows and knighted them 'Assistants for Coordination.' Their job was to go to meetings, look wise, and then give him a one-paragraph report on what, if anything, had been decided. It wasn't long before someone began calling them Odlum's Owls."

"That couldn't have been very nice for them," Emily said, laughing.

"There was a much ruder version," Trosper said. He put down his cup. "For some people one of the advantages to being in the racket is that no one on the outside is ever certain where you stand in the hierarchy. If you've got the cash to support a decent house and do some entertaining, outsiders figure you're important. If you need that sort of thing, the Firm makes a better social platform than a job at State or in the Pentagon where everyone in Washington knows exactly where you rank." He smiled. "Wilder had the necessary tickets—he's bright enough, his wife is rich, and he went to Princeton."

"All the same," she said, "you really ought to telephone him."

Trosper asked for more tea before he reminded Emily of what Maugham had said.

EMILY picked up the telephone. "He just this minute came in," she said. "Score a point for Willie Maugham," she added, her hand over the mouthpiece.

Wilder spoke in a rich baritone. "Sorry I couldn't get to you this morning," he said. "But I was rather caught up with LBJ and one of his side boys . . ."

"Who?"

"LBJ—Leslie Barking-Jones. Where have you been the last few months?"

"LBJ . . . of course, I should have known," Trosper muttered.

"I was talking to LBJ when Placide dashed up . . ."

"Who?"

"For heaven's sake, Alan—Placide Gandy, Peter's wife. She had something for you."

"That's odd . . ."

"She had a letter from Peter, but she couldn't find you in all that crowd. She gave it to me as second best."

Trosper was baffled. "You'd better drop it in the mail."

Wilder laughed. "It's all wrapped up, Scotch tape, two envelopes—real Category One, Denied Area, security stuff. I hardly think Peter would approve my trusting it to Her Majesty's postal service."

There was no point in telling Wilder that if Gandy had followed real Category One procedures, the letter would have been casually sealed and inconspicuous. He might even have used a postcard with one of the Firm's old "Request Contact" codes scrawled on it.

"If you can do lunch tomorrow," Wilder said, "I'll be able to tell Peter that I gave your letter the complete to-be-passed-by-hand-of-cleared-courier-only treatment. Come to White's."

"If you wish," Trosper said.

"We can have a chinwag, and you can tell me all about your new job."

Chinwag indeed. Trosper wondered if Wilder wore his bowler while telephoning, or on the blower, as he would surely say.

"At one o'clock," Wilder said. "You know where White's is?"

"If it's still where it has been for the last two hundred years, I think I can find it," Trosper said.

4

LONDON

TROSPER hated to be late, even for what he knew would be a long two hours of gossip and interrogation. He didn't give a damn who had what job in the Firm, and he wasn't in the least interested in how well Wilder might think Duff Whyte, the new Controller, was doing. He hurried up St. James's, glanced appreciatively at the bowed windows, and sprinted up the steps to the paneled door. The club porter hesitated for an instant and then said, "Mr. Trosper, sir. It's good to see you again."

"Hello, Martin. You're looking fit." It was true. The porter was no exception to the rule that whatever other changes might have occurred, well-established English functionaries and servants always seemed frozen at the age one had first encountered them.

"Will you be back with us again, Mr. Trosper?"

"Yes, Martin, just as soon as I get settled in a bit. Right now, I'm meeting Mr. Wilder."

"He'll be in the bar, sir." He hesitated a moment. "I read about your good news. Your lady's father, Colonel Beaufort, was with us for years. My very best wishes."

"Thank you, Martin. That's very kind."

The number of people who bothered to read social announcements was an endless matter of surprise. It was Emily's mother who had insisted on the announcement and notice in the *Times*.

"PETER was actually on his way to our flat when it happened."

Trosper looked up from his plate of potted shrimp. "I hadn't heard a thing about it."

"A mugging like that is not the sort of thing the press takes much notice of over here." Wilder took a sip of the Hock he had described as "sensibly full-bodied."

"Was Peter hurt at all?"

"I don't think so. At least he didn't make anything of it in the note he sent explaining why he had missed our little drinks party," Wilder said.

"Didn't Placide say anything about it when she spoke to you at the memorial?"

"Not a word," Wilder said. "She dashed up, thrust the letter into my hand, and whispered that Peter had told her to give it to you as soon as possible. She couldn't find you in the crowd and decided to trust me to pass it along." He took another appreciative swallow of wine. "I suppose that may have been the only decision Placide ever took on her own."

"It's odd he didn't mail it," Trosper said. "If Peter doesn't have my address, he could easily have got it."

"I had expected to see Peter at Bunty's services," Wilder said. "As I understand it, Bunty was still a fan of Peter's, even though they were both involved in that flap in Paris."

Trosper glanced across the table at Wilder, who was grinding pepper onto a remaining morsel of smoked salmon. He wondered why Wilder, who was intelligent enough, and wily in a quiet way, persisted in presenting himself as a fool. Trosper had known General Myles for fifteen years, but had never referred to him as Bunty. He knew that what Wilder called the flap in Paris was one of the most successful defensive operations the Firm ever ran. Thanks largely to Peter Gandy, a kidnapping had been aborted so deftly that one of the goons who attempted to set it up realized that he had no alternative but to defect. As it turned out, this thug had been involved in at least one assassination, and had come straight from old Colonel Khoteyev's outfit. He gave the interrogators the only firsthand information the Firm ever got from the Kuchino poison shop.

Wilder perceived Trosper's silence and said quickly, "Of course, what I meant was the tangle with the French police after the car crash."

"The General respected Gandy," Trosper said, "and he had good reason to do so."

Like many whose careers had been on the periphery of operations, Wilder had the annoying habit of foraging for gossip. He was like a puppy nuzzling for handouts, and it irritated Trosper even more to realize that he had almost given Wilder enough data to make his next telling of the tale even more effective.

"Club grub," Wilder muttered as he took a bite of the grilled sole.

"Mine's delicious," Trosper said.

"What about Placide? I've always thought she was something of a lefty."

"I've never known her that well," Trosper said. "But I doubt she's ever been very political."

"That's as may be, but I don't think I've ever seen her without one of those pins she wears. At Bunty's memorial she had a big 'Vivisection Is Torture' button on her coat."

Trosper laughed. "She probably thought some of those geriatric brass hats would have had strokes if she had sported her 'Ban The Bomb' and 'No Nukes' badges," he said. "On the other hand," he added, " 'Boycott U.S. Chicken' might have gone over pretty well."

"Frankly, I never could understand how Odlum let Gandy get away with it," Wilder said.

He should not have come to lunch. He should have told Wilder to mail the damned letter and have done with it.

"Get away with what?"

"You know as well as I do," Wilder said. "Placide always made a point of avoiding every social contact with anyone in the Firm, she's an out-and-out vegetarian, and in my book just as eccentric as they come." He composed his handsome features into a frown. "That's just the kind of personality profile that makes Moscow Center sit up and take notice."

Trosper forbore comment on Wilder's operational wisdom and mumbled, "That's not exactly grounds to fire her husband, one of the best case men in the racket." He knew that Darcy Odlum, the first Controller, and the man the Director of Central Intelligence had recommended that the President choose to establish the Firm, had proposed Gandy for the National Security Medal.

"If you ask me," Wilder said, "I doubt that Placide even knows what business Peter was in."

That, Trosper thought, should at least have taken care of any possible security problems.

"Keeping to themselves the way they do, I've always wondered what they talked about when they were at home," Wilder said. "I can't see Peter chatting about the spooks he was running, and I can't imagine he has much interest in the effect Placide thinks hair spray is having on the Van Allen belt."

Trosper looked up from his plate. Wilder was over fifty. His tanned, youthful features were nicely set off by his lean figure, dark, double-breasted suit, boldly striped shirt, and heavy silk tie. From his expensive haircut to his glistening black shoes, he looked custommade. It was true, Trosper realized as he glanced around the room, that these days only rich foreigners could afford to dress like Englishmen.

"It's nothing I've ever pried into," Trosper said resignedly, "but I've always supposed that Peter and Placide were in love, and that they made their own world, and kept it separate from everything else." He took the last bite of sole.

"Let's have some cheese or a sweet," Wilder said. "After that, we can take coffee outside." He paused. "I'd rather not open the letter here. Someone might think it was business." He looked approvingly around the cheerful room. "I suppose it's a hangover from the military—'No shop talk in the mess,' and all that sort of thing."

Trosper asked for a piece of Wensleydale.

"JUST as I said," Wilder whispered. "All wrapped up like a Category One exercise." He handed Trosper the envelope.

It was on personal stationery, with "Gate Cottage, New Lane, Gerrards Cross, Bucks" embossed on the back of the envelope, and heavily sealed with transparent tape. Only Placide, Trosper realized, would have thought to seal the letter with the cellophane tape. Aside from making the envelope conspicuous, Peter would know that it is as easy to lift and replace the tape as it is to steam open and reseal an envelope.

Gandy wrote in black ink, with a felt-tip pen. "Dear Alan," it read. "It seems odd, this late in the game, but I have reason to believe that I have been hit. If I'm right, it must have been something fancy, like the Markov umbrella business a few years ago. My doctor has been rather at a loss, but it seems to me that things have gone downhill too fast just to be the result, as the doc seems to be convinced, of a few too many whiskeys too often. Whatever the cause, I'm told I haven't much time left. If you can come by, we might have a chat. All things equal, I'd suggest you make it before the end of the week. Cordially, Peter."

Beneath his signature, Gandy had scrawled "Krusia flourishes . . ."

It was an authentication used by Duff Whyte and a handful of the older case men in their rare personal correspondence. Krusia was the most beautiful girl in Podvolochiska when Ignaz Reiss and Walter Krivitsky were schoolboys in the tiny Polish border village. She died a few months after Krivitsky and Reiss joined the newly formed Soviet intelligence service. At the height of Stalin's purges, when Reiss was planning his escape, he used Krusia's name as a bona fide in correspondence with his friend Krivitsky. Reiss and Krivitsky defected, and both were gunned down by Stalin. It pleased Whyte's sense of history to keep the beautiful Krusia's name alive.

Trosper read the letter again. He folded it, tapped it gently on the table, and thrust it into his breast pocket.

Wilder was miffed. "I say, not even a glimpse for the faithful courier," he spluttered. "What is it, 'Top Secret, For The Controller's Eyes Only, Codeword Platinum'?"

Trosper shook his head.

"Or has Duff Whyte changed all that? Is it Plutonium, or maybe Pumpernickel—something too hot to share with the honest messenger boy?"

"It's personal, Paul," Trosper said softly. "Peter's ill. He wants to see me. That's all."

"You'll forgive me, Alan, but I simply do not believe you. You and Duff Whyte have always been thick as Damon and Pythias. No one believes that story about your retiring. There's not a chance Duff would let you sit around here pretending to write some damned book about sailboats."

"About fighting ships," Trosper said.

"I don't give a damn what you say it's about. I know perfectly well—everyone knows—that you have a string direct to the great Duff Whyte. Not only that, the Brits know it too. You should have seen the way LBJ stared at you when you waved the other day. He's no fool. He knows what you're up to."

"I'm out of it," Trosper said. "Even your LBJ must know that."

5

GERRARDS CROSS

"It's not the oncoming cars that bother," Placide said, her hands clenched on the wheel. "It's those in back, always tooting and dashing past one." Like a bicycle rider on her maiden trip in traffic, she stopped at each intersection and, ignoring her own right of way, bewildered other drivers by beckoning them through stop signs. She had met Trosper at the station in an ancient Hillman Minx.

"It's not far, just at the edge of the village," she said. "But the house isn't like us a bit. It was my Aunt Margaret's. My mother died in thirty-seven, she was English. When my father—he was Canadian, a chaplain during the first war—became a roaring pacifist and got interned just before the blitz, Aunt Margaret took me in. She died a few years ago, and left the house to us. I'd have chosen something a bit less grand, but I know we were lucky to inherit it."

She was even shorter than Trosper remembered, and the top of the steering wheel seemed to be directly in her line of vision. As she drove, she bobbed up and down in the driver's seat, straining to see above the wheel and then ducking to squint beneath the rim. Perceiving Trosper's grim expression, she turned and said, "I used to have a dictionary to sit on, but someone pinched it."

Trosper nodded, his eyes fixed on the road.

"That's because I hate locking things up," she said. "I suppose whoever took it really needed an unabridged, even if it was quite shabby and out of date. I hope it was a student, or perhaps a young writer." She smiled, presumably at the image of an impoverished poet thumbing the worn volume, and said, "Whoever took it probably puts it to better use than I did."

She wore a green Barbour waterproof that reached to her knees, a heavy, roll-collar Irish sweater, and stout shoes flecked with mud. Her gray hair was braided, and loosely coiled at the top of her head. Wisps hung at the sides, and when she halted the car to give a confused driver the right of way, she tucked loose strands back beneath the coiled braid. Under way again, her knuckles were white with the strain of holding the wheel.

As Placide swerved the Hillman across the highway and into the narrow country lane, Trosper glimpsed the contorted face of the driver who had been about to overtake the slow-moving little sedan. Placide smiled and waved politely as the man braked and clutched at the wheel.

"You *see*," she said gently, "he's quite angry." Still in fourth gear, the Hillman labored to pick up speed. "It *really* is the ones behind who make all the fuss."

Trosper released his grip on the dashboard and slumped back in his seat. "How is Peter?"

Placide glanced anxiously toward Trosper. "Was it all right, what I did? Giving the letter to Mr. Wilder?" She kept her eyes on the road ahead. "Peter thought you'd be at General Myles' service, but when I couldn't find you, I felt lost and turned to Mr. Wilder instead." She bobbed her head as if expecting a rebuke from Trosper.

"That was just right. Wilder gave me the letter the next day."

"I'm glad," Placide said. "I've never mixed in Peter's business affairs, and I never wanted to know about his work." She hesitated and then said, "And I wouldn't now. It's just that he's so terribly sick." With a quick motion, she dabbed a tear from her eye. Her voice broke. "There doesn't seem to be anything that can be done about it."

"What has the doctor said?"

At the corner of the hedge-lined driveway, Trosper saw a discreet wooden sign with *Gate Cottage* carved into the weathered board.

"He says it is only a matter of a few days. Along with the terrible infection, the fever, and then the treatment, it seems that Peter's heart is worn out."

"I am so very sorry," Trosper said.

"You'll scarcely recognize Peter, he's so thin and weak. But he's been putting his things in order, and writing notes for me on how to handle the checkbooks, taxes, and things like that." She brought the car to a halt on the gravel driveway. "Don't be alarmed when he dozes off. Just let him sleep—he'll come awake again after a few minutes." She turned off the ignition. "I know Peter's friends think I'm not quite housebroken, but I am sure I'll be able to cope with those things. It's the missing of my darling man that will be the hard part."

Trosper held her hand as he helped her out of the car.

"I KNOW I look like hell," he said apologetically.

Peter Gandy hitched himself up on the chaise longue, and pulled the quilt over his legs. He wore flannel pajamas, unbuttoned at the neck, and a sporty tweed cap. His face was so thin and drawn that his teeth seemed to protrude.

"First there was the fever, nearly boiling out what little brain I had left. Then, when they tried radiation, and chemotherapy, my hair came out in patches." He touched the cap. "It's a bit less off-putting than my scruffy pate, and it keeps me warm."

They chatted until Trosper said, "Why would anyone hit you now?"

Gandy's eyes flickered around the cheerful, booklined study as if he were trying to impress it on his memory. "It's a fact of life in the racket, you know that," he said. "After a long run in operations, there's bound to be wreckage strewn about, bits of unfinished business that someone might feel should be tidied up."

The chintz upholstery of the comfortable chairs, brightened by the rays of the winter sun that glanced through the casement windows, contrasted sharply with Gandy's pallor. The case man squinted at Trosper and said, "Don't tell me *you've* never wondered who might be ringing the doorbell?"

It was a valid point. Although Trosper had not mentioned it to Emily at the time her mother published the wedding announcement, his interest in keeping his name out of the press was more than mere modesty. "One of the walking wounded, someone who limped off the battlefield, is that what you mean?"

Gandy shook his head. "Not at all. If it's what I think, at least two goons and a damned fancy poison were involved. A stunt like that here in England, with everyone in an uproar about terrorism, could only have been ordered by someone with real authority."

"With due respect, old friend," Trosper said with a smile, "wouldn't that be a lot of trouble just to teach you a lesson—some two years after you left the racket?"

Gandy coughed and pressed a handkerchief to his mouth. A spasm racked his wasted torso and his chest heaved as he struggled to control the coughing. He was so thin it seemed as if the collarbones might punch through his bleached white skin.

Gandy threw the handkerchief aside, took several deep breaths, and said, "Sorry, I thought I was through with all that." He took a sip from the tumbler at his side. "Whiskey," he said. "It's as good a medicine as any at this point." His white hand seemed almost translucent and shook as he put the glass down. "It wouldn't be just me," he said. "There will be side effects. Word will get around. In a while, everyone will know about it—our British cousins, the NATO crowd, even the French. In the end it will be like one of those villages in India when they find a pug mark on the path. Everyone is reminded that there are still tigers out in the deep grass. The villagers hunker down, and stay close to the fire—at least for a while."

Trosper wasn't convinced. The racket had spawned its own conventions—unwritten, but universally accepted rules. For Moscow, Soviet defectors and renegade or troublesome agents were fair game. But because murder would beget murder, and good case men were hard to replace, normally prudent operatives on either side of the secret war were, by and large, a protected species.

"Aside from giving us all a warning," Trosper said, "is it possible that someone wants to cover something up? Maybe erase a bit of memory?" He smiled. "You aren't sitting on any secrets the Firm should know about, are you?"

"I suppose we all have a few things that we left out of the

reporting," Gandy said, his voice trailing off.

Trosper shook his head. "I'm not talking about some embarrassing little detail that you decided to forget—it would have to be damned important to make Moscow set up a stunt like this in England." He fixed his eyes on Gandy and waited a moment before saying, "Tell me straight, is there anything at all, any unfinished business that might have caused this?"

Gandy turned to look out the window at the garden where Placide, clippers in hand, hovered over a clump of privet like a nervous barber. He turned back to Trosper. "The last Soviet case I had was Antelope, the young diplomat in Geneva, and it came to term almost before I could get it going." Gandy's chest heaved and he struggled to suppress a cough. "Christ knows, I've hit Moscow a couple of good licks, and I suppose that through the years they've pasted together a pretty thick book on me. But if they wanted me out, and were prepared to break the rules, the time to have done it was years ago, while I was still active."

He reached for the tumbler at his side. "Two years and not a peep from anyone. Then, for no reason, I spot someone at the side of the road, halfway between Gate Cottage and the White Horse, Toby Wright's pub. He was mucking with his bike chain, but he took a very careful look at me."

Gandy shook his head slowly. "I didn't give him a thought at the time, but there was something askew about him—maybe it was because he didn't wave, or say hello the way the locals do. It wasn't until I spotted the goons outside the club in Hans Crescent that I remembered it. Even then, I wouldn't have noticed them if it hadn't been raining so hard that no one in his right mind would be standing on the corner."

"It doesn't make sense, Peter," Trosper said. "No sense at all."

Gandy grunted, mumbled an obscenity, and took a gulp of whiskey. "Stalin was a sore loser, but I had scarcely got up to speed before he croaked." He put the glass on the table beside him. "It's hard to believe that any of the present crowd would bother me just to take revenge." He shook off a cough and said, "No one runs operations on that basis." He closed his eyes and lay back.

Trosper pulled the quilt up over his shoulders. "You're right, old friend," Trosper whispered. "No one runs operations that way."

PLACIDE brought lunch into the study. Gandy asked after old friends and they gossiped idly as she mixed a salad and served a roasted vegetable loaf with boiled potatoes and peas.

"In a way, I hate having to offer you this kind of food," she said. "But I can't eat anything that was alive and I can't bring myself to cook animals either." She cut into the loaf. "It's supposed to taste just like meat of some kind," she said. "But I know it doesn't really." She looked apologetic. "If you can't manage that, I can make an omelette, or fry some eggs. There's a man here who supplies all of us local veggies with unfertilized eggs."

Trosper shook his head. "This is just fine, and it will do wonders for my cholesterol count."

PLACIDE cleared the dishes. As she began to fuss with the pillows behind Gandy, he closed his eyes. Asleep, he seemed more skeletal than when awake.

"He has so looked forward to seeing you," she said with an anxious glance at Gandy. "This is the longest he has been awake for nearly a week."

"What exactly has the doctor called it?"

"He says it is like a general malignancy, and all through his system." Her eyes watered. "He's never seen anything like it."

"Did Peter remind him of the umbrella incidents?"

Gandy's eyes opened slowly and he snorted. "Of course. And I told him about the poisoning of Nikolai Khokhlov in Germany, and that poor Hungarian in Vienna. At first the doc thought I was crazy. But after I admitted that I'd been in the racket, he checked with London—I suppose with public health, or the people who investigated the Bulgarian, Markov. Last week, he brought two men from London. When they began nattering about more tests, I knew they were hopeless." Gandy's eyes fluttered and his voice faded. Trosper wondered if he had fallen asleep. But Gandy began to speak again. "I thought of calling the Firm in London, but then I realized that if I had to explain it all to Charlie Pottle, I would be buried before he got word back to the head office. That was when I wrote you."

"I'll call Duff Whyte tonight," Trosper said. "He'll get the best people in Washington. The Agency monitors this sort of thing and there will be someone at National Health who has studied their goddamned poisons. Duff can have someone here within a day."

"Not to be melodramatic, Alan, but it really is too late." He closed his eyes.

"It's never too late," Trosper said. He took Gandy's limp hand and held it.

"I'm glad you could come down," Gandy said, his eyes still closed. "I appreciate it."

Trosper leaned closer to Gandy. "There must be something more," he said. "Give me a clue, something to work on."

Gandy lay still. "I wish I could. But there's nothing, not a damn thing . . ."

The shadows in the garden had deepened. The cold rays of the late afternoon sun barely touched the shrubs along the side of the house.

With an effort, Gandy opened his eyes. "I hate going out like this," he murmured. "I'd like to have stayed around long enough to see how a few things come out."

As Trosper pulled the quilt up around his friend's chest, Gandy began to speak softly. His eyes were closed. Trosper could not hear. He bent closer. " . . . something wrong in Geneva . . . Antelope couldn't have bothered them that much . . . maybe you can hit the bastards another lick . . ." Gandy's voice faded, and he fell silent.

Reluctantly, Trosper released his friend's hand and tucked it under the quilt.

"I've called Mr. Slade," Placide said. "He helps with the garden and runs a little jitney service. He can take you to the train." She smiled apologetically and said, "I like to be here when Peter wakes up."

6

GERRARDS CROSS

"THE Bull," Slade said without taking his eyes off the road. "I'm told the rooms are small, but the inn has been in business the better part of three hundred years." Trosper had decided to spend the night at Gerrards Cross and asked Slade about accommodations.

"Most of the Yanks . . . seem to fancy it." Slade glanced anxiously at Trosper. "Mr. Gandy liked it better before they did all the changes to bring in the London crowd, but even so most *Americans* head straight for the Bull." As if to erase "Yanks" Slade emphasized "Americans." "Mr. Gandy says the food is pricey but probably the best in these parts. He said the bar's been tarted up, but it's still comfortable." Slade turned to Trosper. "It's mentioned in your guidebooks."

Slade was about five feet eight and, Trosper guessed, sixty-five or more—old enough to have done five years' service during the Hitler war. His face was an almost perfect oblong, his square jaw parallel to the flat tweed cap pulled down on his forehead. His light blue eyes contrasted sharply with his complexion, tanned to the color of oak.

"Do many tourists come through here?"

"It's seasonal," Slade said. "In summer, there are quite a few. But there aren't any big attractions here in Gerrards Cross. Most of the Yanks are just passing through. If they stop, it's usually to visit Old Jordans, and to see the Quaker meetinghouse there. They say it was used for illegal meetings by the Quakers who stayed behind when your lot, Puritans I think, left for the States." Slade's brow furrowed as he struggled to remember. "They say that some of the planking in the meetinghouse came from the little ship they sailed in. After the trip the ship was dismantled in Ipswich. I suppose they carried the planking here to save money."

"You mean the *Mayflower?*"

"That's the one."

"The Bull sounds fine," Trosper said.

Slade slowed the Volvo and turned off the main road. "How is Mr. Gandy?"

"He's not well," Trosper said. "Not well at all."

"He's a good man," Slade said deliberately. "It's rotten what's happened to him. First the mugging in London, and the police doing nothing about it. And now, this sickness. It's not right what's happened to him."

Slade drove carefully, like a work slowdown, signaling each turn, keeping the immaculate Volvo exactly on the posted speed limits. "He's a quiet man," Slade said. "I know he's a stranger, that he's not from these parts. But most around here would never know that. Mr. Gandy has the knack of getting around quietly. Sometimes it seems like he's making a recce—a reconnaissance—always checking little things, asking questions, taking the trouble to understand the way things are done."

"Peter's got a taste for that," Trosper said softly. "And he's had a bit of practice."

"Not that I mean to take anything away from Mr. Gandy, but Mrs. Gandy has helped," Slade said. "She's Canadian, but she grew up here, right at Gate Cottage." He paused and seemed to be nodding agreement with his own observations. "She's got a mind of her own, all the crusades she takes on, protecting animals, worrying about the bomb, helping at the church. Shy as she is, she's dead set on what she thinks is right." Then, remembering he was talking about a married woman, Slade flushed.

"If I want to move around a little tomorrow," Trosper said, "is there someplace I could rent a bicycle?"

Slade thought for a moment. "Hereabouts most of us have our bikes. There's no need to hire what you've already got or can borrow."

"What about tourists, someone who might have come along by train and is only planning to be here for a few hours?"

"Hire-cars, that's what they want," Slade said. "They're in too much of a hurry to pedal and take a look at things."

"Suppose," Trosper said softly, "that someone didn't have a license to drive. Isn't there someplace near the station he could hire a bicycle?"

Slade glanced at Trosper and turned quickly back to the road. "Old Haggett's is nearest the station. Before his son came into the shop and began changing everything to motorcars, Haggett did nothing but bicycles and motorbikes. Now young Tom's concentrating on auto repairs." Slade shrugged. "But Haggett's still got a few bikes out back."

Trosper nodded but said nothing.

"He's crusty," Slade said. "You have to take it gently with old Haggett—even if all you want is to hire a bike." He gave Trosper another appraising glance.

"Haggett's sounds fine," Trosper said. "It's not a bicycle for me, I just want to ask about a bike or two that might have been hired a few weeks ago."

Slade pointed across the road to a small red sign. "There's the Bull," he said, gesturing toward the low, white building. "Seventeenth century, same as the meetinghouse at Jordans." He turned the Volvo into the car park.

"It's past opening time," Trosper said. "Why don't you come in for a drink? Then, if they don't have a room, you can take me to one of the other places."

SLADE put the dimpled glass mug on the tile-topped table and wiped the back of his hand across his lips. "Exactly what is it that you might want from Haggett?"

"I'm curious about a couple of fellows who might have rented bicycles here a month or so ago."

Slade pulled a small pipe and tobacco pouch from his pocket.

"I'm not too sure about the date," Trosper said, "but it could have been early December, say the sixth, give or take two days."

"Visitors?" Slade didn't take his eyes off Trosper.

"As you say, there wouldn't be much reason for anyone *here* to hire a bike."

Slade lit the pipe and tossed the match into the ashtray.

"Has this got something to do with Mr. Gandy?"

Trosper picked up the tapered glass of chilled lager. "Peter thinks he noticed someone near Gate Cottage here in Gerrards Cross, tinkering with a bicycle, a few days before he was robbed. He didn't pay any attention at the time, but later he remembered that the man didn't seem to be from the neighborhood here."

The bar had all the marks of the recent redecoration. The wood paneling was muted and in the half-light took on a rose shade. Light flickering from the fireplace reflected off the horse brasses and bits of tackle mounted on the walls. There was nothing wrong with the new decoration, but it was easy to imagine why Gandy would have liked the old bar better.

Slade picked up his glass and for a moment looked through it at the fireplace. "The first time I ever came in here was with my dad, in thirty-nine, the night I joined up. It's not his kind of place, not at all like our local, but he wanted to stand me a round—to take notice of my leaving. He'd been through the fourteen–eighteen war, and I think he wanted to say something, maybe even to give me some advice. But all he talked about was football." Slade glanced quickly at Trosper. "We stood each other a pint, the first I had ever bought him. When we got home, he put his arms around me and gave a hug that nearly took my breath. But he never said a thing."

Slade kept his eyes on the fire. "This is the first time I've been back since." He sat with both hands lightly clenched on the tabletop. "It's gone even more fancy than it was then." He turned away from the fire to face Trosper and said, "Memories can trip a fellow up."

Trosper nodded.

"I take it you've known Mr. Gandy for some time?"

"We've worked together from time to time."

"It's a long way from London," Slade said thoughtfully. "December isn't the best month to be biking around this corner of Bucks."

"That's what Peter thinks."

Slade got up and walked to the bar to order more beer. He put the lager in front of Trosper and sat down. He cupped his hands around the pint of mild and bitter.

"Am I right that you think what happened, the robbery and all, had something to do with Mr. Gandy's work?"

"I'm not sure, but I am going to find out."

"Haggett is a difficult old sod, but not so bad that I can't help you get around him," Slade said. "It's too late now, but I'll pick you up tomorrow and we can see what he's got to say."

FOR Trosper, breakfast was the most reassuring of meals, and few ever compared with those served in a good hotel. Aside from the inevitable jigger of canned grapefruit juice, English breakfasts were the best. The eggs were always fresh, and English sausages—they were Bowyers at the Bull, not the old-fashioned Palethorpes that Trosper would have preferred—are never better than on their native soil. He had finished breakfast and was in the lounge, leafing through the *Economist*, when Slade pushed through the door.

"All set?"

Trosper picked up his coat.

"You still got bikes for hire?"

Slade had led Trosper through the garage to the bench where Haggett was adjusting the gears on a new bicycle.

"What's the matter, petrol got too dear for you?" Haggett glanced at Slade and reached into his back pocket for a handkerchief. He blew his nose loudly.

"This is Mr. Trosper," Slade said. Haggett dabbed at his nose and nodded in Trosper's direction.

"Mr. Trosper's come down from London. He's a friend of Mr.

Gandy. You know Mrs. Gandy, she's still got her aunt's old Hill-man."

"She'd have it longer if she'd learn to shift down . . ." Haggett bent over the bicycle.

Slade glanced at Trosper and grimaced in frustration. "We'd like to ask about a fellow who rented a bike here, in the first few days of December . . ."

Haggett straightened up. He pushed his wire-frame glasses back on his nose and squinted thoughtfully at Trosper. "Why?"

Slade's face flushed. "You heard that Peter Gandy got hurt when he was robbed in London?"

Haggett nodded. "He feeling better?"

Slade shook his head. "Mr. Gandy thinks he saw one of the fellows who robbed him right here in Gerrards Cross a couple of days before it happened. He was messing with a bike, right near Gate Cottage. Since Mr. Gandy didn't think the fellow was from here, maybe he rented the bike."

Haggett wiped his hands on an oily rag and walked to a desk in the corner. He flipped open an account book. "Things are slow in December," he said. "Slow most of the time, when you think about it." He studied the book, turning the pages carefully. "It was two fellows who rented from me," he said, running his finger down the page. "The third of December, and cold as I remember it."

"Have you got their names?" Slade asked patiently.

"You can get burned in rentals. I get identification, cash deposits, and take no checks."

"Who were they?"

Haggett bent closer to the accounts book. "One's Doliner, R. The other was Meyers, G. Both from London."

Slade looked over Haggett's shoulder. "I'll just copy down their addresses, if you don't mind."

"Did they say why they were renting bikes this time of year?" Trosper asked.

"They said they had come down from London by train. They wanted two bikes for the day. Said they were thinking about renting property, and wanted to take a look around before talking with any house agents. Said they could get a better look at things if they didn't drive."

"What did they look like?" Trosper asked.

"They were city people, all right. The one with the gammy arm kept quiet. Nothing special about them, maybe a bit too quick to offer a deposit and to pay up."

Slade handed Trosper the slip with the addresses. He turned to Haggett. "They came only once?"

Haggett pursed his lips in irritation. "Turn the page, and you'll see they came back a couple of days later. Same story."

Slade picked up the accounts book. "The fifth. They came back on the fifth."

Trosper thanked Haggett for his help.

"They weren't English," Haggett said. "They both struck off in the right lane. Like a couple of Yanks, on the wrong side of traffic."

Trosper thanked him again.

"If you see Mrs. Gandy," Haggett called after them, "better not say anything about the changing down. She's a nice lady, and she's got enough to worry about."

Slade winked at Trosper and slipped into the Volvo. On the way back to the Bull, Slade said, "Do you Yanks mind being called Yanks?"

Trosper laughed. "I don't. It reminds me who I am."

7

LONDON

"PETER died an hour ago." Dr. Arthur Spokes was calling from Gerrards Cross. "I've been with him for the last thirty-six hours, but there wasn't a damned thing I could do. It was as if he were dodging a surveillance—he just slipped away."

"What about Placide, is she all right?" Trosper asked.

"I think so. If not, I'll give her a little something." There was a pause. "What about the autopsy? I haven't any idea how they arrange these things over here."

"Peter left a note with Placide requesting an autopsy," Trosper said. "I suppose all his doctor has to do is give it to whoever arranges things like that."

"Right now, I don't think the Limey doc is too keen on asking for *anything,*" Spokes said. "If you ask me, someone upstairs has stepped on the quiet pedal."

"I wouldn't be surprised," Trosper said.

"I think you should speak to Charlie Pottle in London, at least fix it for him to have a chat with the two fellows who came down here a couple of weeks ago."

"Not now," Trosper said. "I'll telephone Duff tonight. He'll have to handle things from here in."

THE conference room opened off Barking-Jones's crisply modern office on the top floor of a drab office building, fifteen minutes by cab from Duff Whyte's hotel.

"Since I asked for this meeting," Duff Whyte said pleasantly, "I suppose I had best state my business." He smiled across the polished conference table at Leslie Barking-Jones and his personal assistant, Harry Flood.

"Please, Duff, this should be as informal as we can make it." Barking-Jones turned to Flood, "But I suppose I must remind us all of the ground rules—this gathering is deniable, completely off the record."

"Agreed," Whyte said.

Flood glanced across the table to Trosper. "No memoranda of conversation? No reference to our session in any cables or dispatches?"

Trosper nodded agreement. Had it been the usual meeting between chiefs of service, it would have been the responsibility of the side-men, Trosper and Flood, to prepare the minutes.

"I am here," Whyte began, "because there is good reason to believe that my friend Peter Gandy was hit—murdered."

"It's not *all* that clear, Duff," Leslie Barking-Jones said quietly. "I mean it's not been *proved* that Gandy was murdered." He turned to Flood at his side. "I say, Harry, could you . . . er . . . make a signal? Tell Marjorie we'd like tea." He smiled brightly at Whyte. "Harry's never got over his hitch on that destroyer. He's even got me talking that nautical gibberish."

"I have the same problem," Whyte said with a glance at Trosper.

"Tea all 'round?" Flood asked.

Whyte nodded.

Trosper assumed it was a rhetorical question.

"Do you mean, Leslie," Whyte said impatiently, "that I'm supposed to believe . . ." There was a knock on the heavy door. It swung open and a plump, gray-haired woman backed into the room with a large tea tray.

"Mrs. Douglas," Barking-Jones said. "You're timely indeed." He waved his hand toward the end of the conference table. "Just drop things there, we'll cope from here in."

Whyte grunted.

Trosper said, "Hello, Mrs. Douglas. It's good to see you again."

"Why hello, Alan . . . er . . . Mr. Trosper." She smiled shyly and hurried out of the room.

Barking-Jones glanced up, a flash of irritation crossing his face.

"Alistair Douglas and I worked the Plaid case out of Berlin for a few weeks," Trosper said. "He took me home for Marjorie's steak and kidney pie at least once a week."

Whyte dropped a cube of sugar into his tea. "To begin again," he said. "There is ample reason to believe that Peter Gandy was murdered, and that it was a Moscow Center operation."

"I'm not sure we can agree," Barking-Jones said softly. "There doesn't seem much reason, or any motive, for Moscow Center to stage a sophisticated stunt like that just to eliminate Peter Gandy, good man though he certainly was."

"The autopsy shows traces of that stuff . . ." Whyte paused, trying to recall the chemical composition of the poison. He could not. "It's the stuff we call Apricot—and it's not something he's likely to have picked up from an unwashed glass." He waited a moment and added, "The formula's right here in our report."

"It was a *faint* trace, Duff. Not something we could go into court with." Barking-Jones picked up an elaborate tin cookie box. "Here, Harry, do the honors, get the biscuits started."

"According to Dr. Spokes, the postmortem also showed a bit of what seemed to be a radical form of phosvitin," Whyte said. "That's one of the substances medicine is suspended in when it is supposed to be absorbed slowly into the system."

"There was also a faint trace of the plastic-like stuff that pills are wrapped in to delay the absorption of medicine—or poison—in the body," Trosper added.

Flood glanced at Barking-Jones and then spoke to Whyte. "The plastic you speak of is about as common as aspirin. It could have come from any one of fifty or more pills that Gandy might have picked up—as you say in the States—over the counter, at any pharmacist's shop. This is less true of phosvitin—if that is really what it was. But the fact it was present is scarcely evidence of crime."

"It was a *version* of the common stuff," Trosper said. "A stronger trace was found near the neck wound. It was meant to suspend the poison for a *very* long time. Our people have never seen anything like it. My guess is that the man behind Gandy, the one who cut him, didn't use a knife at all. It must have been some kind of device that projected the poison—possibly even in pellet form—into the wound." He pulled an envelope from his pocket and passed it across the table to Barking-Jones. "Here's Doc Spokes's lab report." He glanced toward Flood. "If Gandy hadn't become suspicious, or if the stuff had worked just a little more slowly, there wouldn't have been any indication of murder."

Whyte waited until Barking-Jones had glanced at the report, and then said, "The two men who rented bicycles at Gerrards Cross? What have you got?"

"The addresses were both for blocks of flats," Barking-Jones said. "The police vetted the places backwards and forward. There is no record of anyone with even slightly similar names ever having lived on the premises." He paused for a moment before adding, "And of course we had no records trace of either name."

"What about physical descriptions? Couldn't anyone at Gerrards Cross, the bicycle shop, or elsewhere remember having seen them?" Whyte asked.

"We got nothing at all. The description from the bike shop was so general as to be useless." Barking-Jones glanced at Trosper. "Does this confirm your investigation?"

"It was not an *investigation*," Trosper said stiffly. "On behalf of a friend's wife, I was merely trying to identify someone who might have fingered my friend for robbery, possibly murder. I'm sure that the Firm's head office has forwarded the bits and pieces I turned up." He knew there was nothing more certain to get the British back up than the idea of a foreigner poaching on the Queen's turf.

From across the table, Flood winked at Trosper. It was a friendly suggestion to simmer down. Trosper raised an eyebrow in acknowledgment and added milk to his tea.

"If you forgive me," Whyte said with elaborate courtesy, "it doesn't seem likely that two men who were merely reconnoitering real estate at Gerrards Cross would bother to mask their identities, and have the wit to pick two spurious addresses calculated to be difficult for the police to check."

"Quite right," Barking-Jones said. "The story makes little sense. Moreover, there *are* slight indications of possible foul play." He took a sip of tea and said quietly, "And, in the privacy of this room, I'll admit that it does add up to the suggestion of a professional hit."

"Which brings us up to date," Flood said. "Except, that is, to add that we've been damn lucky to keep this out of the press." He looked at Trosper. "The last thing the shop needs is for Fleet Street to begin howling about spies who have gone quietly to ground in the home counties and then been assassinated for their trouble."

"Harry's right," Barking-Jones said. "We simply cannot risk having your TV fellows sticking their cameras into our business here."

Moving slowly, Whyte got to his feet. He walked to the window and stood looking down at the traffic-clogged street, four stories below. He was six feet three inches tall, and thin enough to be called lanky. His soft, gray flannel suit was a perfect imitation of the casual, unpadded cut that Brooks Brothers had perfected in the thirties. Despite the years he had spent abroad, Whyte affected a completely American appearance. Along with suspecting that the Controller had talked an English tailor into making his suits, Trosper had long been amused by the thought that Whyte's resemblance to Gary Cooper was a bit contrived.

The Controller turned and walked back to the conference table, glanced at his untouched tea, and said, "As far as I am concerned, Peter Gandy *was* murdered. He was murdered because of his work for my service." He sat down.

"Duff, there's something I must tell you," Barking-Jones said softly.

"Yes?"

"I am sorry to say this, and believe me, I'm talking out of school . . ." Barking-Jones folded both hands around his teacup. "My committee, and you may include my Minister, have agreed on this. Along with all the publicity the Agency is getting in Washington, and over here for that matter, and the witless messes that the French keep getting themselves into, we've run into a spot of trouble ourselves. Fortunately, nothing has leaked, but it's truth that we're going through a rough patch right now. This is not the time for any scandal. I am under the strictest instructions that nothing is to rock the boat."

"And?" The Controller did not take his eyes off Barking-Jones.

"With all this pressure, I have been given no choice but to attempt to ease around this incident."

Trosper could see the muscle in Whyte's jaw harden as he made the effort to keep from speaking.

"I am sorry," Barking-Jones said.

"It's not an *incident,* and Peter Gandy's body is not something that can be tucked quietly under the rug," Whyte said softly. "It's murder, plain and simple." He glanced from Barking-Jones to Flood. "I don't give a hoot what the Moscow thugs do to one another. And as far as I'm concerned, they can murder any of their own agents they think troublesome—they've been doing it since the twenties. But Moscow Center will never, and I mean *never,* get away with touching one of my people." He glared across the table. "Before I'm through with this I'll break a few of their goddamned vodka bottles." He took a deep breath and glanced at Flood. "And rattle some teacups, if it comes to that."

"Duff, I don't disagree . . ." Barking-Jones's hands fluttered as if he wanted to reach across the table to calm Whyte.

"It's one thing for *us* to refer to our work as 'the racket'—that's in-house talk," Whyte continued loudly. "But the responsibility for keeping our governments, and such allies as we have left, informed of Soviet intentions and capabilities is simply too complex to be left to a few diplomatic observers and a cohort of analysts."

"Controller," Flood said quickly. "There's more to be . . ."

Whyte waved his hand to silence Flood. "There's more to this than the murder of a good man. If we let them get away with it, they'll do it again and with less hesitation. Before long we'll all be playing vigilante and too busy to keep shop." Whyte sat straight in his chair, both fists clenched on the table in front of him. "That might even be part of what Moscow has in mind—they can get ninety-five percent of what they need to know about us overtly, and they know we have to steal just about everything we need to know about them." White's face was clouded with anger.

"I'd like some more tea, Harry," Trosper said loudly. "And if you have some ice, drop a couple of cubes in my Controller's cup."

Whyte whirled to face Trosper. Then, noticing Trosper's grin, Whyte's expression softened. He turned to Barking-Jones. Shaking his head slowly, he said, "Sorry about that. I should know better than to try to teach a cousin how to suck eggs."

"Now that our respective governments have spoken their pieces, and the decks are cleared," Barking-Jones said, "maybe we can talk a little shop."

IT was after seven. Trosper pushed his chair away from the long table and walked to the window. The street, four floors below the conference room, was choked with taxis inching their way toward the theater district.

"As host," Barking-Jones said, "perhaps I should sum up."

Whyte nodded.

"It is agreed that on a completely nonofficial basis, the Firm will investigate the death of Peter Gandy. Alan Trosper will handle the field investigation, and conduct whatever relations are necessary with my office through Harry here."

"Agreed," Whyte said.

"It is also agreed that there will be no written notice of his activity passed to my service."

Whyte grunted.

"What if Alan needs some specific support from our side?" Flood asked.

"As of the moment," Trosper said, "there's only one possible clue, and it doesn't involve any British interests."

Barking-Jones got up from the table and walked to a breakfront cabinet. "It's time to mend the main brace, as Harry would say. Will whiskey do?"

8

LONDON

Duff Whyte looked across the dining table at Alan Trosper and wondered how Moscow Center's version of a personality file, a *spravka,* would describe his friend. At best, he was not an easy man to characterize. "Various false identities on record. Speaks French, German, heavily accented Russian. No distinguishing marks. Regular features. Dark hair cut short, traces of gray. Possibly identical with A. J. Trosper, Silver Medal, U.S. Olympic sailing team." But a *spravka* opened with the more vital physical characteristics—"Height, six feet. Weight, two hundred pounds . . ." And, of course, the figures would be in metric measurements. Unfortunately, Whyte had never been able to transpose inches and pounds accurately into the metric equivalent. "Eyes dark. European (Anglo) appearance. Born U.S. circa . . ."

From across the table Emily interrupted his reverie. "Duff, you're grinning like the cat in the hat. Is it a secret?"

Whyte raised his glass to Emily. "It's scarcely a secret, but it is amusing to see how domesticated Alan is acting these days." He turned to Trosper, who was thrusting at a roast of lamb with a long carving knife. "I must admit that it becomes the old bachelor."

"I've watched fifty maîtres d'hôtel do this at least three times each," Trosper said. "But everywhere I slice there's a bone." He looked at Emily.

"Take it from the side," she said. "Better yet, let me do it."

Trosper waved the offer aside. "From now on it's meat loaf when we have guests."

LATER when they were alone, Emily said, "Duff is exactly as you described him. I like him."

"I've read that wives usually hate their husbands' best friends."

"That's male chauvinist nonsense. Only a foolish woman would be jealous of a man's friends." She pushed her reading glasses up into her hair and put her book on the bedside table. "How far back do you two go?"

"Forever. Duff brought me in. One place and another, we've shared some interesting times."

"And who brought Duff in?"

"He was the first person Darcy Odlum hired after the President and the DCI asked him to set up Research Estimates Incorporated."

"There's one thing you didn't mention."

"Oh?"

"You didn't say how much Duff looks like that old cowboy actor . . ."

Trosper knew who she meant but said, "Leslie Howard?"

"No, silly, you know the one I mean—Gary Cooper."

"Some people think Duff affects it a bit. Anyway, Cooper only looked like a cowboy. His father was a judge in Wyoming somewhere, but his mother insisted young Gary go to a fancy English public school—Dunstable, I think."

"Another illusion shot," Emily said.

She was quiet and then said, "Do you mind going back?"

"I'm not *going back*. It's one thing to try to tie the can to whoever killed Peter, it would be something else to go full time into the racket again." He wanted to turn off the bedside light. It would be easier to talk about himself in the dark. "When I signed on, I'd been looking for a job with more future than sailing other people's boats. I liked the idea of living abroad for a while, and the little I could tell about what Duff was offering sounded more interesting than some executive training program. Even so, I didn't plan to stay very long. Then, almost before I realized it, the work took over, and I was committed—not to say obsessed with it."

He touched Emily's hair. "When Odlum died, Duff was shunted to one side, and Walter Bates came along. That was when I realized how stale I was. It was time to get out, and that's what I did."

"No regrets?"

"I've missed it some—mostly the people, and the pressure." He was silent for a moment. "I suppose I enjoyed the secret authority as much as most people do, and there's a sort of romantic satisfaction in dealing secretly with things that seem important."

"Isn't your manuscript important?"

"Writing a book about fighting ships is more agreeable than peddling tacky yachts to people who probably should stay on shore. But I'd be kidding myself if I thought it amounted to much more than a hobby."

"I'm sure Duff would like you to come back . . ."

Trosper shook his head. "Memory is a real charlatan. Listening to the old boys reminiscing about the racket, I've never once heard anyone mention the downside—the headquarters staff always jockeying for position, the auditors arguing about every penny spent from special funds." Now he was wide awake. "Nobody remembers the charades and maneuvering they had to go through before being able to spend an hour stroking some ratty little clerk who is hawking state secrets because his boss hates him."

Trosper decided it would be pretentious to admit that what he really savored was the occasional opportunity to deliver the straight story to the White House. That, and the chance to work with the authentic heroes, the agents in place who knew what they were fighting for, and understood the odds against them. In the end, it was the achievements of these agents that made the hours of wasted motion, the lying, the compromises, and the whole bloody racket worth the candle.

He turned out the light.

"WE will be serving dinner in half an hour." The white-coated steward set the double old-fashioned glass on the table beside Whyte's seat and twisted the top from two miniature bottles of Jack Daniels. With the two miniatures between the fingers of his other hand, he emptied both bottles simultaneously into the ice-filled glass. "I'll just leave the water here," he said.

"It's worth ordering a double just to watch you do that, Donald," Whyte said.

They sat facing each other in heavy club chairs. The webbed seat belts were the only evidence that the chairs had been modified for the airplane.

Trosper picked up his drink. "I could get used to traveling like this."

"It's just because the security people are getting windy about the hijacking that we can hitch a ride on one of the White House planes." Whyte took a sip of his drink. "But there's no free lunch— Donald will collect for the food and drinks before we land."

Whyte glanced toward the forward section where a cabinet officer and his shirt-sleeved aides were secluded. "Any time you see one of those command chairs, it was taken from a plane that was fitted out for President Johnson."

Trosper peered into the forward section. He could see what looked like a cross between an Eames chair and an expensive, leather-covered, barber's contraption, with electronic controls for adjusting the height, back, and footrests. A telephone hung beneath the left arm.

"Lyndon was still in the Senate when he saw the chair an admiral had made to use on the bridge of his carrier. Johnson never forgot it, and when he got to the White House, he insisted that every plane he used be fitted with one."

Whyte reminisced until the steward came back. "It's roast beef again tonight, Mr. Whyte," he said. "But there are still a few bottles of the cabernet sauvignon on board."

It was only after dinner when the coffee was served that Whyte lowered his voice and said, "At our . . . er . . . non-meeting with our opposite numbers—a dreadful expression—you mentioned that you had one clue, something that might have to do with Gandy's death." He looked expectantly at Trosper. "What was it you had in mind?"

Trosper hunched forward and attempted to pull the heavy seat closer to Whyte. The chair was bolted to the floor. Whiskey spilled from his glass. Trosper bent to blot his shoe with a handkerchief.

"The only operation Peter mentioned was a young Russian, codename Antelope," Trosper said. "By late afternoon, Peter was fading fast. He was worried about how Placide would get along, and asked if I would look in on her once in a while. Then, when I thought he had dozed off, he changed gears, as if he had suddenly remembered something. He mumbled, 'Something wrong in Geneva . . . Antelope couldn't have bothered them this much . . .'" Trosper pushed his coffee cup aside. "That was all he said."

Whyte leaned back and brought his fingertips together in a cathedral. "I'll be damned," he muttered.

"Peter must have realized there was more to it than he had managed to indicate," Trosper said.

"There's *always* more," Whyte said quickly. "Another page, another file, maybe a dozen files. You know that as well as I do."

"I remember Mercer mentioning Antelope when we were in Vienna on the Aksenov case," Trosper said. "Wasn't it Antelope who practically threw himself at us in Geneva? From what I heard, it wasn't that much of an operation."

Whyte grunted. "That's right. Antelope was a bright young fellow who went straight to the Foreign Office from the university. He came looking for us a few weeks after he was posted to the Soviet Mission in Geneva." Whyte paused, as if he were taking the time to thumb through his personal card file. "Antelope probably meant well, and God knows he seemed to loathe the Russian gerontocracy. But he was so determined to convince us that the Soviets were no damned good that his lectures used up most of the time he could spend in the safe house. Before Gandy could get him in line, Antelope was called back to Moscow. You'll have to check, but my guess is that he never did tell us anything much."

Whyte picked up his glass and began to study it like an antique dealer examining a piece of fine crystal. Trosper recognized the maneuver. Whyte was about to change the subject.

"Texan or not, President Johnson always drank scotch, Chivas as I remember it," White said. "I always liked Lyndon and respected him." He took a deep swallow of the bourbon. "As a matter of fact, I still miss the bigger-than-life old gent."

Life would be easier, Trosper thought, if Whyte would stick to a point long enough to finish a thought. But the Controller used asides like a chicane, a series of baffles to slow the flow of his conversation and to let him slip away from a topic he was not ready to develop. There was no point in wheedling. Trosper would wait.

"Wheels down in forty-five minutes." The steward rattled the breakfast tray like a surrogate alarm clock. Trosper woke with a start, clutching for the book which tumbled from his lap. His tongue was thick as a barkeep's wallet and his eyes burned as his body struggled to oxidize the alcohol he had consumed.

"There *is* one more fact that may bear on your problem," Whyte said. It was as if the Controller had not broken off their earlier conversation, but Trosper could see that he had washed, shaved, and changed his shirt and tie. Given a choice, Trosper would have preferred to brush his teeth and have coffee, maybe even a therapeutic glass of milk, before being faced with any facts at all. But if Whyte wanted to talk, Trosper would listen. "Yes?" he said, his voice resonant with hangover.

"Did you ever know Ben Frost?" Whyte said softly. "Bates used to call him the golden boy."

Trosper thought for a moment and shook his head. "He might have been at the Fort when I lectured, but I'd remember if I had ever met him," he said. He laughed. "Frost must have been quite a piece of work to win that much recognition from Bates."

"I wouldn't have called Frost the pick of the litter, but then Bates rarely asked for my views." Whyte lifted the thick china cup and sniffed the faint aroma. "I may be the last man on earth who actually appreciates American coffee." He took a deep swallow and said, "Frost went to Geneva as Gandy's caddy. That was his only field assignment. He quit right after he got back to the head office. That must have been three years or more ago."

Trosper forced himself to take a forkful of what looked to be scrambled egg. "What happened, did he fall out with Bates?"

"Not at all. Bates did his best to keep him."

Two could play this game. Trosper pried the top from a plastic container and began deliberately to butter a piece of limp toast. He'd be damned if he would ask another question.

Whyte put the empty coffee cup on his tray. "I thought you might have heard . . ." His soft voice, barely audible above the resonance of the four engines, trailed off.

"For Christ's sake, Duff, drop the shoe. What is it I might have known?" So much for resolve, Trosper realized wearily. He dumped milk into his coffee.

"Six months ago young Benjamin Franklin Frost touched one of Tommy Castle's back-channel trip-wires."

Trosper put down his cup. He recognized Whyte's euphemism and knew that the trip-wire was probably a human sensor, one of the agents that Castle liked to secrete quietly in place. Castle was the Controller's Chief of Special Operations. Trosper scarcely knew him.

Whyte motioned to the steward. "Have we got time for some more of that coffee, Donald?" The steward hurried toward the galley at the rear of the plane.

"It was in Mexico," Whyte said. "And it was a positive make. It seems Frost was there several months." Whyte turned to peer out the window beside him. Thick gray clouds rolled beneath the plane. "I suppose the miserable weather down there means we're over the coast of Maine," he said pleasantly.

By Trosper's reckoning, they were over Maryland, but he would not rise to Whyte's bait and defend his favorite state.

Whyte busied himself with the coffee. Trosper handed his tray to the steward and buckled his seat belt.

The plane slowed and dipped its port wingtip into the cloud cover. As the aircraft lurched into a broad, slow turn, it seemed to hunker down, bracing itself for the final approach. There was a grinding sound and the big plane bucked as the landing gear swung into place and caught the full blast of air rushing beneath the fuselage.

Whyte watched as the plane dropped through the thick gray cloud and the rain-soaked Virginia countryside came into view. He turned to Trosper. "As a matter of fact, when I took over from Bates I found the Geneva office a little out of sorts. I sent George Fuller out to replace Buster Rodman, not that it seems to have made much difference. The place still seems rather soft."

Whyte surrendered his empty cup to Donald and buckled his seat belt. "Along with checking into Gandy's files and the Antelope case," he said, "you'd better have a chat with Castle as well."

Trosper nodded.

"Castle thinks Peter Gandy had gone sour," Whyte said.

"Is that all?"

"He doesn't think much of Ben Frost either."

9

WASHINGTON, D.C.

TROSPER tossed his reading glasses onto the desk and walked to the window. After four days of studying the smudged and torn carbon copies that formed the record of Gandy's earliest cases, his eyes were raw. The flimsy carbons were torture enough, but not so taxing as the fading, brittle pages produced by the primitive copy system that in the early days a long-forgotten administrative expert had inflicted on the Firm.

There was one consolation. His work was moving faster now that he had pursued Gandy's career into the era of the high-grade copy machine, the Xerox age.

He pushed the heavy curtains aside. Wisconsin Avenue, one of the few streets in the capital to have successfully confounded all the solutions posed by two generations of traffic engineers, was as always choked with automobiles. He rubbed his eyes, and wondered if they glowed in the dark like the ash-covered coals of a charcoal fire.

It was 7:30, past time to secure the office, and think about a drink and dinner. He scooped the bulky dossiers from the desk and stuffed them into the safe. After a final glimpse of his notes—a scant half-page of carefully penned observations and, as he knew, not worth the nine hours' swotting—he dropped the lined yellow pad into the safe drawer.

EARLIER that day, Trosper had reported to Duff Whyte's office. He couldn't remember the last time his day had started at 8:30 in the morning.

"I can see no practical way to keep your friends downstairs

from knowing that you're here." The Controller sat behind the battered desk from which General Donovan had directed OSS operations.

"Then I'd better have some cover," Trosper said, "some reason for leaving the U.K. to luxuriate in one of your back rooms."

"You're here to research some old material, files that Bates left behind."

Trosper nodded absently. An utterly transparent cover story might be best after all: the office gossips wouldn't touch it. He glanced around the room, checking the changes Whyte had made in the Controller's office. The high-kitsch, Southeast Asian artwork favored by Bates had been replaced by a Winslow Homer seascape and a collection of Civil War sketches. The chrome-and-walnut desk that had proclaimed Bates a presidential appointee had vanished.

As Controller, it was Whyte's prerogative to lay down the operational guidelines on any operation. Trosper spoke quickly to seize the initiative. "I'll start with Peter's personnel and service records. After that, I'll scan the last two or three years of his cases, and take a good look at Antelope." He would leave it to Whyte to mention Castle.

Whyte led him to an office opening off the corridor connecting the Controller's suite with the private file room. Trosper sniffed at the worn desk, dial telephone, manual typewriter, and the shabby, four-drawer safe. The travel posters were fixed to the metal wall by strips of magnets that looked like licorice sticks. He tore two pages from the wall calendar, and glanced at Whyte. "Home at last," he muttered.

An outsized sofa, covered with worn imitation leather, crowded one side of the small room. Trosper remembered that it had been hastily requisitioned to soothe a querulous Soviet intellectual who, while under interrogation in a safe house, had claimed he could think best flat on his back. The seven-foot sofa turned out to be the defector's most lasting contribution to the Firm.

"You can call for the registry files you need through my secretary," Whyte said with an apologetic glance at the utilitarian aspect of the room. "As long as the material comes through my office, no one will have any idea what you are working on." He fixed Trosper with a speculative look. "I'll tell Tommy Castle you're here."

MORE than any of the passive aspects of the racket, Trosper enjoyed quarrying in old files. Viewed with hindsight, the wisdom and the folly of the case men groping for answers leaped from the pages. After a decade, the most fiercely contested doctrinal battles and the struggles within the hierarchy assumed their true value; most could be dismissed as curious footnotes.

The stiff cover of the battered folder was labeled *201: Gandy, Peter Zygmunt* and classified Secret/TABYR. Stamped in red ink across the front of the file was the caution *For Approved Access Only.* This was a level of jargon that could only have been concocted, Trosper was certain, by Oliver Gravell, the personnel chief Walter Bates had brought into the Firm from "real life"—in this case, the head office of a Hartford-based insurance company. As part of what the former Controller called his struggle to bring the Firm into the twentieth century, and incidentally to help erase Odlum's memory, Bates had levered a handful of experts laterally into the Firm—and onto the shoulders of the established staff. But the bewildered efficiency experts and the administrative innovators had vanished along with Bates. Like the footprints of dinosaurs frozen in prehistoric clay, only an occasional trace of the outsiders' activity remained unerased in the files.

Trosper thumbed back through the pages of the personnel folder until he reached Gandy's original application for employment by Research Estimates Incorporated. In the upper right-hand corner of the personal history form, a twenty-four-year-old Peter Gandy stared obediently at the camera. The harsh lighting, crisp focus, and sterile backdrop mandated by the mug-shot protocol were calculated to burn away pretense. Beneath the untested confidence of the young Gandy's expression, the photograph caught a hint of candor. As Gandy's face matured, the forthright expression had become a useful cloak for the skepticism with which experience had taught him to view the world.

Trosper had studied hundreds of mug shots, and had learned to value them. Like certain snapshots, the photographs sometimes captured truth. He never mused over a mug shot without thinking how much he would have liked to see one of Shakespeare.

"Peter Zygmunt Gondelski, born 19 March 1929 . . ." He was the youngest of four children. His father, a self-employed carpenter in Baltimore, died in 1947, the year Peter entered the University of Maryland on a football scholarship. Two events marked his freshman year. Tired of correcting the spelling and pronunciation of his name, Peter Gondelski applied to have it changed to Gandy. In November, when it became apparent that his right knee, damaged in the second freshman football game, was not likely to respond sufficiently to warrant the expense of the necessary surgery, Gandy was politely informed that his scholarship would end with his freshman year.

Gandy, who had no hope of continuing without some form of subsidy, turned to his studies with the same intensity he had used in football. That spring, his application for an academic scholarship caught the attention of Douglas Purcell, professor of European history, veteran of OSS, and a close friend of Darcy Odlum. The scholarship was granted.

By the time Gandy was graduated with honors in history and languages (Polish, Russian, German) Professor Purcell had arranged a graduate fellowship for a year at the Free University in West Berlin. The impact of Berlin and the reality of the cold war had, as Purcell expected, jarred Gandy's plans for a career in journalism. When he returned from Berlin, and told Purcell that he was thinking of applying for the Foreign Service, the professor invited him for dinner with Darcy Odlum. In 1953, Gandy's application to Research Estimates Incorporated was accepted.

TROSPER took a final lingering look at the bare top of the desk and the upended In and Out trays. He pushed the safe shut, spun the dial. "Another day, another *douleur.*" It was old Mahoney at Fort Mudge who used to say that, and said it so often it had become a trademark.

He plucked his coat from the rack and bent to make a final check of the locked safe. The telephone rang. It was the first call of the day.

"Mr. Trosper?"

"Yes."

"I'm so glad to have caught you . . ." Her voice was husky. "Alyce Pinchot," she said.

It had been a long day. The assumption that her very name was explanation enough irritated Trosper, and he would be damned if he would admit recognizing it. He paused before saying, "Yes?"

"Mr. Castle asked if you could drop by on your way out."

At least one thing hadn't changed. Castle's hours were famous. It was quarter to eight. According to the corridor gossips, it was Castle's custom—rain or shine—to get to his office in time to glance at the morning cable traffic before going out for lunch. Few had any idea when Castle called it a day.

"I was just about to leave," Trosper said, instantly regretting the hint of apology that crept into his voice.

"That will be all right . . . I'm sure," she said. "We're in 4-B, just below Mr. Whyte. The guard will direct you."

"Of course."

He picked up his coat, remembered to leave the lights burning, and stepped into the corridor. Although he begrudged his reaction, Trosper could not suppress a flicker of anticipation. What the hell, it would be the first time he had ever had occasion to discuss the murder of one colleague and the possible disaffection of another with Thomas Augustus Castle.

10

WASHINGTON, D.C.

EXCEPT for the light from two desk lamps, the office was dark. In the gloom, Trosper strained to make out the picture on the wall behind Castle's desk. It was a copy of a painting of Cornwallis's surrender to Washington at Yorktown, and a token of membership in the Yorktown Club—a group of OSS veterans who had worked closely with the British in World War Two.

"It was an effort," Castle said slowly, "but we put a thread on Master Frost."

Trosper did not conceal his smile. The common term was "a string" and it meant that a person had been put under a surveillance so light that the most the watchers could hope to learn was whether their prey was preparing to break camp. Trust Castle to come up with something more tenuous than a string. But string or thread, Trosper did not understand why Castle had used his own facilities to find Frost. It was a function of the administrative staff to maintain address files on former employees.

"From what Duff Whyte said, I assumed Frost was still in Mexico. Has he left?"

"It seems he was there a month, maybe six weeks ago, but he has left," Castle said.

"What was he doing in Mexico?"

"I can tell you what he has *said* he was doing," Castle answered deliberately. He sat erect in a high-backed leather chair. The desk top was bare except for an ink stand, a leather-bordered desk blotter, and an open crystal ice bucket filled with needle-sharp yellow pencils. When Castle tilted back, his face was half hidden in shadow and only his slim hands and long tapered fingers remained in the cone of light on the desk top. It reminded Trosper of a magician he had seen in a Milan nightclub. Dressed completely in black, performing in front of a black curtain, with only his seemingly disembodied hands exposed to the single spotlight, the man conjured on a black velvet table, close to the audience.

"Frost said that he was researching a book on American foreign policy." Castle sniffed. "What more logical place to delve into the complexities of American foreign policy than the public library in Mexico City?"

"Where is he now?"

Castle eased himself forward and put his elbows on the desk. He laced his thin fingers together. For a moment, light from the desk lamps caught the gold rims of the reading glasses that hung just below the bridge of his nose. He remained silent.

It was probably too much to have expected the Chief of Special Operations to answer three direct questions in sequence. But Trosper understood the uses of silence and felt no need to break the quiet. He would wait for his host to speak. Finally Castle said, "Have you got plans for dinner?"

It seemed unnecessary to say that if he had plans for dinner, he would not be sitting in Castle's office at 8:30. Trosper shook his head. "No plans at all."

"There's a place I know that's not too bad for this part of the world," Castle said. "We can try it, if you agree."

Trosper nodded compliantly, and wondered if in Castle's parlance "this part of the world" meant Georgetown, the District of Columbia, the East Coast, or the Western Hemisphere.

THE *patron*'s blue double-breasted suit was cinched tight. The high collar of his mauve shirt seemed to disappear beneath his earlobes. A lavender tie, wide as a dickey and flecked with purple threads, spread across his narrow chest. The Frenchman acknowledged Castle's whispered introduction with a tight smile, and reached to shake hands with Trosper. "Marcel," he said, exhaling deeply. Trosper's eyes watered as he recoiled from a miasma of garlic, goat cheese, and sour red wine. *"Enchanté,"* he gasped.

Castle had driven his shining black Cadillac across Key Bridge and along the Lee Highway to a row of shabby shops strung out along a service road beside the highway. The six tables were at the rear of a delicatessen. Refrigerated glass cases filled with cold meats, sausage, cheeses, and pâtés lined the sides of the shop. A shoulder-high partition held shelves of canned French delicacies and separated the dining area from the store. It was like a well-appointed speakeasy, hidden at the back of a neighborhood shop.

Trosper reached for a slice of crusty bread and listened as Marcel turned to Castle and began to speak in French. Castle responded fluently, his language studded with argot, and as he warmed to the conversation, his voice echoed the metallic Marseilles accent that flavored Marcel's speech. When Castle's hands came into play, flashing responses to the Frenchman's vivid gestures, the masquerade was complete. He was as French as Marcel.

The casual transformation reminded Trosper of one of Malcolm Muggeridge's jeering comments. The most egregious of the innumerable failings of intelligence officers, Muggeridge had scoffed, was their universal yearning to be known as legendary.

If there was a trace of truth in the observation, the hankering for status, legendary or otherwise, in the secret world had always struck Trosper as a most desperate ambition. At best it was only the war-time operatives whose achievements might eventually be trumpeted by historians. In peacetime, the annals of espionage rarely amounted to more than a handful of discreetly ghosted defector memoirs, a congeries of newspaper clippings footnoting blown operations, and a string of noisy editorial allegations of malfeasance. By consigning its success stories to the secret archive, the racket consumed the best of its own history, and left its heroes unsung.

But even if Castle was an exception to Muggeridge's sour wisdom, and did not strive for Olympus, Trosper knew that he had at the least enlivened the folklore of the trade. His disregard for bureaucratic convention was notorious, and the subject of countless stories. These anecdotes, the choicest of which, Trosper suspected, were created by operatives who had never known Castle, usually showed him to be a fuddled genius, at best an anachronism. But there were other stories as well, and these, Trosper knew, hinted at the reason Castle retained his license.

What Trosper knew of Castle's personal history came from corridor gossip. His father, an American officer in the First World War, had married a Frenchwoman—variously rumored to have been a countess, a beautiful peasant girl, an heiress, a *poule de luxe*—and remained in France as a businessman. Although Castle and his older brother grew up in France, they were sent to an English public school before matriculating at an American university. Both Castles had served in OSS, the older brother in Southeast Asia, Thomas Castle in Europe.

Trosper's first encounter with Castle came before Darcy Odlum's death, when, without explanation, Trosper was ordered from Berlin to Washington and whisked into the Special Operations offices. It was mid-afternoon before Castle returned from lunch and began with scrupulous courtesy to question Trosper about the operation he was developing in East Berlin. Castle talked around the subject, but it became immediately clear to Trosper that his agent had somehow stumbled into one of Castle's ultra-secret operations. When Castle was satisfied with Trosper's answers, he outlined a series of instructions that would completely change the objective and scope of Trosper's case. Furious, Trosper asked for an explanation. Castle shook his head. "Your operation touches on another activity," he said quietly. "One that, for the moment at least, has rather a priority."

Trosper had spent weeks establishing the operation, and had no intention of having it radically redirected without an argument. "I could discuss this more intelligently if you gave me the background," he flared.

Castle shook his head. "I appreciate your cooperation, it really is important."

Trosper started to protest, but Castle cut him off. "The Controller left word that he wants to see you this afternoon," he said. "Why don't you ask Miss Pinchot to see if he is free now."

"THIS is ridiculous," Trosper snorted. "I'm not someone's caddy, and I can't run a serious operation without some idea of what the devil I'm dealing with."

Darcy Odlum took off his rimless glasses, fished a foulard square from his breast pocket, and began to polish the oval lenses. He squinted at Trosper, and said, "Oh yes you can."

At dinner that same night, Odlum was more expansive. "A few months after I set up shop, the Director of Central Intelligence took me to lunch. As the Director put it, Tommy Castle needed more elbow room than the Agency could give him." This meant, Odlum explained, that Castle's approach to operations was snarling the Agency's bureaucratic procedures.

"With that the Director offered him to me—all I had to do was agree to Tommy's concept and ground rules. It's been painful at times, but I've never regretted it." At this point Trosper expected the Controller to slip back into his glass-polishing routine—a sure sign of irritation. But Odlum did not make a move until he said politely, "And I know you will understand why I am not going to make an exception for you."

Castle's concept, as Odlum explained it, went back to the time when secret intelligence was a cottage industry, with fewer practitioners, slower communications, and much less activity. "In those days," Odlum added wistfully, "one good chief could keep all the threads in his own hand, each operative could work independently, and there was no need for the elaborate coordination that is all but strangling us today."

The rules were that Castle would operate in complete secrecy, his files, operational activity, correspondence, and budget to be known only to the Controller. There would be no coordination with any other element of the Firm, and no accounting to anyone but the Controller. Just as the Firm was separated from the overt agencies—CIA, NSA, and the military intelligence services—so was Castle's activity to be separated from Research Estimates. In effect, Castle would build a service within a service, a cover within a cover.

Because of the security compartmentation of the Special Operations office, Castle would also undertake any activity so sensitive that it might not prudently be entrusted to one of the Firm's line components.

Odlum accepted the proposition, but with the understanding that the Special Operations office would be limited to a maximum of five case men. "At the moment," Odlum said, "Tommy has only four, and things are going well."

"That's great," Trosper said. "But what are special operations?"

"Special operations are to intelligence collection as a string quartet is to a marching band," Odlum said. "You've seen those football games between UCLA and some Texas university where at halftime they have bands, two hundred strong, weaving up and down the field?"

Trosper nodded politely.

"In a way, the musicians—all more or less playing the same tune—remind me of case men and agents milling around some of our intelligence targets. It's a miracle that they don't trample one another to death. In comparison, special operations—penetration, control, deception, counterespionage—are like a string quartet, a handful of fellows playing some of the most intricate music ever written. The marching bands and the fiddlers each have a place, but I learned long ago that they can't play on the same bandstand."

Still smarting from the encounter with Castle, Trosper contemplated reminding Odlum that Castle's ground rules might be seen as self-serving. What better cloak for the occasional, and in Trosper's experience inevitable, pratfall than security so rigid that there could be no peer review of the operations? As Odlum rambled on, Trosper opted for prudence.

The next day he returned to Berlin.

It was Marcel who ordered the meal. "*Quenelles de brochet* with a light *Nantua* sauce, just a touch of crayfish?" Castle nodded. "Then a *poulet grillé* with a *gratin dauphinois?*" Castle glanced at Trosper. They both nodded.

"A glass of Macon Lugny, I've got an open bottle, and then a Graves, perhaps a bottle of your Haut Brion?"

Castle nodded agreement and said, "Marcel lets me keep a few bottles in his cellar. He likes to say he is Corsican once-removed, but as you can tell, he grew up in Marseilles. In the old days, his father was quite useful. All he ever asked of us was that Marcel be brought over here. Some of the old man's enemies have long memories."

The *quenelles* served, the waiter hurried back to the table flourishing a pepper mill. Castle plucked the mill from the waiter's grasp and handed it to Trosper. "There's enough bad service in this country without waiters insisting on grinding pepper," he said. "They wouldn't dare toss salt all over one's food, slosh ketchup around, or even put sugar in the coffee—it's just the damned *moulin* they think Escoffier gave them authority over."

Finally Castle began to talk. "About Gandy's death? There's no mistake there, I suppose?"

"There can't be any doubt. If the poison had worked the way the Kuchino lab probably promised it would, I doubt that Peter would have suspected anything."

"I suppose it is difficult to test that sort of thing these days, even at Kuchino," Castle said.

Trosper watched as Castle mopped up the last of the sauce with a bit of bread. He must have been at least sixty-five, but despite his close-cropped white hair, he looked ten years younger. The worked buttonholes in the sleeve of the dark suit suggested that the garment was custom-made. But the suit fitted so badly, Trosper wondered if even a French tailor could have allowed it to leave the premises. Perhaps the cover shop's tailor had run it up as a disguise.

"Tomorrow, after you've finished the Antelope files, come and see me again." Castle poured the remaining wine. "We have to illuminate the Gandy affair, and steps will have to be taken to . . . er . . . resolve the Frost matter." Reluctantly he pushed his empty plate aside.

Trosper leaned forward, closer to Castle. "There's something we both had better understand. I have a life of my own now. The *illumination* of Gandy—whatever that may mean—is your problem. Peter was a good friend of mine—all I've agreed to do is to tag the bastards who killed him."

Castle reached into the side pocket of his jacket and pulled out a slim Hermès leather notebook. The corners were edged in gold. He opened it and took out a folded sheet of notepaper. He pulled a fountain pen from his pocket, unscrewed the top, and, in bold script, made a note on the paper. "I've been told to lose eighteen pounds," he said. "My counselor seems to think that if I keep a careful record of everything I eat, it will have an inhibiting effect." He sighed and shrugged his shoulders. "Do you recall if there was a sauce with the *quenelles?*"

"Oh, yes indeed," Trosper said cheerily. "Marcel said it was *Nantua.* The base is a béchamel, with butter, cream, and a dollop of crayfish butter added." Trosper was not in the mood for rhetorical questions.

Castle signaled for coffee. "There is something I want you to keep in mind." He paused while the waiter poured the coffee. "The Antelope case, never of any importance in itself, evaporated a month after Antelope was called back to Moscow—we never heard another word after that. Gandy was retired a month or so after the case closed down. Frost, his caddy, came home and resigned so quickly that no one on the operations staff even had a chance to talk to him." Castle tapped his finger on the table for emphasis. "Some two years elapse and Gandy is cut down by a pair of Moscow-sponsored thugs." Castle closed his eyes for a moment. "None of which makes any sense whatsoever."

The waiter returned and laid a leather folder beside Castle's coffee cup. Without looking at the bill, Castle signed the check and handed it to the waiter.

Castle pushed himself back from the table. "I do not like loose ends," he said. "And in my position, I cannot tolerate unanswered questions that reflect on serious matters."

"I take your point," Trosper said.

Castle made a careful entry in his notebook and snapped it shut. He glanced at Trosper over the rims of his half-glasses. "So, with any luck at all, we may find that our various objectives coincide . . ."

"But I hear that you have never put much store in luck?"

"That's true," Castle said. "But I'm always willing to learn."

11

FLORENCE

"Our boys never think about their aspect," the street man said.

Trosper took a deep breath, inhaling the aroma of the *fonduta* topped with paper-thin shavings of white truffle. He poured a glass of wine from the carafe, and glanced across the table at the little man nursing a cappuccino.

"They slap on a mustache, or a beard, and, God should save them, horn-rimmed glasses. They never think about their walk or silhouette—the things that really matter. They lope around like they've got trust funds, real Peter Prepschools." He made a tight gesture with his hands. "A pair of cheap pumps a size too small, even a stone in one shoe would change the aspect more than anything they glue on their face."

Teddy Vermont had come well recommended, but Trosper did not like to talk shop with anyone he didn't know. There was something lewd about it, like kissing a stranger.

"Faces don't mean much anyway—not unless the comedians have cameras, or you're working up close." He turned, and for the first time looked directly at Trosper. "I've asked Mr. C. to let me talk at the Fort—there are some things I could show them." He laid his forefinger alongside his nose and winked. "Some of those professors could use a little street work."

Perhaps he's just lonely, Trosper thought. Street men usually work in a team.

"For openings, take eyebrows. Heavy, they change the face as much as a mustache. But the first thing beginners think of is to glue on a mustache." He snorted. Without moving his head, his glance flickered around the crowded cafe. He leaned closer to Trosper. "Think about it."

Trosper made a sound that could be taken as a promise, and stifled a groan. What is it, he wondered, that makes everyone in the racket think that he has discovered absolute truth, and why do they all think they must reveal it to me?

Still, as a street man, Vermont was an interesting specimen. He was about five feet six, a perfect height. A tall observer could be expected to report that he was five-four. A shorter witness, accustomed to estimating his own height generously, would probably think Vermont was five-seven or more. His dark hair lay flat against his head, making it easy to slip into the wig that would be part of the equipment he carried when on the street. A moment of privacy, in a telephone booth or dark doorway, would be enough for him to pull on the wig and slip into the lightweight raincoat tightly folded in a deep pocket of his jacket.

One thing was certain. There was nothing outstanding about Teddy Vermont—neither his appearance, nor his clothes, nor his mannerisms. With no handles at all, and nothing about him to fix on, he was the very model of a street man, nearly invisible.

Vermont pulled his chair closer to the table and murmured, "Don't forget the eyebrows . . ."

Trosper realized he had been caught taking inventory and laughed.

"TEDDY VERMONT is the best street man in the racket," Castle had said. "He's in Florence. He'll look for you at da Celestino, in the Piazza Santa Felicità, Thursday, Friday, and Saturday. Have a late lunch there. Teddy will join you for coffee around two-thirty." Castle touched a button on his desk and Alyce Pinchot came in with coffee and a plate of cookies.

"Have a *langue de chat,*" Castle said. "They seem less calorific in French than plain English shortbread fingers."

"Teddy *Vermont?*"

"Like the state—he chose the name when I brought him over here in forty-eight. He decided that Vermont was the Anglo version of his family name—Gruenberg or some such." He paused, and then said, "I suppose it is easier to spell than Massachusetts."

"Teddy?" The half-light in Castle's office inhibited Trosper's conversation.

"He's a great admirer of the first Roosevelt, 'Walk softly' and all that," Castle said. "When I fished him out of Vienna he spoke four languages, and could scarcely write his name—he still doesn't have much of a knack for slang." Castle smiled, remembering some personal joke, and took another cookie.

"Teddy comes from a village tucked hell and gone away in the southeast corner of the Polish Ukraine. The Russians took it in thirty-nine, and the Nazis overran it in forty-one. Later, on one of the transports taking Jews to Treblinka, the men clawed a vent out of the side of the boxcar. At night when the train slowed, they managed to push three of the smallest children through the hole. If Teddy hadn't been a runt, as he puts it, his father couldn't have wedged him through. It was the last he saw of his family. He thinks he was eleven years old."

Castle leaned forward and put his elbows on the desk. He brought his fingers together in a delicate inverted V, and said, "Imagine, little Jewish kids, too frightened even to scream, dropped ass over teakettle from a moving train." He pushed himself back from the desk. "Teddy thinks he was the only survivor. A peasant family found him and worked him like a pit-pony for a few months. When he got his bearings, he took off. Staying alive in Poland meant learning every trick—he black-marketed with the Germans, and ran messages for the AK." Castle peered at Trosper. "That was the Polish Home Army, the principal resistance force."

Trosper nodded politely.

"By the time the war ended, he was in Warsaw," Castle continued. "He scrounged off the Russian troops until forty-seven when he saw his first American movie. He decided on the spot that this was the only place to live. He made it out of Poland, across Czechoslovakia, and into Austria on his own. In forty-eight, when I picked him up, he was sleeping beside the furnace in an officers' club in Vienna, and working the black market for the crook who ran the mess."

As Castle tilted his high-backed chair into the shadow, the rims of his half-glasses caught the light from the lamps at the side of the desk. "It seemed to me that Teddy deserved a break, and I brought him over here. My wife and I dusted him off a little, and put him in school. He was a quick study, but after all the early hugger-mugger he knew he wasn't cut out for anything that involved even a few minutes of office work."

Castle glanced at the empty plate and pulled the slim leather notebook from his pocket. He looked up at Trosper. "Do you remember how many cookies I had?"

Trosper shook his head.

"It couldn't have been more than two, maybe three," Castle said. He made a careful entry, studied the notebook for a moment, shook his head sadly, and turned back to Trosper. "Teddy was quite apologetic about it, but he said he had had all the schooling he could tolerate. Since the Nazis had been paid off, he wanted to have a go at the Russians—he calls them comedians. We tried to talk him out of it, but all he wanted was a place in the racket."

"If you've got Frost's address," Trosper said, "wouldn't it be easier just to telephone and say I want to drop by for a chat? All I'm going to do is ask a former employee a few questions about Antelope, a case that scarcely got off the ground." It was expensive folly to use operational facilities unless secrecy was essential.

"On the assumption that we rarely know where even the most routine activity will lead, I prefer to get things under way in a professional, clandestine manner," Castle said stiffly. "At the outset of what seems to be a commonplace affair, it's often tempting to relax security and to do a few simple things efficiently . . ." He paused as though the mention of efficiency in connection with secret operations was a mortal sin. "But we've all learned that it is often impossible to refabricate security once a case is under way."

There were times, Trosper knew, when no matter what the provocation, it was best to remain silent.

Castle pulled his heavy chair forward, bringing his face into the light. "Try the truffles at Celestino. They're as good as at Passetto's in Rome and half the price."

Trosper knew that he had been dismissed. He said goodnight to Miss Pinchot as he closed the door.

"He's shacked up on the Lungarno Guicciardini, a fancy place for a young fellow," Vermont said. "Since I've been on him, he doesn't seem to be doing anything special. He stays home until around one when he goes out for lunch with his squeeze. Then, late afternoon, they go back to their pad. They come out for a promenade around seven—by the look of them, they have at it in the afternoon." Vermont shrugged. "Off the tip of my head, I'd say she's quite an enthusiastic piece of business." He pursed his lips appreciatively. "A little thin maybe . . ."

Castle had not mentioned a woman. Trosper did not conceal his surprise.

"Has she been here all along?"

"I've been on him since a few days after he got to Italy," Vermont said. "The most I know is that they were together in Rome when I first picked him up."

"How did you find him?"

"The boss, Mr. C., told me he was in Rome."

"And?"

Vermont glanced at Trosper and took a sip of coffee.

"How did you *locate* him?" It could take days for a single street man to find his pigeon in a city with as much tourist traffic as Rome.

"A friend on the cops, I've known him a while, checked the hotel registration slips—thanks to the terrorist punks, they're getting more efficient now, they've even got computers."

"Did Castle tell you anything about the woman?"

Vermont looked around the restaurant. "Listen," he said, "out here, we don't use names."

There was no one within fifteen feet of the table.

"Sound practice," Trosper admitted.

"About the woman, that's something else," Vermont said. "Mr. C. never tells anyone anything like that. He expects you to find these things for yourself." He smiled slightly and said, "You're lucky he lets you know what he wants done."

"And a hundred flowers shall grow in the garden of operations," Trosper murmured.

Vermont stared for a moment before saying, "And, he never confirms what you tell him. That's so there's no way you can find out what cards he's holding."

Trosper tapped lightly on the table. "There's something we'd better get straight right now." He glared at Vermont. "I don't give a good goddamn what cards Washington is holding, or how Mr. C. briefs his people. But I'm the boss here, and I haven't got time to play hide-and-seek with you."

"It's just that Mr. C. thinks it's better security that people uncover things on their own, without him telling everyone everything . . ."

It was as if the street man had not heard Trosper speak.

"When I ask you a question, I expect a straight answer, and all the information you've got." Trosper had difficulty keeping his voice down. "Is that clear?"

"Mr. C.'s been burned before trying to keep everyone in the big picture," Vermont said. "That's half what's wrong with security—before anyone can make a move, he has to tell everyone else what's coming on . . ."

"Coming down," Trosper mumbled. "The expression is what's coming down, not what's coming on."

Vermont did not acknowledge the correction. "Her name is Angelica Church," he said. "She's an American, but I've never seen her passport." He shrugged. "She's five-eight, blond, and about thirty-five—older than Frost. That's all I've seen, except that she speaks some Italian and seems to know her way around Italy pretty good." He took a sip of coffee. "The apartment is owned by an American, Mrs. Willwood. I've never seen her. It's an expensive address, so maybe she just lets Frost and the woman use it."

"What about at night, does he go out?"

"Most nights they leave their joint about seven, walk half an hour or so, stop at a newsstand and buy the *Paris Herald* and a couple of English papers. Then they stop for drinks. Two or three nights a week they have dinner, most often at a place called Cammillo. They seem to think it's a local hangout—but it's not much different from every other expensive *trattoria* in Florence, and just as full with tourists."

"Is he drinking much?"

"Just wine. I don't know about controlled substances, but he looks like the type."

"When can I find him alone?"

"Depends how much time you want," Vermont said. "In the morning, she goes shopping, and makes a stop at the central post office to pick up mail. He stays in the apartment. You get there at ten, you could have an hour alone with him. Otherwise, three weeks I've been on them, she never lets him out of her sight."

TROSPER walked slowly, glancing at the heavy, unrevealing doors of the buildings lining the street. The raw morning air stirred wisps of cold mist from the slow-moving Arno.

As he pulled a handkerchief from his pocket and blew his nose, he glimpsed the watch he had moved to the inside of his wrist. There was nothing more certain to alert a surveillant to a pending contact than to see a target check his watch. It was a minute before ten. A hundred yards ahead, a solitary figure, a mesh shopping bag swinging at his side, walked toward him. Like the adagio movements in ballet, slow walking and loitering are the most difficult street tactics. Vermont was a chore to work with, but he knew his job. The slouch-brim hat he wore would be easy to roll up and stuff into one of the deep pockets that Trosper assumed the street man had sewn into his clothes.

"She's gone five minutes. You got maybe an hour," Vermont said softly as they passed. He did not break his pace or glance at Trosper as he whispered the message. It was as deft a brush contact as Trosper could remember.

Trosper quickened his gait. He turned into the arched stone doorway, and bent to study the names on the polished brass plate beside the glass door leading into the lobby. Before touching the button beside W. Willwood, he pushed against the door. It was ajar. Congratulating himself on this bit of luck, he moved quickly up the worn stone stairs. On the second floor, still following Vermont's instructions, he turned to the left. He glanced at the name plate on the heavily varnished door, and pushed the bell twice. Two short rings.

"*Aspetti un momento. Vengo subito.*" The voice was male, the accent American. Score another point for Vermont.

Ben Frost was six feet, and thin. He wore a russet turtleneck sweater, pleated gray flannel trousers, and leather moccasins. His dark hair was worn long, and emphasized his pale, girlish complexion. He stepped back, apparently surprised to find a stranger at the door. Staring through wire-rimmed, aviator-style glasses, he moved forward to block the door. Then, apparently recognizing Trosper as an American, he smiled uneasily.

"What is this," he said, his smile fading, "magazine subscriptions or insurance?"

Trosper moved to step into the apartment. "Not to worry, it's not even vacuum cleaners," he said. "I'm perfectly tame."

Still blocking the entrance, Frost studied Trosper. "I know I've seen you . . ." His glance lowered to Trosper's polished brogues. "I'll be damned, the well-shod Alan Trosper," he said.

Frost swung the door open and said, "I suppose I should be flattered. At least they think I warrant the first team."

12

FLORENCE

"IT's your nickel, or perhaps here, in Machiavelli's backyard, I should say *gettone.*" Benjamin Frost motioned Trosper to a sofa and dropped into a deep leather chair. A portable word-processor and a printer with perforated paper spilling from the back stood on a stand at the side of an immense desk. The blank electronic eye of the computer screen was at odds with the heavy formality of the book-lined study. "It must be something important to bring you to Florence."

"In truth," Trosper lied, "it was rather an afterthought. I'm passing through on other business."

Frost hitched himself up in the chair. "I may be an afterthought," he said, "but somebody must have made an effort to find me."

Trosper crossed the room and stood beside the tall, double windows. For a moment he watched the scattering of pedestrians hurrying along the Lungarno Guicciardini. Bundled up against the damp chill, they walked with their faces averted, as if to avoid acknowledging the heavy clouds scudding over the city. Trosper turned away from the window, and smiled pleasantly. "It wasn't any trouble."

"I might as well tell you right now that I'm not interested in resuming a challenging career that will involve travel and possible residence abroad." Frost's voice was crisp with irritation. He glanced around the room and spread his arms expansively, as if to convince Trosper that the richly furnished study was proof of his well-being.

"It's not that," Trosper said.

"Then why do you come pussyfooting around like Captain Midnight? You might have telephoned or even dropped me a note."

"Something has come up," Trosper said. For a moment he wondered how many times he had heard that worn phrase murmured in a late-night telephone call. "Alan, I'm glad I could get you this late," the caller would begin. "Is there any chance you could drop by? Something has come up." The familiar words had signaled more operational mischances and catastrophes than Trosper cared to remember. He stepped away from the window and eased himself into a heavy chair. "I'm looking into a case you were involved with. For the moment it's a bit sensitive."

"Now I really am surprised." Frost got up, pulled the study door ajar, and in Italian called loudly for Maria to bring two *caffè con latte*.

"I'm interested in Sergei Bondarev, codename Antelope, the young Russian diplomat you and Peter Gandy were handling in Geneva."

Frost sniffed. "Peter Gandy handled Comrade Bondarev," he said sharply. "It seems I hadn't been seasoned enough to be trusted with anything more than carrying Peter's bags and keeping the safe house clean." He threw his leg over the wide arm of the chair and reached to take a cigarette from a box on the desk. "You'll have to talk to Peter about anything of substance."

"Unfortunately, that's not possible."

"What's happened? Has the whiskey finally got to him?"

Frost sounded like a querulous ten-year-old commenting on an inadequate birthday gift.

"Peter's dead. He died three weeks ago."

"Oh . . ." Frost's voice caught. "I'm sorry . . . I liked him. He really understood the racket." He fished a large linen handkerchief from his pocket and blew his nose. "I haven't heard a word from him since I left. I suppose it's the rules of your stupid game . . ." He dabbed at his nose and pocketed the handkerchief. "Had he been sick for some time?"

"No, not very long at all," Trosper said.

There was a discreet knock at the library door and a billowy, black-haired woman swept into the room. She eased a heavy silver tray with two huge cups onto the desk, mumbled what seemed to be an apology, and surged out of the room like a flood tide rushing through a narrow gut.

"Do you have Peter's address . . . I mean his wife, or family? I heard they were living in England somewhere. I suppose I should write . . ."

Trosper scribbled the address and took a sip of coffee. "Tell me about Bondarev."

Frost dropped sugar into his cup. He stirred the coffee slowly, taking the time to compose his answer. "Bondarev spoke good French, he was a bright, good-looking guy, and, now that I think about it, quite sophisticated for a young Russian. Despite all that, he wasn't a very rewarding fellow. Beneath the fetching exterior there was a fanatic streak—he was obsessive, and gave the impression he was possessed by hatred. If he had ranted about cats the way he went on about the Soviet government, you'd have thought he needed a shrink. Bondarev was so extreme it made you want to hear the Soviet side of it."

"That comes through in the file, perhaps not so strongly . . ."

"It was driving Gandy crazy. The meetings were irregular, ten to fifteen days apart, depending on when Bondarev could get away. Like all Russian diplomats, it was hard for him to shake free of his pals at the Soviet Mission." Frost pushed his cup aside. "When he did get around to coming to the safe house, and settled down to business, Gandy could hardly ask a question without touching off another lecture on some sort of Soviet perfidy."

"I've read the file," Trosper said.

"Gandy knew he had to let him ventilate—the need to blow off some of that steam was probably one of the reasons Bondarev came to us. But once he got started he never seemed to have time for anything but this raving."

"Could it have been deliberate—something Bondarev did to keep from having to answer Peter's questions?" Swamping a case man with irrelevant data was a trick invented by the first double agent in history.

"Sure, of course Peter considered that possibility, but almost from the beginning he was convinced it was just Bondarev's nature . . ."

Frost's voice trailed off as he studied Trosper. "I tried to warn Peter that if the guy really was obsessive, he should be careful not to oversell the case to Washington. It seemed to me that anyone with so much steam in his boiler was a bad risk. Sooner or later he was certain to pop off in the wrong place." Frost thought for a moment, and said, "I suppose that's what happened in the end."

"How well did *you* get to know Bondarev?"

"I was introduced to him at the third session Peter had with him," Frost said. "A real big deal—my very first encounter with an agent in place." He cocked his head, and glanced sideways at Trosper. "Of course Peter made sure that Bondarev understood I was just a substitute, someone who would take over in event that Peter, the great agent handler, got run over by a bus." Frost finished his coffee and put the cup on the desk. "Christ, before I signed on, I had romantic illusions about what old Baden-Powell called 'the great game.' Nobody thought to tell me that the game was one part movement and twenty parts waiting for a phone to ring. I never did get used to it, and I don't see how Peter or any of you guys stood it all those years."

"We've had our moments," Trosper muttered. And it was Kipling who called it the great game, he reminded himself.

Frost raised his eyebrows and moved his shoulders just enough to suggest a shrug. It was a gesture that any graduate of the body language seminar would have translated as polite skepticism.

"Aside from the big introduction," Frost said, "I was almost always in the back room—riding shotgun and making sure the audio gear was working."

"*Almost* always in the back room . . . ?"

"Except for the last time, when Bondarev called for an emergency meeting. Peter couldn't make that one."

"It's not much like Peter to miss *any* meeting, let alone when an agent hits the panic button," Trosper said.

"Bondarev telephoned around seven that night. Peter was out, but I took the call. We had given Bondarev four or five codewords to signal different kinds of emergencies—everything from immediate evacuation to his having some hot documents that would need urgent copying—but he had obviously forgotten all of them. All he said was that he had to see us urgently and would be at the safe house within an hour. It took Bondarev less than an hour to get to the safe house. He was in a swivet. He'd been selected for intensive Japanese language study and had to report in Moscow within a week." Frost laughed. "Even in Russia, it's the bachelors who get jerked around."

"Was there any confirmation, any collateral information, that would confirm his assignment?"

"A week or so after he left," Frost said, "one of the young Soviet diplomats remarked that one of his pals had just been recalled for a two-year course in Japanese. It could only have been Bondarev."

"Why couldn't Peter make the meeting?"

Frost ignored the question. "I knew it would take half an hour to get across town to the safe house, and another twenty minutes to set up the audio gear. I also had to check the Mayday book. It was a near thing."

"Didn't you have a drill for emergency meetings?"

"Of course we did," Frost said. "Peter was a stickler for doing things by the book. We had alternate commo—by mail to a drop right in town. And we had a fallback system—with a manned, twenty-four-hour phone. The Mayday book was complete—envelopes with two or three different currencies, communication setups that he could use almost anywhere he might be sent, escape procedures—everything was perfect. Aside from his drinking, Peter wasn't about to violate any of the protocol laid down at the Fort."

"How much was Peter drinking?" Booze was one of the occupational hazards of the racket, and it had a way of catching up with older case men.

Frost inhaled deeply and paused to grind his cigarette into an ashtray. "Peter was having trouble. He hated the changes Bates was making in the Firm. He could see that the new management was getting rid of the old gassers—and he knew he didn't have any real support from the people who were handling the Bondarev case at home." Frost stopped short. He blinked his eyes rapidly as if he were struggling to guess Trosper's age. Apparently satisfied, he continued. "The desk people were pushing for quick results, for almost any product that would make Bates look good at the White House. Peter kept telling them that it takes time to develop a serious case." Frost took another cigarette and lighted it. "I think he sensed that Bondarev would be his last assignment. Maybe he thought that if he made something of it, Bates would have to keep him on to handle the case." Frost studied his cigarette. "Maybe all he wanted was to prove to himself that he could hit one more home run before he was sent to the showers. But no matter how he tried, he couldn't get Bondarev off the ground."

"How much was he drinking?"

"I don't suppose it matters much now," Frost said slowly, "but the fact is he was sloshed when Bondarev called for the emergency meet." Even Frost knew that missing a meeting was one of the cardinal sins.

"Didn't anyone in Washington ask why you had handled that meeting by yourself?"

Frost shook his head. "If Peter were alive, I wouldn't have told you any of this." He cocked his head and looked sideways at Trosper. "If you're putting me on about his death, you're a real shit—not that I would put it past some of you people."

"He's dead all right," Trosper said.

"Then he died broke," Frost said.

"Not at all," Trosper said. "As far as I know, he was in good shape financially."

Frost shook his head. "That's not what I meant. I remember Peter saying that for people who were pushed out of the racket when they were too young simply to graze on a pension, and too old to find something else, it was like dying broke. I suppose he meant unsatisfied, emotionally spent. I'm sure Peter felt dishonored when Bates told him there was no more room for him." Frost flicked the ash off his cigarette. "Maybe it was self-respect Peter was talking about. When Bates dropped him, I think Peter lost his sense of achievement. In the closed society you guys live in, I suppose that sort of thing means a lot. Christ knows your racket doesn't offer any tangible recognition."

This was midnight talk, the sort of chatter that went down more easily when lubricated with whiskey. Trosper glanced at his watch. He wanted to get on with it, to finish before the girl came back. "About the final meeting?"

"I managed to get Peter to the safe house, but he was too drunk to function," Frost said. "So I just left him in the back room with the audio gear. He slept right through the meeting." He shrugged and shook his head. "It was sad, seeing a good guy fall apart like that. In a way, I suppose it was one of the things that soured me on your racket."

What a perfect world this golden boy expected had been made for him.

"Do you recall anything special that Bondarev reported, anything that was more important than his ranting against the system?"

"It's been a long while now," Frost said irritably. "You've read the file, surely you can judge that sort of thing better than I can at this point."

"Did he report anything at all on Moscow Center?"

Frost thought for a moment. "He mentioned a disarmament expert who showed up almost unannounced at the Soviet Mission. He was to be there for only a few days. One of Bondarev's young chums spotted him as a Moscow hotshot."

"What name did he use?"

Frost rolled his eyes in irritation. "We reported all this . . . I think his name was Aleksandrov. I know we asked Washington about him."

"Did you find out what he was doing in Geneva?"

"That wasn't our job. We were in Geneva on a temporary assignment. Peter was supposed to establish Bondarev as an agent and then hand him over to someone else for the long haul. I was sent along as Peter's caddy—to learn what I could and to help with the dog work. The follow-up on anything local that we turned up was the responsibility of the Geneva office. We had nothing to do with it."

"Knowing Peter," Trosper said, "I find it hard to think he would let the two of you twiddle your thumbs for three or four months in a city like Geneva, without doing a bit of operational exploration."

"Peter didn't want to poach on the local office's game park."

There was a rattling of keys and the sound of the apartment door opening. From the hallway a throaty female voice called confidently for Maria.

If Castle weren't calling the shots, Trosper grumbled to himself, we'd be sitting in a comfortable cafe, fifty fervid Florentines would be arguing with one another, and we would have had a quiet, uninterrupted chat. Instead, we're suffocating in a library that smells like an ashtray, and are about to begin talking shop in front of the lady of the house.

"You mean neither of you saw anyone at all while you were holed up in Geneva?" Trosper asked quickly.

Frost pulled himself from the chair and turned toward the study door. "It was no big deal, but I did have a couple of sessions with a German pal of Peter's."

"How come?"

"Peter and I were having dinner in the old town one night when this fat guy came over and gave Peter a big hello. Later, Peter explained he had known him in Berlin, when they were both at the university. The guy had wangled some kind of a scholarship. He was supposedly studying history, but picked up a bit of cash working as a tipster for some of the news services in Berlin."

"What was he doing in Geneva?"

"He gave Peter the whole story, chapter and verse," Frost said. "He had fixed himself up in Geneva, covering the U.N. for half a dozen little newspapers, and had been hanging around the press room long enough to catch a little work for some of the TV outfits that didn't keep anyone in Geneva." Frost smiled. "Foxy old Peter told me that every intelligence service in Europe had had a line on him one time or another."

"And?"

Frost moved slowly toward the door. "I was so bored sitting around that damned apartment that I asked Peter if he minded if I saw a little of this guy. Peter said the guy was a merchant, one of the professional tipsters who hang around the fringes of the racket, peddling themselves to all takers. He told me to stay away from him."

"But you did see him?"

"Some time later I talked Peter into letting me see him, as a sort of training exercise, a way to get my feet just a little wet. We had a couple of meals, and it turned out exactly the way Peter said it would. The guy probed a little about my cover—I had a solid commercial deal. He asked a few questions about Peter, just discreet enough to make me wonder if he knew Peter was in the racket."

Frost pulled the door open and called, "I've got company, sweetheart, but ask Maria for some more coffee and come on in."

It could only be the devil who scheduled interruptions.

Angelica Church was tall, with long, racy American legs. She had a Manhattan look, one step closer to real life than the models whose photographs sold everything from frying pans to men's socks. Her blue eyes were immense, and she didn't seem at all pleased to see Trosper.

They chatted about life in Florence until Frost said, "Tell me about Peter, if it's not something so secret that I'm not allowed to know."

"He appears to have been hit by a virulent malignancy of some kind," Trosper said. "In the circumstances, it may have been just as well that he went as quickly as he did."

Frost turned to Angelica. "You remember my telling you about Peter Gandy, the fellow I worked with in Geneva? He died a few weeks ago."

"Why should that be such a secret?"

Angelica Church was too tall to be petulant. And too intelligent, and too good-looking as well.

"It's *not* a secret, it's just as Alan said." Frost turned to Trosper as if to apologize for having used his first name.

"It was kind of you to come so very far to ease the blow," she said. "Will you be staying for lunch?"

"Angie, for Christ's sake . . ."

Trosper glanced at his coffee cup. He liked Italian coffee, it was almost as good as that in Vienna. But he could take a hint as quickly as the next fellow. He pushed the cup aside. "Thank you, but I'd better go," he said. "I've got a train to catch."

At the door, Frost helped Trosper into his coat. "I'm sorry about Angelica," he said. "It's just that she gets a little paranoid about your line of work. I guess I shouldn't have admitted I was ever involved. If she hadn't been so damned persistent, I never would have said anything."

"Do you remember what they used to say at the Fort?"

Frost grimaced. "Not all of it . . ."

"Cover comes first, last, and always." Trosper smiled at Frost. "That really is an important bit of doctrine." There didn't seem to be any point in adding that every time he violated the rule, he had come to regret it.

"It's just that she hates everything to do with it," Frost said. "Sometimes I think she's convinced I'm still tied up with you guys . . ."

"What *are* you doing?" Trosper asked. "I noticed the word machine in the library." It was the least he could do for Castle.

"I'm working on a book," Frost said. "When I left the Firm, my father still wanted me to go to law school, and then join his office. But there are so many lawyers these days, I couldn't see myself standing in that line. I took some time off, went to Mexico, met Angie, and the rest is history."

"A novel?"

"Hell no," Frost said. "I'd like to try fiction, but I'm as ambitious as the next guy, and I can't see myself lining up behind all the English majors who think they're the new Hemingway." He cocked his head to the side. It had become an irritating mannerism. "You can tell them that I'm working on a serious book on Mexico—if that's what you were sent here to ask."

"I'm in Europe on other business. There is some interest in Bondarev—and that's why I stopped to see you."

As they shook hands, Trosper said, "What was the German fellow's name?"

Frost laughed. "You guys really are depraved—it was Brodsky,

Anatol Brodsky. He's a Pole, maybe a Ukrainian who picked up West German citizenship after the war. Everyone calls him Tolya."

Trosper waved, and hurried down the stone stairs.

"He's just a merchant," Frost called after him. "You can take my word for it."

"I'll remember," Trosper said.

On the whole, it had not been the best of mornings.

13

FLORENCE

THERE are countless good reasons to rejoice in the electronic age, but in Trosper's view, the most substantial was the decline and near demise of secret ink. He loathed secret ink and its messy, uncertain components and fussy techniques. As a means of clandestine communication, secret ink was an anachronism even before Pliny the Elder recommended the milk of a tithymallus plant. Too much pressure on a stylus and the message could be read with the naked eye; too little pressure and the ink would remain invisible forever. If too much ink was used, the restored message looked like a miniature reproduction of a de Kooning. Even the best technician could not produce more than hen tracks if a parsimonious spy used too little ink. Until Moscow had come up with a variation of the transfer system so good that versions of it were quickly adopted by the opposing services, Trosper would as soon have scratched a message in the snow with a ski pole as attempted to write it in secret ink.

The love letter, scribbled in an intimate mix of French and English, was addressed to John Doughty and signed Jeanne. It was part of the luggage litter, a sheaf of business and personal correspondence that had been prepared to authenticate Trosper's cover legend—John Doughty, Marine Marketing Consultant, Boston, Massachusetts. Along with a plea that John call as soon as he arrived in Paris, there was a touching declaration of Jeanne's continuing affection. The mock love letter was so much more imaginative than those the documents people usually prepared that Trosper wondered if Castle had asked the prim Miss Pinchot to write it. But maybe not so prim. The love letter could only have been shaped by unhappy experience.

He laid a sheet of hotel notepaper on the polished desk top and positioned Miss Pinchot's letter on it. Impregnated with the secret writing formula, the letter acted as carbon paper. Any slight pressure against it left a faint trace of secret ink on the plain sheet beneath it. Unlike the system recommended by Ovid, in which the secret fluid—"new milk"—was applied directly to the document, no fibers were disturbed and no telltale trace of moisture could be detected. Only the most sophisticated laboratory could uncover the chemical tracing left by the carbon.

Trosper placed a second sheet of hotel stationery on top of the love letter. Using a blunt pencil, he began to print his message lightly on the top sheet. REQUEST SOONEST FULL TRACE ANATOL BRODSKY, POLISH, POSSIBLY UKRAINIAN, NATURALIZED WEST GERMAN. D.O.B./P.O.B. NOT KNOWN, BUT ENTERED GERMANY END WW2. JOURNALIST, ACCREDITED GENEVA UN PRESS OFFICE, PRINT AND TV. ATTENDED UNIVERSITY WEST BERLIN WHERE MET ZEBRA CIRCA FIFTY. ALLEGEDLY KNOWN INTEL MERCHANT. TAFFRAIL AT HOTEL DU LAC LAUSANNE EARLIEST THURSDAY TWENTY-ONE. KRUSIA KISSES ALL. TAFFRAIL.

He had taken the workname Taffrail from the pseudonym of a British naval officer who had turned to writing sea stories and an occasional espionage novel. Captain Taprell Dorling, R.N., had retired in 1929. He knew ships, and his relentlessly pukka view of the secret world delighted Trosper. It was Castle who had chosen "Zebra" as a pseudonym for Gandy.

He took the sheet from beneath the love letter and placed it face down on another sheet of hotel paper. In five minutes, the bottom sheet would have absorbed an even fainter whiff of the chemical transferred from the Pinchot letter. And that, Trosper admitted with a shrug, should satisfy all of Castle's security notions.

Trosper tossed the treated letter into his suitcase, tore his penciled message to bits and flushed it down the toilet. He checked his watch and removed the paper from beneath the original copy, wrote a simple cover letter on the reverse side, and stuffed it into an envelope. The letter should reach Castle's drop by Thursday. The restored message would be on Castle's desk an hour later.

He slipped out of his double-breasted jacket and dropped it on the hotel bed. He took the left sleeve, glanced approvingly at the four neatly worked buttonholes, and unbuttoned each. He turned the sleeve inside out. At the hem of the sleeve, two inches of the lining had been folded under before being stitched. Taking a pair of tweezers from his shaving kit, he worked the flat points through an opening in the lining between the buttonholes. He probed until the tweezers touched a loose bit of folded silk. Gently, he eased the silk out. It was oblong, about twice the size of a postage stamp. Four columns of what looked like evenly spaced dots were neatly inscribed on the silk fabric.

Holding his reading glasses a few inches from the silk, Trosper could read the photographically reduced list of codewords to be used when he telephoned the number Castle had given him. The hours he had spent studying transcripts of the tapped telephone calls of supposedly wary professionals had long ago exhausted Trosper's tolerance of the telephone as a means of conveying any message more secret than an order for groceries. Castle's telephone procedure was better than most, but it was scarcely a substitute for enciphered cable traffic. Still, it was Castle's show, and Trosper would as usual play by the rules.

The area code 312 was for Chicago. Trosper guessed that the unlisted phone hung in a coat closet of one of the Firm's retired secretaries. After four rings the answering machine switched on and Mrs. Wilfred Forsyte announced in a high nasal voice that she could not come to the telephone at the moment. That, Trosper told himself, would have been a safe bet. Mrs. Forsyte existed only in the imagination of a security support officer. Attached to the Chicago telephone was a Bookie, a device the Firm had adapted from bookmakers anxious to put a hurdle between themselves and the police. The silent switch automatically transferred incoming calls to another telephone number—in Washington, Trosper assumed—where business was actually transacted.

If the caller wished to leave a message, the voice continued,

she—or perhaps even he, Mrs. Forsyte added with a giggle—
should begin to talk after the beep.

Dutifully, Trosper dictated his message to the machine. He had
met Teddy, the open code message would tell Castle, and inter-
viewed Frost. An urgent request for traces would follow by mail.

He glanced at his watch. A mere two hours. But then nobody
had said that life in the glamorous secret world would be without its
price.

14

GENEVA

"I DON'T know what you think you're up to—and obviously Castle isn't going to tell me—but if you try any stunting here, I'll be on the horn to Duff Whyte ten seconds after I learn about it," Fuller said. He was a nervous driver and had begun to fret as soon as he eased the Peugeot into the late afternoon traffic.

Trosper nodded sympathetically. "Not to worry."

"That's easy for you to say, but I'm carrying the can," Fuller said. "Wednesday, just after midnight, my commo man calls. I get dressed and drive back to the office. There it is, an Expedite, Eyes Alone cable from the Controller." He turned to Trosper. "The very first message I ever got directly from Duff Whyte. I thought World War Three had started."

Trosper began to laugh. The Geneva office was George Fuller's first independent command, and the responsibility lay heavily upon him.

"It's not funny. I drove halfway across the canton just to be told that I'm to lend all necessary support to none other than Alan Trosper."

"I'd have thought by now they would have learned to arrange for messages like that to arrive during office hours."

"Oh sure, of course," Fuller said. He turned into a row of parking places in front of a low-slung modern apartment building. A stylized mural of Lac Leman and the Jet d'eau covered the front of the building. "And they didn't have to wait until fifteen minutes after I had got back to the apartment before sending another one, the longest cable I've ever seen. This was slugged *Eiderdown* and I had to decipher it myself. Twenty-six pages of traces on that shopworn swindler, Anatol Brodsky." He glared at Trosper. "Codeword

TEAK, no less. But for little me, just a second trip across town."
His voice rose slowly, his fingers drummed on the wheel.

TEAK was the Special Operations designator.

Fuller turned the key and opened the apartment door. He lowered his voice. "Bunky will be cooking—we'd better slip into the study." He winked at Trosper. "My bride doesn't like to be disturbed when she's working her magic."

The apartment was in Trélex, a few kilometers from Geneva. Real estate was hard to come by in the Geneva area, and Fuller admitted he had spent months finding it.

Fuller tossed the sheaf of paper onto the coffee table. "I suppose you and Castle think you know what you're doing, but I wouldn't let anyone touch a peddler like Brodsky with forceps and rubber gloves, and the locals won't stand for any monkeying around."

Trosper picked up the wad of cabled printout.

"At the moment," Trosper said, "I'm only interested in reading the traces."

"The Washington office seems to forget that along with everything else on my plate, I have to maintain security here, and that's not easy with touring cowboys dropping in every week," Fuller said. "What's more, I don't know why you insist on coming way out here. I've got a very comfortable safe house on the Rue de Lausanne. It's one of the few things Buster Rodman left for me. He must have spent a fortune furnishing it."

"I'm sorry, but on this trip I'm trying to stay away from safe houses," Trosper said. "A *safe* safe house is about as hard to find as a martini in Mecca."

Fuller growled his disagreement.

"I'll just read this material and get out of your hair," Trosper said.

"Brodsky's a merchant, that's as much as anyone needs to know about him." Fuller closed the study door.

Trosper began to read. It was 5:30. It would take at least an hour to study the file and form an impression of Brodsky. He would like a drink but if he asked for whiskey, Fuller would mark him down as another old lag drowning in booze. If he didn't ask for whiskey, he would be offered an aperitif. Trosper would as soon sip slurry from the bottom of a goldfish bowl as soda-water tainted with colored syrup. He continued reading.

Anatol Brodsky had stepped out of the Berlin shadows in 1947 with an offer of a half-kilo of uranium ore purportedly mined by the Russians in East Germany. The package, flown to the Pentagon in a lead-lined box, turned out to be low-grade iron ore. As Jack Holder pointed out in an analysis completed years later, Brodsky's first operation set the pattern for all his future activity. The target was well selected—the Western intelligence agencies were all under pressure to determine the quality of the uranium the Soviets were mining in Silesia. The means by which the ore was ostensibly obtained, the identity of the agent who procured the material and that of the courier who delivered it to West Berlin, were shrouded in such mystery that even Brodsky, the alleged honest middleman, claimed he could not learn the details. And the operation was expensive—in those days, $8,000 would have been a heavy payment even if the ore had been the real thing.

Brodsky, it appeared, was heartbroken, and at least as surprised at the result as were his chagrined sponsors.

It was not until East Germany came on the political boil, and demonstrations were breaking out, that Brodsky reappeared in the Firm's record. In a late-night barroom conversation with a young American writer who claimed, but not very convincingly, to have chosen Berlin as the place to finish his first novel, Brodsky mentioned that he had met the brother of a colonel high in the Ministry of State Security in East Berlin. As an earnest of how the Soviet zone of occupation was coming apart at the seams, Brodsky confided that the colonel was completely disaffected. Weeks later, as the young writer put it in the final report, "It was an expensive operation, but we sure learned a lot . . ."

Lessons like that, Trosper sniffed as he turned another page of the file, had been learned at least once a year by every over-optimistic intelligence service in history.

In 1968, when the Czech spring blossomed in Prague, Brodsky blossomed again in the Firm's files, this time offering contact with Anatol Dubcek's best friend and sole confidant.

His most recent brush with the Firm involved a code machine supposedly liberated from Soviet intelligence headquarters during the Hungarian uprising. Rather a lot of cash had changed hands before Holder's research determined that however fierce the fighting had been in Budapest, no Soviet offices were known to have been looted.

Without exception, each of the scams attributed to Brodsky had a twist of sincerity, and a subtle turn of imagination. Each was threaded with enough scattered facts to have dazzled two generations of case men, and to convince their ever-hungry headquarters that despite Brodsky's participation, the new scheme would strike pure gold. He played no favorites; one NATO client was as good as another, and the neutral powers were as well served.

Trosper flipped another page and began to smile. It took a kind of genius to have ridden the crest of every intelligence fad of the past thirty years. Brodsky was an authentic relic of the cold war, a museum piece.

"Bunky's finished in the kitchen. Is it time for a drink?"

Trosper pushed the papers aside and nodded gratefully. "It is indeed, but I'm afraid I'll have to go over these papers once more before I leave."

Fuller looked disappointed as he called loudly for Bunky. She was an anorexic creature, young beyond her years and keenly aware of her position as wife of the office chief.

"Alan still has some reading to do, Bunky, so we'd better not ply him too strenuously."

"We're completely into aperitifs," Bunky said, brandishing a bottle of Punta y Mes. "What with all the delicious wine here, it seems silly to blunt our palate with anything stronger." She nodded her head encouragingly. "And we almost never use ice."

"Of course."

On his knees, Fuller rummaged in a cabinet beneath the bar. "Perhaps you'd like something stronger," he called. "Some sherry, or a glass of Malmsey? I'm sure there's some left."

"Uh, Campari and soda if it's right there," Trosper said grimly.

"Ready in a jiff." Fuller plucked a dusty bottle of Perrier from beneath the bar and struggled to his feet. He glanced at Bunky. "Damn it, sweetie, this looks as if it's been opened." The bent cap was loose, and the bottle was half empty.

"Golly, I knew there was something we needed." She turned to Trosper. "We divvy up, George takes care of the bar, and I try to cope with the soft drinks."

"It doesn't matter," Trosper said. "I'm sure it will be fine just the way it is." Flat soda water was as valid a reason for domestic confrontation as any Trosper could imagine.

He finished the drink and turned gratefully back to the papers on the coffee table.

"If you like," Bunky called from the door, "join us for dinner. I'm sure there will be enough to go around."

For a moment Trosper saw the prospect of a late dinner at Au Bec Fin slipping away. "Don't you bother about me. I had a huge lunch," he said, thumping his stomach for emphasis. "I've still got some reading to do. You go ahead and have dinner—I'll just finish this file and scuttle back to the hotel."

Bunky looked relieved. It was almost seven.

Trosper went back to his reading.

In the closing paragraph of a 1972 analysis and comment on the Brodsky file, Jack Holder had added a warning: "Given Brodsky's well-documented history of fabrication, it would seem certain that Moscow Center has identified him for what he is. For our part we must be careful not to underestimate Brodsky. He is intelligent and clever, and has on occasion shown considerable charm."

Trosper thought for a moment, and then scrawled "Well said, old friend" alongside the warning.

15

WASHINGTON, D.C.

"WHY Brodsky?" Castle thrust his heavy torso forward and plucked a needle-sharp yellow pencil from the bucket at the corner of his desk. He began to sketch an intricate design on a yellow pad.

"He's the only lead I have," Trosper said.

The heavy draperies masking the high, double windows behind Castle's desk were pulled slightly apart. Two shafts of the early afternoon light slanted into the dark office and along the sides of his desk. The chiaroscuro effect distorted perspective. It was as if the desk sat between two radiant pillars, and Castle were guarding the shadowy entry to an ancient temple. Trosper could not see Castle's face as he hunched over the desk and began to darken the jagged lines of his design.

"For what it's worth," Trosper said, "Frost thinks his contact with Brodsky was sterile, that there was no reason for him to suspect Frost was anything but a businessman."

"I can't believe that," Castle said. "Old hands like Brodsky create the world in their own image. If Brodsky saw the Angel Gabriel talking to Gandy, he'd be convinced that the Lord's right-hand man had got into the racket." As Castle looked up from his doodling, the light from the desk lamps traced the rims of his half-glasses. "What's more, I might think the same thing."

Castle tossed the pencil into his Out tray and took another from the bucket. "There's not a chance Brodsky didn't assume that Frost was a protégé of Gandy's." He bent forward again, concentrating on a detail of his design. Then, apparently satisfied, he tossed the pencil aside and looked up at Trosper. "Is that all Frost had to offer?"

"That and the booze. Frost said Gandy missed the final meeting with Bondarev. The only other news is that Frost said he talked Gandy into letting him have dinner with Brodsky."

"But nothing came of it . . . ?"

"Frost said they chatted about Germany, the U.N., and the high cost of living in Switzerland. I got the impression he was disappointed that, aside from a couple of questions about Gandy, Brodsky wasn't even interested enough to pry, or maybe make a proposition."

"What about Bondarev's reporting?"

"I have to agree with Frost that it's all in the file, and none of it worth a damn. Just bits and pieces on the Geneva rezidency, a few pages on the Moscow hierarchy, and a couple of paragraphs on Aleksandrov, the visitor from Moscow."

Castle looked up. "True name Pyotr Lukin. An interesting fellow, but there's no reason to believe he would have anything to do with Bondarev."

Trosper had had enough cat-and-mouse. If Castle wanted to pretend he had not read, and probably studied, the trip report, there was no point in going over the details orally. He shrugged. "I'm going to have a chat with David Barlow. He'll be able to flesh out my report."

Castle pulled a sheaf of cables from the In tray at the corner of his desk, and bent forward to study them. Trosper had been dismissed.

THE office was on the top floor, at the end of the corridor. The door was marked Restricted Entrance. Trosper handed his pass to the secretary. She wrote Trosper's identification number, security code, and time of arrival on a roster. Then she smiled and said, "Mr. Barlow is expecting you."

"I liked that stunt in Budapest," Barlow said as he swung his feet off the desk. He marked his place in a thick dossier, and with an apparent effort got slowly to his feet to shake hands. Trosper had forgotten how languid the Controller's Special Assistant for Soviet

Affairs managed to make himself appear.

"We had our share of luck," Trosper muttered.

Barlow was lanky, and wore a tweed jacket, flannels, and a rose-colored button-down shirt. His heavy black mustache was a fraction too short to be called a handlebar. Office gossip had it that Barlow possessed even more high-security clearances than the Controller, and that he was the only man in Washington who read every scrap of reporting on the U.S.S.R. Moscow Center was his passion.

They chatted until Barlow asked, "What bit of—shall I say *piecework*—brings you back?" He reached into his desk drawer and drew out a cut-glass fruit bowl full of brightly colored chocolate-covered peanuts. "I'm still not smoking," he said.

Reluctantly, Trosper took some of the candy. Despite its taste, American chocolate had its full share of calories. "I'm curious about one of the old-timers," he said. "In Geneva a couple of years ago, Pyotr Lukin popped up. He used the cover name Aleksandrov. Our friend Peter Gandy was in Geneva at the time and asked for traces. The desk sent out some preliminary information, but because Lukin was only on temporary duty in Geneva, and Gandy left a few days later, no details were ever sent out."

Barlow's eyes flickered with interest. "If it's Pyotr Semyonovich Lukin you're interested in, that's the big league. He's always been a bit of a mystery to us. But let's have a look at the file." He scribbled on a memo form and pressed a button at the corner of his desk.

"THERE's damn little in this file," Barlow said without looking up from his desk. "Lukin is a senior colonel, a veteran, dating back to the war."

Trosper nodded.

"Aside from a couple of clippings from *Red Star,* the bulk of it—maybe ten pages—is Top Secret, Codeword Platinum. You'll need a new clearance to read it all." He looked up, and smiled apologetically. "I'm sorry about this, but I'll have to get an okay from the Controller before I can let you look at it."

The thin dossier was bound in a green plastic folder. Stapled inside the front cover, Trosper could see the brown envelope labeled "photographs." It looked empty.

"If Tom Castle can clear me, there's no reason to bother the Controller," Trosper said.

Barlow raised his eyebrows. "Well, well, well . . . You *have* been getting around. I'll arrange the clearance tomorrow. Meanwhile, I'll give you some of the data orally—actually it's just background on a handful of operations we think he ran."

"This is disappointing." Duff Whyte glanced again at the last page of Trosper's trip report and snapped the folder shut.

"That's right," Trosper said. "There's almost nothing to work on . . ." He hesitated a moment before saying, "There's something else I'd better mention to you . . ."

Whyte looked up. "Yes?"

"Peter Gandy and I go back a long way, I liked him a lot."

"So did I."

"I just can't make myself believe that he went sour," Trosper said. "I'm not sure I can be very objective about it."

"All I asked you to do was to find out who killed Peter and why they did it," Whyte said. "If you find out he was sour, then you can start worrying about being objective . . ."

An insistent buzzer interrupted, and a light flashed on the telephone beside Whyte's desk. It was the high-security, inside line. Trosper fell silent.

Whyte picked up the phone. "Yes . . . yes . . . Can you give me some slight notion of what is . . . Yes . . . Yes, I understand . . . He's here now." He put down the phone. "It's Tommy Castle, he'd like to see you." Whyte smiled and shook his head. "This is probably the most secure telephone this side of the Oval Office, and Tommy still wouldn't even give me a hint what the hell he's talking about."

Trosper got up and moved toward the door. "Let me guess—something has come up?"

"His exact words."

Whyte stood up. "I want you to use a caddy, someone who can run your errands. Give one of the young things a little fresh air, and a chance to forget some of the nonsense they get pumped into them at the Fort. Talk to Personnel—Fred Tuttle will have a file on the right person."

"THIS is not satisfactory at all," Castle said. He waved Trosper to a chair, and waited until Miss Pinchot pulled the door shut behind her. "Someone has put eyes on Ben Frost."

"Eyes?"

"Street surveillance," Castle muttered.

"If it's not a state secret, how long has this been going on?"

"At least two days. There was a message from Teddy this morning."

"I left Teddy in Lausanne with orders to case Anatol Brodsky— what the hell is he doing back in Florence?"

"If he hadn't been there, we *might* not have known about the surveillance." Castle moved his head slightly to one side. The almost imperceptible gesture might mean that Castle would not answer any more questions, or merely that he was dismayed at the turn of events.

"Does he have an idea who might be responsible—the Italians perhaps?"

Castle tilted back in the high leather chair and folded his hands. "There's no reason to assume any of the Italian services are involved." He looked at Trosper. "But that's something I'll run to ground in the next few days."

"Do you have a *notion* who might be behind it?"

Castle pushed himself farther away from the desk. "It can only be connected with your visit."

"There's no way any outsider could have taped my visit. I was in pseudo, my plane landed in Rome, I took the train to Florence. I saw no one but Teddy, Frost, his lady friend, and their fat maid." Trosper was irritated. "There's really no point in my continuing with this if you force me to play with half a deck."

Castle's expression did not change.

"If you can't tell me why Teddy went back to Florence when he was supposed to be on Brodsky," Trosper said slowly, "I'm the wrong man for this job."

"The Controller warned me that you were set in your ways," Castle said. "I told Teddy to go back to Florence because I think Frost is the key to your problem." He smiled slightly. "Brodsky is a merchant. He's never been involved in anything but a series of swindles, some clever and some not so clever. The key is Frost. As far as I am concerned you can investigate Brodsky on your own time."

Trosper got up and walked to the door. "Since it is my own time," he said, "that's *exactly* what I'm going to do."

16

WASHINGTON, D.C.

"SHE'S a woman," Trosper blurted.

Fred Tuttle looked up from his desk. "That's right."

"I don't need a secretary—I need an assistant, one of your bright young men," Trosper said. "I've got my hands full. There's a job to be done in New York, and probably something in Europe. The Controller said you were assigning me a caddy."

"These days our bright young men are bright young *people*," Tuttle said. "Some people are *women*. The racket is now an equal-opportunity employer. Figure it out for yourself."

"I don't believe this . . ."

"Read the file, Alan. She was one of the best in her class. Just give her a chance. She might even work out."

"This is ridiculous . . ."

FIVE feet five inches, 125 pounds, mouse-brown hair, blue eyes, heavy horn-rimmed spectacles, a gray flannel skirt and jacket, white blouse tied at the neck with a red ribbon, and a heavy black leather handbag. At twenty-five, Ida Rowan was a bit plump, but all business.

"I've read your file," Trosper said. "You certainly made an excellent impression at the Fort." He would refrain from remarking on the difference between the classroom and field work.

She nodded. It was not an eager, encouraging nod, merely a polite acknowledgment of Trosper's remark.

"You have Russian and German?"

"Yes, I've had four years of Russian and three of—"

"I mean, do you *speak* Russian?"

"*Ya govoryu po-Russki na chetverku.* That means I can handle routine negotiations in the language. *Uebrigens besitze ich diese Faehigkeit auch in der deutschen Sprache.*"

Her Russian accent was better than his, her German grammar perfect.

"But I have trouble writing Russian script . . ."

"You won't need to write any Russian," Trosper said. "But it will be more convenient for you if you can go by car—do you drive?"

Other women might have smiled and nodded pleasantly. Ida said, "Yes," and opened her handbag to get at her license.

"That's fine," Trosper said, waving away the proffered proof. He stopped talking and for a moment studied the file on his desk. It was an opportunity for Ida to fill the silence with an observation, pithy or inane. She looked attentive but remained silent, refusing to be drawn.

Nettled, Trosper scanned a few pages, and flipped the file closed. He looked up at Ida and asked, "Have you ever been to the Hamptons?"

"I don't think I've even met them," Ida said thoughtfully.

"I mean East Hampton," Trosper said.

"I beg your pardon?"

"East Hampton, Southampton—they're towns way out on Long Island . . . New York."

Ida's face flushed. "I was there once, for a weekend. It rained so hard I really didn't get an idea of the place." She was silent for a moment. "Actually, it was kind of dismal."

Trosper scented a romantic weekend gone wrong, but said, "You'll probably find it easiest to fly to New York and rent a car. It's about a hundred-mile drive to East Hampton from the airport."

Her nod displayed a cautious enthusiasm.

"I want you to study this," he said, picking up the folder from his desk. "It's the basic data on Colonel Grigory Pavlovich Aksenov, formerly chief of Department Twelve of the First Chief Directorate, Moscow Center. He's the man I want you to interview."

Ida glanced quickly at the file, and pulled a spiral notepad from her handbag.

"Er, Miss Rowan . . ."

She looked up from the notebook.

"This is classified codeword material," Trosper said. "You're going to New York to interview a former KGB colonel. I'd prefer that you remember some of what you need to know and not carry notes to the meeting."

"Cryptic notes?"

"Any notes."

Ida blushed again, and for a moment lost her composure.

"I'm sorry to be so difficult," he said softly. "But you will be more confident if you have the data squarely in your mind." He smiled encouragingly. "Besides, it will make a much better impression on the Colonel—and he's a much tougher nut than I am." So much for having been a mean bastard to a young woman who was behaving perfectly. "You'll have plenty of notes to bring back with you."

He picked up the phone. "How about a cup of the Controller's dreadful coffee and a couple of my stale cookies?"

IDA ROWAN eased the rental car into the flow of traffic. She was certain of one thing. The great Alan Trosper had not *asked* for her. Mr. Tuttle had as much as admitted that she had been *assigned* to Trosper, and that she would continue as his caddy only if she worked out. It didn't change things in the least that he had deigned to give her a chance. For all his reputation, Alan Trosper was clearly a male chauvinist. Still, she doubted that anyone in her class had as yet been given as much responsibility as he had handed her. As she settled down behind the wheel, she began to ponder the material she had read.

Like her classmates at the Fort, Ida Rowan had studied the sterilized version of the operation that resulted in the defection of a senior Moscow Center officer and his escape from Budapest. Neither the Russian's nor the case man's name was given in the training file, but it was common knowledge that Alan Trosper had personally arranged the escape, and that the operation had been done on a shoestring, and in defiance of specific orders from the then Controller, Walter Bates. She had not learned Colonel Aksenov's name until she read the file Trosper had handed her.

Ida was surprised when she read that Aksenov and his friend Franz Radl had asked to be resettled in Key West. Their idea of getting as far away as possible from the Russian winter, and indeed everything Russian, was sound enough. But the notion of a recently displaced Moscow Center colonel and one of his Austrian operatives opening a boutique in Key West seemed bizarre.

By Ida's quick count, it had only taken Aksenov and his friend six weeks to give up the boutique idea. They had then spent most of the summer checking health-food stores from one end of Florida to the other. At this point in her reading, Ida had looked up at Trosper. "Health-food stores?"

"I'm afraid I may have given them the impression that nuts, berries, and potions of all sorts are big items down there," he explained. "Aksenov started life as a student at the Bolshoi Ballet. The idea of strenuous exercise stuck with him all his life. And seeing the way most of his contemporaries in Moscow Center ate and drank, he was always very careful with his diet."

In September Aksenov had called the Firm. It was embarrassing, he said, but neither he nor Radl had realized that Key West weather was hot and humid all day, every day, at least five months a year. If the Firm had no objection, he and Radl planned to move to East Hampton, New York. They had kept in touch with Nancy Cunningham, the woman who had helped in the escape from Budapest, and who lived on Long Island. She had mentioned an acquaintance who was about to follow his girlfriend to Portofino and was desperate to sell his East Hampton health-food shop.

"They seem to have settled in quite well out there," Trosper said. "I suppose the winter reminds them a little of home, and the summer crowd must keep them amused."

"Is THERE something special?" he asked.

He was short, about five feet six, and so thin he seemed almost fragile. His heavy tweed jacket hung loosely from his shoulders, accentuating his slight build. A dark blue shirt made his pale blue eyes look even lighter.

"Mr. Komar?" she asked. The instant she heard the words she spoke, she realized she was off on the wrong foot. Just because she had driven the length of Long Island to interview a Soviet defector in East Hampton was no reason to assume that the first person who spoke with an accent was a former Moscow Center operative. It wasn't even a Russian accent.

"No, no, he's not here," he said. "Is there service I can do?" He gestured vaguely at the shelves lining the shop.

"Do you expect him soon?" she asked.

"I don't really know when he . . ." Then, noticing her confusion, he said, "I'm Adler, the Adler portion of Komar Adler Health Food." He pointed to a rack of tins beside the cash register. "We've just received a shipment of *organic* pet food. For dogs, cats, and such." He picked up a blue jar. "This is new. Special for goldfish—no preservatives, no chemicals, and no artificial coloring." He smiled tentatively. "But perhaps you do not keep fish?"

Ida Rowan blushed and put out her hand. "I'm Jane Johnson. I think Mr. Komar expects me."

Adler's smile broadened. "Of course, I should have known—and so many Johnsons in your service." He moved toward the back of the shop. "Alex is upstairs. He's been expecting you."

Adler's face was thin, and deeply lined. He wore his sparse hair brushed forward, like the busts of Julius Caesar. The description fitted Franz Radl, the Austrian friend of Colonel Aksenov. But Ida Rowan would make no more assumptions.

"When we first came to Long Island, we lived upstairs, but it's not good living above a shop," Adler said. "We were lucky to find a small house. Now we keep the upstairs as an *atelier.*" Adler turned. "The stairs are a little difficult—let me lead the way."

"You drove?"

"Yes, from New York."

"That's best. The train is an affront."

If the idea that her first operational assignment would be as Trosper's caddy had startled her, the notion that her first task was to question a defector was unnerving. As she struggled to keep from seeming to take stock, it did not seem possible that the slim man who rose to shake hands could be identical with the Russian dancer who had been parachuted into Nazi-occupied Vienna, and who had survived to fight his way from field agent status to chief of Department Twelve, one of the most senior positions in the Moscow Center hierarchy.

It was even difficult to believe that Colonel Grigory Pavlovich Aksenov—think of him as Komar, she corrected herself—was more than sixty, and one of the most important defectors in recent years. His thick gray hair, flecked with white, was close cropped and shaped to show his attentive brown eyes and thin, aquiline nose to advantage. The brass buttons on his blue blazer were polished, and a blue foulard was knotted loosely at the open collar of his pink poplin shirt. In lieu of a belt, his pleated, gray flannel trousers were secured with a casually knotted yellow necktie.

He motioned her to a *bergère* covered in nubby raw linen. Without touching his hands to the arms of the chair facing her, he sat down. Two years at Miss Plumbly's school of dancing and out-of-date manners, Ida reminded herself, and she had never learned to sit without seeming to hit the chair as if she been dropped from a forklift. She shifted uneasily, and pulled herself up, back straight, stomach tucked in. Then, remembering Miss Plumbly's advice for moments of stress, she leaned forward slightly, lowered her eyes, and took two deep breaths. She exhaled slowly and opened her eyes. She found herself staring at Komar's crotch. She gasped and quickly raised her head.

He sat erect, his back not touching the chair, his feet roughly in the fourth position. Not for nothing had Aksenov—Komar, damn it—begun life as a student at the Bolshoi. She felt as if she had gained twelve pounds since coming into the room.

"We have tea about this time," he said, smiling. "English tea. Not Russian. Would you like something?"

"Anything," she murmured. "Anything at all."

———

HE took the empty cup from the table beside her chair. "Now, perhaps, your business?"

She nodded gratefully. "Mr. Trosper, arrghh"—as she groaned, her eyes closed in embarrassment—"and . . . ah . . . Mr. Warner, have both asked me to find out if you could add any details to what you first reported on Colonel Pyotr Semyonovich Lukin." She knew that her face had turned scarlet. In posing the first question of her operational career she had given Komar the true name of her boss, the man who, as Mr. Warner, had smuggled Komar out of Budapest. She slipped into Russian. "Lukin sometimes uses the workname Aleksandrov. You mentioned him in your debriefing, but Mr. Warner thought that you might have a few more details."

Komar leaned back in his chair. "Your Russian is excellent, much better than my poor English." He smiled and continued softly in Russian. "It's quite all right, Miss Johnson, Alan Trosper and I are old friends now. Even before he told me his name, I knew that Warner was just a pseudonym."

She nodded several times, and pulled the spiral notebook from her bag.

KOMAR sat quietly as Ida shuffled through the pages of notes she had taken during the interview. As if to jog Komar's memory, she began to read occasional phrases aloud. "He came out of the war with an excellent record . . . couldn't have been more than eighteen when Stalin personally awarded him the Order of the Red Banner, First Class."

She turned another page and stopped. "The *gossip* you mentioned . . . ?"

Komar spoke slowly. "It was none of my affair—I never paid much attention to it. But we all heard things after the war. Ivan Ivanovich really didn't deserve this or that decoration. Boris Borisovich shouldn't have got credit for the Berlin operations." He shook his head. "It really didn't matter much. So many of the best men had died. What difference that some of the survivors were given a little credit that they didn't deserve . . ." He was silent for a moment, and then said, "But I must be careful not to line your files with gossip. I must only give you facts."

"Specifically—the gossip you heard about Lukin?"

Komar studied Ida Rowan. "You will do well," he said. "Your Russian is outstanding. With a little more experience, perhaps . . ."

Ida Rowan blushed as she realized she was tapping her pen on the notebook like a schoolmarm impatient for an answer. Trosper had not mentioned gossip; if Komar didn't want to go into it, Ida would not push for an answer.

"But Lukin stayed on with the partisans until . . ."

"All I know is that he went north from the Ukraine and was still active behind the lines in Germany when the war ended. It took courage to do what he did."

"And then?"

Komar hesitated as he struggled with his memory. "It was probably 1949 before Lukin was assigned to *Spetsburo,* the special operations outfit—kidnapping, murder, and such—organized by General Pavel Antolevich Sudoplatov. Old Sudoplatov was in charge of the Partisan Directorate, and after the war he hung on to his best men. He was impressed with Lukin's war record, and saw to it that he finished his education, and got an NKGB commission."

"Wasn't Sudoplatov arrested in fifty-three?"

Komar nodded. "When Stalin died, Beria saw to it that many of the older officers were removed. Only after Beria was ousted did the service settle down, and the work go on. The *Spets* became the Ninth Department, and when the service was reorganized in fifty-four, the Ninth became the Thirteenth Department."

"And now it's Department Five?"

"That's right, but as I told you, Lukin had left by 1975."

She flipped a few more pages of the notebook. "That's when he went into Department Sixteen, cipher procurement?"

"What you must remember is that Lukin has a great yearning for position—status as you call it. He wanted to be rid of his reputation as a tough, a specialist in murder and kidnapping. He married

General Molchanov's daughter, and tried to improve his position by being posted abroad, as first secretary in some nice embassy." Komar shook his head. "But his work had marked him. It was not so much that he looked as if he had just stepped out of one of the *boyevaya* outfits—the strong-arm fellows who do the really dirty business—it was the way he thought. The service was changing, his kind of violence was no longer the answer. He would not easily accept direction, and he made people nervous. No one in the First Directorate would consider putting him in an embassy, particularly since his wife has left him."

"But he continued to work?"

"There is always a little . . . er . . . *cleaning up* that has to be done, and I suppose it amused some of the big bosses to keep him around—much the way it pleases some people to have a dangerous dog, like a Doberman or a Rottweiler, around the house."

"If Lukin realizes that, he can't like it very much."

"Quite true," Komar said.

"I still don't understand why they would use him for something as sensitive as recruiting code clerks."

Komar thought for a moment. "For all his faults, Lukin is a good operations man. He has learned English, and speaks German well. I suppose he is best on special assignments or with only one other man. Department Sixteen works like that."

"I still don't understand . . ."

Komar looked impatient. "Most of the officers in Department Sixteen have a technical background—they spend half their careers studying fancy cipher machines, and working on computers. Recruiting hostile communications personnel is the highest priority for every intelligence service. But because every country takes special precautions to protect these people, recruitments are rare. As a result, some officers in Department Sixteen have relatively little street experience."

She shook her head, "But . . ."

"My guess is that Lukin made such a fuss to get himself out of Department Five and into something he thought more *kulturny*, that the chief had to give in. Lukin was sent to Department Sixteen in the hope that he would add operational toughness and practical experience to the fancy boys and their machines."

"How did he work out in the new job?"

"I never really knew Lukin, but from what little I ever heard, he had done well."

Ida Rowan made another note and closed her book.

As they walked downstairs, Komar said, "I suspect you find my appearance surprising?"

She managed a tentative smile. "You are rather different from what I expected."

"When Alan Trosper helped us get started here, he explained something he called protective coloration, like animals whose coats change color with the seasons. He wanted me to make a complete change from what I suppose he considered my . . . er . . . unfortunate military manner and appearance. I've done the best I can to blend into this odd Long Island community."

"I'd say you've made a success of it."

Komar glanced at Adler, who was busy closing the shop, and whispered. "Now if I can only get Franzi to change his appearance a bit. He still looks exactly the way he did in Vienna—like a coffeehouse intellectual." Komar shook his head. "And he refuses to take the health-food business seriously enough."

At the door, Komar took Ida's arm. "There's one thing you must make clear to Alan and your people." She nodded. "Lukin is a dangerous man. He's a killer and he may even be a little mad."

Afterthoughts, Trosper had told her, were often the most important, and when she had stopped her questioning, she should let the conversation spin on for a while.

"He is of the old school," Lukin said sadly. "The bad old school. Some of his habits come from the partisan days. They were hard days and he was very young. It was the wartime experience, and the work he did in the wild years right after the war, that shaped him."

It was after seven, and the wintry streets of East Hampton Village were empty except for a cluster of brightly jacketed young people under the marquee of the movie house.

Komar took her hand. "Our people do not like Lukin. They use him, but they don't like him. He has been lucky to find protectors, senior officers who have grown so far away from operations that they have forgot what kind of trouble he can cause."

He pulled the latch on the shop door. "Lukin has one friend, an agent who has worked for him since the early days. In my office we had a saying. We said every case man recruits in his own image. Unconsciously, we all seem to like people who remind us of ourselves—or what we would like to be. We always called Lukin's man Golo—but his name is Leditsa." Komar released her hand. "He is just a crude version of Lukin."

"Golo Leditsa," she said. "Is that a pun? Doesn't it mean freezing rain?"

Komar nodded. "In East Hampton we call it sleet." He chuckled at his own irony. "Comrade Sleet makes a perfect tool for his mentor Lukin."

He opened the door. "Come back soon, and let me hear more of your beautiful Russian accent."

Ida Rowan blushed and pulled her collar high around her neck. *"Ya obeshchayu,"* she said. "I promise."

17

FLORENCE

"No more Captain Midnight?" Frost asked, a nervous smile touching his lips.

"I try to learn from my mistakes," Trosper said. He had telephoned to ask Frost for another meeting.

Frost tugged the heavy door aside, and beckoned Trosper into the apartment. "Angie's in her room," he said. "We've got the place to ourselves, at least for the moment."

Trosper shook the rain from his hat, dropped his wet coat on the ornate chair beside the door, and followed Frost into the library.

"Maria's out for the evening, but she left some coffee in this contraption." The glistening, four-sided thermos looked like a silver-plated milk carton. Frost poured two cups, and turned to Trosper. "What is it this time?"

"It's still about Geneva," Trosper said. "I've got a few more questions . . ."

"I've told you everything I know about Comrade Bondarev," Frost said, drumming his fingers on the arm of his chair.

Trosper dropped sugar into his coffee. He had not come to talk about Bondarev.

Frost's hands fluttered and the coffee spoon rattled in the saucer. "Look," he said. "You have the entire file in Washington. It's all there, cables and dispatches, the whole story. There's no point in badgering me like this. It makes me nervous." He lit a cigarette.

"Sometimes things get left out of reports," Trosper said. "Not necessarily deliberately, sometimes just forgotten. You were under pressure, you had to cover for Gandy, it was an important case, the first agent you ever met . . ." Trosper checked himself. He did not want to reassure Frost.

"Nothing was left out of the report. It took me all night to draft

the cable—a damned long cable. In the morning Gandy had so-
bered up. He checked my draft, and turned it over to Terry Nash."

"Who?"

"Nash, the commo man in the Geneva office. The young guy
with the Jaguar."

"A Jaguar?" Most commo men drove family sedans.

"A twenty-year-old two-seater, if it matters," Frost said.

"Not the least conspicuous vehicle for his line of work," Trosper
said.

"Come off it—he's a bachelor." Frost shook his head in disbelief. "Don't you people ever think there's a simple answer to
things—must it always be sinister?"

"Not always sinister," Trosper said.

"Look," Frost said irritably. "Either Bondarev really was named
for Japanese study, or the black hats uncovered his contact with
Gandy—either way, he gets called back to Moscow." He shrugged.
"Unless you people hear from him, and pretty soon, you'll have to
admit that the Bondarev case is dead."

"There's no statute of limitations on counterespionage, none at
all," Trosper said. He waited before saying, "And I don't like loose
ends, no matter how old."

"What loose ends?"

"Too many loose ends," Trosper said. Though it was none of
Frost's business, there was also a murder. *And*, as the thought
slowly formed, there was also a less than productive office in Geneva.

"Whatever went wrong—if anything did go wrong—it wasn't
my fault."

"No one has blamed you for anything," Trosper said. "It was
Gandy's case."

Mollified, Frost said softly, "If Bondarev really was headed for
Japan, he should have been posted by now."

"We would have spotted him if he had been assigned to Japan—
or anywhere else for that matter," Trosper said.

Frost ground out his cigarette. "I guess that will have to be your
problem."

Trosper nodded. He recalled Duff Whyte saying that knowledge is power, secret knowledge is more power. Trosper had added his own codicil to the truism: the best secrets mature like fine wine. Gandy's murder was a strong hole card, but once it was on the table it could never be withdrawn.

He finished his coffee and cradled the cup in both hands. What would Karl von Clausewitz have advised a commander who had only one shot in the locker? His advice could only have been to cut and run. Not very useful, but then the German military had never had much luck with spies.

He waited until Frost, impatient with the silence, seemed about to speak. Then he cleared his throat and put the empty cup on the coffee table. It was just enough movement to forestall Frost speaking, and to give him a few more moments to wonder what Trosper was after.

What would Sun Tzu have counseled? Trosper was familiar with the 2,500-year-old text, but none of the ancient Chinese espionage wisdom seemed to fit. "What you said about Geneva doesn't make sense."

"What the hell do you mean?"

Keep the ball in the other court. "It doesn't add up."

Frost stared at Trosper. He opened his eyes wide and flared his nostrils—an involuntary attempt at intimidation.

"Just what is it that *you* can't add up?" Frost's question had a hollow bravado.

Force the opponent to make his own mistakes. "None of it makes any sense."

It was time to make Frost concentrate on what Trosper *might* know, and to impel him, in his uncertainty, to magnify the weight of Trosper's secret knowledge. Trosper was motionless. Watchful. Disbelieving. Unblinking. If he was right, and if there was a flaw, a covered blemish, it was time for this unblooded young man to point to it.

"Why I left the Firm when I did?"

Not even close. Trosper raised his eyebrows.

"There weren't any girls, any serious girl anyway, or anything like that, if that's what you're driving at."

Trosper waited. Shrugged.

"Why I covered for Gandy?"

Trosper watched, implacable, until he moved his head, a slight negative signal.

"You mean about Brodsky?"

Bingo.

Trosper nodded.

Frost twisted sideways in the big chair. Another few inches and he would be in a fetal position.

"To tell you the truth . . ."

"That's exactly what I have in mind," Trosper said.

The door opened and Angelica Church stepped into the room. "Is this a good time for our little chat?" she said brightly.

"Angie, sweetheart, come in, sit right here," Frost said.

Trosper smiled manfully. Only once before had his life passed before his eyes.

Angelica Church perched lightly on the arm of the chair beside Frost. Her long legs were drawn up, her knees and ankles were together as if she were negotiating a high-speed maneuver on parallel skis.

"What I want to know is just where you people think you get off putting us under surveillance?" she demanded. Frost beamed his approval.

Trosper glanced wistfully at his empty coffee cup, and then at Angelica. He shook his head and said, "Not possible."

"It damned well is . . ." Frost's hand shook as he filled Trosper's cup.

"What kind of surveillance—telephone, mail, someone on the street?" Trosper asked politely.

"A goddamned street surveillance," Frost said. "I mean we can see what's going on in the street, but there's no way we could know about the telephone or the mail."

"How long has it been going on?"

"Not that it could be news to you, but I spotted the fellow four, maybe five days after you arrived unannounced," Angelica said.

"It *is* news to me," Trosper said. At least it was news that an amateur like Angelica Church thought she had spotted street surveillance.

"I want to know what's going on . . ."

"Tell me about the surveillance."

"It's a professional job," Frost said. "There's one guy who's been at us off and on all the time . . ."

"If it's only one man, it isn't all that professional," Trosper said quietly. "And, certainly not if he's been at it every day."

"But it's true," Angelica said.

"Maybe not every day," Frost said.

"How often then?"

"We've made him twice for sure, and maybe one other time," Frost said.

This was more like it. "Why would anyone be interested enough in you or Miss Church to put you under surveillance?"

"You're the one who took the trouble to find us and to make two trips here to talk about some Russian who was probably dragged off to Siberia two years ago," Angelica said. "Why don't you tell us what's going on?"

Trosper turned to Frost. "What about you and Miss Church? Are you both all right with the Italians?"

"Of course we are," Angelica said sharply. "Our permits are good for another six months."

Trosper glanced at Angelica. "Could your family be worried, or perhaps a—"

"This is my aunt's apartment, and my parents know perfectly well where I am." Angelica's eyes flashed. "And since you're probably too genteel to ask, I don't have a jealous husband either."

"Then that's the best I can do," Trosper said. "I don't know who it was, or what he wanted. But he had nothing to do with my office." With Castle in the act, Trosper would not risk denying anything about the Firm as a whole.

"Don't you think it's a remarkable coincidence that you come snooping, and a week later someone starts following us around?"

"I can't believe the two facts are related . . ." Trosper let his voice drift off. He flicked a bit of lint from the shaped instep of his

polished black shoe and glanced quickly at Angelica. Light from
the library floor lamp touched Angelica's high cheekbones, softening her expression. Trosper wondered for a moment about her relationship with Frost, and recalled Hemingway's advice about not
speculating on the bedroom scenes of one's acquaintances.

"Are you going to tell us or not?" Frost demanded.

"I've told you—I know nothing about it."

"All right," Frost said. "We've given you a chance. Since you've
got nothing to say, I'm going to the Italians tomorrow. The hell
with you people . . ."

"That," Trosper said, "is positively the last thing you should do.
After the Italian security services—probably both DIGOS and
SISDE—have finished crawling right up your nose, some smart
fellow will decide you're a couple of dilettantes who've been swan-
ning around with the terrorists, and want police protection from
your revolutionary playmates. When the Italians give you the boot,
they'll put you both on an Interpol watch list, and you'll be there
till hell freezes."

Frost got up. "What a bunch of bastards you people are."

Trosper glanced at Angelica. It was his best I-am-just-too-polite-
to-ask-you-to-leave-us-the-hell-alone-for-half-an-hour expression. He
waited. Proof positive, there was nothing to telepathy. He turned
to Frost. "I'd like to go back over some of the things you said
about Geneva."

Frost touched Angelica's shoulder. Blessed relief, perhaps he
had intercepted the message. "This really is company business,
Angie. It would be better if you left us alone."

As she got to her feet Angelica said, "There's just one more
thing."

Trosper nodded.

"My father has very good connections in Washington. If I tell
him you're trying to push us around, he'll have plenty to say to a
certain senator."

"Angie, please . . ." Frost got up to open the study door.

"All right," she said. "You can tell me about it later." She was
too tall and lean to underline the statement with a switch of her

behind, but the thought was there.

"You have to excuse Angie," Frost said. "She's always been a great one for having her own way." He smiled and shook his head wonderingly. "But she's a real woman, and like every prize, worth all the effort."

Trosper managed to nod.

"I suppose it's time for a drink. Scotch?"

"Yes, please."

"I'll try to pry some ice out of that damned refrigerator."

Frost disappeared down the hallway.

The doorbell rang.

Frost called from the kitchen. "That will be Maria, without her keys as usual. Will you open the door, *per favore?*"

Trosper pulled the heavy door ajar.

The man didn't look anything like the maid. He was five feet ten, heavyset, and had been standing in the rain. His shapeless raincoat, broad-brimmed hat, and thick crepe-soled shoes were wet. He wore heavy black gloves and stood, feet apart, leaning slightly forward.

Trosper stared for a moment, and said, *"Prego?"*

The man stared back, his eyes blinking with uncertainty. "Signor Froust?" he asked, peering more closely.

Trosper edged back from the door.

The man raised his right hand in a clumsy salute. Then, with a lopsided grin, he corrected his pronunciation slightly. "Signor Fross?"

As Trosper stepped back, his eyes glimpsed the open packet of Pall Mall cigarettes half-hidden in the thick glove on the man's left hand.

"Mister Fross?" He spoke louder, and raised his left hand slowly, as if to offer a cigarette from the open pack.

Trosper lunged forward and with both hands grabbed the man's wrist, shoving the gloved hand up and away from his face.

There was a pop, as if a toy cap pistol had been fired, and a softer echo from the high ceiling. Bits of paper and tobacco drifted down from the cigarette package.

The man swung a clumsy right-hand blow. Trosper ducked and kicked savagely at the goon's knees. He was too close. The toe of his shoe caught the man's shin and tore upward toward the knee.

Growling with pain, he wrenched his arm free of Trosper's grasp and staggered a step backwards. With a curse, he thrust the torn cigarette package at Trosper's face. Trosper recognized the matte aluminum box now only partially concealed within the red paper. He twisted violently, and dropped to his knees.

But there was no sound. The device was empty or a second charge had misfired.

Trosper pitched forward, scrabbling to grab the man's ankles. Through the torn trousers, he could see blood oozing over the raw shin as he yanked at the heavy black shoes.

The man fell backwards against the balustrade, his thrashing legs tearing free of Trosper's grasp. Struggling to catch his balance, he dropped the weapon as he stumbled, lurched sideways, and rolled down the few stairs to the half-landing below.

Trosper lay flat at the head of the stairs, his vision blurred and his chest heaving. If the bastard has another weapon, Trosper realized, it won't be cyanide gas in a custom-made concealment device.

The goon rolled to his side and pushed himself against the wall. Without taking his eyes off Trosper, the man struggled to regain his breath. For a moment he seemed to be considering the possibility of charging back up the stairs. Gasping for breath, he heaved himself to his feet. He took a final look at Trosper, and with a clumsy movement, bent to scoop up his hat. The wet rubber soles of his heavy shoes made a sticking sound as the goon moved unsteadily down the stairs to the ground-floor landing.

Trosper heard the street door scrape as it was pulled open. He stared at the torn cigarette package. The old-style gas guns, meant to be concealed in a cigarette pack, used compressed air to spray cyanide vapor into the victim's face, and were considered useless at more than four feet. That much he remembered. What he could not recall was how long it took for the gas to dissipate.

It had been at least a minute, probably longer, since the device had been fired. He would give it another thirty seconds for good measure. He counted to thirty. And then to thirty again before he pulled himself to his feet. He picked up the cigarette pack, wrapped it in his handkerchief, and eased it gingerly into his side pocket. As he stepped back into the apartment, he glanced in the hall mirror. Still breathing heavily, he straightened his tie and brushed the dust from his trousers.

Frost called from the kitchen at the end of the apartment hallway. "Maria, is that you?"

There was a rattle, and Trosper glimpsed Frost, backing cautiously through the kitchen door, balancing glasses, a bottle of scotch, and a siphon on a large silver tray. "Was that Maria?" he called.

"No," Trosper said. "It was a man. He was looking for someone else."

TROSPER took a sip of his drink. "About Brodsky?"

Frost looked closely at Trosper. "Are you feeling all right? You look sweaty, a little feverish . . ."

Trosper pulled a foulard from his breast pocket and dabbed at his forehead. "It's a fever I had years ago," he lied. "Every now and again it kicks up a hot flash or two." He was still having trouble controlling his breathing, and his elbows felt as if they had been hit with a baseball bat. His knees were bruised, and to his dismay, the toecap of his right shoe was scuffed.

"Brodsky?" he asked.

"There's nothing so special about him," Frost said. "He's a peddler, with a file four inches thick. When I told Terry Nash—the code man—that Gandy and I had bumped into him, he laughed and said he'd met Tolya and that everyone in Geneva knew him." Frost stopped to light another cigarette. He grinned at Trosper through a cloud of smoke. "Nash was no dope. He was too well qualified to spend all his time sweating over other people's cable traffic. He has his eye on better things. He even ran some name searches directly with the Washington office—he'd just type up a cable, and send it. When the answer came in, he would keep it in his office. Old Buster Rodman never even knew about it."

"He told you all this?"

Frost nodded. "We got to be friends, I've even invited him here for a weekend."

"Did you mention his sending his own cables to Gandy?"

Frost hesitated, his confidence ebbing. "There wasn't any point . . ." He shook his head. "No, I didn't tell him."

"No point in telling Gandy, your boss, the man who was handling an in-place Russian agent, that the code clerk in Buster Rodman's office was bumming around Geneva? That he was running name searches in Washington files behind Rodman's back? No point in mentioning that Master Nash was on a first-name basis with a creep like Brodsky?"

"Look," Frost said. "Things had changed a lot from your time. Bates had new ideas . . . the Firm was more like the old days, when the OSS guys were encouraged to take a lot of initiative."

Trosper stared at Frost. "Not that it matters much, but OSS got by on initiative because there was a war on, and they had no choice but to write the rules as they went along." He leaned forward, closer to Frost. "Tell me the parts you've left out."

"There was no big deal, I've told you everything."

Trosper got up and walked across the room to the double windows. He had skinned both knees and his elbow was beginning to swell. He pushed the draperies apart and studied the rain-drenched street. He turned back to face Frost. "There's something I'm going to tell you."

Frost raised his eyebrows. Trosper ignored the implied skepticism.

"There is good reason to believe that Peter Gandy was murdered." Trosper spoke slowly, giving equal weight to each word.

Frost blinked, and moved his shoulders as if ducking a punch. "That's nonsense . . ." He shook his head. "Why would anyone want to kill Peter?"

"It was a professional job . . ."

"You're lying," Frost said, his voice tense.

"It had all the benchmarks of Moscow Center . . ."

"This has nothing to do with me . . ."

"As of now, I think it has to do with Bondarev," Trosper said. "But only Gandy and you had anything at all to do with Bondarev."

Frost shook his head.

"And that makes it very important that you tell me everything you know about Bondarev and anything else that might have gone on in Geneva," Trosper said.

"Look," Frost said. "I don't owe you people a damned thing. I left the business because I hated it. I've told you everything I know about Bondarev, about Geneva, and about Gandy." He stood up. "Now it's past time that you get the hell out of here."

Trosper stood up. "There's just one more thing . . ."

"The hell with you and that whole damned Firm of yours."

"I don't know the man you think was surveilling you," Trosper said, "but he might have been the fellow who rang the bell a few minutes ago. He's not from my office and he wasn't looking for me. In view of what happened to Peter, it might be a good idea if you and Miss Church were to take a vacation, get away from Florence for a while. Maybe even leave Italy for a few weeks."

"That's crazy," Frost said. "We're just getting settled here."

Trosper pulled his handkerchief and the crumpled cigarette package from his pocket. He dropped them on the table beside Frost. "Your visitor left his calling card."

Frost stared, then picked up the device. "For Christ's sake, it's just like one of the things they showed us at the Fort."

Trosper nodded. "A bit old-fashioned now, but the real thing." He wrapped the handkerchief around the weapon. "The man mistook me for you. If I hadn't spotted this thing, I'd be dead and the coroner would have called it a heart attack."

"How the hell did you get it away from him?" There was a hint of admiration in the question.

Trosper stuffed the weapon into his pocket. "I'll be at the Excelsior until mid-afternoon tomorrow," he said. "If you think of anything pertinent, and decide to call, remember my name is John Doughty."

"There isn't any more, I've told you everything I know."

Frost was lying, but Trosper had had enough. It was already a night to remember.

As Trosper picked his coat off the chair by the door, Frost said, "What should I tell Angie?"

Trosper pulled on his coat. "Tell her I think someone is going to murder you."

18

FLORENCE

"It complicates things a bit, your being a young woman." Trosper took the last bite of his scampi, and a sip of wine. His delayed reaction to last night's trauma and his failure to move Frost had shaken him. He realized he had been silent through most of lunch.

Ida Rowan blinked. "What?"

"I just meant both of us staying in the hotel, and meeting for lunch, separate rooms notwithstanding." He should have known better, he realized belatedly, than try to make spontaneous small talk with Ida.

"There *are* other hotels," she said calmly. She wore contact lenses in place of her heavy spectacles, and was turned out in a navy blue suit. It occurred to Trosper to wonder if it had been made for her—adding a hint of height, smoothing down the hips.

"On the chance that bloody-minded Frost would agree to meet me here, I wanted you on hand to deal with the recording." After clearing customs at the airport, Ida had gone to the Rome office to exchange her travel papers for a cold passport and supporting documents. She had also picked up a pair of miniature short-range radio transmitters and a tape recorder.

"I suppose it was the divine Miss Church who insisted Frost make me come to the apartment—I think she likes to monitor things," Trosper said. What he wanted, Trosper realized, was the chance to discuss the case with someone whose judgment he trusted.

"If I were some young guy, and we were staying in a hotel like this and met for lunch, or even had breakfast together, do you think people would assume we were business colleagues or a couple of gays?"

"I've never been sure what Italians think," Trosper murmured. If all the young women graduates of the Fort were as relentless as Ida Rowan, Moscow Center was in deep trouble.

"Then why do you care whether a hotel clerk thinks you're shacking up with me or some guy? Surely you're not that concerned about your sexual identity?"

"Damn it, we're not here to discuss my sexual anything." He stopped short when he realized he was blushing. "This is business," he continued calmly, "and it's not going all that well." Then, managing a slight, conciliatory smile, he said, "It's your reputation I'm thinking of. You're young enough to be my daughter." He could feel his blush deepening as he realized he sounded like a parody of Amelia Bloomer.

"But you wouldn't worry about anyone's reputation if your caddy were some male hunk right out of training?"

Trosper managed to keep smiling. "I'm sure you're right. But I've never liked this sinister goddamned city, and as of last night, I really loathe it." He rubbed his swollen elbow. "I've got a lot on my mind. I'm not sure exactly where we go from here. And if it hasn't occurred to you, I'm not entirely accustomed to working with sensitive young women." If he were ever again invited to the Fort to lecture the plebes, his talk would be on the uses of silence. Precious, golden silence. Silence as a weapon. Silence as provocation. Blessed silence as a balm . . .

Ida spoke again. "If it will make things easier for you, just think of me as one of the guys." She blinked rapidly and added softly, "Most of the guys do . . . "

Trosper could only hope that the young porter threading his way between the tables had a message for him.

FROST'S telephone manner was cheery, and businesslike.

"Mr. Doughty? John Doughty?"

"Yes," Trosper said. "John Doughty." At least Frost had remembered his cover name.

"Oh, good, I was hoping you hadn't left yet. I've been thinking about our talk last night . . ." Frost spoke with the heartiness of an actor delivering a few lines of exposition in Act One.

Trosper murmured a response.

"I wonder if I might see you for a few minutes before you leave? I think there may be a bit of unfinished business . . ."

"I'm in room 306, come by at four." Trosper managed to keep the enthusiasm out of his voice. "I'll have tea sent up."

Frost hesitated—perhaps to get Angelica's consent—before saying, "Okay, I'll be there."

IDA looked up from her *coupe jacques* as Trosper slipped back into his chair. He signaled for the check. "We've got to move quickly," he said. "Frost is coming to my room at four, and I want the meeting recorded. We'll also need to know if anyone is on Frost's tail."

Ida nodded politely.

"You've got half an hour to set up the audio . . ."

Ida nodded.

"My guess is that Frost will come on foot. As soon as the audio is set up, can you position yourself to see if anyone is behind him?"

Ida Rowan pushed the empty ice cream dish to one side and picked up her handbag. "I checked the area yesterday," she said. "There's a little statue and some stone benches where the Ponte alla Carraia meets the Piazza Goldoni. If Frost leaves from his apartment, he will almost certainly cross the Ponte Carraia. I can easily cover the bridge and anyone who might be behind him from the benches." She hesitated. "But I'm not so sure I can identify the tail . . ."

"If he's there, he'll probably be on the other side of the street from Frost, well back, a hundred yards or more," Trosper said. "He may be thickset, moon-faced, heavy shoes, raincoat, and almost certainly will be wearing a hat." He paused before saying, "What I want is a good description. Don't under any circumstance try to follow him."

"I'll rig the transmitters first, then get to the bridge."

Trosper signed the bill.

Ida stood up. "I hate to mention this," she said with a smile, "but unless you come with me to your room, I'll have to ask the clerk to give me your key." Her smile broadened. "It's going to look like an assignation, any way you handle it." She beamed at the maître d'hôtel and patted Trosper's arm reassuringly.

19

FLORENCE

TROSPER turned away from the double windows looking out over the Piazza Ognissanti and stepped to the dresser. Ida had placed one of the miniature transmitters in his open shaving case on the dresser. It was concealed in a half-empty box of antacid tablets, but should have adequate volume. He knelt to examine the second transmitter taped beneath an end table beside the chair Frost would use. There had been no time for a test, but if everything worked, the crude stereo transmission would be received by the small radio and tape recorder in Ida Rowan's room.

"Look," Frost said. "That thug with his damned cigarette case puts a different face on things." His flannels and blazer were rumpled. A light gray turtleneck sweater added to his pallor and gave Trosper the impression Frost had spent the night arguing with Angelica Church.

"But maybe you were just putting me on?" Frost cocked his head to one side, and seemed to be soliciting an affirmative response.

"Not about Gandy, and not about the goon last night."

"Why would anyone want to kill me?"

"There's no accounting for taste," Trosper said.

"But I haven't done anything. . . ."

"Maybe, if you can bring yourself to tell me a straight story, I can sort something out," Trosper said.

"Are you really sure about what happened to Gandy?"

"There's *no* doubt," Trosper said. "Peter was murdered with a poison that was meant to simulate a natural death. And there's no reason to believe the murder was committed as revenge, or even as a warning to the rest of us. Someone wanted Gandy out of the way without creating suspicion." He waited before saying, "And as of last night, it's also clear that someone has the same plan for you."

Frost took a deep breath, and exhaled noisily. It was as if he had hoped Trosper would deny everything.

"Now, how about telling me what you've come to talk about?"

Frost toyed with his teacup. "There's something about Brodsky that I didn't mention last night," he said. His glance darted around the room, avoiding eye contact.

Trosper remained silent. The golden boy would have to pay his own way.

"I never even told Gandy about it." Frost shook his head and looked expectantly across the table. Trosper said nothing.

"Up to a point, what I told you about Brodsky is correct," Frost said. "I mean, I really did check the file, and I knew Brodsky was a merchant. If I'd had more to do in Geneva, I probably wouldn't have bothered. But aside from Bondarev, he was the only real live spy I had ever laid eyes on." He looked at Trosper, soliciting encouragement. When he got none, he added, "That was why I asked Gandy if I could get in touch with Brodsky, maybe have a meal and get some sense of an intelligence hustler."

"You told me Gandy had agreed," Trosper said patiently.

"I shouldn't have tried to lie like that," Frost said, shaking his head. "I did ask Gandy, but he went off like a hand grenade. He said I was not to have anything whatsoever to do with Brodsky. Then he gave me a lecture about how we were in Geneva on a big case, and that we had no business trolling in the local sewers."

"But you did see Brodsky?"

Frost nodded. "I bumped into him—believe me, I wasn't looking for him—at the Cintra, a sherry bar across the river from where the U.N. crowd hangs out. It's one of the places Terry Nash put me on to."

"He does get around . . ."

"We had a couple of drinks, and decided to have dinner," Frost said. "It was just as I told you before—Brodsky was completely tame. He asked a couple of questions about what I was doing in Geneva, but I had a solid commercial cover, and he didn't seem interested enough to probe. He didn't even ask how I had happened to meet Gandy." Frost shrugged. "We had dinner at some *raclette* joint, and split the bill. I was home by eleven."

"The first time we talked," Trosper said, "you said you'd seen Brodsky twice . . ."

Frost smiled. "Not bad—I couldn't remember if I had told you we met a couple of times." He hitched himself up in the chair. "It was the second time when it hit the fan."

"When was this?"

"Two, maybe three weeks later . . ."

Time enough for Brodsky to have checked with his handler, and for the handler to report to his control and get instructions.

"Did Brodsky call you, or was it another . . . er . . . *chance* meeting?"

Frost looked warily at Trosper. "Every couple of weeks or so, Nash and I would have a drink and drive out along the lake to one of those fish joints near Lausanne. This night he telephoned and said he might have to stay late at the office, and that if he didn't show up by eight, I would know he couldn't make it."

"Nash didn't show, and Brodsky happened by?"

"That's right," Frost said.

"And you two went along for dinner?"

Frost nodded. "Right from the outset, Brodsky was different from the first time we went out, ordering drinks, insisting on an expensive meal, and paying more than his share." Frost shrugged. "He came on like some horny old guy trying to put the make on a chick." He stopped abruptly and glanced at Trosper. Then, apparently satisfied that Trosper was not offended, he took a reassuring sip of tea. "I should have known what was coming, but the truth is it didn't even cross my mind."

Trosper poured more tea. There was nothing to be gained in pressing Frost.

"By the time we finished dinner, I was a little drunk, but not drunk enough to forget exactly how Tolya got around to it. We had left the restaurant and were walking toward the Ba-Ta-Clan, that's a nightclub." Frost splashed milk into his tea. "We were just chatting when, clear as a bell, he said something like, 'I've been watching you, and I can help.' At first I thought I'd misunderstood him."

"What did you think he was going to do? Recommend a good tailor?"

Frost leaned forward toward Trosper. "I'll tell you one thing—when it happens it's sure as hell different from the lectures and security crap they hand out at the Fort."

"I suppose it can seem that way," Trosper said.

"When Brodsky said he could help, I said something cynical like 'I can sure use all the help I can get.' That's when he said, 'Let's go to my place, we can have a drink and maybe go to the nightclub later.' He had two rooms—nicely furnished, with a couple of pretty good pictures." Frost ran his hand through his hair. "By this time I was really interested in finding out what kind of a scam he would try to pull. He poured a couple of drinks and let fly . . ."

"Did you give a thought to his taping your little tête-à-tête?" Trosper asked.

"Of course I . . ." Frost fell silent, and then began again. "To tell the truth, it never crossed my mind."

"And?"

"Brodsky started his pitch—what else?" Frost reached across the coffee table to pour himself the last of the tea. "Until he got going, I wouldn't have believed the pressure, or even that I would sit there listening to him."

"What pressure exactly?" Trosper asked.

"I couldn't believe they knew so much about me—they had me coming and going." Tea spilled into the saucer as Frost put the cup back on the table. "They even thought I was broke."

"Were you broke?"

"Geneva's expensive as hell—if I'd been living on my salary and per diem, I would have been broke all right. Along with everything else, I'd been chasing this girl . . ." Frost glanced around the room as if he expected Angelica suddenly to materialize. Then, with a self-conscious smile, he said, "A nifty little Italian, she was working in a bar—Nash had struck out with her, but she came on nicely with me." His smile faded. "If I hadn't had a little money coming in from my trust, I sure would have been stony."

"What exactly did Brodsky say?" There would be time enough to identify the girl.

Frost shook his head. "He said he had a proposition for me."

"And?"

"I wasn't so drunk I'd forgotten that he was a con man. So, I said something smart like, 'What have you got, a formula for changing lead into gold?' This made the bastard laugh. Then he said, 'That's it, you've got it exactly right—I really can help you change lead into gold.' Then he started laughing again." Frost squirmed in his chair. "You know it wasn't anything like the stuff they hand out at the Fort. This was real life. Everything Brodsky said underlined how much those guys know about their business. He had an answer for everything. Like a presidential press conference, all the responses had been thought out—whatever I said, he had an answer. He had all the answers."

"The pitch?"

Frost shook his head. "It was almost unbelievable. He wanted me to sign on with Moscow Center—it was just as simple as that. All I had to do was to stay in place and work both sides of the street."

"What did you say?"

"I told him he had it all wrong, that I was just a businessman, that I didn't have any secrets. I started laughing, and tried to make a joke of it, but he just ignored my talk about business." Frost ran his hands through his hair. "Before I knew what was happening, he had me completely conned—I'd forgotten my cover and was arguing with him on his level, operative to operative."

"What did he offer you?"

"Brodsky's no dope. He began nice and easy, explaining that politics had nothing to do with it. He said plenty of our people knew there wasn't a nickel's difference between Washington and Moscow. I told him he was talking nonsense, but nothing slowed him down. He said the more we know about one another—East and West—the less chance we all have of getting our ass fried in another war. 'I've been through one war,' he said, 'and believe me, you won't want any part of the next one. Right now, you've got to take care of yourself—and not end up like Gandy. I know as much as you do about your shop. You won't be doing any harm—it's all part of the game.' "

"What did he offer?"

Frost leaned back in his chair, resuming his man-of-the-world pose. "I suppose it was the usual formula—career help and money. They would feed me an occasional agent, nothing fancy, just enough to make sure I would get along in the service. There'd be money enough to make things easy, and an escrow account. Somewhere along the line he said, 'Best of all, you won't have any problem when you decide to get out. We've learned a lot about you guys, and we know that it's no good trying to keep someone on the job once he's made all the dough he wants.' "

Trosper laughed. "They'd let you out all right, but you'd have to be ten years into retirement or dead."

"I know that," Frost said petulantly. "It was about then that Brodsky got crafty, and started painting a little ideology over his proposition. Stuff like, 'What's happened to your generation and all the talk about one world? Don't you know that no one wants war except those maniacs you have in Washington?' "

"That's not much of a pitch," Trosper said.

"The bastard kept prattling on about *glasnost* and the Gorbachev revolution, socialist free enterprise—like in Hungary—help for our third world brothers, all the usual crap," Frost said. "If he had really understood me, he'd have known I don't give a damn about any of them—black, brown, or beige."

"Have you told Miss Church any of this?"

"Do you think I'm crazy?"

"What about the hook?" Trosper asked.

"The what?"

"The hook—the reason they thought you could be had, and why you wouldn't blow the whistle." Impassive and unblinking, Trosper managed to keep eye contact with Frost.

Frost thrust himself back in the chair, pulled his legs up, and locked his arms around them, comforting himself. He began to speak, stopped, and then began again. "It was a straightforward recruitment pitch—the new look, cash-and-carry espionage, like the Walkers and those other shitheads. But there weren't any threats."

"Yes there were," Trosper said evenly. This was the moment to be right, and he savored it. "There's always a hook."

Frost's face flushed, and seemed to swell as if he were choking back a sneeze.

"He wasn't asking you to join some goddamned fraternity, he was talking treason."

Frost flinched and closed his eyes. "I swore I was through with this damned business." He opened his eyes and glared at Trosper. "I should have thrown you out the first time you came around."

"But you didn't," Trosper said softly. "And that's because you wanted to know what I was after." He paused and his voice hardened. "You were also trying to make up your mind about getting something off your chest."

Frost shook his head. "You're pretty damned smug, just sitting there like that." He half rose from his chair and then slumped back. "Didn't anyone ever whistle at you? Are you so goddamned pure nobody ever bothered? Haven't you got any idea what it's like to go through something like that?"

"Now that you know what I want, you can stop the crap and tell me about it."

Frost leaned back in his chair and stared at the ceiling. "Christ, I thought I knew Gandy pretty well . . ." As he began to speak, Frost closed his eyes. "Brodsky told me Moscow knew all about Gandy and me, and all about Bondarev as well. He said they had Bondarev under control and that if I didn't act sensibly, Moscow had a big operation all set to go. They were going to shake the Firm to pieces."

Trosper's jaw tightened. He could feel the muscles swell as he set his teeth.

Frost spoke quickly, as if he were ripping a bandage from a

painful wound. "I wasn't ready for anything like that," Frost mumbled. "The training was no good . . . It wasn't right to let me go up against guys like that."

"You're the one who wanted to play spy with Brodsky," Trosper said softly. "Gandy ordered you to stay away from him."

"The hell with Gandy," Frost said. "It wasn't fair what happened."

Trosper wondered why anyone thought that playing fair had anything to do with secret operations.

"What was Brodsky threatening?"

With his arms locked around his legs, Frost pressed his face against his knees and began to rock back and forth. "He said the big boys—that's a quote—were prepared to blow the whole story of Gandy and me *blackmailing* poor young Bondarev into being a spy. He said they would make a diplomatic protest straight to the Secretary General at the U.N. in New York, and that they had pictures, and all the crap necessary to prove their case. At the U.N., they were going to release the whole story to the press. He said Bondarev would be a hero, a young man brave enough to resist our blackmail, and to turn himself in to his own people."

"But nobody blackmailed Bondarev—he approached us."

"Hell yes, but when Brodsky began talking about the blackmail, he reached behind the sofa and fished out a big manila envelope. Sure enough he had a fistful of photographs of Bondarev and this young girl. He said Moscow would prove that we set him up, took the pictures, and tried to use them to blackmail him. The pictures looked exactly as if they'd been taken clandestinely in some cheap hotel room—grainy, slightly out of focus, but nothing left to the imagination. Just Bondarev having at this girl—a little S and M, and some everyday sort of sodomy." Frost managed a faint smirk. "A few shots were tame enough for the scandal sheets to publish—the others were more for collectors."

"And all of them staged?"

Frost unwound, pulled himself upright in the chair, and looked around the room. "You wouldn't have a drop of whiskey by any chance?"

Trosper took a bottle of scotch from the dresser drawer and poured a drink. "Water?"

Frost nodded. "My guess is that they took the pictures in a studio somewhere and made them look as if they were real." He pulled a package of cigarettes from his pocket and fumbled for a lighter. "When they uncovered Bondarev's contact with us, they probably made him pose for the pictures." Frost made an obscene gesture, and said, "All the same, he looked enthusiastic enough . . ."

"You said Brodsky had pictures of you and Gandy?"

Frost inhaled deeply and blew the cigarette smoke toward the ceiling. "Not the same kind, if that's what you're driving at. They were good shots of Gandy and me coming and going into the safe house." He laughed. "If Buster Rodman is still in Geneva, you can tell him there's one safe house he can write off."

"Where is it?"

"On the Rue de Lausanne, a nice apartment a few hundred yards from the Gare de Cornavin."

"What did Brodsky threaten *you* with?"

"He said that when the story was released, with pictures of Gandy and me, our careers would be ruined, and the Firm would be in the middle of a scandal big enough to bring the White House down on the Controller's head." He bobbed his head, inviting Trosper to offer him some encouragement. He got none.

"How did you leave it with Brodsky?"

"By the time he brought out the pictures, I was stone sober. We talked for a while, mostly me asking questions about what would be in it for me, and how risky it would be—at this point he was coming on like a regular guy, he couldn't have been more reassuring." Frost grimaced and stubbed out his cigarette. "I admitted a few things, like not always agreeing with our foreign policy, but by then I was just trying to find out enough to give Gandy a complete picture. Finally, I said I'd think it over."

"And?"

"Hell, I was afraid he'd go through the roof, maybe even hustle a couple of thugs out of the closet. But he didn't. All he said was that his people would cooperate with me, but they would not put up with any crap. He said if I breathed one word of the approach, they would know about it."

Frost gulped the remains of his drink and balanced the empty glass at the edge of the table beside the tea tray. He stared at Trosper, for the first time looking him straight in the eye. "There's something else I better tell you," he said slowly. "You're not going to like it." Frost cocked his head to one side, softening the flicker of defiance.

"Try me."

"They had me completely boxed in."

Trosper waited.

"Look, maybe you really are here to sort out Bondarev, and fix whoever killed Gandy. If so, you'd better face the facts."

"What facts?"

"Brodsky told me, and then he proved it—Moscow had Bondarev under control. They knew Gandy cold and they had me chapter and verse."

"That's an old dodge, you know that," Trosper said. "They fake having all the answers, convince their dupe that he's only got one way to go—and that's the one they've chosen for him."

"Look," Frost said. "I may not be the best case man going, but I'm not dumb. And I'm not a dupe . . ."

"What was he after?"

"Christ, you're acting like Kim Philby's pals must have done. They couldn't believe that one of their own had gone sour. You've got the same idea about Gandy." Frost waited. "Do you know what I'm talking about now?"

"No."

"There was only one place they could have got so much stuff on me . . ."

There had to be more than one place, Trosper told himself.

"Gandy," Frost said loudly. "Peter Gandy, goddamn it. They must have got to him a while back—maybe even years ago." Frost stopped, and took another cigarette. He studied Trosper's face for a moment and said, "Maybe it was only after he realized that Bates was going to retire him, he made some kind of a deal. Then when he got the Geneva assignment, he hit the jackpot. He gave them Bondarev's head on a plate. They would have paid plenty for that . . ." Frost twisted uneasily in the stiff chair. "I told you, you weren't going to like it."

"Go on."

"That would have made Gandy's reputation in Moscow . . ."

"Almost certainly."

"As I see it now," Frost said, "Gandy knew he had to work fast if he was going to make another deal, another quick killing. The Russians couldn't let Bondarev stay in business, and when that case folded, Bates would almost certainly retire Gandy. After that, the most Gandy could hope for was a little clandestine consulting with Moscow Center—he wouldn't have access to anything new, just personal background stuff on some of his old pals, and chit-chat on old operations. He knew he couldn't pay the rent peddling that stuff. Perhaps that's why he thought maybe, just maybe, I was worth an approach. If it worked, it would have been a coup. If it didn't work, well maybe he'd get some points for trying. Perhaps he didn't give a damn about that or anything but a bonus for having set me up."

Frost walked to the dresser and poured himself a drink. "Perhaps you'd better give that a thought or two . . ."

"You thimble-wit," Trosper said. "Of course I've thought about it. I've thought a lot about it. I might even have come up with answers if you'd given me some of the facts." So much for self-discipline, he realized.

Frost managed a slight, feminine smile, and stepped into the bathroom to run water into his drink. "You know," he called, "I'm not really cut out for this business."

"The thought has crossed my mind," Trosper said. "But let's get back to Brodsky. You don't need me to sort out your personality problems."

"All Brodsky's concern for me might have been effective, except that while he was talking, I kept wondering how they had collected so much information on me, and fighting the idea that Gandy had sold out."

"Could Brodsky have been *trying* to suggest that Gandy was their man?"

"He's not that subtle." Frost's confidence had come back in a rush. "He simply didn't realize that he'd pressed me so hard that he'd blown Gandy." Frost swirled the whiskey in his glass. "What a rotten business you guys are in. I really liked Gandy and until I realized he had gone over, I respected him as much as anyone I ever met."

Trosper was silent.

"I guess he was just used up—maybe he'd been in the business too long. Maybe he just didn't give a damn anymore." Frost shrugged dramatically, and cocked his head to one side. "Maybe he just needed the money, like Benedict Arnold . . ."

"Perhaps."

"The one thing sure is that the recruitment pitch was set up so as to convince me that I was completely boxed in and that Moscow Center was damned well informed on the Firm."

"And Brodsky just let you walk away?"

"Look," Frost said, "if Gandy was their man it would explain why they killed him, wouldn't it? I mean, he might have screwed them in some way. Maybe he was threatening to blow some operation that he had set up, and trying to milk them for a lot of dough. It would be like them to snuff him for that, wouldn't it?"

Trosper mumbled a noncommittal response.

"When I told Brodsky I needed some time, and that I'd meet him again in a couple of days," Frost said, "I still expected the door to burst open and the goons to come tumbling in. He obviously didn't like this very much, but he came on sweet as pie—'Take a day, but make absolutely sure you do come back' was all he said."

"And so you just went home?"

"I was too nervous to go back to that miserable apartment Rodman had put me in, so I called my little Italian. I figured that if anyone could take my mind off my troubles, she could. No harm done."

"Next day?"

"Gandy was smooth as glass, no sign at all that he had anything on his mind but getting Bondarev on the track." Frost paused, waiting for another question from Trosper. There was none, and he said, "It would have been better if I could have talked to someone."

"But you said nothing to Gandy?"

"I didn't dare to, not in the circumstances."

"To the Italian girl?"

Frost shook his head.

"To your buddy, Nash?"

"I'd scarcely discuss it with a commo man."

"But you saw Brodsky again?"

Frost fumbled with a cigarette. "Look, I went to meet Brodsky in some little joint just off the Rue de Rhône. I was some scared, but I said straight out I had no interest in his goddamned proposition. As far as I was concerned he could tell Moscow Center to go ahead with a publicity campaign, anything they could dream up. I told him our case file would prove to any congressional committee that we were on the level, that there hadn't been any blackmail, and that the only disgraceful behavior had been on the Moscow side."

Frost beamed and then seemed to simper. It was as if he expected a round of applause. But Trosper had known too many agents who had toughed their way through lethal situations in areas less benign than downtown Geneva. The most he would give Frost was a slight, encouraging nod.

"Then I told him I hadn't said anything to anyone about him, and that I wasn't ever going to tell anyone about his offer. I told him—and this is holy truth—that the intelligence racket was not for me, and that I was getting out of it just as soon as I could." Frost set his empty glass on the tea table. "I told him that if I ever laid eyes on him again, I would beat the crap out of him—and I didn't give a damn where he might be at the time."

Frost's smile returned. "He was some surprised, I'll tell you that. He had probably spent an hour telling his control what a job he had done on me, and how he had me completely in the bag. When he realized I meant what I said, he went red, and began to thrash around so much I thought he was going to fall off his chair. He couldn't come up with a coherent sentence. He just sat there, spluttering threats in English and German."

"*When* did this happen?"

Frost thought for a moment. "You know, I didn't keep a diary or anything. That's one thing I took away from the training—no personal notes, no diary, no journals, ever." He was confident again. "But you can date it from the time Bondarev left Geneva—it was two, maybe three weeks before he was called back to Moscow." Frost paused before saying, "Cause and effect?"

"I shouldn't be surprised," Trosper said. "The truth now—did you tell Gandy about it?"

Frost's confidence ebbed. "God's own truth," he said slowly, "I did not tell Gandy, and until this minute, I've never mentioned it to a soul." He peered intently at Trosper. "The most I did was send a cable on my own to the Firm asking for background on the intelligence outfit Brodsky said he was with during the war—a 'FAK' or something like that. But I left before we ever got an answer, if one was ever sent. All I wanted was to get as far away from the whole mess as I could."

"As a matter of curiosity, what did you think would happen— that it would simply blow over?" Trosper's clenched jaw was beginning to ache.

"Look, I was on my own, completely on my own," Frost said. "I had to think my own way through it. As it was I came up with the right solution. I decided that if I told Gandy, and if they had Gandy in their pocket, I'd be in rotten trouble. But if I didn't tell Gandy, then Moscow would probably decide not to do anything." He shrugged. "After all, if they made a big stink about Bondarev being blackmailed, and put out a lot of publicity about Gandy and me, it would be Gandy who would be used up. Since he was their creature, I figured they might think he still had a little mileage left."

"Even after you got back to Washington, you didn't see fit to tell anyone that Gandy might have gone sour?"

"There was no way to do that without telling the whole story," Frost said.

"Didn't you think it might have been worth mentioning that

Brodsky was a bought-and-paid-for Moscow Center agent, and that he had told you Bondarev was under Soviet control?" Trosper realized he had been lightly pounding his clenched left fist against his thigh.

"Look," Frost said. "Bondarev never gave us anything worth reporting. It was clear to me that he never would." He smiled uneasily. "The Firm has a big file that proves Brodsky is a bum. Gandy was going to be retired, and I was surely going to quit. Why pull the house down over everyone's head?"

"Did you have any further contact with Brodsky or anyone from Moscow Center?"

"I never laid eyes on Brodsky again, and I was out of the Firm a week after I got back from Geneva," Frost said. "Until you showed up, I had practically forgotten the whole rotten business."

Frost went to the dresser. "Look, I didn't say anything to Angie about the guy with the cigarette gun. But I did tell her about Gandy being murdered and you trying to find out about it." Frost picked up his empty glass. "Angie's a class six skier," he said thoughtfully. "She's been talking about Kitzbuehl for a month now. So last night, I agreed to go for a couple of weeks. We're leaving tomorrow." He glanced at the scotch on the dresser. "I'll just have half a one for the road?"

He poured the whiskey and turned to Trosper. "I still can't believe it—there's no reason for anyone to want to kill me." Frost's expression was blurred with drink and self-pity. "There's one other thing . . ."

Trosper nodded.

"When you told me Gandy was dead, my first idea was that maybe you guys had found him out and put him away—like you said, just to tidy up a loose end." He turned to the mirror over the dresser and ran his fingers through his hair. "But I guess that's something you wouldn't be at liberty to discuss?" Frost managed a bitchy grin and downed his drink. As he began to move toward the door, he turned back to Trosper.

"Look, I'm sorry to have pulled the chain on Gandy. He used to be a good guy, it's just that he spent too long in your lousy business." Frost fumbled with the doorknob. "He's dead, so it probably doesn't matter, but if I had to choose, I'd still take Gandy over the rest of you guys."

Trosper closed the door. It had grown darker. He snapped on another light and went into the bathroom. He turned the tap and doused his face in the cold running water. It soaked his collar and dripped onto his tie. "The golden boy," he said aloud, staring into the mirror. "He doesn't belong on the same planet as Gandy." He brushed his hair into place and said, "There damned well is another way they could have got the book on Frost."

He splashed more cold water on his eyes. There was no place for tears in the racket.

20

FLORENCE

"WHAT an afternoon," Ida said. "It was even better than if you had busted him right over your knee." She was flushed with excitement. "I mean you had built up all that pressure without Frost even realizing what you were doing. You *made* him think he'd taken the decision all by himself." She helped herself to one of the petit fours that came with the tea Trosper had ordered for Frost.

"You're too generous," Trosper muttered. The long session with Frost had meant he would have to spend another night in Florence. Ida's presence in his hotel room made it difficult to concentrate on packing for an early morning departure.

"There's a baseball player who used to say, 'It's never over till it's over.' " Then, like a parson apologizing for an impromptu sermon, he said, "And that's the lesson for today—budget enough time for the other guy to have the last word."

He pulled the miniature transmitter from the box of antacid tablets and handed it to Ida. "When he thinks the pressure is off, he'll relax a little, sometimes even ventilate a bit. Then—if you've laid the plumbing properly, and are a little lucky—he may even come up with a clue to something he's been concentrating on hiding. Sometimes it will pop right out."

As he dropped to his knees to pull the second transmitter from beneath the end table, he said softly, "Sometimes it's more difficult to keep your own emotions in check." He handed the transmitter to Ida. She would return the audio gear to the Rome office when she picked up her passport.

"To be honest, I'd given up on Frost by the time he telephoned." He plucked a suit from the closet and folded it into his suitcase. "My guess is that Angelica spent most of last night trying to thump the story out of him. By the time he told her part of it, he probably decided he was getting in over his head." Trosper snorted. "That must have been when he decided he'd better keep the dirty bits for me."

Ida took a frosted cookie. "Wasn't Peter Gandy a friend of yours?"

"Yes, he was," Trosper said.

"He had a good reputation, didn't he?"

"One of the best."

Trosper knew that Ida Rowan expected him to make a judgment, or compose an oral epitaph for his friend. But there would be time enough for that.

He took two tubes of shoe polish and brushes from the night table beside the bed and dropped them into a soft draw-string leather sack. Then he bent down and fished two pairs of shoes from beneath the bed.

"How many pairs of shoes do you travel with?"

"Three," Trosper laughed. "Two black, because I don't like to wear the same shoes every day. And a pair of brogues because the weather's always rotten when there's work to be done." He slipped the shoes, stuffed with their numbered and fitted trees, into knitted mittens and stowed them at the bottom of a small valise.

"No slippers?" Ida was obviously trying to keep from smiling.

"Damn it, they're still in the closet."

Ida's smile escaped. "You're the first person I've ever seen who has trees for his slippers."

"There aren't half a dozen bootmakers left who will still bother to turn a slipper," Trosper said stiffly. "The least I can do is treat their work with respect."

He dropped a bundle of freshly laundered shirts into his suitcase, and changed the subject. "One of Master Frost's problems is that when he was a kid, his parents probably got him into the habit of talking things over with them—to treat them as pals, and confide in them, the way the books say happy children should do. Now that he's supposedly all grown up, he still has to talk things over with someone—anyone. This may have made for a nice warm relationship with his parents, but it's the sure mark of someone who ought to stay the hell away from the racket."

The need that some people feel to air private anxieties and to confide in strangers merely to seem sociable never failed to surprise Trosper. He closed the suitcase and snapped it shut.

"When Frost decided he couldn't talk to Gandy, he just folded up. All that nonsense about the training being no good, and his not having enough experience to deal with Brodsky, is a cheap excuse for his own shortcomings." Trosper's frown deepened. "Meanwhile, how did you make out on the street?"

Ida Rowan blushed, and began to rummage in her handbag. "I'm sorry, I meant to tell you right away," she stammered. "There wasn't anyone . . . I mean I didn't *see* anyone who looked anything like a tail." She pulled a roll of 35-millimeter film from her bag. "Here are a dozen dynamite snaps of Florence, and ten pictures of the Ponte Alla Carraia and everyone on it for three or four minutes after Frost passed by."

"You took photographs?"

She looked anxiously at Trosper, and said quickly, "I've tried to establish a pattern. Like every tourist in Florence, I've been taking pictures ever since I've been here." She noticed Trosper's dismay. "I sat on the bench, half hidden by the little statue, and looked busy sketching it. The camera was on my duffel bag. It's a motorized Nikon with a twenty-eight-millimeter lens, I don't have to focus it or wind the film. I had a long cable release hidden in my hand." Her confidence faded. "I was alone on the bench, and didn't even put the camera to my eye—there's no way anyone could have spotted me." She lapsed into silence.

If a male operative had used a camera on a sensitive countersurveillance without permission, Trosper would have sent him home.

"There's something we've got to get straight," he said evenly. "I'm not sure what we're dealing with, but someone is playing for big stakes."

Ida Rowan fished in her handbag for a handkerchief.

"Peter Gandy died less than a month ago. Last night someone

was ready to kill Ben Frost. This afternoon, some two years after the fact, we learn that Moscow Center attempted to recruit Frost. If that operation had worked, Frost's career could have taken him right into the upper echelons of our service. It didn't work, but the recruitment pitch was so well contrived that Frost couldn't bring himself to report it, even though he had plausible reason to suspect that Gandy had gone sour."

Ida Rowan's eyes watered.

"In these circumstances, you should have known that I simply cannot allow any operational moves by you or anyone else that are not cleared with me in advance."

Ida Rowan nodded. "I understand . . . it won't happen again." She dabbed at her eyes with the handkerchief. "I'm sorry," she said. "It's just these new contact lenses."

Trosper damned all equal opportunity employers.

"TRY the pasta *alle vongole,* the tiny clams are a treat, particularly with a taste of white truffle," Trosper said. "And then a *costata o bistecca?* Aside from New York, this is the one place to order beef without feeling like a businessman on an expense account toot."

Ida nodded agreement.

"The Tuscans claim they invented the beefsteak," Trosper said. "Of course they didn't." He picked up the wine list. "With the beef, we'd better have some red wine, maybe a Fattoria Montagliari—a classy Chianti?"

Ida looked a bit more enthusiastic.

Trosper knew he was showboating, but Ida's drawn expression was unnerving. He had invited her for a late dinner at the Buca Lapi, a noisy, cellar restaurant paneled with posters, and filled with people.

"I've always been undecided about martinis in Italy, but I keep trying," Trosper said. "Are you game?" Then, suddenly unsure if the young drank anything but jug wine or designer water, he said, "Or maybe sherry?"

"It seems to me that I've earned a shooter—a nice big one."

"A what?"

"A shooter—a martini." Ida managed a smile.

It was a good dinner, and in the course of it Trosper's nerves quieted. He lingered over the coffee until Ida said, "What now? Was this the condemned caddy's last meal? I mean, am I to be returned to Mr. Tuttle's personnel pool at the head office?"

Surprised, Trosper growled, "There's a squall or two on every cruise. You'll get used to it."

Ida's smile came back and she began to fumble in her lap. For a miserable moment Trosper thought she was groping for her handkerchief. When she produced her napkin, he said quickly, "But you are going back to Washington. I want you to bring the Controller and Castle up to date. If your negatives can be blown up enough to use as mug shots, I want David Barlow to run them through his private rogues' gallery. If he doesn't find anything, and if the prints are good, you'll have to stop in East Hampton and have your new friend Aksenov check them. If Pyotr Lukin is involved in this operation, Frost's surveillant could be Lukin's old sidekick, and Aksenov might recognize him. When that's done, you're to come to Zurich." Trosper paused. "Okay?"

"Yes, but . . ."

"You're also to tell the Controller to send an Eyes Alone message to Geneva telling George Fuller that he's to give me all the support I may ask for and on an Eyes Alone basis. Tell him to make sure that the message is sent so that it arrives during office hours and that Fuller must decipher it himself."

"Yes, but what if they ask about your plans?"

Trosper shook his head. "Whyte has the whole Firm to run. He's got too much on his plate to have to worry about my plans." He finished his coffee. "For the moment, I think I'll just let Castle figure things out for himself." Trosper imagined Ida struggling to balance what she had been taught at the Fort and Trosper's approach to field work. Fresh from the training courses, she would know that proper procedure called for Trosper to submit a detailed operations plan to Whyte and Castle for advice and clearance.

But Ida could not be expected to know the probable extent of the security problem. Gandy's murder and the goon's attempt to kill Trosper, even though he was not sure that he had the right victim, were absolute proof of the equities someone perceived to be at issue.

Trosper waited until the waiter left the table before saying, "What I'm going to tell you is for your ears only. It is not to be mentioned to another soul, not even Castle."

Ida dabbed butter onto a piece of hard roll. "What about Mr. Whyte, the Controller?"

"Duff won't ask, but if he does, you can tell him."

Ida nodded.

"No matter what anyone told you at the Fort, the heart of our racket is penetration. Our job—the job of any intelligence service—is to get inside the opposing camp." He tapped gently on the table. "In the end it doesn't much matter how many scouts and observers you have sniffing around outside the target. The information that will really help the policymakers is inside, and you can't get it by peeking over a fence, or even by taking snapshots from a satellite."

Ida seemed to agree.

"You get that information by penetrating the target."

Ida nodded.

"There are only two reasons why Moscow Center would even consider risking murder."

Ida glanced nervously around the room.

"Either they're trying to protect a penetration operation of their own, or they suspect and are trying to uncover a penetration of their service."

Ida blinked rapidly.

"Because the action all seems to be here in Western Europe, on our side of the fence, the chances are that Moscow is protecting one or more of its own highly productive penetration operations."

"But . . ."

"The fact that Gandy and Frost are involved suggests that the penetration involves our staff, our communications, or possibly some fancy and very productive audio operations," Trosper said. "Maybe, all three."

Ida looked doubtful. "But what if . . ."

"Because there may be a penetration, I can't risk transmitting detailed operational plans when there's a leak somewhere along the line—in Europe or perhaps even in Washington."

Trosper leaned closer to Ida. "And that's why this hasn't been business as usual." He finished his coffee. "Given these conditions, I've got no choice but to keep a free hand." And, he thought, to risk his own mistakes.

"But if Mr. Castle insists . . . ?"

"He won't—it would be beneath him to ask a mere . . . er . . . caddy for information." Trosper sighed with relief at not having said a mere woman, and signaled for the bill. When the waiter left the table, Trosper asked, "How well do you get on with Freddy Tuttle, the personnel maestro?"

"About average I guess, maybe a little better. I thought he liked my record in training, but then he said he had gone out on a limb suggesting that you take me as caddy."

"It wasn't exactly a suggestion," Trosper said.

"Then make it a little better than average . . ."

"In that case, there's a TABYR file I want you to read and take notes on . . ."

"That's not possible, only supervisors can read the personal files," Ida said primly. "You'll have to ask Mr. Whyte's permission."

"If I wanted to go through channels, I'd send a cable," Trosper said. "Tell Tuttle anything you want, but get your hands on the file."

"But . . ."

"Training evaluations, psychological test records, performance reports, the works."

"Yes, but . . ."

Trosper glanced at the bill and dropped a credit card onto the tray. He smiled at Ida and said, "There's one more thing—please tell Castle that I want the Musician to meet me in Zurich on Wednesday week. He can telephone me at the Dolder."

"A musician?"

"*The* Musician, Mozart Riley—they'll know who I mean."

Trosper got up and pulled Ida's chair back from the table. "I don't give a damn what you say," she muttered, "I'm going to write this down."

"It's good to be back." Trosper looked across the dining table to Emily, and gently swirled the Château Petrus in his glass. It was a wedding present, one of his best bottles, and right for the occasion. Trosper wanted to tell Emily how good it was to be home. But it was a word he couldn't use. It had been beaten to pieces and molded into a concept by real estate brokers and advertising votaries. Trosper settled for, "I used to think I could bump around hotels forever. Now it's not so easy."

"I was beginning really to miss you," Emily said. "Those skimpy little letters and only six telephone calls after you left Washington . . ."

"Lots of letters, and a dozen calls," Trosper lied. "Besides, it's not all that cozy calling from a booth at some drafty post office."

They had coffee by the smoldering fireplace. Trosper poured himself a Glenlivet. He preferred the heavy, unblended scotch to brandy after dinner. Emily glanced up as he splashed a jigger of siphon water into the glass.

"You look absolutely guilty," she laughed. "It's not a crime, it's not like putting ketchup on crepes suzette."

"In truth, I've never agreed that water is the only thing to mix with whiskey," Trosper said. "A little seltzer points it up, and makes it easier on my digestion." He took a sip. "Fifty years ago, half the purists who make such a fuss about water in their whiskey were dousing their brandy with ginger ale."

"Tell me about the beautiful little drummer girl you're working with?"

Trosper took a deep breath. "I thought you'd never ask." Still uncertain if the flicker of jealousy he detected was real or teasing, he chose prudence. "Actually, I suppose I've learned more from her than she has from me . . . but it's not been easy."

21

WASHINGTON, D.C.

"You want *what?*" Frederick Tuttle, Chief of Personnel, looked as if Ida Rowan had asked for an unvouchered expense account.

"I'm just telling you what Mr. Trosper told me . . ."

The telephone rang. Tuttle picked up the receiver and listened for a moment. "Dammit all, he's one of only two people on the entire roster who has even so much as set foot in Pyongyang," he shouted. Tuttle dropped the receiver, apologized to Ida, and rushed out of the office.

Ida remained quiet for a moment. Then she clenched her fists, closed her eyes, and groaned aloud. Tuttle's outburst had driven the presentation she had so carefully rehearsed completely out of her mind.

She began aimlessly to leaf through the copies of *House and Garden* carefully arranged on the coffee table in front of Tuttle's gleaming chrome-and-teak desk. The magazines were no help.

Ida got up to study the rows of photographs lining the wall on the far side of the room. A young Tuttle with Eisenhower on the golf course. Tuttle being handed what looked like a medal by Allen Dulles. Tuttle in black tie, and seated at a head table, two chairs to the left of President Kennedy. A graying Tuttle, grimly serious, leaning toward Henry Kissinger, whose head was bent forward as if in intense concentration . . .

It was no good. Her confidence had vanished. She should have tried to steal the damned file.

"God save me from silly people," Tuttle groaned as he slipped back behind the desk. "It wasn't until I said that the man I assigned to him was two years older than Alexander the Great when he conquered the known world that Wheaton agreed he could have the job." Tuttle rolled his eyes and muttered, "Make the mildest-mannered man chief of the smallest office in the shop and ten minutes later he's acting as if he has four stars on his shoulder and is late for a meeting in the Oval Office . . ."

Ida nodded as she desperately tried to reconstruct her presentation.

"Now," Tuttle smiled, "what were you saying?"

It must be a trick, she told herself. Fifteen minutes after the outburst, he couldn't have forgotten her mission. "I don't quite know how to bring this up . . ."

Tuttle slumped back in his chair. "Start anywhere, I can assure you I've heard everything." Twenty years earlier, and he would have recognized this opening as leading to a tearful and heart-scalding admission of pregnancy. But Ida Rowan looked entirely too practical to be pregnant.

"This is rather sensitive . . ."

"Use your own words." Tuttle studied Ida. She didn't seem to be Alan Trosper's type, but secret operations make strange bedfellows.

"The file, Mr. Tuttle . . . ?"

"You want *what?*"

She wished Tuttle would stop saying that.

Tuttle scowled. "Now I remember, you want to *read* a personal jacket classified TABYR and make *notes?*"

Ida nodded, grateful that the double door guaranteed privacy as Tuttle's voice continued to rise.

"If Alan Trosper can't remember that TABYR files are restricted, *you* should be able to do so."

"I recall your lecture at the Fort very well," Ida said.

"Then you'll know it's out of the question."

"The only thing I know is that Mr. Trosper directed me to read the file, and he expects me to do so."

"Just tell Alan what I said, he'll understand." Tuttle's voice had dropped several decibels.

"Mr. Trosper is a senior officer. He's on a very sensitive assignment . . ." Ida's voice caught. "I'm probably not even authorized to tell you that . . ."

"I don't care if Alan thinks he's the Scarlet Pimpernel," Tuttle said. "It is not possible."

Ida clutched her leather handbag with both hands. "I won't leave this office until I have done as I have been told." She damned Trosper and hoped that the Chief of Personnel could not see her lip tremble.

IDA snapped her notebook shut and got up from the table beside Tuttle's desk. She picked up the file, tied the ribbon that bound it, and said, "I'm sure Mr. Trosper will appreciate your cooperation, Mr. Tuttle."

Tuttle groaned. "You can also tell him that for the twenty minutes you've taken *transcribing* that file, I have not been able to use my own office."

"I haven't transcribed anything, Mr. Tuttle. I've just taken the notes that Mr. Trosper asked for."

"Tell Alan to try that on the Controller when he fires us both." He waved Ida toward the door.

"Is it safe to assume that Mr. Trosper gave you a complete rundown on his plans?" Duff Whyte smiled at his irony and reached across the scarred desk for a tobacco pouch. He began to busy himself stuffing tobacco into a long, slender pipe.

Ida Rowan felt her face go scarlet. "No, sir, he didn't say a word about his plans." Up to that point, she had thought the briefing was going well. "I know he wants tight security—that's Category One, Denied Area Operations Level," she explained. When she saw the Controller nod to acknowledge his understanding of the term, her color deepened. "I know he thought you would understand his not being able to communicate his plans in detail . . ." The last of Ida Rowan's confidence evaporated as she realized she was explaining secret operations to the Controller. Silently she cursed all chauvinists, particularly Trosper, Tuttle, the smug Thomas Augustus Castle, and now Duff Whyte.

From his chair to the left of the Controller, Thomas Castle growled, "I've heard that in the field, survival is the infinite capacity for suspicion." He had not looked up from the complicated design he was inking onto a notepad since having recognized his introduction to Ida with a firm handshake. "Actually, Darcy Odlum told me he read that in a novel. I've been trying to find it ever since."

There was a moment of silence while Ida and the Controller contemplated Castle's observation and then Whyte asked, "Do you have the impression that Frost will have anything more to say about Brodsky or Gandy?"

"Mr. Trosper likes to say there is always something more, but he hasn't specified anything at all."

"Do you think he will have anything more on Frost?" It was Castle's first question.

She thought for a moment and said, "Frost and his girlfriend are just about to leave for a vacation in Austria. Mr. Trosper suggested they get away from Florence for a while."

"What did he say about Gandy?"

Castle spoke so softly Ida strained to hear. "He didn't say anything," she said. "I think he's under a lot of pressure, moving all the time, and not having an office or anything . . ."

"What are your plans?" Whyte asked.

"If it's all right, sir, I plan to fly to New York this afternoon, and then drive out to see Colonel Aksenov in East Hampton. Mr. Barlow could not identify the men in my photograph." She glanced at Castle, still busy with his sketch. "After that, I'm to go directly to Zurich."

The Controller leaned back in his chair. "Did Alan say anything at all about the Musician?"

"No sir, just that his name was Riley."

The Controller turned to Castle. "I don't know about this—Switzerland's a damned quiet country . . ."

Castle added a flourish to his drawing and for the first time looked up. "Riley will be in good hands," he said. "Besides, there are some first-class book dealers there."

If Mr. Castle had the slightest curiosity about Trosper's plans, Ida realized, he had concealed it to perfection.

Whyte turned back to Ida. "I'll get the necessary cable to Geneva," he said. "And I will see that Moe Riley reports as directed."

When Ida realized she was nodding to the Controller as if encouraging a timid schoolboy to repeat the list of his homework assignments, the color flashed back into her face.

22

ZURICH

"It will be best if you don't stay in Geneva," Trosper said. "Lausanne, or someplace along the lake will be better."

"Then I'll stay in Lausanne. More people . . . more cover."

Wolfgang Amadeus Riley was not a strikingly tall man, just a jot over six feet, Trosper guessed. But because much of his weight was above the hips, he gave the impression of bulk. In 1945 Corporal Pat Riley had married a local girl while stationed in Salzburg, and the only demand she had ever made upon him was the naming of their son.

Riley gazed unblinking at the view across the snow-covered garden stretching from the terrace of the Hotel Dolder. He took a sip of coffee, and gently put the delicate porcelain cup back upon the glistening saucer. He moved carefully, as if each motion were the result of an elaborate intellectual process.

"Will I need a car?" Riley spoke as deliberately as he moved.

"You'd better rent one here rather than in the Geneva area."

Riley nodded. Slowly.

"What about your cover?"

Riley turned to Trosper. His face was unlined, and calm, his dark blond hair was cut short. Only his lively, bright blue eyes hinted at the vitality behind his placid expression. "I've always liked books," Riley said. "Now in my spare time—we're not on the road all that much these days—I've slipped into the trade." With a flicker of pride he added, "W. A. Riley, modern first editions . . . letters, manuscripts . . . specializing in Joyce, Yeats, O'Casey, Fitzgerald, etc."

Trosper had forgotten how carefully Riley weighed his words, and how cautiously he eased them onto the scales.

"Mr. Tuttle keeps after all of us . . . to be sure we have some other line of work . . . once we leave the racket." He turned to look out across the garden. "I've done business . . . with dealers here . . . and in Lausanne and Geneva . . . I've written . . . they expect me." He fell silent as if analyzing another mass of data before saying, "I see no cover problem."

"That's great," Trosper said.

Riley's stint as a middle linebacker in the NFL was brief, but well publicized. Wolfgang Amadeus ignited no useful spark in the sportswriters' imagination, but his three initials made an acronym that did. For the two brief seasons before it became clear that his legs could tolerate no more punishment, "War" Riley became even better known than his agility and upper body strength warranted. Trosper recalled the lead to one columnist's story. "This afternoon the Washington Redskins learned that war is hell. But unlike the bloodbath that inspired General Sherman's observation, 'War' came to the Redskins' backfield on two rickety knees . . ."

Riley finished his second season, but his knees were gone, and a month later his reserve commission was activated. After two years in Special Forces—where accommodation was made for his knees—Captain W. A. Riley joined the Firm. From the moment he entered training, Riley was known as Mozart, or the Musician. Although he had no objection to the nicknames, and greatly admired his eponym, those who didn't know him well found it prudent to take no chances. He was also known as "Moe."

Trosper finished his briefing. "Any questions?"

Riley shook his head. "No."

Trosper reviewed the communications plan, and said goodbye to Riley.

This was one of the moments that Trosper savored, the slight movement that signaled the operation was under way. It was as if the dock lines were loosed, his craft had slipped free and was beginning slowly to respond to the helm. The mix of uncertainty and anticipation was part of what he most hated giving up when he thought he had left the racket forever.

"Starting right now," Trosper said, "I want you to stay on him—just as tight as necessary."

"Take risks?" For a moment Teddy Vermont took his eyes off the crowded cafe and glanced at Trosper.

"You've got two days, if we're lucky maybe sixty hours maximum," Trosper said. "I want total coverage. Use your judgment."

"I need backup, some people with cars . . ."

"We can't use people with cars in Switzerland, and there won't be any backup."

"It's a hard town to get around in . . ."

"It's just as hard for him as it is for you," Trosper said. "My guess is that he has a set pattern, and probably moves routinely between the same four or five points every day he's in Geneva. When he leaves from one place, it's up to you to figure where he's going. You shove off and pick him up at the next most plausible point."

"It will be a red leather day if you can bring this off."

"Red letter . . . ," Trosper muttered, and began a final review of the communications setup.

"All set?"

Teddy Vermont nodded. "I'll give it a good shot anyway," he said.

They shook hands. Trosper signaled for another cup of coffee and picked up his newspaper. At the door, the street man slipped into his shabby raincoat and tugged a tweed cap from his pocket. He stepped onto the sidewalk. Trosper watched through the window as Teddy Vermont took two steps among the scattered pedestrians hurrying along the sidewalk, and disappeared. At the Fort, surveillance doctrine was specific. If you're not sure you can pass for one of the crowd, don't trust your luck.

Teddy Vermont had his own technique, and it didn't have anything to do with passing. The veteran street man seemed simply to erase himself.

23

GENEVA

GEORGE FULLER's driving style was no match for the Swiss traffic. He drove tentatively, as if so accustomed to following his wife's directions that he had lost the power of decision. But it was Trosper, not Bunky, in the front seat, and Trosper had no intention of supervising Fuller's efforts to navigate through the clotted Geneva traffic.

"It gets worse by the month," Fuller said.

"It's bad everywhere," Trosper said. "You should see what Florence is like."

"I mean the office," Fuller said. "Business is lousy."

"That's more or less why I'm here . . ."

Fuller's foot slipped off the accelerator as he turned to Trosper. "You're taking over?" The color drained from his face. "What a really rotten way to handle things. The least they could have done would be to call me home, to let me tell them my side of the story . . ." The Peugeot coasted to a halt. Behind, a frantic taxi driver flashed his lights in a furious signal.

"Christ Almighty, George, watch what you're doing."

Fuller stepped on the gas and the car stalled. Cursing, he turned the ignition key, shifted into first, and stomped on the accelerator. The car bolted forward and stalled again. "Foolish . . . funky . . . French car."

Trosper wondered if Bunky had forbidden Fuller the "F" word.

The Peugeot sputtered and began to move forward.

"It's nothing like that," Trosper said. "But there is a problem." As the small sedan began to inch forward, the taxi flashed past, braked sharply, and slipped in front. Fuller muttered a complaint.

"Is there someplace we can talk, where I can at least share your attention?"

"I told you last time I've got a house on the Rue de Lausanne . . ."

"It's blown."

"It's not—"

"It was blown before you got to Geneva," Trosper said softly, "and I won't go near it. Drop me here, get rid of the car, and meet me at the Amphitryon bar in half an hour."

Fuller started to speak.

"Meanwhile, you might as well know that Teddy Vermont is in town and Mozart Riley is in Lausanne. Ida Rowan, my caddy, is on the way. I'll need some accommodation for her . . ."

"Damn it, I warned you about this. The Swiss simply won't let you get away with anything like—"

"We'll need a quiet place for an interrogation. Maybe for a couple of days, and with a good taping setup."

As Fuller pulled the car into a bus stop, a heavily clad Swiss policeman motioned him away. Trosper pushed the door open and got out. "The Amphitryon, half an hour . . ." Fuller pulled away from the curb.

"This is the most expensive bar in Geneva," Fuller moaned.

"I'll put the drinks on my account—'safe house rent' ought to satisfy the auditors," Trosper said. At a table in the distant corner of the bar, a plump young Englishman in a black suit and a cerise shirt bent close to a rouged blond. If they hadn't been holding hands, Trosper would have guessed she was his grandmother.

"In the absence of a safe house, it seems to me we're less likely to see anyone we know here than in some *zinc* in Eaux Vives." He ordered another Campari and soda for Fuller and a second martini for himself. Without taking his eyes from his raddled date, the Englishman wrested a bottle of champagne from the ice-choked bucket, and with one hand and no drop wasted, filled their glasses.

"We'll kick off tomorrow night, about ten-thirty at your place," Trosper said. "That will give you time to get things squared away with Bunky." He paused for a moment and said thoughtfully, "Women always like to know about these things in advance."

"I don't know what you've got in mind, but there's no way you can use my apartment," Fuller said. "It took me four months to find it."

"If you've got something better, now's the time to let me know . . ."

"You'll blow me right out of the water . . ."

"Unless you've got a place just as big, and absolutely clean, we have no alternative," Trosper said.

"Damn it . . ."

"Ida and the Musician will be with me," Trosper said, "and I think you and Bunky had better count on our being there for two days. It might be best if Bunky were to take a trip. Does she ski?"

"She doesn't ski, and she doesn't hang-glide either. What's more, she's not likely to agree to turn her apartment over to you and your flying circus."

TROSPER glanced at the porcelain clock at the end of Bunky's immaculate living room. "It's about that time," he said, pushing his coffee cup aside. "Please call Nash, and tell him to come pick up the cable." Fuller grunted and started toward the telephone.

"How long will it take him to get here?"

Fuller continued dialing and said, "About twenty minutes, give or take."

Trosper turned to Ida. "You'd better give the audio a final check." She nodded, and stepped into the hallway leading to the bedrooms.

"Terry, I'm glad I caught you," Fuller said in a cheerful telephone voice. "If it's not too late, come on by the apartment. I'm just about to open a bottle of the burgundy I picked up last week . . . Good enough . . . I'll pull the cork."

It was as good an open code as most.

Fuller turned to Trosper. "*Now*, will you tell me what the hell is going on?"

Mozart Riley looked up from the book he was leafing through.

Ida stepped back into the room. "The audio is loud and clear. Both recorders are set."

Mozart Riley put his book aside.

"There's a great big leak in your bucket, and I think I'm just about to plug it," Trosper said softly.

24

GENEVA

The fireplace at the end of Fuller's long living room was so clean that Trosper wondered if it had ever been used. The polished brass andirons reflected the bright chintz love seat at one side of the fireplace. The coffee table looked French and fragile. In the far wall, a picture window above the dining table allowed a glimpse of Mont Blanc, or so Fuller had said.

Trosper slumped in one of the tweedy chairs facing the love seat, an unread copy of the *Journal de Genève* spilling from his lap. This was the run-up to takeoff, the final few moments before the point of no return, and the last chance to act on second thoughts. No longer could Trosper suppress the realization of how much he would have profited from testing his plan and vetting his assumptions with someone whose knowledge of the racket he could trust— Odlum, Jack Holder, Duff Whyte, even Castle. But Odlum and Holder were gone, and Whyte had been lofted so high into the stratosphere that it would have been unfair to saddle him with tactical decisions. Only Castle, secretive, Olympian Castle, had been available. If it weren't for his own wiseass pride, Trosper knew, he could have taken the time to lay his assumptions before Castle, and got the second reading that might have made a difference. If only Castle had *asked* what he thought . . . But Castle had his own pride, and was too full of himself and his private secrets to ask a mere colleague what was going on.

Doubt smoldered in Trosper's mind. He did not understand how Castle had learned that Frost and his paramour were under surveillance. More to the point, he was not sure why Castle first suspected that Gandy had gone sour. Perhaps it was a reflex conditioned by the Kim Philby fiasco. Castle had known Philby and had lived through the aftermath of the Englishman's treason. But it was past time for brooding, and far too late to think through every possible contingency.

Trosper hitched forward and gathered up the newspaper. He glanced at Ida, in a straight chair beside the door, plucking rhythmically at a patch of needlepoint stretched drumhead tight on an embroidery hoop. *I was out of all this*, he reminded himself, *and as happy as I have ever been. If I'd left well enough alone, I would be home, finishing dinner and a good bottle of wine. But I'm in Geneva, and when my caddy isn't about to burst into tears, she's damned well sewing.*

Fuller, sent out by Whyte to put the Geneva office back in the running, stood by the picture window, his thoughts, Trosper decided sourly, largely occupied with Bunky and her squeaky clean salon. If Fuller had put as much effort into the office as he had into dancing to his wife's tune, there might not have been any need for stunting in quiet old Geneva.

In the far corner, in front of a sparse shelf of books, Mozart Riley had wedged himself into a club chair and was tenderly turning the pages of a fragile brown volume. Trosper caught his eye. "A new acquisition?"

Riley nodded. *"Nurse and Spy in the Union Army* . . . S. Emma E. Williams . . . 1865 . . . first edition . . . scarce but not rare . . . this one came from . . . Colonel Ronge's own library . . . signed by the old gent himself . . ." Riley went on to explain that Ronge had been one of the Austrian officers who apprehended Colonel Redl in 1913, after the Colonel had betrayed the Austro-Hungarian mobilization plan to the Russians.

The Muscian was well into a discourse proving that these mobilization plans were the most secret of all documents before World War One when Trosper headed him off. "Anything notable in the tradecraft line?" He cleared his throat, masking the tension in his voice.

Riley nodded, slowly. "Page 106 . . . before she signs on . . . I'll read it . . . Quote . . . 'Next came a *phrenological* examination . . . and finding that my organs of secretiveness, combativeness, etc., . . . were largely developed . . . the oath of allegiance was administered . . .' End quote . . ." Riley chuckled and carefully turned another page. "Perhaps . . . we should pass that along to the Firm . . . Doc Boeser may not . . . have considered phrenology."

For a moment Trosper hoped that Moscow Center had the room bugged.

The bell rang, and a spurt of adrenaline extinguished Trosper's second thoughts.

Fuller stepped into the entrance hall to touch the button that would buzz the ground-floor door open, Mozart Riley put his book gently aside and with three loping strides slipped into the coat closet beside the entrance. Ida glanced quickly at Trosper, and darted out of the living room, along the hall, and into the study where the tape recorders were set up.

With an effort, Trosper remained in his chair by the fireplace.

Two quick taps, and Fuller opened the door.

"Come in, Terry," Fuller said heartily. He shook hands and said, "There's someone here who wants to talk to you."

Damn you, Trosper raged silently. Get him into the room and out of his coat before you tell him something's up.

But before Nash could react, Fuller guided him across the narrow hall and into the living room. Trosper stood up, folded the newspaper, and dropped it onto the coffee table.

"This is Mr. Doughty, John Doughty," Fuller said. "He's here from Washington."

Terry Nash was bundled in a loosely buttoned trenchcoat. The long belt hung free. He wore no hat, the better, Trosper guessed, to keep from mussing his carefully arranged dark hair. Trosper took a step forward to shake hands with Nash. The commo man remained motionless in the middle of the room.

"I thought you had an urgent cable . . ."

"I have, I have," Fuller said quickly. "But John wants to talk to you. He's here from the head office . . ."

"I came for a cable . . ."

"This is important, Terry," Fuller said. "Come on in, let me take your coat, and get you a drink . . ."

"I don't like to drink before I start working on a transmission." Nash stood motionless, staring at Trosper.

"There's plenty of time, John wants to have a talk with you before the cable goes out."

Nash shook his head. "I'm sorry, but I've got a late date. Just give me the cable now. I can talk with him in the office tomorrow."

"There's plenty of time, Terry," Fuller said. "Just take off your coat and sit . . ."

"I *told* you I have a late date," Nash said. "If there isn't any cable, I'm going on about my business."

Over Nash's shoulder, Trosper could see Riley move silently to block the door behind the commo man.

"It's important that I talk to you now," Trosper said.

"I work enough overtime as it is," Nash said loudly. "I've got some rights to a life on my own. If you haven't got a cable, I'll see you in the office tomorrow . . ."

"Take off your coat and sit down," Trosper said.

Riley moved closer. He was taller than Nash and despite the bulk of Nash's trenchcoat, he seemed just as broad.

"It's the middle of the night . . . ," Nash said.

"It's barely ten-thirty," Fuller said.

"You people can drift into the office at noontime, I have to be there before nine o'clock . . ."

"Sit down," Trosper said.

Nash took a step backward. "I've got a date. I'll see you people in the office." Without taking his eyes off Trosper, he took another step backward.

Riley peered over Nash's shoulder and raised his eyebrows in a silent question. The moment of decision. The time to be right. Trosper took a deep breath, sighed, and nodded.

Mozart Riley grabbed the shoulders of Nash's trenchcoat with both hands and yanked it down to his elbows. There was a tearing sound as the tightly sewn buttons ripped away from the front of the coat. With his left hand, Riley held the coat tight, trapping both Nash's arms in a makeshift straitjacket. With his right hand, Riley reached around to frisk Nash's coat pockets and waistband. As the startled code man struggled to tear his arms free, Riley twisted the raincoat tighter, lifted Nash free of the floor, and thrust him face down onto the rug. Nash twisted to protect his face, and screamed, "What the fuck . . . you crazy bastards . . . let me—"

Still holding the raincoat tight, Riley followed Nash to the floor, landing with both knees on Nash's buttocks. He bent close to Nash's ear and hissed, "Now, shut up."

Nash's legs thrashed wildly, and he twisted to pull free. "Let me go, you sons of bitches . . ." With his free hand, Riley jammed Nash's face into the carpet. "I'll get all of you . . ." Nash's voice was only partially muffled. Riley looked across the room to Trosper. Reluctantly, Trosper nodded. Riley let go the trenchcoat and with his left hand flipped Nash over onto his back. Using his massive right hand and wrist like a mallet driving a ten-penny nail, Riley struck a short chopping blow that landed an inch below Nash's solar plexus.

Trosper flinched as he heard Nash's hoarse scream stop as suddenly as if he'd been throttled.

Fuller gasped, and lurched backwards. "Oh, my God," he said, his voice cracking.

Riley eased himself to the side, pulled the torn trenchcoat open, and methodically continued to frisk the body. Satisfied, he got slowly to his feet. "He's clean." Then glancing at Fuller, who seemed on the verge of tears, he turned to Trosper. "A couple minutes . . . he'll come around."

He reached under Nash and pulled the twisted raincoat free. He examined the lining and torn fabric where the buttons had been, and muttered, "A Burberry . . . Nothing but the best." He shook his head. "A cheaper coat . . . the buttons would have come off . . . and no damage." He bent down, and unbuttoned Nash's double-breasted blazer. With one hand, he took hold of Nash's belt and trousers and lifted his waist free of the floor.

Fuller brightened as he heard the sudden, rasping intake of breath. As Riley repeated the movement, lifting Nash's waist above his heaving chest, he turned to Trosper. "It helps the breathing . . . happens all the time . . . on the field . . . even in practice . . . all he's got is the wind knocked out. . .and a sore chest."

Riley opened Nash's blazer and fished a black pinseal wallet from the breast pocket. He flipped it open, glanced at the faint gold trademark, and sniffed. "Swaine, Adeney . . . London." He glanced at Fuller. "A classy kid you've got here." He tossed the wallet to Trosper.

"God Almighty, Alan," Fuller croaked. "Was that really necessary?" He tugged a neatly folded white handkerchief from his pocket and wiped his face. "I mean, damn it, he could have been killed right here, with Bunky in the bedroom."

If Fuller could not understand the importance of getting a suspect's attention, Trosper decided it was not the moment to explain it to him. "See if there's a notebook, or papers, and take his watch and keys," he said. Riley began to rummage through Nash's pockets.

"Look," Fuller said. "Couldn't we postpone all this until we call a doctor, or something? We could say he's fallen downstairs . . ."

Later, when he remembered the scene, Trosper would recall wondering how Fuller's hair had got mussed. It was always the irrelevant things that he remembered about violence.

"I mean," Fuller said, "Terry and I have been working together all this time. He's even been a good friend to Bunky and all . . ."

"Time is short. Good friends or not, I have no intention of questioning someone who might be carrying a gun."

"No papers, no notebook," Riley said.

Nash's breathing was coming in short gasps and he struggled to sit up.

Trosper turned to Fuller. "Why don't *you* catch *your* breath, and then go back and tell Bunky that everything's all right in here?"

It had all the makings of a long night.

25

GENEVA

Nash leaned back on the love seat and dabbed at his swollen nose with a blood-stained linen handkerchief. "The hell with you and your trained ape." His face was streaked with tears. His hoarse and rasping voice added conviction to his bluster.

"You're going to be seeing a lot of Mr. Riley," Trosper said patiently. "I think you should make a serious attempt to keep things on a civil basis with him." Trosper turned to Riley, who was seated with his back to the door opening into the hallway. "Tap on the study door, and ask Johnson for a tray of ice and a towel for our visitor," Trosper said. He took a legal-size yellow pad from the coffee table. "Now, let's get started . . ."

"Who do you people think you are, treating me like this? You don't have any authority to do this to me."

"Not that it makes much difference to you, but I am deputized as a federal marshal and I have a warrant for your apprehension for espionage," Trosper said. "If you make me serve it, I'll do so and take you straight to the Swiss authorities. You'll be extradited to the United States within forty-eight hours." Trosper leaned back in his chair. "If that happens, the press will know about your arrest by noon tomorrow."

"I'll blow you and the fucking Firm right off the map . . ."

"Not until your case comes to trial," Trosper said. "And that will take some weeks." He smiled and said, "By then, you'll have had plenty of time to think it all over."

"Legally, you can't hold me . . ."

"Legally, I'm not holding you."

Mozart Riley stepped back into the room and handed Trosper an icepack and a towel.

"You're free to leave any time Mr. Riley agrees to let you go," Trosper said. He wrapped the icepack in the towel and leaned across the coffee table to hand it to Nash. "Use this," he said. "It will keep the swelling down." All things equal, it was important that by morning Nash not look as if he had been in a fight.

Nash glanced down at his blood-flecked shirt and necktie, and stuffed the handkerchief into his pocket. He winced as he pressed the towel-wrapped icepack gingerly against his nose and bruised cheek.

"Now," Trosper said, "let's get down to business."

"The hell with you all . . ." Nash's voice was barely audible from behind the icepack.

Riley moved slowly across the room and stood with his hands on the love seat behind Nash. "Shall I have him stop talking like that?"

Trosper shook his head. "Not yet . . ."

Except for the noisy burst of violence, and the bruises on Nash's face, it had been satisfactory. Nash had not reacted like an inno- cent man. He had not protested or even questioned the allegation of espionage. All his concern was directed to violence and being held illegally. He had not challenged the "federal warrant," or the equally bizarre notion that the Swiss police would agree to extradi- tion within forty-eight hours. Nash had reached for the icepack like a prisoner accepting a cigarette from an interrogator. It was a clear signal of a crumbling will. In a country where most apartment dwellers were forbidden to flush their toilets after ten at night, there had been no complaints from the neighbors about the noise. Nor would there be any more noise; the wary eye Nash was keeping on Riley suggested he was not about to test Mozart's temper.

In a more easily controlled circumstance this would be the mo- ment to isolate Nash in a solitary cell. When the excitement and hugger-mugger of arrest subsided, and the rush of adrenaline slowed, even the toughest prisoners began to grasp the reality of their plight. Isolated from human contact, left with no means of measuring the passage of time, the defenses of even the strongest crumbled. But this was Geneva, and anything but the controlled circumstance specified in the interrogation manuals.

Trosper beckoned to Riley. "I'm going to check with Johnson on my call to the States, and I'll be away for a while. Keep an eye on things while I'm gone." Leaving Nash alone with Riley was as close as Trosper could come to the real thing.

Riley nodded and pulled a small straight chair from the far corner of the room. He placed it midway between the hall door and the love seat and sat down. He tugged a pair of horn-rimmed reading glasses from his breast pocket and with a pencil began checking items in the glossy catalogue of Lacoste Frères, L'art ancien, Livres Rares, Quai des Bergues, Genève.

Trosper paused at the door. Perched on the small chair, Riley looked even more massive than he did on the move. With the stubby pencil in hand, and the granny glasses pulled down on his nose, he might have passed as an overweight professor.

Nash sat with his face half masked by the icepack. He dabbed at his stained shirt, and squinted balefully at his captor.

IDA ROWAN tossed the earphones onto the bed and flipped the speaker switch. She adjusted the volume, but no sound came from the living room. "Are they all right in there?"

"It's time to give our chum a few moments of silence, the better to contemplate his situation," Trosper said. "Riley won't speak to him until I go back."

"Who is Johnson?"

Trosper laughed. "There isn't any Johnson, I just wanted to be sure Nash knows he's completely outnumbered."

Ida nodded. "The call to Washington?"

"There's no call either," Trosper said. "I'll send a cable as soon as we have Nash sorted out."

"Have you really got a warrant?"

Trosper wanted to wash, and would have changed his sweaty shirt if he had remembered to bring another. He also wanted coffee and something to eat. He would not touch the amphetamine before morning.

"Are you really deputized?"

He also wanted some fresh air. As he struggled to open the frosted window he said, "No, of course I'm not deputized, and I haven't any warrant." He was rather pleased with his improvisation, and if it had been anyone but Ida—who he assumed would think he was bragging—he would have admitted as much. A rush of cold air gusted in through the narrow opening he had forced in the window. "And the Swiss would probably pop me into the pokey if I showed them one. They come on like William Tell if they think anyone is messing around with their sovereignty."

If Ida were a man, Trosper would have asked her to make coffee and bring him something to eat. But rather than risk violating the Firm's touchy equal opportunity code, he resigned himself to doing without. "I'll keep an ear on the machines," he said. "Please ask Fuller to come in."

"No, I haven't the slightest idea when this will be over," Trosper said.

"If you had let me know more about what you had on your mind I could have planned better," Fuller said.

"If I had told you, we'd still be arguing about it." And you might have had trouble playing your role, Trosper thought.

"I mean, what am I going to tell the office?"

"Tell them anything you want, but absolutely nothing about Nash."

"But I can't just . . ."

"Can't your secretary handle the ciphers?"

"She's got a lot of other things to—" Fuller stopped when he saw Trosper's expression. "She's just a little slow, that's all," he said prudently.

"Will she be able to keep her mouth shut?"

"She hates Nash," Fuller said. "I think he made a pass . . ."

"What about the other case men?"

"There's only Rusty Higgins. Chet Davis is in the States, and Harry Collins is on a job in Berlin." Fuller shrugged. "It's no wonder I can't get this place off the dime, everyone always on call to some other office . . ."

"Tell Higgins that Nash has been called on an emergency job." Trosper's stomach rumbled. "Could Bunky brew some coffee, and maybe whistle up a little something to eat?" Trosper knew it was the wrong verb the moment it escaped his lips.

Fuller shook his head. "She's just taken a sleeping pill," he said. "This has shaken her almost to pieces."

"You've told her about Nash?" Now, Trosper had heard everything.

"No, no, of course not. I mean about using her apartment like this."

"This place," said Trosper deliberately, "on which you pay no rent, is company property."

"If you don't need me here, I'll make something," Ida said quickly.

"A lot of coffee, scrambled eggs, rolls, strawberry jam and butter." Trosper spoke quickly before Fuller could raise an objection. He reached for the monitor and turned the volume up. There was a background hum, but Trosper thought he could hear Riley turn a page. "You did a good job with the audio," he said to Fuller.

"I'll just go in and check on Terry," Fuller said.

"Damn it, George, the last thing I want is for him to see a friendly face," Trosper said softly. "He's got to begin thinking he's between a rock and a hard place. *I'm* not even going back in until I'm sure he's begun to sweat."

"GREAT eggs, good coffee," Trosper said. Ida beamed.

"It's like Bloomingdale's in there," she said. "Every utensil ever made."

There was a rustling sound on the monitor and then Nash cleared his throat. Trosper lowered the volume on the small black box. It had been more than an hour, and Nash had not said a word.

"I want a drink."

Trosper imagined Riley shaking his head.

"Just water, for Christ's sake."

Another rustling sound. Nash squirming on the love seat.

"I want to talk to Fuller. He's the boss here."

The monitor was dead quiet. Trosper doubted that Mozart had even looked up from his book.

"You guys aren't going to get away with this . . ."

Nash's voice seemed to taper off. Trosper glanced at Ida. "Just an hour and twenty minutes—they don't make 'em like they used to."

Ida looked baffled, but managed a smile.

"I'll let him cook for another half-hour," Trosper said.

26

GENEVA

"I WANT the whole story," Trosper said. "The first time around, I'll take it in the short form." He leaned forward in his chair and took a yellow pad from the coffee table. "Tomorrow you can write it all down."

Nash shook his head. He had taken off his tie and folded it carefully at the side of the coffee table. His rumpled blazer was still unbuttoned. Even if allowance was made for bravado, Nash was in better shape and more self-confident than Trosper would have wished.

Mozart Riley pulled his chair next to Nash.

"You people are crazy," Nash said, his voice thick. "What's more, you're not going to get away with it." He leaned back and casually crossed his feet on the polished coffee table. "There's not a damned thing you can make me—"

With a barely perceptible shift of his weight, Riley leaned forward and swung his left arm like a scythe. His open hand whipped Nash's feet across the table with enough force to spin him off the love seat and onto the floor beside the coffee table.

Riley turned to Trosper. "Shall I have him begin to mind his manners?"

Trosper shook his head. "Not yet . . ."

Nash's mouth opened, but before he spoke he glanced at Riley. He closed his mouth and eased himself back onto the small sofa.

"There's something you had better begin to understand," Trosper said. "As of right now, you're looking at half a dozen charges of espionage. Short of a series of child murders, that's as tough a rap as anyone your age is ever likely to face."

Nash shrugged, and attempted to pat his mussed hair back into place. In profile, he seemed strong, even handsome. Glimpsed from the front, his face was so narrow it seemed crowded. Heavy eyebrows threatened to eclipse his small dark eyes, crammed tight against a nose that was interesting in silhouette but thick and fleshy when viewed full-face. Nash's loose, heavy-lipped mouth occupied too much of the area above his chin.

"In about ten minutes, Johnson and his team will be leaving for your apartment," Trosper said. He spoke softly, and tried to keep eye contact with Nash. "You can start cooperating now by telling me exactly what gear you have stashed." He glanced at the door as if expecting the mythical Johnson to open it and ask permission to begin the search. "If you don't cooperate, they'll take your place apart an inch at a time."

"I want a lawyer," Nash mumbled. "I'm not going to say a word until I have a lawyer."

"If you make me put you under arrest, and turn you over to the Swiss authorities, you'll be able to hire all the lawyers you can pay for," Trosper said. "You'll be big news, a headline on the front page of every newspaper from Geneva to Melbourne. I wouldn't count on Moscow Center making one of their front men available, but if you can't afford a lawyer, you'll probably rate a public defender. Or, maybe your family will be able to help?"

Nash's eyes flickered, but he remained silent.

The notes Ida had taken from the TABYR personal file had given Trosper all the background on Nash he needed.

"Once you hit the press," Trosper said, "it will be too late for any positive cooperation, and you'll be left with only one card to play."

"What card?"

"You can plead guilty," Trosper said cheerfully. "You'll recall that's exactly what Chief Petty Officer Johnny Walker and his brother did a couple of years ago. By agreeing to a complete debriefing and saving the cost of a trial, they both got off with multiple life sentences." Trosper shrugged. "But now that I think about it, it might not have been such a good deal—neither one of them will be back on the street in this century."

Despite his bruises and swollen nose, Nash's face was ashen. "I want to talk to Mr. Fuller, he's my boss."

"Yesterday," Trosper said slowly. "Yesterday, you could have talked to Mr. Fuller. Now, it's too late." He waited before saying, "You've got no alternative but to talk to me."

Nash's shoulders began to heave. As he struggled to mask his sobs, he bent forward, burying his face in his hands and gulping for air.

"If you're gonna puke, you'll do it in a wastebasket," Riley said. "You mess on Mrs. Fuller's rug, I'll fucking wipe your nose in it."

Trosper glanced at Riley, appreciating the bit of theater. It was the first obscene word he had ever heard him use.

Nash sat straight up, his eyes red and moist. He stared wildly at Riley. "You guys, you don't know anything. Man, you don't know what it's like . . . your colleges . . . expense accounts . . . this dog work punching out cables." He lurched to his feet, staring at Trosper. "This is the end of everything I've tried to be, and you just sit there with that smug look on your . . ." Then, like a frenzied child throwing a tantrum, he smashed his foot down on the fragile coffee table. The top splintered and a broken leg skittered into the fireplace.

Mozart Riley shot to his feet, his eyes on Trosper.

Trosper nodded. He hoped there would be no marks on Nash's face.

The short right hook landed an inch above Nash's polished belt buckle, slamming him backwards until his rump caught on the arched back of the love seat. It toppled, spilling him onto the rug.

Riley stepped around the overturned sofa and set it upright. He reached under Nash's shoulders and dumped him back into his seat.

Trosper remembered Fuller and Ida in the back room with the monitoring gear and said softly, "All secure. No problems."

He glanced at Nash, sprawled semi-conscious on the chintz. He looked smaller than when he had first come into the room, and younger than his twenty-six years.

Riley began gently to try to piece the broken coffee table together. He looked up at Trosper and shook his head. "Totaled," he said.

"It's about time for a drink," Trosper said for the benefit of Ida. "If you put three scotches and some soda on a tray, I'll take it from you at the door."

Mozart shook his head.

"Make it two," Trosper said.

Nash whimpered as he struggled to pull himself into a sitting position. His eyes were glazed and his breath was coming in short, rasping gasps.

Trosper remained silent until there was a tap on the door. He opened the door, carefully blocking Fuller's attempt to peer into the room, and took the tray.

"For heaven's sake, Alan, the neighbors will raise Cain about all this racket and—"

"If they complain, tell them it's your anniversary, and you and Bunky are having a spat," Trosper hissed as he closed the door. He took a drink from the tray and offered it to Nash. "You'd better take this." Nash's hands shook as he reached for the glass.

Trosper took a long sip of whiskey. "You know," he said, "there wasn't any need for this, no need at all." He pulled the yellow pad from the wreckage of the coffee table. "I've told you straight out that you're in about as bad a jam as is possible. You should have realized that by now." Trosper took another sip of whiskey. "What I have to do is work out a way to salvage some of the pieces. If you cooperate, maybe, just maybe, we can stuff some of this back up their nose. If so, it'll probably be the only chance you're ever going to have to help yourself."

Nash took a sip of whiskey and began to cough.

"Do you take my point?"

Nash twisted sideways and eased a crumpled handkerchief from his pocket. He wiped his eyes.

"And no more nonsense?"

Nash took another swallow of whiskey.

It was almost two o'clock. It would take four hours to unravel Nash's story.

Trosper pulled a ballpoint pen from his pocket.

"How did you first meet Brodsky?" he began.

27

GENEVA

THERE was no fight left in Nash, and, Trosper hoped, no more tears.

"I'm going to have something typed up for you to sign," Trosper said. "After that you can sack out for a while."

Nash stared vacantly at the shattered coffee table and nodded. His eyes were bloodshot and bleary. His expensive poplin shirt was stained with stale sweat and he needed a shave.

Trosper dropped the yellow pad and ballpoint pen onto the table beside his chair. He had twenty-two pages of double-spaced notes, his head ached, and the night-long resupply of coffee had soured his stomach.

Mozart Riley eased himself off the straight chair. He glanced ruefully at the coffee table and with some care began to flex his cramped knees.

"There's one more thing," Trosper said, "and this is the last time I'm going to remind you."

Nash raised his thick eyebrows and made a show of concentrating on Trosper.

"You have one chance of mitigating the mess you've made of your life."

Nash snuffled and reached for his handkerchief.

"If you give me any reason to think I have to worry about you making a run for it, you'll go straight back to the States."

"My passport is at the office. You've got my money, the keys to the apartment, and my car . . ."

"I mean," Trosper interrupted, "no stunts of any kind." He decided not to make a specific reference to suicide.

"But you *are* going to help me?"

Trosper shook his head. "You've got it backwards—*you're* going to help *me*. Then, if things work out, the judge will be told that you have cooperated."

"That's not much of a deal . . ."

"It's not a deal. You don't have anything to say about it."

"But . . ."

"Can't you get it through your head that the moment Moscow Center learns what happened last night, you're wasted?" Trosper said. "From their point of view, you were damned well paid. The fact you were pocketing a lot more cash than the case men handling your operation is not likely to endear you to those guys either. It doesn't much matter how well you earned your keep—that was yesterday. From their point of view, what happens from now on is *your* problem."

Nash's eyes filled. "Brodsky promised that if anything went wrong, I'd be resettled anywhere I wanted." He blew his nose and dabbed at his eyes with the soggy handkerchief. "I suppose that doesn't count now . . ."

"Maybe after you get out of prison," Trosper said helpfully. "Perhaps then Brodsky and his friends will do something for you." He waited before saying, "Of course they don't let guys like you hang around the big tourist cities, but you can probably get something in Volgagrad or Kiev. Maybe Minsk, that's where they dumped Lee Harvey Oswald . . ."

"I never believed Brodsky anyway," Nash said.

It was time to get back to business, to ease Nash into the next phase. "You said Brodsky never *pressed* you about any of your commo colleagues?" Trosper began. "But he did question you on everyone in the office, every visitor, everyone you knew in Washington?" Nash nodded confirmation. "And you told him everything you knew about everyone?" Yes, Nash had told him about everyone.

"You gave him chapter and verse on Gandy?"

"Yes."

"And your pal Frost and his carousing around Geneva?"

"I told you all that last night, at least a dozen times," Nash said, his thick lips pouting. "Brodsky told me Gandy was dangerous and to stay away from him. It was different with Frost, Brodsky was all hot to trot with Frost. He even had me fix him up with a little Italian barmaid, and paid for it—that dumb-ass Frost thought she had eyes for him. Then Brodsky had me arrange it so he could bump into Frost. But a couple of weeks later, he lost interest entirely and told me to back off. It was no sweat because a little while after that Bondarev was called back to Moscow, and Frost and Gandy left for Washington." Nash's voice began to rise. "I'm just not going to go over the Bondarev story again. I've admitted it, if I had it to do again, I wouldn't do it. Just don't forget that Bondarev would've done it to me twice as quick . . ." Nash's voice broke. "Anyway, Brodsky said that nothing would happen to Bondarev because of what I did." He managed to glance defiantly at Trosper. "I'm not going to talk about that any more."

Exactly right, Trosper thought. And now for something I really do want to talk about. "You said Brodsky let you breeze right past the zeroes, the guys he might expect you to know best?" Trosper waited until Nash's defiant frown had faded before adding, "You don't really expect me to believe that, do you?"

"Zero" was shop talk for cipher clerk or code man. Commodore Hamilton, the retired naval officer Bates had made communications chief, disliked the expression, and attempted to stamp it out. He had failed. The cipher clerks still referred to themselves as zeroes and most signal centers, still called radio shacks, were marked with hand-lettered signs proclaiming Ground Zero.

Nash twisted sidewise on the sofa, the better to show Trosper his profile and to avoid eye contact. "What you said is not exactly what I meant. Brodsky asked plenty about all the commo guys I might know, but I convinced him that I hadn't been around Washington or anywhere else long enough to get to know anyone too well . . ."

Trosper shook his head. "What about the guys who spell you here, who take over when you're on vacation? Are you trying to tell me he never asked about *them?*"

"There's only one, he comes over from Vienna . . ." Nash ran his fingers along his stubbled jaw.

"But Brodsky *did* ask you about him?"

"Some . . ."

This was more like it. "What's his name?"

Nash studied his black Italian moccasins, and without looking up said, "He's really not involved in this. There's no reason to get him into trouble."

"You're the one who's in trouble—face down in it—so stop the damned nonsense."

"If I convince you he's not involved, can we keep this just between us?" Nash glanced quickly at Riley as if to include him in the agreement.

Trosper dropped his yellow pad and leaned closer to Nash. "Life isn't long enough for me to sit here listening to this crap. How many times do I have to remind you that you're looking at *life* in the can?" Trosper had learned to use his temper as a weapon. He had little use for spontaneous eruptions and it irritated him to realize he was flexing both hands as if restraining himself from grabbing Nash. "There's no way on earth I'm going to make any kind of a deal with you."

Riley got lightly to his feet and moved closer to Nash. It was another neatly executed bit of theater, intended to leave Nash confused as to whether Riley was going to restrain Trosper or hit Nash.

"All right, all right," Nash said with a calming gesture.

Riley walked to the window, flexing his stiff knees.

"Snow?" Trosper asked.

Riley nodded. "At least six inches."

Trosper turned to Nash, "Let's get on with it—what's your Vienna friend's name?"

Nash wiped his mouth with the back of his hand. "Jordan, Ralph Jordan . . ."

"And?"

"It got started a year, maybe fifteen months ago when Tolya began pressing me for what he called *leads,* " Nash said. "He wasn't interested in the guys in the Geneva office, and always told me to stay away from the people who outrank me. But like you suspect, he always jumped at any scrap of info on the commo people, the zero guys."

"And so you fed him your friend Jordan?"

Nash nodded. "Brodsky kept squeezing, telling me that the big boss wasn't satisfied, and was threatening that I wasn't earning my money. This worried Brodsky. You don't have to be in the Ivy Leagues to see that those guys scare him shitless."

"Did he make threats?"

"He'd tell me what tough guys they are, how they had gone through the war, and didn't give a damn about anyone. Then he began to cut back on the money, and I could really feel the pressure on my life-style."

"When did you introduce Jordan?"

Nash shook his head. "I never *introduced* him, I just told Brodsky that I thought Jordan could be had."

"How?"

"It was easy. I started feeding him the straight stuff—Jordan's got a kid, he's ambitious and wants to get along in the Firm. Like most married guys, he'd like to have enough bread to get away from the old lady once in a while. I figured if Brodsky's people could check, they would find out the obvious things and think I was telling the truth about the rest. After that, I went on with stuff I figured they couldn't check so easy. I told Brodsky that Jordan was broke, that his kid was costing an arm and a leg, his old lady was giving him hell, and he was desperate to find a better job. Stuff like that."

Nash looked expectantly at Trosper, and got no response. "Jordan only came here three or four times a year, when I was going on leave or there was a lot of extra work. We always had an overlap before I took off and after I got back. I'd tell Brodsky I was taking Jordan out for meals and that we were hitting the bars, and how much he was going for it."

"Was this true?"

Nash grinned and shook his head. "Jordan's a real tight-ass. The once I even got him out to a bar, he thought I was crazy spending francs like that." His grin broadened. "I needed the money, so I

stuck Tolya for a lot of phony expenses for boozing with Jordan.
One time I said I'd fixed him up with a date, five hundred francs.
Brodsky asked for a receipt, but I said those girls didn't give receipts. He knew that anyway, and was just trying to hold me down.
I had them convinced I was really softening up straight-arrow Jordan, and that it wouldn't be long before he was ready for an offer to
earn a little on the side."

"Didn't Brodsky ever ask to meet Jordan?"

"That's a good question." Nash waited, as if he expected Trosper to acknowledge the compliment, and then began again. "I was
really scared that he'd insist on a face-to-face and then make some
kind of pitch himself. But I finally realized Brodsky had no intention of risking a meet with Jordan—he was afraid something might
go wrong, that Jordan would blow the whistle on him, and we'd all
go down the chute." Nash thought for a moment. "You know,
Brodsky was even afraid to see me. Like we only met about six times
a year. Otherwise, I just put the Minox film and a piss-ant message
saying I was okay in the dead-drop, and got my dough out of another drop."

Trosper yawned, and turned to Riley. "It's beginning to feel like
breakfast time . . ."

Nash's eyes brightened.

Trosper picked up his notes. He handed Nash a sheaf of paper.
"After you have something to eat, and a break, I want you to start
typing your story—chapter and verse from the first time you met
Brodsky. You can use the portable over there."

"I DON'T see why you think you have to be so tough on Terry,"
Fuller said. "I mean, you might have offered him something more
than a word to the judge if things work out right."

They were sitting at the breakfast table in Bunky's gleaming
kitchen. Nash and Riley were in the study, Nash asleep, and twist-
ing fitfully. Riley dozed by the door. Ida Rowan had showered and
made breakfast, and was closeted with Bunky in what Fuller referred to as the rose bedroom.

Trosper looked up from the cable he was drafting. "I want Master Nash to *know* that he hasn't got a friend in the world. I want him emotionally flat on his ass. Maybe then it will be time to offer a little something." Trosper glared at Fuller. "Right now his attention span is so short, he recharges his battery every time he looks out the window or has something to eat."

"What about Brodsky?" Fuller asked.

"When they find out Nash is burned, Brodsky's case man will offer him a chance to cut and run," Trosper said. "But that's only if Moscow is sure he can get away before being arrested—any old trollop who speaks as many languages as Brodsky can earn his keep in East Germany, maybe in Poland. It's Nash who's dead meat."

Trosper initialed the draft, and tossed it to Fuller. "Seal this and have Rusty Higgins take it and copies of my notes to Daisy for transmission to the Controller, Eyes Alone."

Fuller's face fell. Daisy, the central communications office, was a five-hour drive from Geneva.

"Until the waffle-bottoms have sorted out their cipher machines, or brought in new ones, there's not going to be any traffic to or from Geneva on this case, or on any new business," Trosper said patiently. "Nash has sold every cable he put his hands on. The fact he *says* he hasn't rigged the cipher machines is not particularly reassuring."

Fuller did not protest.

EVEN in sunlight, driving in Geneva was a stress test. In rush hour and in snow, a twenty-minute trip across town could take an hour. Fuller's apartment in Trélex was on the opposite side of town from the office. Trosper's hotel was midway. Time was becoming a problem. Nash could not remain out of sight indefinitely. The logistics of keeping six people in the apartment had already become difficult; the nervous wear and tear would soon become apparent. There were eight inches of snow on the ground and it was still coming down. Trosper tried to recall a really important operation that had occurred in good weather, or even broad daylight. His head throbbed as he contemplated Teddy Vermont.

———

It was 2:30, the luncheon crowd had dissipated, and it was too early for the hot chocolate and pastry enthusiasts to congregate at the Pâtisserie du Rhône. Trosper decided to ignore the possibility that a glass of chocolate milk would help settle his stomach and took a sip of mineral water.

"The trick with a *coupe Danemark* is to keep the chocolate from getting into the whipped cream and making it all soupy."

Teddy Vermont sat on the edge of his chair, carefully ladling the melted chocolate into the hollow he had formed in the mound of French vanilla ice cream. "At the end, when there's not much ice cream left, you take each rosette of whipped cream separate, with a spoonful of chocolate and melting ice cream . . ." He looked up at Trosper. "This is good stuff, but I'd swap all the ice cream in Switzerland for a supply of McDonald's milkshakes."

With an effort, Trosper put the thought out of his mind. "What about your pigeon?"

Vermont leaned back from the table, and with an almost imperceptible movement checked the position of the waiters. "It's like he owns the town."

"For example?"

"Not once did he even look over his shoulder." The street man fixed his eyes on the ice cream. "He uses buses, he walks, he has a little car. But it's like he thinks he's the invincible man."

"The invisible man?"

"That also . . ." Vermont eased a spoonful from the metal cup. "If he's with the comedians, he's been here too long. They should call him back for refresher courses."

"What does his day look like?"

"He must make coffee at home because he heads straight for the U.N. press room about ten every day. Around noon he goes out, catches lunch just off the Rue de Mont Blanc. Then he goes back to the U.N. About five-thirty he has a *Stamm* drink with a couple of guys, press I think. Then he heads home."

"Where is that?"

"He's got a second-floor apartment on the Rue des Eaux Vives.

It's a middle sort of place, not fancy."

"Does he live alone?"

"I've checked his doorbell three times, half an hour after he left in the morning. No answer."

"Mail?"

"I've been getting his box open with one of those little gadgets the magicians are so proud of. But it's not so easy here. These Swiss mind your business like it's their own."

"And?"

"Nothing. Some bills, a couple letters that looked like business—I've got the return addresses and description in my pocket. I haven't had time to open anything."

"What about friends?"

"Aside from the people he lunches with, I haven't seen anything. One night he boozed a little in the Argosy, an expensive nightclub for our friend. But he seemed to know one of the bar men, and just signed his tab. I'd guess he steers people there once in a while, maybe gives some free RP."

"PR, surely," Trosper said.

The street man glanced around the restaurant and said, "What you need is to get on his telephone."

"We could also check with his neighbors, and talk to some of his colleagues in the press room, but we're not going to," Trosper said sharply. "What about women, is there anyone he invites to the apartment?"

"From what I've seen, there's no women at all, certainly no squeeze."

"What time does he get home?"

"As far as I can tell, he usually eats in. He gets there around seven. Turns on the TV, makes something to eat. The TV goes off about eleven, thereabouts. I can't tell for sure, but I think he usually falls asleep in the living room. Then later, reads in bed. The living room fronts on the Rue des Eaux Vives, and you can tell when he douses the lamps, but you can't see the bedroom light."

"Can you get into the apartment?"

Vermont glanced around the room, and whistled softly. "I can get in most anywhere if the lock's not trapped." He laid his forefinger alongside his nose. "You know the comedians have got some stunt where if you stick the wrong key or a pick into one of their locks, it freezes and your key or pick is stuck there unless you break it off . . ."

"Yes, yes," Trosper said. This was an old device and to Trosper's knowledge had never been issued to agents.

Teddy said, "If I go in, I should have backup. I don't want some local looney-tunes calling the cops."

"What about the downstairs door, the one leading into the building?"

"I've already done that," Vermont said. "It's an expensive lock, real shiny—I can go through it with a ripe banana, maybe ten seconds, broad daylight."

"I want you to take him right around the clock tonight," Trosper said. "Stay just as close as necessary."

WASHINGTON, D.C.

"SOMETHING must have gone down by now," Castle murmured into the high-security phone. "Have you heard anything?"

Duff Whyte glanced at the sealed envelope. It was classified Top Secret/Eiderdown, and addressed Controller, Eyes Alone. The envelope was stamped "By Hand of Officer Courier Only."

"Mrs. Thornton just brought a cable. You'd better come up and have a look at it."

Whyte put the phone down. Before he had finished rereading the cable, Castle slipped into the chair beside his desk.

"Every cable in and out of Geneva from June eighty-five, photographed, and turned over to Brodsky," Whyte said.

Castle muttered an oath in French.

Whyte handed the cable to Castle and walked to the window. With his back to Castle he said, "Nash left the undeveloped film in a drop, twice a month. Alan didn't say when Nash made the last delivery, but effective right now, the Geneva office is totally compromised."

Castle began to read, running his finger down the cable. "No quarrel with paragraph two—'Nash insists Brodsky made recruitment and remained Nash's only live contact.'"

"No matter how high-grade the stuff he's turning over, there's no reason Moscow would use a staff man to handle a bought-and-paid-for mercenary like Nash in Geneva," Whyte said. He turned away from the window and stepped back to his desk.

Castle continued to read. "What about paragraph eight? 'Nash claims Brodsky's case man considered Nash too valuable to risk attempting to get access to office central files, bugging cipher equipment, or tampering with pouch communications.'"

Whyte nodded. "They're right again—and that's why none of our security inspections ever found any problems." Whyte tapped his fist lightly against the desk. "There's no reason for the rezidency to risk bugging the office, or going after the staff, as long as they're reading all of our mail."

Castle said, "If you agree with Alan's recommendation that we send a security officer with a warrant for Nash's arrest and repatriation, I'd better brief Justice this afternoon."

"Talk to Tony Broder—see if he'll send a marshal along with our man. Have them both stand by at Daisy, I don't want us to be any more conspicuous than necessary in Geneva."

Without looking up from the cable, Castle said, "I don't like to admit it, but I agree with Alan's assessment . . ."

Whyte looked up.

"'It now clear that since June 1985 Moscow Center has considered Geneva office an asset rather than a threat.'"

"Mercenary little *salopard* . . ."

Castle turned to the last page of the cable. "What about this last sentence? 'View possible exploitation Brodsky, strongly recommend you do nothing to disturb Geneva office routine for next several days.' Does that mean what I think it does?"

Whyte managed a faint smile. "It means Alan Trosper is going to nail Brodsky's ass to the wall." Whyte's smile broadened. "And I for one would like to be there to see it."

28

GENEVA

"LET's get the logistics out of the way first," Trosper said. He glanced around the kitchen. Eighteen hours of short-order cooking and coffee-making for six people had begun to leave a patina of grime on the spotless room. The fearful symmetry with which Bunky's mortal hand had framed the vast array of copper and iron cookware had been violated by hastily washed, dingy pots and pans suspended at random among the other as yet untouched utensils.

They were seated around the kitchen table. Fuller had both arms on the table and was listlessly doodling in a spiral notebook. Riley sat straight up in a kitchen chair, his eyes fixed on the door leading to the hallway and the bathroom where Nash was showering. Ida was alert, her eyes on Trosper.

"Tonight we'll need a big car, something with four doors, local plates."

"Betty, my secretary, has an old Chevy," Fuller said. "It's about as big as anything we might be able to rent here."

"We also need a second car, preferably not a rental . . ."

"My Peugeot," Fuller said. "We might as well make a clean sweep of the Geneva office . . ."

"And radio commo between the two cars . . ."

"I've got a couple of good Maggie and Jiggs in the office," Fuller said quickly.

"I can rig and test them," Ida said.

"It's almost four now. I'm going back to the hotel and flake out for a couple of hours." Trosper stifled a yawn and turned to Fuller. "I want you, Riley, Ida, and Nash in the Rue de Lausanne apartment by nine. Teddy will call me there."

Fuller nodded.

"Park both cars close to the apartment."

"There's no one on the street," Fuller said. "There hasn't been this much snow here in five years."

Trosper picked up his coat. "Try to get some rest, and eat something. But no booze." He rubbed his eyes. It had been thirty-two hours since he'd slept, with another long night to come. He was glad he had not taken the amphetamine. He needed three, maybe four hours' sleep. The first pill would come tonight after the midnight charge of adrenaline had burned out.

As he stepped into the living room, Trosper glanced around. The customary safe-house detritus—dirty ashtrays, yellow pads, coffee cups piled onto a butler's table, drawn curtains—and the pervading stale air were unmistakable. Chairs carelessly pulled out of place, and the end tables serving as substitutes for the smashed coffee table, had skewed the decorator balance of the room. With a groan Trosper remembered that he had completely forgotten Bunky.

"Damn," he muttered. He turned to Fuller. "I'd better go in and apologize to Bunky. The least I can do is say I'm sorry about all this . . ."

Fuller grinned self-consciously. "She's left for a few days. She slipped out this afternoon before you got back. She'll stay with Kitty Webster in Munich until this blows over . . ."

The irritation that flashed across Trosper's face prompted Ida, in the doorway to the kitchen, to make a reassuring gesture.

"Actually, Alan," Fuller said quickly, "when I told her Terry had gone sour and ruined everything I've been trying to do, she took a sort of spell. Then, when she came around, she began to rave about killing him . . ."

From behind Fuller, Ida stuck out her tongue, crossed her eyes, and puffed out her cheeks. It was a perfect imitation of Harpo Marx. Trosper got the message, kept a straight face, and said, "You warned her about keeping quiet?"

"Of course I did," Fuller said. "Bunky's a special woman, but she's got plenty of common sense. She won't say a word to anyone."

Ida nodded her enthusiastic agreement.

Trosper turned up his coat collar and stepped out into the snow. Never again, he promised himself. Never again without a proper safe house and a holding area that the lady of the house doesn't call the Blue Room.

29

GENEVA

"Get his legs down, for Christ's sake," Trosper shouted into the palm mike. "Get them down."

Brodsky's feet were sticking straight up over the back seat of the blue Chevrolet, fifty yards ahead of Trosper in Fuller's Peugeot. The expanse of white flesh between the top of Brodsky's black snow boots and his trousers caught the Peugeot headlights like bizarre reflectors.

Until Mozart Riley, who had hidden on the floor behind the front seat of the borrowed Chevrolet, reached across and pulled Brodsky backwards over the front seat, things had gone almost according to plan.

"This is Mr. Eskimo," Teddy Vermont had begun. "I'm telephoning to say that my friend got in at seven-thirty. Now eleven-twenty, the lights are out, he's in the sack, and I'm froze."

"Okay," Trosper said. "I'm glad you guys are all well. Have you heard any weather reports?"

"The snow has just about stopped. But there's not a car on the road."

"Well done, my friend. Let's keep in touch."

Trosper put down the phone. He would have liked to go over his plan once more, and to be certain he had allowed for at least the most likely contingencies. But there was no time. He stifled the rush of uncertainty and beckoned to Nash. "Now," he said. "And no mistakes. No improvising."

Nash propped his pocket notebook open and began to dial. Trosper picked up the monitor that Ida had rigged on the "safe-house" phone. After the fifth ring, a muted click. "Brodsky . . ." The accent was guttural, harsh. "Brrodski."

"Tolya, you awake?" Nash's voice was high-pitched, cheerful.

"It's after midnight, why should I be awake?"

"It's only eleven-thirty." Nash sounded even more cheerful. "It's me, Victor. Wake up, Tolya."

A long pause.

"Come on man, I've got big business . . ."

"Business starts in the morning . . ."

"This is the best yet," Nash said. "A minimum of three one-minute spots a week. Good syndication, with a contract option. This is the best yet. Wake up, Tolya."

It was an open code. The number of TV spots indicated the degree of urgency.

A muttered curse in German.

"Tolya, there's no time. We've got to get this set tonight. I'm leaving first thing—"

"We can meet in the morning . . ."

"Tolya, listen. This is the contract we've been after for months. I got to leave first thing. It really can't wait."

More muttered German.

"I'll pick you up at the usual place."

"Moment . . ."

Nash covered the phone mouthpiece and glanced at Trosper. "I'll bet he's gone to look out the window. He hates snow . . ."

"Pay attention," Trosper ordered.

"Victor, there's a lot of snow. Morning will be better."

"Tolya, I'm leaving tomorrow morning. It's tonight or we miss out . . ."

"Vienna," Trosper scribbled on a pad. "Mention Vienna."

"Tolya, listen. I've heard from my Vienna customer. He's ready to deal. When he learned I was going to Vienna temporary, he called me. I've got to be there tomorrow, and I've got work in the office before I go."

Trosper nodded approval.

"You got your stupid race car?"

"That car's no good in this weather. I borrowed a Chevy, much better in the snow. I'll meet you in fifteen minutes, the usual place." He hesitated, and said, "It's a big sedan, and I'll be the only car on the road in this weather."

A long pause. "Too much snow. Pick me up here, right in front. You know the address?"

Nash was silent until Trosper signaled approval.

"Sure, Tolya, that's easier. But be ready. Fifteen minutes. I won't be able to park there, the plows are all over the place, so be out front."

Brodsky hung up.

Trosper tossed the earphone onto the desk. A scant thirty seconds into the operation and his plan was already out of kilter. If Brodsky had agreed to his usual meeting place with Nash, the cars could have gone out of Geneva on the route Fuller had reconnoitered. The hell with it, he would improvise a route and hope for the best.

Trosper remembered to nod a grudging approval to Nash.

Fuller, his face flush with enthusiasm, clapped Nash on the shoulder. "Well done, Terry, that was a good job."

Mozart Riley and Ida had gathered their coats.

"All set," Trosper said. "Except for the pickup point, it's the same drill except we go straight out the Rue des Eaux Vives and if need be turn off along the Rue de Contamines."

Fuller glanced at Riley. "Moe, have you got a weapon?"

Riley shook his head. "I don't need anything . . . one little move . . . our friend thinks he's a hit-and-run accident."

Trosper scanned the tense faces. "All set?" He turned to Ida. Her face was drawn. "Once more now, what if we flap?"

"I'll either see what's happened, or be told about it by radio from the Chevy," she said quietly. "Unless there are other instructions, Nash will drive the Peugeot back to Trélex." She patted her heavy handbag, and turned to face Nash. "You'd better remember that by the time you and I are in the car alone, your friend Tolya will know exactly who sold him out."

"Listen, I'm not going to make any trouble," Nash said.

Ida tossed her head.

". . . any *more* trouble," he mumbled.

"Hit him, for Christ's sake, whack him out . . ." Nash's voice was loud and clear above the muffled crashing sounds beamed from the miniature transmitter in the Chevy.

"Shut up . . ."

Trosper could not tell whether Riley's advice was meant for Brodsky or Nash.

"Now, close up," Trosper barked. "Parking lights only."

The Peugeot bucked, and shot forward. As the car moved close to the Chevy, Fuller touched the brakes, and the small sedan slid to a stop, inches from the Chevy's rear bumper.

"Perfect," Trosper muttered as he leaped from the front seat, heading through the snow to the Chevrolet.

"Get out, Terry," Fuller shouted into the radio. "Ida, up front, quick now." Fuller swung the front door open and sprinted toward the Chevrolet.

Ida slipped into the Peugeot's front passenger seat. She pulled a canister of Mace from her handbag and watched as Nash lurched out of the Chevy driver's seat and held the door open for Fuller.

"Split, damn it," Fuller yelled at Nash, who stood peering at Riley, bolt upright in the back seat. When Nash leaned closer to the rear window, attempting to see Brodsky, Fuller shoved him toward the Peugeot. Nash's low shoes slipped on the snow and he fell backwards. "Get up, God damn it, and get into the Peugeot . . ." Fuller grabbed Nash's arm and pulled him to his feet.

"Let's move out," Trosper said, keeping his voice down.

Fuller eased himself behind the wheel.

Nash skittered along the snow-slick street to the Peugeot.

Over the radio Trosper could hear Ida whisper, "This is Mace. One squirt in your direction, and you're flat on your back for five minutes."

"Get that thing out of my face." Nash's voice rose.

"Two squirts, and you're out for the night," Ida promised.

Trosper spoke into the hand mike. "Knock it off back there."

"We're ready to move," Ida whispered into the radio.

"All clear ahead," Trosper said. "You can move right along."

Trosper turned to Riley in the back seat. The big man sat straight up, his feet resting lightly on the dark blanket covering Brodsky on the floor.

"All clear?" Trosper asked politely.

Riley nodded, and wiped the perspiration from his forehead. "I think his glasses got broken."

"Does he understand about keeping quiet?"

"I believe he does," Riley said.

Through the back window, Trosper could see Nash hunched over the Peugeot steering wheel. Then Ida's voice on the radio, "The motor's running, you idiot . . . just stop messing with the starter . . . ease it into reverse, hold it, and then gently forward . . ."

Then a furious Nash. "Girlie, I've got an open competition license. I can race any sports car in Europe. I could drive this crap can straight up Mont Blanc without any advice from you."

A rustle of movement came over the transmitter, and then an unmistakable groan.

"Christ Almighty, she's Maced him," Fuller said.

Trosper strained to see through the back window. "Damn, damn, damn . . ."

Then from the Peugeot, "You silly little bitch—you hit me one more time with that bag, I'll bust your ass . . ."

"Thank God it wasn't the Mace," Fuller sighed.

"If you can manage to get moving, just concentrate on trying to drive, if you please." Ida's voice was a full register lower than usual.

A few seconds later Ida picked up the transmitter. "All set back here."

The Peugeot began to move.

"Not a single freaking car on the road," Fuller said. "It's all this gorgeous snow . . ."

As the small sedan made a slow U-turn, Trosper could hear Nash complaining to Ida about his wet feet.

Trosper spoke softly into the tiny transmitter. "You're *still* on the air, Red Rider."

Fuller laughed.

"This is over and out," Ida said primly.

The snow had stopped.

30

GENEVA

TOLYA BRODSKY was older than Trosper had imagined, and despite his bulk, more muscular. He was about five feet nine, and larded with fat. It was a strong man's fat, and bulged around his chest and above his waist. His face was so fleshy that his huge head seemed to sit directly on his shoulders. If Brodsky had a neck at all, it had disappeared, compressed beneath the burden of his face and cranium.

Brodsky had bent double to struggle out of his heavy galoshes. Freed of these encumbrances, his feet, in shiny, mouse-gray shoes, seemed perilously small for his body. As he fought to catch his breath, Brodsky rubbed his rheumy, pale blue eyes and peered at Trosper. Then, after running his hand through his short white hair, he touched the etched red line across the bridge of his nose where the glasses had hung. "I can't see too much without my glasses."

"For now, there's nothing you need to see."

Riley pulled a pair of heavy horn-rimmed glasses from his pocket. They were in two pieces, broken at the bridge. He grimaced and silently mouthed, "Glue?"

Trosper shook his head. It was after midnight. He had only a few hours to skim the essential elements of an interrogation, which if done in depth could take weeks. "If there's coffee, we'd better have some," he said to Riley.

"What happened," Brodsky asked. "Did you people get luck, did someone walk in?" He pulled a handkerchief from his pocket and wiped his eyes. "Maybe Sergei the sly has decided to try your side for a while?"

Brodsky's sanguine assumption that he was in a position to ask questions was not encouraging, and for the moment Trosper would not give him the satisfaction of asking for Sergei's last name and patronymic.

"If you really want to know, I expected something like this," Brodsky said. "It couldn't go on forever. Something was bound to happen." He shrugged. "But I thought it would be the Swiss. With them it could be harder to make a deal." He had complained about his back and sat wedged into the corner of the love seat in front of the fireplace. "Who are you people?" He grunted as he pulled himself forward and put the empty coffee cup on the end table. "The Firm?"

"Does it matter?" It pleased Trosper to answer Brodsky's four questions with a question.

"I suppose not," Brodsky said. He eased his trousers and crossed his legs. There was an indelicate spread of white flesh between the bottom of his trouser leg and his black, ankle-high socks.

"You know, it doesn't snow much in Geneva, not this much in the last five years," Brodsky said. "Now, two storms right together. Did you wait for it, or did it just happen?"

Brodsky had begun to talk as soon as Riley had thrust him through the door of Fuller's apartment. This was a good sign, and partially compensated for Brodsky's unwelcome self-assurance.

"I want to do this backwards," Trosper said. "We'll begin with what you've got on your plate now, and work back to the beginning." It would have been better to start chronologically, but time was becoming important.

"What's the deal?" Brodsky said. His English was accented but fluent with traces of both Anglo and American cadences and mannerisms. "I mean, what's in it for me if I cooperate?"

"As of now, nothing."

"Then what if I just tell you to piss off?" Brodsky peered in Trosper's direction. "There's nothing you could do about it in Geneva." He turned and attempted to focus on Riley. "And I'm not planning to make trips . . ."

Trosper shook his head. "You've got a limited residence permit, press credentials, and a kind of life. You're pretty well known, but up to now no one's been able to prove anything. Now we've got all the evidence we need. You're a Soviet agent. That ruins you as a journalist, and even if the Swiss don't prosecute, you'll be expelled and never allowed back."

"You willing to swap your Geneva office just to hurt me?" Brodsky delivered the question with some dignity.

"The Geneva office is long gone," Trosper said. "The only reason it's still open is to keep you people on the string for a while . . ."

Brodsky squinted and tried to focus his eyes. "I want to know what my cut will be," he said. "There's plenty I can tell you once we agree on a deal . . ."

"Let's get started . . ."

"Nash is just a jerk," Brodsky said. "You could feel sorry for him."

"I know about Nash," Trosper said. "What else are you up to?"

"A taste," Brodsky said. "I'll give you an hors d'oeuvre. After that we cut a deal."

Trosper hoped Brodsky could not see the satisfaction that slipped into his expression.

"CLERKS," Brodsky continued. "They like officers better, but they're happy with secretaries. The women always know which boss is broke, who's drinking, and who's whoring around. What's more—and Sergei's got this on the brain—secretaries get transferred. With luck they could land in a hot office, somewhere there's real information."

"I'm quite familiar with their theory," Trosper said. He was satisfied that Brodsky had begun to talk. Detailed questions would come later.

"They must have a book, something someone wrote for the big school in Moscow. So Sergei always says go for the minorities—gays, blacks, drunks, Mormons, Arabs, Jews—anyone who could have a grudge." Brodsky shrugged and managed a self-deprecating grin. "Or somebody like me, fat, heavy glasses, ugly . . . maybe even disappointed. It's dead simple, but it must work or they wouldn't keep pushing on it."

"Nash doesn't fit those criteria . . ."

Brodsky peered more closely at Trosper. "I told Sergei a dozen times that there's two kinds of people you can work, weepers and dreamers. Weepers are lonely-hearts, desperate for friends. The trouble is you have to dig them out of their nest before you can begin to show them some sights, so to speak. The dreamers get around more. They save up and then go out to have an adventure. But they're just dumb suckers like most people." He belched and swallowed several times. "I got stomach acid. My pills are in my coat pocket."

Trosper shook his head. "We'll find you something here . . ." He motioned to Riley.

Brodsky snorted. "If you're worried about suicide, you've got the wrong guy. I've been through it all—barefoot." He nodded, approving his own observation. "I learned something in the war—I survived what killed a lot of people." He pressed his fingers against his eyes. It was as if he could squeeze them into focus.

"What about our U.N. Mission here in Geneva?"

"Look, I've already given you plenty. How about my deal?"

"You were saying . . ."

Brodsky sighed. It was a long whistle of a sigh, orchestrated with self-pity. "The trouble is I'm too old for the people they told me to go at. What I wanted to do was older people, people disappointed with the way things turned. Those people I know about."

Riley handed Brodsky a glass of water and two pills. "Chew them and then take the water."

"I could use a real drink . . ."

"Let's get back to what you're doing."

"They really like Nash," Brodsky said. "He's a big case . . ." He corrected himself quickly. "*My* big case. Sergei said I had scored for peace." He shook his head. "Scored for peace, ha!" With an ingratiating smile, he took Trosper into his confidence. "I wonder if they really believe that stuff?" He groped in his pocket and pulled out a package of small Dutch cigars. "Anyway, it worked like I told them. I spotted him and a bit of fluff in a bar one night. He spoke some French, but he was American, clear as glass. I figured he was a clerk, maybe in the U.S. Mission here in Geneva. He didn't look like anyone very serious. I could hear him chatting up this little meatball. I got interested when she started talking about his car. He had this old two-seater, and fancied himself a race-driver. So I had two things going, the guy's a chaser and he's got more fantasy than brains."

A lifetime of hustling had taught Brodsky his trade.

"I bought a couple drinks, and he recites his cover story like it's a lesson he had learned—he's a big-shot trainee in some international firm, and even wants me to believe they'll send him to Harvard Business School after Geneva." Brodsky was speaking more freely now. "Dreamers get romantic pictures about anything to do with media. All I had to say is that I usually drop around the bar on Monday night, after I file my copy. Right away Nash says he's also been thinking about journalism—more headroom than business, or so he thinks." Brodsky snorted. "In three weeks I've got him writing little economic fillers for me. I pay him a hundred francs a shot, and he thinks he's also learning journalism."

Brodsky peered blearily around the room. "Listen, I could really use my glasses. This way, it's like I'm talking to the wall. I'm getting a headache, too."

And you can't see what kind of an impression you're making either, Trosper thought. "Tomorrow, we'll figure something out," he said.

"There won't be tomorrow unless I get a deal . . ."

"You were saying?"

Brodsky inhaled deeply and blew the smoke in Trosper's direction. "Nash can't write shit, so I begin to squeeze him. Like I figured, he's lazy as hell, and in a couple weeks he's just copying political and economic stuff from the briefings your head office sends out. I'm telling him how his writing is improving, and he's signing receipts for the money he's getting."

"What about your case man?"

"He's pissing lots of good advice, like 'Be careful' . . ." For a moment Brodsky savored the smoke from his cigar. "After I had a pile of the stuff Nash was handing out, I tell him, 'Cut the shit, I know who you are, and what you do.' He blubbers around for a while and I tell him, 'From now on, I want the cable traffic, and no more bullshit.' It was easier than I expected."

"What's Sergei's name?"

"Sergei Antonovich Varentsov, Second Secretary in the Mission here. He's on his first assignment abroad, and not too bright."

"Before him?"

Brodsky pulled himself forward on the sofa, trying to bring Trosper into focus. "Before Sergei it was Boris Kruglov."

"Was it Sergei or Boris who told you Nash was a cipher clerk?"

Brodsky's face clouded.

Trosper waited. It was an important question.

"Nash was in the business all right, anybody could see that. But he didn't have the *Format,* the background, for operations, just a little French." Brodsky leaned back on the cushions. "You people don't use male secretaries. So what else could he be?"

"Who told you he was in communications?"

Brodsky lowered his voice. "Your friend didn't have to pull me over that seat. An invitation would have been as good. In the snow and all, I couldn't have done anything. Now my back hurts—it could be a disk." Brodsky's massive face became a canvas of pain. "I could really use something to drink."

"Get him a whiskey," Trosper said to Riley.

"Cognac," Brodsky said quickly. "You're not drinking?"

"My back's all right," Trosper said. "How long was it before you were told he was a code clerk?"

Brodsky rolled his eyes, and stared in Riley's direction. *"His* back's all right," he grumbled with heavy irony.

"Who told you he was a cipher man?"

"Someone—maybe Moscow—spotted it right off that I had a clerk in a deep cover office," Brodsky said slowly.

"And?"

"Look," Brodsky said. "When you get beyond a twit like Sergei, these are serious people. They're nobody to screw around with."

"Did someone come out from Moscow to talk about the case?"

"Now we deal," Brodsky said. "I'm not talking any more until we work something out."

"The deal is that you tell me the whole story, right now."

"No deal, no more talk," Brodsky said.

Riley eased himself out of the club chair at the side of the room, and walked slowly to the fireplace.

Brodsky peered blearily at Riley. "I'm supposed to be frightened?" he said. Without his glasses, all of Brodsky's gestures were skewed, even his attempt at a sardonic grin miscarried. "This is Geneva, you can't put hands on me. Tomorrow morning, I'm back in my apartment and I go to work like always." Seeming to sense an advantage, he said, "I've been through a war, I've seen fifteen-year-old kids hung like chickens at the market, a dirtier business than you can imagine. I was in a prison camp when we were starving. Now I'm sixty-five and living quiet in Geneva. I don't scare easy any more."

"Tell me about Ben Frost."

Brodsky blinked with surprise, and like a fighter who has taken a punch, bobbed his head. "I set him up pretty good, but when I got down to it, the pressure didn't work, and Tolya Brodsky was in the shit again."

"Gandy?"

"My old pal from Berlin? Gandy the operator?" Brodsky broke into a sly grin. "They had him pegged as one of one of yours from way back, they told me to stay away from him."

"Who told you?"

Brodsky shook his head.

"Why did they tell you to stay away from him?"

Brodsky remained silent.

"You're giving me no choice," Trosper said slowly.

"What choice? Make a deal, and I'll tell you what I know . . ." Brodsky hitched himself up on the sofa.

"One word from my service, and you're totally compromised in the West. And if you don't talk now, there'll be no alternative but to burn you black with Moscow Center."

"Dream some more," Brodsky said. "All that's happened is Nash sold us out. That's part of the game. Nash isn't the only Moscow agent that's ever turned."

Trosper shook his head. "With young Nash looking at life in

prison, you can bet your hat and ass that we're not going to let you walk away."

"So go ahead, tell Moscow I made a big mistake and you smart guys caught us up . . ." His voice trailed off. "Look, Tolya Brodsky's not such a big deal—you already got that punk Nash . . ."

It was time to let Brodsky know that Nash had broken completely. "What about your other cases—Jordan, for example."

It was a moment before Brodsky could ask, "Jordan, the Vienna guy Nash has been hustling?"

"It's the others I'm interested in . . ."

"There aren't any others, and that's a fact," Brodsky said. "After I got Nash going, Boris, he was my first contact, was anxious I keep my nose clean." Brodsky waited before adding, "And that was okay by me."

This was plausible—the handling of one code clerk was as much responsibility as Moscow Center was likely to entrust to any one agent. "Possibly true, but the fact is you went for Frost *after* you had Nash in hand."

Brodsky's head snapped up, and he stared intently at Trosper. "That bastard Nash, I told Boris to keep him out of the Frost thing. Anyway, it was Moscow pushed the Frost deal."

"But you're the one who goofed," Trosper said.

"It wasn't me," Brodsky said. "It was Moscow and Nash."

"What did Nash have to do with it?"

Brodsky leaned back on the seat. "He gave me the inside stuff on Frost, his spending, all that crap. Then I busted my ass setting up a *lastochka*—a swallow, an easy bit of fluff—for Frost."

"Nash gave you everything on Frost?"

Brodsky frowned. "I had one meal with Frost and already I knew him better than Nash ever did."

"You got nothing from Boris on Frost?"

Brodsky shook his head.

"Didn't Moscow send anything on Frost?"

"How would I know what Moscow sent? I never got anything that didn't come from Nash. All Moscow did was push to get Frost recruited . . ."

Which, Trosper told himself, might at least suggest Gandy had not sold out. Except that Moscow would never have given Brodsky the slightest hint that there was another, independent source reporting on Frost.

"Then, all at once, Boris starts talking about a hook, something that will make Frost come across. From what he said, maybe someone in Moscow got big ideas after the job I did on Nash."

"Why did you think you could take Frost?"

Brodsky shook his head. "I told them it wouldn't work, but Boris was under all this pressure."

"From the rezident, the local boss?"

Brodsky hesitated. "I don't know, maybe from somewhere else . . ."

"Moscow?"

"Maybe," Brodsky said.

"But the rezident would have had the last word. If he said no, Moscow isn't likely to have overruled him, particularly in a quiet place like Geneva."

"Maybe, but there are some guys in Moscow have more muscle than others," Brodsky said softly. "Specialists, guys that have been around for a while."

"What was the hook?"

"It was my little swallow, Teresa, the bar girl I'd been working on." Brodsky managed a slight smile. "We waited until Nash had delivered a couple long cables from your head office to Gandy. Like always, after Gandy read them, Frost was supposed to get hold of Nash and give back for safekeeping in the office. But this is Frost's big date with the girl. I'd rigged it so Nash doesn't show up, and Frost has no choice but to keep the cables in his pocket. He goes out on the town with the girl. After dinner and some boozing, she takes Frost back to her apartment and dumps some Moscow beddie-bye into his drink. She gets him into bed, and he passes out. The girl calls Nash. He opens the envelope, photographs the cables. Then he stuffs them back in one of the same envelopes he brings from the office." Brodsky nodded his head in satisfaction. "All the while, Teresa thinks Nash is just stealing business secrets from a competitor."

Trosper was impressed. An operation like this involved a mass of detail and careful coordination. "And it went like clockwork?"

Brodsky nodded. "Except I told them a dozen times that Frost is a guy who doesn't care a damn. He's just interested in getting along easy."

"And?"

"A couple weeks later, I have Nash set it up so I can accidentally have dinner with Frost. I get him a little boozed and take him to my place. I tell him we know all about Gandy and him. Then I make a big pitch that he should sign on with my guys, and pick up some easy money. Like I figured, he wasn't much impressed—I always suspected he had some money on the side, something Nash wouldn't know about. Then I tell him about Bondarev, the Russian you people thought you had recruited, being under Moscow control, and about a big stunt we're going to run against the Firm for blackmailing our innocent young guy. Frost blinks a couple times, but as far as I could see, he still wasn't impressed. Then I tell him we never would have known about Bondarev, except for the cables in his pocket the night he shacked up with our little swallow, Teresa Hotpants."

Trosper nodded. Brodsky had begun to brag. This was more like it.

"When I tossed the photocopies of the cables on the table, Frost began to pay attention. He knew damn well he'd as much as killed Bondarev and maybe given the Firm a big kick in the ass just for a little bit of fluff." Brodsky laughed. "That's the first time Frost ever realized this was life, not just games."

"And?"

"That's when we should have jumped him, used some muscle to make him tell us a few secrets, maybe just scare the shit out of him." Brodsky frowned. "But Moscow said no rough stuff in Geneva, just talk him around." Brodsky glanced in Riley's direction. "You guys could take lessons."

Trosper nodded.

"I talked all right, and Frost agreed to see me again in a couple of days. But just like I told them, once the pressure was off, Frost wasn't scared any more." Brodsky gulped the last of his brandy. "I would have bet twenty to one Frost would tell me to piss off. That's just what he did. He told me to go to hell." Brodsky twisted his face into an ironic I-told-you-so gesture of disbelief in the stupidity of other people. "I put on a big act like I was surprised, but I knew this game was over."

"What did Moscow say?"

"What would you expect? Bondarev leaves town in a hurry, Boris my case man is called back, the Moscow guy who thought it was such a hot idea maybe gets a kick in the ass, and old Tolya, who told them it wouldn't work, is face down in the shit." Brodsky snorted. "So for a while I get all my instructions in a dead-drop. All I do is pick up Nash's film from another drop and leave his money. After that I stuff the film in the third drop. Three or four months go by. Then, like nothing ever happened, along comes a new chum, Sergei the sly, and I'm back in business again."

Brodsky pushed himself back in the love seat and strained to see Trosper more clearly. After a moment he said, "I don't know who you are, but you've pumped enough free information out of me." He began to toy with his empty glass. "As of right now, though, I'm finished talking. If it's all the same, you can either drop me back in town, or call a taxi. Whatever you decide, I'm through talking."

Trosper shook his head. "Do you really think I'm just going to buy Nash a ticket home, and close the Geneva office?"

"Nash is a punk, it was bound to happen."

"He's likely to get life in prison."

"Nash is your problem."

"As may be, but now Moscow's got a problem," Trosper said. "When they realize that a valuable guy like Nash is down the toilet, they'll begin to worry about other things that can go wrong, and whom to blame." Trosper paused before saying, "And that's about the time I arrange to drop enough clues to burn you in Moscow."

"So what? It isn't the first time an agent went sour."

"But Moscow Center doesn't like to lose an agent like Nash, and when they do, the first thing they think is that someone sold him out. They won't be able to piece it all together until they pick you up. And they *will* pick you up."

Brodsky shook his head. "That's crazy . . ." He dabbed at the sweat on his forehead.

Trosper turned to Riley, and in the same tone said, "Please get me a whiskey, this party's about over."

Brodsky managed to laugh. "I'll tell them myself that you're going to screw us . . ."

Now Trosper laughed. "You do that, and in about three weeks there'll be a polite summons for a talk with one of their senior fellows, someone who wants to *help* you clear things up. Not Sergei, and not anyone from his branch. It will be someone from the Second Chief Directorate, one of the hard guys from the counterintelligence side. Your meeting will be in East Berlin if they think you're as dumb as you're acting. Or Vienna, if they figure you've got brains enough to try to stay on our side of the fence."

"That's tough talk," Brodsky said ironically. "Real scary . . ." He had begun to sweat heavily.

"If you've got a cat, you'd better make sure someone will come in to feed it before you go to the meeting, because you're going to be away for a long while . . ."

Trosper was coming up to the breakpoint . . . maybe one more shot.

"As of right now you haven't got a friend on either side of the fence, not here, and certainly not in Moscow where you're still wanted for war crimes. That's one of the reasons they took up with you in the first place—you've got no place to go. And that means they know they can control you."

Trosper leaned back in his chair. Ask me one question, and you're finished . . . just one goddamned question . . .

Brodsky dabbed at his eyes and squinted at Trosper.

Time, Trosper reminded himself. Give him time . . .

The door opened and Riley came in, balancing a tall glass on a small serving plate. Trosper took the glass and nodded thanks.

Brodsky pushed back on the love seat and wedged himself into the corner.

Just ask one question . . .

Trosper took a sip of whiskey.

Brodsky cleared his throat.

Now, damn it . . .

Brodsky wiped his eyes, and took a deep breath. "What's your proposition? What the hell is it you're angling for?"

Trosper smiled pleasantly. He took a long swallow of his drink. "I want you to arrange it so I can have a chat with the guy in Moscow, this specialist you've been dodging around about."

"Oh shit," Brodsky said, blinking rapidly and trying to focus on Trosper.

"The best place to do this is Vienna," Trosper said cheerfully. "Your chum will feel safer there."

"You're out of your mind," Brodsky said. "If you want to play games with those guys, you might as well do it in Leningrad as in Vienna."

Trosper smiled politely. "I was thinking that when you tell Moscow that Nash's buddy Jordan is ready to do business, this might interest the big fellow," he said. "After getting burned a couple of years ago when everything went wrong with you and Frost in Geneva, maybe this go-around the hotshot would want to take charge himself, just to make sure everything is right."

"*Guter Gott,*" Brodsky muttered. When he reached instinctively to touch his glasses it was like an actor fumbling for a misplaced prop.

31

WASHINGTON, D.C.

"It's not too late to pull them back," Castle said. "What do you think?"

Duff Whyte leaned back in his chair and tossed the cable onto his desk. "Alan agreed to find out who killed Gandy and why. If he says he has to do it in Vienna, I think we should go along with him."

Castle pushed the gold-rimmed reading glasses higher on his nose and began again to study the cable. Without looking up at Whyte he said, "He's already taken this a long way, and closed a big leak."

"And someone tried to murder Frost," Whyte murmured. He pushed his heavy chair back, and with an apology to Castle, put both feet on the corner of the desk. "I've heard Alan say that quitting too soon is like swimming *almost* all the way to shore."

"I have the feeling that Alan wants to pay them back for having killed Gandy," Castle said.

"I shouldn't be surprised."

"This is a secret operation, not a personal vendetta," Castle said. "It isn't our job to punish those people."

"I think Alan understands that."

"He already has Brodsky pretty well in hand," Castle said. "He's a bigger fish than I thought."

"And Nash gutted the Geneva office—that's not exactly my idea of a balanced equation."

"We'll be lucky if we can keep Nash and Brodsky in the bag for another forty-eight hours without someone noticing that they're out of circulation." Castle peered closely at Whyte.

"As of now, Alan thinks he can get out of Geneva without any rumble from the local service."

"This time of year it could take at least eighteen hours for them to drive to Vienna," Castle said. "By now the thug in Florence will surely have made his report, and Moscow will be tipped that we know someone tried to murder Frost."

"Which means we've got about forty-eight hours before Moscow *begins* to tie things together," Whyte said. He got up and stepped to the window behind his desk. He pulled the heavy curtains aside and peered into the courtyard below. He had known Thomas Augustus Castle for something more than twenty years. There was no reason now, Whyte told himself, to assume that his friend would ever change his ways. It was simply not possible for Castle to come straight to a point. Without turning around, Whyte said, "Send an urgent cable to Hamel in Vienna. Tell him to give Alan whatever support he wants." He turned to face Castle. "Tell Alan to stay just as far away from the Vienna office as he can, and remind him to keep an eye on the clock."

Castle reached into the soft leather portfolio he had brought with him. "I had Miss Pinchot type this before I came up. I thought it might be what you want." He dropped the draft cable on Whyte's desk.

Whyte studied the draft. "Some day you'll play devil's advocate once too often, and I'll take what you say at face value." He scrawled his signature at the bottom of the cable and handed it to Castle.

Castle heaved himself to his feet. "They say vigilance is the price of liberty—you've never taken anything at face value." He turned and walked to the door. "Someone around here has to keep you on your toes."

GENEVA

"Est *ce que je peux parler avec Monsieur Petkov, s'il vous plâit?*" Brodsky put his hand over the mouthpiece and turned to Trosper. "Even when we tested this it took forever for her to check their file. You have to wonder how many calls like this they get every day."

Trosper motioned for Brodsky to remain silent. They were in the

Rue de Lausanne safe apartment and he monitored Brodsky's call with the device Ida had rigged. In a moment the telephone operator at the Soviet Mission came back on the phone. *"Il n'y a pas de Monsieur Petkov ici à la Mission,"* the operator said. *"Il n'y a personne ici qui s'appelle Petkov,"* she repeated.

"Merci, Madame. Je me suis trompé encore." With a deft insinuation of sorrow edging his voice, Brodsky added, *"Je vous demande pardon."* He grinned at Trosper. "Now she passes the message to Sergei. Then he alerts his boss, and runs to the public phone booth to wait for my call."

"His section chief or the rezident?"

Brodsky blinked and touched his glasses. With a flicker of anxiety Trosper reminded himself that Brodsky was little more than a cutout for Sergei, and that Sergei was at best only a messenger between Brodsky and Moscow Center.

"Sergei won't take any decision on his own. He's scared so shitless of his boss that he'll tell someone up the line, maybe a section chief, that he's got an emergency message on a big case."

"All the better," Trosper said. As he attempted to curb his churning anxiety, he cursed himself for having failed to ask Fuller for the file on the Geneva rezident. Working on the outside, and without easy access to the counterintelligence dossiers, was like playing chess against an opponent whose key pieces were as transient as moving shadows glimpsed in a mirror. He should have taken time to study the files and learn what experience the rezident and Sergei's section chief had had, and what the various defectors from Moscow Center and the local agents might have reported on them. He should have made the time to interrogate Brodsky. He should be more certain of Nash.

But there wasn't any time.

BRODSKY glanced again at his worn, pocket address book. "Sergei tried to tell me this number is for a safe phone, but it's in the same series of numbers on every pay telephone in the area of the U.N. offices. All Sergei the sly does is get into the booth and wait for my call—which I'm supposed to make in exactly an hour and ten minutes after I've telephoned the Mission." Brodsky's smile broadened. "We never used this emergency system except as a test. Sergei will piss himself when he gets the message."

"Since this is a real message, let's let Sergei cool his heels in the booth for an extra twenty minutes or so," Trosper said.

"KEEP it simple," Trosper said, putting the monitor to his ear.

"Sergei's going to stall for time so his boss can consult the Center and they can tell Vienna to get everything arranged."

"That's the point," Trosper said. "I'm not going to give them any time. The faster I can get them moving, the less time they have to think about what they're doing."

Ida peeked around the corner from the kitchen. "I'm going to make some coffee . . ."

Trosper glanced at Ida. "As soon as we're off the phone, just bring the coffee in here." He turned back to Brodsky. "Simple and straightforward."

Brodsky nodded and began to dial. "This will probably have to be in English—I'm never sure that Sergei gets anything straight in French, and he won't let me speak Russian on the telephone."

Trosper nodded.

Sergei picked up the phone at the first ring. *"Allo . . . ?"*

"Bonjour, Georges. Ici Konrad. Je m'excuse de vous avoir fait attendre, mais . . ."

"In English," Sergei commanded. "And no names Comrade, just your messages . . ."

Brodsky turned to Trosper and whispered, "No names, but he calls me Comrade . . . tight security."

"Your message please . . ."

"I want you to know that Comrade Pierre has been ordered to Vienna for four days . . ."

"Comrade who?"

Brodsky put his hand over the mouthpiece and said, "He can't even remember Nash's telephone alias . . ." Trosper signaled Brodsky to pay attention.

"Comrade Pierre," Brodsky said. "You may remember his peculiar auto?"

"No details, Comrade, no details on the telephone."

"I repeat, Comrade Pierre has gone to Vienna for four days," Brodsky said loudly.

"Good, good, I understand."

"The comrade will be there for four days," Brodsky said. "I'm leaving in an hour. I can stay there for two days."

"Two days, Comrade?"

Brodsky grimaced and raised his voice. "Four days for Comrade Pierre, two days for Comrade Konrad." Brodsky waited before saying, "I am Comrade Konrad."

Trosper could not conceal his smile.

"What is your message, Comrade? I've been in this phone booth for forty minutes and there's a woman, probably Swiss, who's been pounding on the door . . ."

A malicious grin spread across Brodsky's face. "Do I have the right number? You said this was a secure telephone . . ."

"No details please, Comrade."

"I only want to do what is right, Comrade."

"What is your message, Comrade Konrad?"

"In Vienna, Comrade Pierre's friend Paul is ready to sign, Comrade. I will need a telephone number or a *Treff*. I must meet the comrade who will handle the contract details and—"

"Out of the question, Comrade Konrad," Sergei said. "There's not time . . ."

"Comrade, this is important," Brodsky said. "We've talked about this business for months. There's even been expenses. Now Paul is ready to sign our contract. But he will leave soon for his new assignment. We must not waste time making the deal."

"There's not time . . ."

"I have an hour," Brodsky said. "Put the Chief on, I'll talk with him."

Trosper heard a sharp intake of breath. Then Sergei said sharply, "On this telephone I am chief . . ."

"I repeat, I have one hour before I leave for Vienna. I need a telephone number or a rendezvous point there. I am Comrade Konrad and this is the business Pierre has been discussing with Paul for a long time. Now we must move before Paul changes his mind and leaves for his new assignment in—"

"You will call me here in exactly one hour," Sergei interrupted. "I will have a message for you at that time."

Brodsky put down the phone. "He rang off before I could tell him our Vienna friend's new job will be in Washington," Brodsky said apologetically.

"It's all right," Trosper said. "That's the first question the rezident will ask Sergei—and when he can't answer it, they won't be able to send a flash to Moscow until they've spoken to you again." Despite the anxiety, Trosper managed a smile. "This time, we'll let Sergei wait a little longer in the phone booth."

Ida stepped into the room with a tray. Trosper winked at her. "Every few hours makes the cheese more binding."

Brodsky's huge face brightened. From the moment Riley had fixed his broken glasses with quick-drying epoxy glue, Brodsky had begun to respond to Trosper's direction.

32

AUSTRIA

THE train slowed as it skirted the jagged foot of the mountain at the edge of the valley. Fresh snow, banked high along the track, blotted out the view. Ida sat beside Brodsky, facing Trosper across the dining car table. Preoccupied, Trosper continued to stare out the window, ignoring the waiter who asked if they would have aperitifs before dinner.

"What will you have?" Brodsky asked, leaning politely toward Ida. "I think I'm ready for a whiskey." Ida hesitated and said, "A sherry please."

From the moment Trosper had introduced Ida—Victoria Greene in her new ID—as his assistant, and explained she would accompany them to Vienna, Brodsky had been fascinated. The instant Ida left the room, he asked, "Is she really with your service or . . . ?" He punctuated his question with a gesture and man-of-the-world leer. Later, after he heard her speak German to the waiter, and had bluffed her into a few words of Russian, he was transformed. Mrs. Grundy herself could not more perfectly have expunged the scatology from Brodsky's conversation. In Ida's presence, Brodsky's manners, which to Trosper had seemed an amalgam of abrasive newsman and safe-house-smart huckster, became avuncular and courtly, verging on the Edwardian.

They traveled by rail to avoid leaving the paper trail mandated by airline controls. Trosper enjoyed train travel and one of his lingering memories of Europe in the late forties was the sense of luxury at little cost generated by the accommodations and service in the surviving first-class compartments. Later, as Western Europe shook off the aftereffects of war, and business and tourist travel began to boom, the new first-class carriages were downgraded to an embellished version of what had been second class. Now, the diminished amenities were merely a pleasant alternative to the pervading misery of air travel. Trosper particularly missed the old *wagons restaurants,* with their sparkling napery, hefty silver-solder cutlery, and deft, polyglot waiters. Though he would not willingly have admitted it, he had even delighted in the elaborately pretentious *cartes* and wine lists. The new dining cars were efficient, the menus modest, the food indifferent, and the wine ordinary.

Trosper's efforts to stifle his impatience to be off the train impinged on his struggle to catalogue the loose ends that bedeviled his planning. He had no doubt that Riley could keep Nash in hand as they drove with Fuller to Vienna. He was satisfied that Brodsky had made a change in affiliation—loyalty was not a word Trosper associated with Brodsky—and for the moment at least was convinced that his immediate future was more secure in Trosper's hands than with the representatives of Moscow Center. Nor did he worry that Teddy Vermont would miss their Vienna *Treff.* Vermont might, Trosper realized, even be on their train. He glanced around the lightly populated *Speisewagon,* and satisfied himself that Teddy was not, at least, within eyeshot.

"WHAT's going to happen?" Nash asked. He sat beside Fuller in the front seat of the big Chevrolet. In the back seat, directly behind Nash, Mozart Riley methodically worked his way through a sheaf of book catalogues. After stopping for lunch near Salzburg, they were now less than a hundred kilometers from Vienna.

"I'm not sure," Fuller said. "Mr. Doughty never talks about his plans."

"I mean what's going to happen to me?"

Riley looked up and fixed his glance on the back of Nash's head. A row of carefully contrived ducktails crested on the high collar that proclaimed Nash's striped poplin shirt to have been custom-made. Although Riley had a professional's regard for mercenary agents, he considered Nash a self-serving turncoat and loathed him.

"I don't know exactly," Fuller said. "But I can promise you that

Mr. Doughty is as good as his word. He said that if you cooperate, and all goes well, he will put in a word for you with the court."

"That's not very much, considering all the risks I took the other night, and what might be coming."

As Riley moved to swing his legs sideways to ease the cramp in his knees, his shoulder bumped against the back of the front seat. Nash started apprehensively, and lurched forward against the dashboard. He turned to stare at Riley.

"There's risks . . . in just about everything," Riley said slowly. "Or didn't . . . your friend Tolya . . . ever mention it?"

Fuller glanced at the speedometer and picked up speed.

TROSPER tossed the menu aside. He had been silent since ordering his meal, absorbed in his plans. Now, still fighting his impatience to be off the train, he began to listen to Brodsky talking to Ida.

". . . and my mother was Russian. She spoke Russian that Turgenev would have admired. My father's family were Austrians, who stayed in Poland when the Austro-Hungarian empire folded its tent. We lived in Krynki, a village at the tip of the old empire, and close to the Soviet border. Before I was ten, I spoke Polish, German, and Russian so fluently I didn't even know which language I was using." Brodsky smiled at Ida. "You want some advice from a real expert?" She nodded. "Don't grow up on a border. Even near a border. If you cross often enough when you're a kid, you begin seeing too many sides to questions."

Ida glanced shyly at Trosper. She had been prepared to hate Brodsky and was surprised by her reaction to him.

"My father was a doctor, a decent man, but he wanted changes in Poland and was a Communist party member. So in thirty-nine, when the Soviets grabbed our part of Poland, he welcomed them. Six weeks later, my father and all the other party officials were deported to Russia."

Ida nodded sympathetically. "But I thought you were with the—"

Brodsky interrupted. It was as if he didn't want to hear Ida say she knew he had been with the Nazis. "I've always been on the wrong side," he said quickly. "First, I was for the Russians. Then all I could think of was to revenge myself for what the Soviets had done to my father. That's why I volunteered for the Wehrmacht." Brodsky paused for emphasis. "Do you know that with all their muscle, the Nazis couldn't even line up a quisling government in Poland?" He glanced at Trosper, who remained silent.

"And now comes the joke," Brodsky said. "The Nazis turned me down—there was no place for Poles in the new order." He laughed. "But being Germans, they kept records. A few months later, when the Wehrmacht was up to its . . . er . . . knees in the Soviet Union, they suddenly found they needed interpreters. And that's when they discovered young Tolya. My three languages made me Aryan enough to be drafted as a helper in the war against the Slavs." Brodsky's heavy face darkened. "I was barely eighteen and classified as a volunteer helper, not even a soldier."

Trosper looked up, trying to see if, behind the thick glasses, Brodsky's eyes showed any sentiment. He decided they didn't.

Ida avoided looking at Brodsky, and toyed with her sherry.

But Trosper, who had never valued self-pity as an emotion, kept his eyes on Brodsky.

"First I was with a Wehrmacht intelligence outfit, a FAK as we called it," Brodsky said. "There was some rough stuff, but not too bad, considering there was a war on, and the partisans weren't exactly choirboys."

Brodsky fell silent while the waiter served *oeufs à la russe* to Ida. Trosper's consommé was too hot to taste. Brodsky, caught up in his story, ignored his potato soup.

"The officer I worked with was one of the good Germans, and that's maybe why he didn't think too much of me. As far as he was concerned, I was just a Polish traitor."

Brodsky paused as the waiter who had poured a taste of the Moselle hesitated, not certain to whom he should offer it. With a gesture, Trosper signaled that the honor was Brodsky's. "I was too young, maybe too proud to try to explain myself to my lieutenant,"

Brodsky continued. "So I just went on, acting like a Nazi, pushing the Russians around. Then, a few days after the lieutenant was killed, our unit was eliminated and Tolya was transferred to the SS . . ." Brodsky smiled self-consciously at Ida.

TROSPER balanced the remaining morsel of hard cheese on a slice of apple and took a final sip of wine. He peered out the frosted window. "St. Poelten?"

Brodsky nodded. "We've got plenty of time for coffee before we get to Vienna . . ."

"I'll be glad to get there," Ida said. "I know it's silly these days, but I was worried about a possible customs examination at the Austrian border. I was particularly worried today."

Brodsky smiled reassuringly. "But here was no examination. There's never any fuss, except Czechoslovakia, maybe Poland."

"It's probably my midwestern upbringing," Ida said. "But even when I *really* was a tourist, just the thought of the border police and the customs people opening a bag used to cow me. This afternoon, even with you two, having the pistol in my bag brought back the same feeling."

Trosper stirred. "You're carrying a gun?"

Brodsky glanced quickly out the window.

Ida flushed. "Just a small one, a 7.35-millimeter . . ."

"And where, pray, did you get a pistol?"

"Mr. Fuller brought it when he gave me the audio things I used in his apartment," Ida said softly. "It was in a sort of kit he had prepared . . ."

Trosper slumped back in his seat.

Brodsky dabbed at the misted window with his napkin.

"I know how to use it," Ida said quickly. "I mean, I've had two courses at the Fort . . ."

Trosper's face flushed. "I don't suppose anyone at the Fort thought to mention that the point of secret intelligence is to outwit the opposition, not to try to outshoot them?"

Ida shook her head.

"For your information, it's the Marines who do the shooting," Trosper said furiously.

Without taking his eyes from the window, Brodsky touched Ida's shoulder reassuringly.

VIENNA

"THEIR train is due at the Westbahnhof at 2100," Fuller said. "We'll need two safe apartments."

"I got the Controller's cable this morning . . ." Hamel was barely able to conceal his frustration.

They were in the bar of the Hotel Bristol, on the Ring, across the Kaerntnerstrasse from the Vienna opera house.

"There's something else you'd better know," Fuller said quietly. "In the last four days my best safe house is gone, two cars are compromised and will have to be dumped. Bunky's apartment looks as if the *Spetsburo* had used it for a May Day all-skate. What's more, I'll be spending the next month closing down the Geneva office."

"Jesus wept, what does he . . . ?"

"Right now, Alan is fighting the clock," Fuller continued. "If things go right, we'll be out of your hair in thirty-six hours. If not . . ." He stopped short. There was no point in speculating on catastrophe.

Hamel finished his drink. "Can you give me a hint as to what's going on?"

"Here's a list of stuff Alan will need by tomorrow."

Hamel glanced at the list. "A 9-millimeter?" He looked quizzically at Fuller. "That's not really Alan's style . . ."

"You'd better think about getting to the Westbahnhof, they're due at nine," Fuller said.

Hamel tugged a thick manila envelope from his pocket. "The address, keys, and a street map are in here, along with my office and several telephone numbers. Under no circumstances are you or Alan to give me any message, no matter how clever the double talk, at my home or office. Call me, have a chat, and then give me the code name for one of the pay phones. 'I'm having lunch with Mary,' or 'Bob is staying for the weekend,' should do it. Give me fifteen minutes to get to either of those phones."

As they shook hands, Hamel mumbled. *"Hals und Beinbruch."* He winked, and said, "Break a leg." With an abrupt thumbs-up gesture, he hurried out of the bar.

33

VIENNA

"Is it all right now for me to say this is some place you've got here?" Brodsky glanced around the room in mock appreciation and yawned as he plucked at the frayed threads on the arm of the overstuffed sofa.

Trosper looked up from his yellow notepad. He had spent the morning attempting to piece together a coherent chronology of Brodsky's career with Moscow Center. Brodsky was clearly so determined to obscure the date and circumstances of his recruitment by the Soviet services that, despite his probing, Trosper realized the gaps and inconsistencies in the account were likely only to be resolved in the course of extended questioning by an interrogator with access to all the files and documents bearing on his stories.

It had been midnight when Hamel dropped them at the safe apartment. After an initial check of the security, Trosper left investigation of the shabby safe-house larder to Ida.

"Eggs, coffee, tea, rolls, jam, and canned o.j. for breakfast," she reported. "Scotch, cognac, vodka, port, beer, two liqueurs, three bottles of Austrian white wine, one of Bordeaux, three Perriers, two seltzers, and a half-pint bottle of bitters." Ida broke into a broad smile. "Of course I may have missed something in the booze line."

"No olives or anchovies?" Trosper had never been in a safe house that did not have a jar of olives and at least one can of anchovies on the shelf.

Ida nodded. "Yes indeed. There's also a tin of pork pâté, a canned Polish ham, and two liters of milk." She smiled and said,

"There's plenty of linen, but not a bar of soap in the whole apartment. There's no butter for breakfast, but we each have a bottle of shampoo and a shoehorn." She thought for a moment. "Shampoo will probably do for the dishes and cleaning up."

Brodsky groaned. "I'm going to have a hot tub, and then a nightcap before turning in."

"It's down the hall on the left," Ida said.

When Brodsky left, Trosper turned to Ida. "It's not exactly in your job description, but if you could make the bed for our friend, it will give you a chance to check his suitcase," he said. "Look for an escape passport, any possible false ID, and a stash of money." Ida nodded. "If there's a concealment built into the bag, it will be in the handle, or along the top, with the opening under the catches or lock." He paused for a moment and added, "Make certain there's no weapon of any kind. I've had enough surprises lately."

"Nothing special in the bag," Ida reported. "Just a copy of this month's *Playboy*—the German edition—and a paperback Plutarch in English."

"A man of parts, our Tolya," Trosper murmured.

"WHAT about this place?" Brodsky asked again.

His reverie interrupted, Trosper focused his attention on Brodsky, sprawled like a camp Madame Récamier on the bulky sofa.

Trosper recognized the sofa as one of the perfect reproductions of early 1930s Grand Rapids furniture manufactured to Quartermaster Corps specifications during the Four Power occupation of Austria. When the occupation ended, and the military staged giant yard sales, the Grand Rapids furniture remained a lingering souvenir of the occupation, and the dominant theme in safe-house decor. In the bleak overhead light, the threadbare upholstery reflected the sepulchral pink tone of an undertaking parlor.

Trosper glanced around the apartment and shrugged. "I've gone through life on the assumption that the best available will have to suffice."

"Which brings me back to my earlier question," Brodsky said. "What's in this for me?"

"If everything goes well from here in, it will be time for you to retire from the racket."

"And then?"

"A thorough debriefing, with you supplying facts that check precisely with our records," Trosper said.

"And after all that?"

"No commitment now, but maybe we can arrange a little post-retirement help . . ."

"That's not satisfactory."

"I'm told Swiss jails are less comfortable than their hotels," Trosper said amiably.

"There's nobody I can't make a deal with." Brodsky noticed Trosper's expression and shrugged. "Well, almost nobody . . ."

"Would it really make you feel better if I told you there would be a whopping resettlement payment?" Trosper asked. "It's no problem to make you promises I know won't be kept." He took the yellow pad from the coffee table. "You've been around, you know that only the head office can make long-running commitments. And no one in the head office is going to do anything unless every-one is satisfied with your work in the next couple of days, and until you're thoroughly debriefed."

"I don't know what the hell you're planning, but when Moscow learns you've got Nash in the bag, what happens to me?"

"If you're lucky, Moscow will consider you a burned-out case and stay well away."

"And if I'm not lucky, what happens then?" Brodsky didn't wait for an answer. "They'll kill me, that's what will happen."

"Not if things work out."

"That's not good enough," Brodsky said. "I want asylum. I insist on asylum."

"I won't make a commitment unless I know it will be met," Trosper said. He had long ago learned not to try to con a con man. Faced with scrupulous honesty, con men were at a disadvantage.

Brodsky's face fell. "The hell with it," he said. "Let's get this over with." He glanced at his watch. "It's about time anyway." He picked up the telephone, and handed Trosper the monitor Ida had rigged.

"At this point, no more horsing around," Trosper said. "We're not dealing with that ass Sergei. This could be the first team, straight from Moscow."

Brodsky nodded. "You can bet on it." He held his pocket note-book open and began to dial. The telephone rang five times.

"Am Apparat . . ."

As if to echo the growled response, Brodsky's voice dropped an octave. *"Hier Konrad,"* he said softly.

"Sehr gut, Konrad. Wir treffen uns an der Ecke Schlachthaus-gasse und Barthgasse . . ."

"An der Ecke Schlachthausgasse und Barth—," Brodsky began.

"Puenktlich um zwanzig Uhr fuenfzehn."

Brodsky glanced at Trosper, who nodded agreement.

"In Ordnung," Brodsky said. *"Zwanzig Uhr . . ."* The contact was broken before he could complete confirmation of the time. Brodsky stared at the mute phone for a moment and slammed it back into the cradle. He turned to Trosper. "Did you get that? I'm to meet them on the corner of Schlachthaus and Barthgasse at eight-fifteen tonight." Brodsky pulled a handkerchief from his pocket and wiped his forehead. "Where the hell is the Schlach-thausgasse?"

Trosper unfolded a *Strassenkarte* and began to check the index. He spread the map across the coffee table. "Here, in the Third District," he said, pointing with a pencil. "It runs straight from the Landstrasser Hauptstrasse past the Viehmacht to the canal." He bent closer to the street map. "Across the canal, the name changes, but it's the same street. It leads to the soccer stadium, and across the Danube."

Brodsky stared at the map. His finger shook as he traced the street. "Shit, shit, shit," he groaned. "They've got the whole god-damned city for a *Treff,* and they meet me on Slaughterhouse Street, around the corner from the bloody stockyard . . ."

"During the occupation it was in the Soviet sector," Trosper said. "Maybe they still feel more at home there . . ."

"That was thirty-three years ago, half these bastards were still in their nappies," Brodsky said. "It's just a lousy Russian joke—and a goddamned omen." He got to his feet. "As of right now, you can all go to hell," he said loudly. "You can go to hell and back. I'm totally through with this whole rotten business. I don't give a shit what you do to me, I don't need any of this. I'm heading back to Geneva . . ."

"Simmer down, Tolya," Trosper said. "I've got your passport, and we've still got a lot of ground to cover before tonight."

"THE meet is at exactly eight-fifteen," Trosper said. "Perhaps you'd better make a pass this afternoon."

Teddy Vermont's expression flickered from bored to baleful. "I never throw my head in the ring without a reconnaissance," he said.

"You'd better stay on the far side of the street tonight," Trosper said, wondering if Teddy had ever taken a word of advice from anyone but Castle.

"It's going to snow," Vermont said. "There's almost no one on foot when it's snowing." Without moving his head, Vermont's eyes made a slow, 180-degree sweep of the crowded coffeehouse. "Anyone who's out in the snow is a real lively wire, and in a hurry to get where he's going. It's almost impossible to loiter about in the snow. It's worse than rain."

"Brodsky and my man will be alone," Trosper said. "Call me at this number as soon as you can after the *Treff.*" He waited before saying, "If you don't spot the pickup, try to make two passes."

"I don't miss meets, even in the snow," Vermont said. He got up and began to pull on his raincoat as he moved toward the door.

"It's your *hat* you throw into the ring," Trosper called after him. "Not your head . . ." He signaled the waiter for the check.

"THERE'S one more thing." Brodsky braced himself against the closet beside the safe-house door as he struggled to buckle his snow boots. "Nash is a punk. He was born a bum and he's going to die a bum." He stood up, his face flushed. "You think you've got a handle on him because he's an American and he spilled his guts the minute you pushed him a little." He touched his glasses, easing them gently back into place. "Just remember, it was Tolya Brodsky who told you not to trust Nash."

"I'll remember," Trosper said.

Brodsky walked across the room and peeked around the curtain from the side of the window. "That's great," he said, staring out the window. *"You'll* remember, but if they pick me up out there, I'll be in Moscow before anyone but you even knows I'm missing." He let the curtain fall back. "I could get my head blown off out there."

"If there were time, we could do it differently," Trosper said. "But there isn't any time."

"It's not my idea we hustle these guys," Brodsky said. "And it's not my notion to trust Nash."

What about trusting Brodsky, Trosper asked himself. What are the odds, he wondered, that a renegade Pole who had been bilking one after another of the Western services ever since he first surfaced in Berlin has changed his ways? And what about Brodsky's affiliation with Moscow Center, so perfectly covered that he was blacklisted as a merchant, and never as a Moscow Center operative? No one, not even Jack Holder in his analysis of Tolya Brodsky's file, had suspected that Brodsky was a deeply covered Moscow Center equity or that he was linked with Lukin, the graduate of General Sudoplatov's old *Spetsburo*. It was only when someone—probably Lukin, Trosper realized—had got too greedy and tried to parlay the recruitment of Nash into the blackmail of Ben Frost that things had begun to come unstuck.

Trosper glanced at Ida. She had the beginning of what Duff Whyte called a safe-house tan. Her face was gray and drawn and despite her makeup, Trosper could see the circles under her eyes. He wondered if she had sensed his doubts.

Brodsky turned away from the window. Ida watched anxiously as he began bundling himself into his heavy black overcoat. "This storm is following us like a stray dog," he said. "It's never going to stop damned snowing."

Behind the thick glasses, Brodsky's eyes brightened as he shook hands with Ida. "Take care," he urged. It was as if he meant the advice for himself.

34

VIENNA

"IF you don't remember anything else Mr. Doughty told you, you damn well remember this," Brodsky said.

Nash peered out the fogged tram window. The snow fell in flakes as big as summer raindrops, and enough had accumulated to slow traffic and hinder walking. Nash turned to Brodsky. "His name is Trosper, Alan Trosper. Everyone knows who he is, but he's such a big shot he can make the head office think no one knows him."

Brodsky shook his head in disgust. "Remember two things. I do the talking. When they question you, make sure you answer exactly what your boss told you to say. Don't act smart and start adding anything. You begin running off at the mouth, you'll be in big trouble."

"If it wasn't for you I wouldn't be in trouble at all." Nash formed his thick lips into a caricature of a pout.

"Second, make sure you tell them just what you told me about Jordan," Brodsky said.

"What I said about Jordan isn't exactly right."

"It doesn't matter," Brodsky said. "Just tell these people what you told me, and follow along with what Doughty told you to say."

"His name isn't Doughty, it's Alan Trosper."

Brodsky jabbed his elbow into Nash. "This is our stop. We get out here and walk a few hundred meters."

It was colder and a sharp wind had sprung up. The snow swirled and capered beneath the yellow streetlights. Like a chilled terrier urging its master to a faster pace, Nash strode half a step ahead. But Brodsky ignored him and picked his way carefully through the snow, his hat pulled far down across his brow, his face half masked by a long woolen scarf. Without slowing his pace, he glanced at each car as it passed along the broad snow-slick street. On the sidewalk on the far side, a bent figure tugged a *luge* into the wind. A suitcase balanced precariously across the high sled required frequent attention and hindered the man's progress.

A dingy, brown Opel slowed, and then picked up speed as it swerved into Barthgasse.

"Jetzt faengst an," Brodsky muttered as he began to hurry forward.

"What?" Nash demanded. "What did you say?"

"Now it begins," Brodsky said. He pulled at Nash's arm, and hurried him around the corner to the waiting Opel.

In the distance, the bent figure on the far side of the Schlachthausgasse made a final adjustment to the suitcase on the sled and began to hurry across the street and on his way.

"YOUR friends showed up exactly on time, an easy meet," Teddy Vermont said. He had taken off his gloves to dial and the kiosk phone was frigid in his hand. "They drove off so slow it looks as if they'll stay right in their car, an old Opel."

"How many people in the car?" Trosper asked.

"A driver and someone in the back seat—the windows were all steamed up."

"Anyone else in the area?"

"There's no one on the street," Teddy said.

"Many thanks, my friend. Call me in two hours."

"You got any use for a sled, a good one, only used once?" Teddy laughed at his joke and hung up without waiting for an answer.

THE rear door of the Opel opened a few inches as Brodsky bent to peer through the window. "In back," said a voice in Russian. "You tell him to get in front."

Brodsky pulled the front door open, and pushed Nash onto the seat beside the driver. As Brodsky moved to wedge himself through

the narrow rear door, his feet slipped and he lurched forward, showering snow into the car. He muttered an apology and eased himself
back on the seat. In the heat of the car, Brodsky's glasses fogged.
He pulled off his thick gloves and tugged a handkerchief from his
pocket. He wiped at his glasses and for the first time could see the
man beside him. "It's you," said Brodsky.

"Of course it's me," the man responded in Russian. He reached
forward and tapped the driver's shoulder. "Move along, slowly."
His voice was harsh.

Nash stared straight ahead, not risking a glance at the driver.

"Does he speak Russian?" The man pointed at Nash.

Brodsky shook his head. "Only English, and a few words of
French."

"Then he doesn't even know what his name means?"

Brodsky was puzzled. "What it means?"

"His name is Nash isn't it? He really is *nash,* isn't he, Comrade?"

Brodsky grunted in embarrassment. "Yes, his name is Nash, and
you know as well as I that he's *nash,* one of ours." It was old
Chekist slang, any person referred to as *nash* was "one of ours"—at
the least a Moscow Center sympathizer, more likely a collaborator
or an agent. Now Brodsky realized he had only heard Nash's name
pronounced in American English and nasally brayed, as in
"Naaash." He had never associated it with the short Russian "a" as
in *nash.*

"You vouch for him, Brodsky?"

"He's paid his way a thousand times over," Brodsky said. "He's
one of yours all right."

In the front seat, Nash stared at the windshield wipers, swinging
like a pair of eccentric metronomes. He turned slightly to the right,
away from the Russians, and asked in a hoarse whisper, "Is everything all right?" Sweat edged along Nash's hairline.

The Russian leaned forward and tapped Nash on the shoulder.
"I am Colonel Aleksandrov. I've come a long way to see you, Mister *Nash.* I must know if everything is as you have reported." He
spoke with a heavy accent.

Nash turned to face Aleksandrov. "Yes, sir. Everything is in order." He bobbed his head, encouraging the Russian to agree with him. "It's like I told Mr. Brodsky, Jordan is ready. It's only a question of money." Nash's head bobbed faster. "It's just lucky I got this temporary duty assignment before Jordan left . . ."

Aleksandrov whirled to face Brodsky. "He leaves?" It was an accusation, not a question.

In Russian Brodsky said softly, "Jordan leaves for assignment in Washington within six weeks. You'll just have to train him here before he goes."

"What's he saying, what's he *saying?*" Nash demanded.

"Why haven't you reported this?"

"I got the news from Nash in Geneva, two hours before I called on the emergency number." Brodsky spoke quietly in Russian. "Your man Sergei rang off before I could tell him what was happening."

Aleksandrov grunted. "He's not my man."

"It's only a question of money, sir," Nash said. "There's a lot more I have to tell you about it . . ." He glanced at Brodsky and said quickly, "I mean about his wife and all . . ."

Brodsky pulled off his hat. As he began to flick the snow from the crown, he put his elbow on the back of the front seat. In a polite monotone he murmured, "Until you're spoken to, you shut your ugly gob." He leaned back and glanced at Aleksandrov, who was apparently preoccupied with the news of Jordan's impending departure.

"Rotten weather for Vienna," Brodsky muttered in Russian. The Opel moved slowly along the monotonous, empty streets.

Aleksandrov peered out the window. "I leave Moscow and it snows in Vienna."

Brodsky translated as Colonel Aleksandrov began to question Nash.

It was twenty minutes before Aleksandrov was satisfied and turned to Brodsky. "Tomorrow, at noon, Golo will pick you three up at the Fersetlstrasse, on the corner just behind the Votivkirche . . ." Aleksandrov gestured toward the driver, and said, "You remember Golo?"

Brodsky nodded. "I remember Golo, but you don't need me for anything."

Aleksandrov's eyes narrowed to a squint. "You'll be there to keep that *jhopa*"—he paused to gesture toward Nash—"to keep that ass quiet and out of things." He tapped Brodsky's arm and said, "Golo will be in the front seat with a driver from the rezidency. They will take you directly to the compound, our guarded housing area, at the old hospital on Peter Jordan Strasse and . . ."

"That's a problem," Brodsky interrupted.

". . . we will have four, maybe five hours, enough time for a good interrogation, to make communication arrangements, and to fix a tight collar for our new friend—something to make sure he knows he's really our creature. After dark, we'll take you out the same way."

"That's not possible," Brodsky said.

Without turning his head, Nash whispered, "What are you talking about, what's going on?"

"What problem, what's not possible?" Aleksandrov demanded in Russian.

"Jordan's afraid." Brodsky began to speak in English for Nash's benefit. "I've gone over this a hundred times with Nash. Jordan says he won't go into the embassy, or any apartment. He says he's afraid he'll be seen."

Aleksandrov cursed in Russian.

"Perhaps he's more afraid of being kidnapped," Brodsky said.

"He'll do what I order," Aleksandrov said loudly.

"Ask Nash," Brodsky said.

"He's scared," Nash said, turning to face Aleksandrov. "He's scared that the Austrian cops have surveillance on all the Soviet buildings."

"You two will be in the back, under a rug," Aleksandrov said. "Only Brodsky, the Geneva newsman, will sit up in the back seat and be seen. He has cover—he's also a TV star—and is going for an interview so he can advise his thousands of listeners what's really going on in the U.S.S.R." The Russian smirked at his irony.

"From what Nash tells me, Jordan won't agree," Brodsky said. He tapped Nash on the shoulder. "You want to talk, now's the time. Tell the Colonel about Jordan."

"It's the first thing he's ever done that's not all right with the Church, with his wife, with someone who tells him right and wrong," Nash said. "He's scared of making up his mind, he's even scared of the Austrians. And he believes all that crap we put out about you people." Nash stopped to see what impact he was having on Aleksandrov. He had twisted sidewise, and was speaking directly to the Russian. "He was like going to puke the last time I argued with him about it."

Aleksandrov pulled himself forward, his face close to Nash's. "He'll do what I order . . ." Nash recoiled, wedging himself against the dashboard.

Brodsky gently tapped the Russian's arm with his glove. "Let's not forget, Jordan's going to Washington in a few weeks. We've been after this fish for a long time. Don't lose him now, *Herr Oberst.*" Brodsky smiled to take the edge off his sarcasm.

With another curse, Aleksandrov shoved himself back in the seat. After a moment he said, "Where does he think I'm going to meet him—the American embassy?"

"Jordan said the best place is his apartment." Nash's voice was a whisper.

Brodsky nodded. "Just to get things started, that's not a bad idea."

Aleksandrov cursed.

"Jordan said it was the only place he would meet anyone," Nash said.

Aleksandrov grabbed the lapel of Brodsky's overcoat. "You've been working with this for almost a year. I take Golo off an important job, not half finished, and I come here from Moscow. I spend time convincing the rezident, young Petrov, that I can use some clerk's living quarters for a meeting without the Austrians' breaking diplomatic relations, and you and this shitface tell me I have to go to some American's apartment?"

"This can be a good thing," Brodsky said softly. "As far as I can see, Nash is right. His friend is scared."

Aleksandrov tapped Golo on the shoulder. "Head back toward

the Ring. I want to drop these people."

"What's he saying?" Nash said. "What are we going to do?"

"Just shut up for a while," Brodsky murmured.

The Opel began to move faster along the empty streets.

After a long silence Aleksandrov asked, "What about you, Comrade, how have you been getting on?"

"I told you before, my nerves are gone, I'm through with this work."

"You lost your nerves in 1945," Aleksandrov said.

Brodsky shook his head. "I can't keep doing this. My luck will run out, you will lose everything we have done."

"You make me sick with your whining." Aleksandrov looked straight ahead, not even glancing at Brodsky.

"I have to stop this work now, before it is too late." Brodsky shook his head. "Everything I have is in Geneva. I've delivered Nash, now you can get Jordan. There's no more I can do. You have to let me go."

"I'll let you go . . ." Aleksandrov twisted to the side and thrust his left arm toward Brodsky. "I'll let you go when these scars are gone."

Brodsky stared at the skin, twisted into knots and gnarled lumps. "That happened before I even saw you."

"Just a little treatment would have made the difference, even your Nazi lieutenant told you to do it."

"If you'd gone back with signs of first aid, you'd have been executed on the spot," Brodsky said softly. "It was the lieutenant who tricked you, not me. I've told you, forget the war, forget the past. You're a big shot, a real Moscow big shot. You should enjoy it."

Aleksandrov shook his head. "You really are a fool, a fat man with a secret. A war criminal with a death sentence, and a *Menschenfresser*, a dirty-mouthed, fat cannibal." Aleksandrov laughed. "What's more, you will do exactly what I tell you." He paused to look closely at Brodsky. "Now, what do you think about Jordan?"

"All I know is what our friend here has told me. What have you found out in Vienna?"

Aleksandrov shook his head. "These new-breed idiots, eight months, and they can't even put anyone near this man. All they try to tell me is he lives like a monk."

"He's married and has a child," Brodsky said. "Nash has always said that."

"So maybe these Vienna idiots think he's a married monk," Aleksandrov said. "One thing they're sure about, he spends no money, and stays in his apartment."

"Nash says he needs money," Brodsky said. "I've never seen a clerk anywhere who didn't need money. You should take Nash's word that Jordan can use money."

Aleksandrov leaned back. In the half-light Brodsky could see the trace of a smile. "Two weeks ago, in Moscow, there was a meeting. General Pyotr Ivanov Korobkov spoke to a select group, colonels and above." Aleksandrov paused. "I was there." Brodsky nodded to indicate he understood the importance of what was to come.

"The best part of Pyotr Ivanov's talk was about motives, and what he called the *Amerikanskaya mechta*—the American dream." Aleksandrov looked closely at Brodsky. "But everything the General said just confirmed what most of us already knew. It's money that works. No matter how reactionary their politics, Americans, British—all these smug imperialists—will work for money. They have this trick of separating their belief from what they do for money. Money is their culture, their only real politics." For a moment he watched the snow rushing past the window. "These mighty Anglo-Saxons come almost as cheap as the Latins they despise." He grunted. "At least the Latins are honest about it."

"So it sometimes seems," Brodsky said, nodding politely. He ignored Nash's demands for a translation.

"You telephone me at three-thirty tomorrow on the number you have, and we will make arrangements," Aleksandrov continued in Russian. "You're an ass even to think I would go to an American apartment." He tapped Golo's shoulder. "Stop here. From here they make their own way."

As Brodsky pushed the door open, Nash turned to face Aleksandrov. In the dim light, Nash's face seemed flushed with emotion as he reached with both hands to grip Aleksandrov's hand. He pumped the Russian's hand. "It will work out, I know it." Surprised, Aleksandrov pulled his hand free of Nash's grasp. He glanced down at his hand, and with an impatient wave, motioned Nash to leave.

Brodsky stepped out into the snow. Nash slipped out of the front seat. As he closed the door, the tires spun and the Open lurched forward and away.

35

VIENNA

If honors were granted for waiting, Trosper told himself, he would qualify *summa cum laude.* He checked his watch. It had been exactly two hours and fifty-five minutes since Brodsky and Nash had left for their meeting with the Russian.

Half dozing in the bulky safe-house chair, memories of the hundreds of hours spent waiting jostled each other. Three weeks in a freezing pension on the Thunersee—explaining that he was finishing a manuscript, and leaving one step ahead of a curious local policeman. Two weeks in a villa on Lake Como, the spectacular afternoon view of the lake humbled by the vision of a nude blond sunbather, tirelessly basting herself with sun lotion on a float fifty meters to the south. Twenty rainy days near the edge of Madame Bovary country, eased only by an occasional excursion for a *Treff* and grim dinner in Lille, the dreariest of French cities.

He imagined an essay, something that might be submitted to one of the intelligence journals in which professors had begun to illuminate the secret world. It would be on the manner of library that might be assembled from the books abandoned in safe houses, hotel rooms, trains, planes, lobbies, and on park benches by the world's secret agents. What insights might the professors draw from an analysis of these volumes?

Trosper shuddered, and glanced sheepishly at Ida across the room. She smiled reassuringly and went on with her needlepoint.

Two sharp rings dispelled his reverie. Three hours and twenty minutes.

Ida put down her sewing and went to the door.

Brodsky wriggled free of his overcoat, stuffed his woolen muffler into the sleeve, and sat down to pull off his snow boots. "So-so," he

said, pronouncing the word *zo-zo* while illustrating it with his hand
flat, fingers extended and rocking from side to side. "Aleksandrov
said he'd come from Moscow. Golo, his pet thug, is here, driving."
Brodsky straightened up, his face flushed from the struggle with his
boots. "Nash was all right. At least he kept his mouth shut, more or
less." Brodsky took a deep breath. "The big news"—he stopped to
peer at Trosper—"and, maybe no surprise, is that Aleksandrov
won't come to Jordan's apartment."

"Oh, dear," said Ida.

"You've danced around this long enough," Trosper said. "I
want the details of your recruitment, and your relationship with
Aleksandrov."

Brodsky took a final bite of the sandwich Ida had prepared and
dropped the remains onto a plate. He took a long sip of wine, and
looked around the room, satisfying himself that Ida had gone to
bed. "In the old days, I got the idea his real name is Lukin, and
once Sergei referred to him that way."

"Then let's call him Lukin," Trosper said.

"We go back to 1943 when the *Herrenvolk* were beginning to
have doubts about conquering the Soviet Union." Brodsky sat with
his heavy body wedged into the corner of the overstuffed Grand
Rapids sofa. "Lukin was picked up trying to cross from a partisan
area into Minsk. I pushed him around—he had a terrible burn on
his arm—but he stuck to his cover story. Fuerst, my lieutenant,
knew he was lying, but because he was brighter than most prisoners, we gave him a choice—an SS hanging, or an easy scouting
mission back into the partisan area. When he decided to live a little
longer, we made him compromise himself by giving us the location
of his brigade headquarters."

Brodsky leaned back on the sofa and crossed his legs. "I thought
Lukin had lied, but the brigade was exactly where he had marked it
on a photomap, and an SS combat team tore them apart. After this,
we sent him on the mission." Brodsky shook his head. "Like most
of the Russians we sent across, he never came back."

Brodsky pulled off his glasses and tugged a handkerchief from his pocket. Squinting, he exhaled on the glasses and began to polish the thick lenses. "You go through a war, you're never the same again," he said. "All these years, and I've never forgotten any of it . . ."

He stuffed the handkerchief back into his pocket. "A few days after this, we were pulling back toward Minsk when our convoy was hit. One mortar round and Fuerst's legs were torn to pieces—I could see the bones where his feet had been. He held my hand like a vise until he said, 'It's all right, Tolya, take care of yourself . . .'" Brodsky slipped his glasses into place and peered around the room. The only light came from the floor lamps at each end of the sofa. "Where's that cognac Ida was talking about?"

Brodsky cupped his hands around the glass to warm the brandy. "After Fuerst was killed, I was co-opted by an SS *Einsatzkommando*. The SS fighting units were as good as any on the front—with better equipment, and an insane sort of morale. But the rear-area security outfits, the SS *Sonderkommandos* and the *Einsatz* units, were killers, as bad as the extermination camp people." Brodsky's frown turned into a grimace. "Lucky Tolya, an interpreter for the biggest collection of swine in this century."

Trosper was impatient. "Lukin?"

"It was a fluke," Brodsky said. "I was forty kilometers east of Berlin when our sector collapsed. We knew the Russians were shooting any *Einsatz* men they could identify, so I had changed into a Wehrmacht uniform. It was a dicey few hours, but I made it into a PW cage. The next day, an informer sold me out, and I was thrown into a special SS enclosure. A few days later a Soviet officer comes stalking through the camp, looking at us like we're rats grazing in an open sewer. He was wearing a junior lieutenant's uniform two sizes too big, and looked like he'd won the war personally. I wouldn't have recognized him, but he stared straight at me for a while and then held his arm up and peeled back his sleeve. Christ, it must have been two years, but the scar and sores would still make you sick."

Brodsky grunted. "Lucky Tolya—the whole damn German

army and Lukin had to spot *me*. Until then, I thought I had a chance."

"But now you had something to swap, some information that would certainly interest the NKVD . . ."

"Oh, sure. I could have told some thick-skulled Chekist that an officer we had recruited was strolling around the camp. They would have shot me first and dealt with Lukin later." Brodsky fell silent, toying with his brandy glass. "I'd already learned not to piss things away, and always to save a few bits and pieces, like emergency rations." He glanced around the room, checking to make sure Ida had not returned. "We were starving in the camp. People were killing one another for a few scraps of potato. There was talk about cannibalism—Lukin still taunts me about it."

"And?"

"The next day, when I thought I was going for interrogation, I was marched to a shed at the edge of the camp. There were guards, a clerk, and—big surprise—a military judge. Right away the judge announced that I was wanted for war crimes in Poland and the Soviet Union . . ." Brodsky shook his head wonderingly. "Tolya, the famous war criminal."

He took another sip of brandy. "About this time the door opened and in came Lukin with a Soviet captain—the real thing, with the light blue NKVD piping on his shoulder boards. I figured they had come in to make sure I got the works. The judge shuffled his papers and asked if I had anything to say, I glanced over at Lukin. He looked straight at me, and shook his head. It was so slight a gesture, I wasn't even sure I had seen it. Then he smiled a little, and did it again."

Brodsky swirled the last drops of brandy in his glass. "Lukin was just a kid when we got him, and he'd behaved better than most prisoners. Fuerst even had the idea that after he left us, he had continued his mission in Minsk. I didn't want to screw him if there was any alternative, so I looked back at the judge and just shook my head."

Trosper reached across the coffee table to pour more brandy.

"Then, the judge read off the verdict. Big surprise, guilty. Death on two charges." Brodsky's eyes brightened with emotion. "It was all bullshit. I was on the wrong side, and with a bunch of real bastards, but the most I'd done was push around a few prisoners. Anyone can tell you, there weren't any Boy Scouts on the East Front."

He leaned back and closed his eyes. "After a while, the judge rattled off some more legal *Wurst,* nonsense, and announced that 'war criminal Brudzinski'—that's my real name, Anatol Brudzinski—was paroled in care of State Security. With this the Captain got up, and Lukin grabbed my arm and hustled me out of the court. Four hours later I was in an NKVD safe house in East Berlin—and as long as I behaved, they would forget about the death sentence."

Brodsky took a final swallow of brandy. "It was like they had bought a slave."

"What was the captain's name?"

"His name was Zotov, but Lukin always treated him like God Almighty."

Trosper glanced at his watch. It was too late to go into the details of Brodsky's career in Berlin. "There were so many agents—double agents—in those days, we'll have to keep the details for—"

"I was never one of that crowd," Brodsky said quickly. "Maybe when I was getting started, you people wrote me off as Tolya the anti-Communist jack-of-all-trades, but that was like a cover; I played it absolutely straight."

Trosper's attempt to appear neutral failed, and the expression drained from Brodsky's face. "Look, for shit's sake, I'm not proud of it, but when the war ended I had a third-hand Wehrmacht uniform, no family, no friends, no education, and no country. The most I had was languages. It wasn't so easy . . ."

Trosper shrugged. He could not sympathize.

Brodsky bristled. "It was Zotov who worked out my job. It was like a cover within a cover. According to him, I was to meet and cultivate as many people as I could, to keep a diary, and to make notes on everything I did, or heard about anyone else doing. The important thing was my assessment of people—everything else was sauce." Brodsky's voice rose with impatience. "I reported on hundreds of people—government, intelligence, newsmen, businessmen, crooks, whores, whoremasters, and politicians—the people who make the world work. And I've done it in Germany, in Austria, and now at the U.N. in Geneva." Brodsky shook his head in anger. "In those early days when most of you were screwing around with the lowest-level spying, this was a damned sophisticated operation. When my cover started to dry up, I took courses at the university, and gradually began to make a go of news work."

"That's all?" It was quite enough, but Brodsky was more forthcoming when on the defense.

"Can't you understand what Moscow Center gets from having a few guys—some at a high level, some like me—circulating around the major capitals?" Brodsky pounded his fist on his knee for emphasis. "For next to no risk, and not much money, they get an informed, maybe even intimate, picture of the people who make up their recruitment pool."

With an impatient gesture, Trosper brushed the argument aside. "But you recruited and handled Nash?"

Brodsky's face reddened. "Zotov was always behind the scenes, Lukin was the middleman. The last time I saw Zotov was in 1983—I don't know if he died or got promoted. But right after that, Lukin took over, and things changed. He got more aggressive, and began insisting that I concentrate on code clerks. It didn't matter a damn how often I told him that if I made one mistake trying to sign someone up, the game would be over, and I'd be no more use to anyone. But he wouldn't listen, it was like he was proving something."

"Proving what?"

"Times had changed, the new people in the embassies were different from the old guys who came along after the war. The new crop was much better educated, they dressed better, and could move around more easily. Maybe Lukin wanted to show he was as good as the new guys. He was smart enough, but he was always too rough, a bully with people." Brodsky sniffed. "Besides, he still looks like a partisan who's borrowed a suit so he can slip into town for a couple of hours—and all the violence is still there, just below the surface."

Brodsky leaned back and swung his feet up onto the varnished top of the coffee table in front of the sofa. "You remember Guy Burgess, Kim Philby's pal, who went off to Moscow with Donald MacLean just before someone finally got wise to Philby?"

Trosper nodded.

"I've read everything there is about him. I've even met a couple of Brits who knew him. Everyone seems to think Burgess was too much of a twit to have been a good spy—he wasn't serious enough, just a flaming faggot and a drunk." Brodsky took a deep breath. "Well, I don't agree. Burgess was all of that, but he was also bright as hell, and a real Commie. Like most of those old-school-tie snots, he knew everyone. When he left Cambridge, I think some bright handler—someone like Zotov—quieted him down, and probably even tried to wean him away from peddling Stalin's politics to everyone he met. After that, I think the Russians ran him exactly the way they ran me—circulate, meet everyone, tell us about them and what they're saying." Brodsky smiled. "It's dead simple, and no risk. The most the Brit security could have found against him was that he was a leftist twit, maybe even a Commie like a lot of his posh pals."

There was more to Guy Burgess than that, but Trosper said, "In the end, he was caught."

Brodsky shrugged. "If Lukin hadn't been so ambitious and forced me into crazy stuff like Nash and Frost, you never would have uncovered me."

"If it will make you sleep any better," Trosper said, "I'll admit that I agree with some of what you say." He smiled. "You've been preaching to the choir . . ."

Brodsky laughed. "Then I'd better say amen." He thrust himself to his feet. "Just one more thing." He looked expectantly at Trosper. "Why are you so interested in Lukin? There must be dozens of guys just like him, maybe some not so tough . . ."

Trosper thought for a moment. "A few weeks ago, Peter Gandy was murdered."

Brodsky's surprise was clear. "Lukin did it?"

"I'm not sure."

"In my experience, revenge is expensive—sometimes too expensive."

"I also want to know why Peter was killed."

"It won't bring him back . . ."

Trosper shrugged. "But if things go right, I'll put the murderer out of business."

Brodsky's jaw dropped. He stared at Trosper, and muttered, "Mother of God." Then, with a quick movement, he whirled in an adroit pirouette, and, with his arms akimbo in a parody of a ballet dancer tiptoeing through a mine field, he minced across the room to the brandy bottle.

Trosper turned off one of the floor lamps, and decided against saying that tomorrow would be a long day.

Brodsky poured two drinks. He handed Trosper a glass and offered a toast. "Break a leg."

Trosper raised his glass. *"Zum wohl."*

As they turned into the hallway and toward the bedrooms, Trosper said softly, "By any chance did you happen to keep copies of the reports and diaries you prepared for Zotov and Lukin?"

In the pale light Trosper could see Brodsky raise his eyebrows in mock surprise. "You mean did I cache them away like a nest egg, or emergency rations?"

"In Geneva?"

"Spies come, and spies go," Brodsky said, "but Swiss banks are forever."

36

VIENNA

As he watched Ida study the menu, Trosper's fingers drummed a half-remembered jazz rhythm on the tablecloth, so heavy and stiff it seemed starched. "*Tafelspitz* is as good as any dish in Austria," he said. "And Sacher's is the best place in Vienna to eat it."

Ida looked up in dismay. "*Boiled* beef?"

"But as you have never had it . . ."

Trosper broke off a piece of *Semmel.* The crusty white roll, which seemed identical but somehow tasted better than those served in any other restaurant in Vienna, was a fitting symbol of the place. The sparkling white-and-gold dining room, the perfectly appointed tables, and the deft service had been fashioned to produce a feeling of well-being, and even to suggest that somehow one deserved to eat there.

It was mid-morning when Trosper handed Hamel the cable slugged Eiderdown/Teak. It would be his last contact with Whyte and Castle before the operation kicked off, and it reminded Trosper of his days in a small boat, watching land disappear over the horizon. It was then that he decided an early lunch at Sacher's might stifle his anxiety, and provide the needed escape from the pinched atmosphere of the safe apartment and its make-do amenities.

But it hadn't worked. He couldn't shake the conviction that the operation was a long chapter of compromises and concessions to security and sound practice. Everything was wrong. There had been too much travel. The problems of working out of safe houses and keeping every detail in his head had multiplied with time. He had no reason for confidence in Nash, and Brodsky was an untested element. He needed a desk in a secure office, and a researcher who could in minutes produce the files he needed to study. Most of all, he needed time. But there wasn't any time.

"Are you all right?" Ida looked at him quizzically.

Trosper nodded and glanced around the room. The only evident tourists were two American couples, the men's faces tanned by high mountain sun, the women lean, chic, and confident. When they ordered a second bottle of wine, Trosper guessed they were celebrating the end of a ski vacation, and waiting for the limousine that would take them to the airport for the flight home. For a moment he envied them.

Ida tossed the menu aside. "What about the venison," she asked, "or hare?"

"Trust me."

She smiled. "You told me that when anyone said that, it was time to stop listening."

IDA dabbed a bit of *Schnittlauch* sauce on the last of the beef and lingered for a moment over the remaining bits of *Geroerstete.* The chive sauce and delicately hashed potato had her full attention until she looked up at the preoccupied Trosper. "What about tonight?" she asked.

Periphrasis was not one of Ida's shortcomings.

Trosper took a deep breath. "We both need a little time off. Let's just finish lunch. There'll be time enough for details when we get back to our home away from home."

Emil hovered behind the young waiter as he cleared the table. If anything, the headwaiter's black tailcoat was more tightly stressed than a year ago. He handed the menu to Ida.

"We'd better have a *Sachertorte,*" Trosper said, and added for Emil's benefit, "They're as good here as in most places."

TROSPER touched the bell twice as he turned the key in the safe-house door. Tolya, visibly nervous, was standing at the double

windows checking his watch. "Two-fifteen," he said glumly. "I
thought maybe you got lost in the snow." As soon as Ida left the
room, he said, "This is shit." His tie was loose, his shirt unbuttoned. "I'm not moving a goddamned inch until I get a commitment from you people."

"We've got more than an hour before you make the call," Trosper said. He picked up a paperback novel and lay down on the sofa.
"If I doze off, please wake me, by quarter past three."

BRODSKY had scarcely stopped dialing before the phone was
answered. He turned to Trosper. "Did you hear that? He said to
call again at five-fifteen." Brodsky's hand shook as he put down the
telephone. "That's another goddamned omen," he said.

"Not at all," Trosper said amiably. "It's a routine precaution.
The most it means is that your friend is a suspicious fellow. He just
wants to be sure that if he's being set up, we won't have time to
make a reconnaissance and to get our support people into place."

He decided against telling Brodsky that he could be right. It
might not be an omen, but if it was a signal, it was a bad one.

WASHINGTON, D.C.

DUFF Whyte picked up the intercom. "Yes?"

"I take it you've got Alan's cable from Vienna?" Castle's soft
voice was unmistakable.

"I've just read it."

"Paragraph three?"

Whyte picked up the cable. "Asylum for the fellow from Geneva?"

"Yes . . ."

"I have no trouble with that."

"I agree," Castle said, "but that's not really the problem . . ."

"Tell me more . . ."

"Alan hasn't mentioned that Brodsky and Nash will have met

twice with the Russian before Alan goes in. If one or both of them have decided he'll be better off in Moscow than with us, Alan has put his neck right in a noose." Castle waited before saying, "Lukin is a bad hat . . ."

"What do you suggest?"

"Bring them home. Alan's taken this far enough. I can have a cable there in half an hour . . ."

Whyte had never heard Castle speak so freely on the telephone. He tilted back in his chair and glanced at the row of clocks along the wall. "It will be going down in four hours . . ." He hesitated for a moment before taking the decision. "Unless there's something new, I will not abort." He leaned forward and began again to study Trosper's cable. "It's show time . . ."

Castle laughed. "Show time" was the Firm's jump-school equivalent of "Geronimo," the paratrooper war cry.

Whyte dropped the cable. "But all things equal, I think you'd better arrange to keep the Vienna circuit open and on line."

"Miss Pynchot has taken care of that," Castle said.

"Why don't you come by about eight—Vienna time," Whyte said. "We can go down to the signal center and keep an eye on things."

37

VIENNA

TEDDY's voice was muffled. "Our friends just pulled in . . ."

Trosper imagined the street man huddled in the kiosk, his hand cupped around the mouthpiece to block the street noises.

He glanced at his watch. Twenty minutes to seven. Brodsky and Nash would slip into the apartment only a few minutes late. It would take him six minutes to get from the kiosk on Waehringer Strasse to the steps running down the Strudlhofgasse. So far, so good.

"What about the street?"

Trosper could hear Teddy's breathing. "I don't know. It's almost stopped, but the stuff's piled all over the place. It's getting colder, there's slush and ice underfoot. People can't walk normal. They're slipping and jumping all over the place. There's no pattern you can check . . ."

"What do you *think*?" Trosper struggled to keep his voice on an even tone. "Is there anyone outside?"

Teddy sighed heavily and paused. Trosper could hear his heavy breathing. "Half an hour, maybe twenty minutes ago, I think I had a make . . ."

"A man?"

Another long pause.

"Big, heavyset, stupid hat, moving very quiet right through the area."

"The man you made in Florence?"

"The same. Maybe the wrong hat for here, but elsewise, he's out of the first drawer," Teddy said. "A real comedian, but good."

"Top drawer," Trosper murmured. Golo Leditsa, a thug for all seasons.

"He was carrying three string bags, like he'd stopped to buy a week's groceries on the way home. He moved slow, picking his way so as not to fall over. If he was working, the most he did was check to see if we got a stakeout or anyone in the neighborhood."

"Are you clean?"

"There's no way he could have seen me," Teddy said.

"What about wheels?"

There was another long pause. "Very little traffic in this weather, and nothing but passenger cars parked out front. No vans. No trucks."

"Anything else?"

"There's a big guy in a car, good spot, not too close, maybe four hundred yards. And there's a woman, doing pretty well . . . but I guess you know all about them."

There was no reason to ask Teddy about observation points. There could be fifty windows with good lines of sight bearing on the front of the apartment building.

"It's like daytime here," Teddy said. "The snow reflects every light. You could get a tan."

"Let's keep in touch."

Trosper stepped into the snow, and headed slowly for the Strudl-hofgasse. He touched the thumper on his right wrist. But there was no reassurance there. Ida had warned him that the radio-controlled signal was temperamental. The wristwatch-like devices were designed for doctors who did not want their golf game interrupted by the noisy call-your-office-right-this-minute type of beeper alarm. The thumpers substituted a silent, unmistakable vibration for the clarion call. But without a test, Ida could not promise that the signal would penetrate the thick-walled buildings common in Vienna.

Thumper or not, Trosper realized sourly, the chances that Ida would spot trouble heading for the building in time to signal a warning were slim.

Loose snow sifted over the side of his waxed brogues and melted against his socks.

38

VIENNA

The elaborate brass bellplate at the side of the apartment door was part of the *"Alt Wien"* garnish that an architect must have thought would both rejuvenate and add character to the tacky, fortress-like, 1940s apartment building. If anything, the embellishments intensified the gloom of the hallway. The apartment number was etched into the brass, but the slot for the occupant's name was empty. Fresh smudges on the polished metal suggested that the card had been hurriedly removed.

Trosper took a deep breath, held it for a moment, and touched the bell. A chime sounded. He could hear a door open, and from within the apartment, the muffled command, "Let your friend in."

There were footsteps, and some fumbling with a chain lock before the door was inched open.

Nash's narrow face was puffy and gray. He wiped at the trace of perspiration along his upper lip, and beckoned Trosper through the door. "He's here," Nash whispered, "right in the front room."

Trosper stepped in and glanced at the door. "Lock it," he said. He had hoped that Brodsky would come to the door. There were questions he might have answered.

Nash eased the chain into place, twisted the drop lock, and stood to one side as Trosper tossed his coat and hat on a chair in the narrow entryway. Through a partially open door to what appeared to be the living room at the end of the hall, Trosper could see Brodsky, his back to the hallway.

"What are they talking about?" Trosper asked.

"I don't know, they're always yakking German or Russian."

"Is the Russian alone?"

"There's just him and Tolya," Nash whispered.

"In the other rooms?"

Nash's glance swept along the hallway. He shook his head. "But there's a plastic toy under a table in the front room—that must mean people live here," he said, proud of his deduction. "The bedroom door was open when we came, but nobody was in there. There's a kitchen, but I don't know about any other rooms . . ."

Patches of sweat ringed the high collar of Nash's shirt. "Look," he said, "you don't need me any more. I'll just go along back to the house. I don't feel so good anyway . . ."

With a quick shove Trosper spun Nash around and pushed him ahead as they moved along the hall.

Lukin stood facing the window at the far corner of the living room. In the soft, reflected light his face was strong, the sharp planes might have been cut by a peasant whittling a rough wooden figure. A square, black suit, with sleeves that hung down well over his wrists, accentuated the Russian's stocky build. With one hand holding the curtain aside, he continued to watch the few flakes of scattered snow that were blown against the double-glazed window.

A moment after Brodsky grunted a response to Trosper's greeting, Lukin let the curtain fall and turned slowly to face the room. Trosper recognized the deliberate movement as a gesture calculated to show that Lukin was so completely in command that he could be indifferent to whoever might enter the room. But when the Russian saw Trosper, his heavy eyebrows knitted in surprise, and his glance darted quickly to Brodsky, standing motionless in the center of the room. Lukin studied Trosper for another moment and said in English, "I expected younger." He peered more closely before saying, "You're not Jordan."

"No, I'm not Jordan," Trosper said in Russian.

Nash sidled away from Trosper until he stood midway between him and Brodsky.

Lukin watched Nash's move and turned slightly toward Brodsky. "Is there something I should know, Comrade Brodsky?" he asked with a smile.

"I told you my nerves were gone months ago," Brodsky said. "And I told you again last night . . ." He shrugged, his movement a blend of resignation and indifference.

Lukin looked across the room at Trosper. "Who are you?" He gestured toward Brodsky and Nash. "What are you doing with this scum?" As he stepped away from the window, his right hand moved slowly across the front of his jacket.

With a quick motion, Trosper slipped the 9-mm Browning from the soft, silk-lined, suede holster under his arm. As he leveled the gun at Lukin, he tried to remember a confrontation in which guns had been drawn but not fired. He could not. Perhaps this would be a first.

Lukin's hand froze and remained motionless until, with a casual movement, he appeared to flick a bit of lint from the front of his jacket.

Trosper turned slightly toward Brodsky. "As of now you have your commitment," he murmured in English. "Asylum." He lowered the pistol and held it loosely by his side. "Do you understand?"

Brodsky acknowledged Trosper's remark with a slight move of his head, and stepped back, farther from Lukin, and out of any possible line of fire. Sweat oozed from his forehead. With his forefinger he dabbed at the moisture trapped by the thick frame of his glasses.

Trosper turned to Nash, whose mouth was working as if he were struggling to phrase an admonition, and motioned him to a chair near the double windows.

With the heavy pistol, Trosper gestured for Lukin to turn and face the wall.

The Russian remained motionless, studying his antagonist.

Trosper repeated his gesture.

Lukin hesitated, and then, seeming to have taken a decision, his mouth twisted, a bona-fide sardonic smile. He turned slowly to face the wall, muttering in a stage whisper, "Cowboys, Yankee cowboys . . ."

The odd locutions of the retired Green Beret sergeant and small-arms instructor at the Fort raced through Trosper's mind. "Subject is at gunpoint. Your left shoulder is toward subject. Your left arm is extended, fist closed. The piece is in your right hand. It is close to your chest. Subject cannot slap it away. The target line is your left shoulder. If you must fire, you will not aim. At three paces, impact will be four inches to the right of your target line. For safety, you will drop your left arm before firing . . ."

Trosper ignored the approved procedure, shifted the Browning to his left hand, and jabbed the muzzle against the base of Lukin's skull. With his right hand he reached around to unbutton Lukin's jacket. He pulled a 7.62 Tokayev semiautomatic pistol from Lukin's shoulder holster. The weapon, discontinued after the war, had become a status symbol among the older Chekists.

He continued the pat-down, running his hands over Lukin's upper body and legs. The stiff, oily fabric of Lukin's suit had the texture of a scouring pad. It was not the clothing Trosper would have associated with an operative of Lukin's seniority and frequent travel. Satisfied there was no ankle holster and no other weapon concealed at the small of the Russian's back, Trosper stepped back toward the center of the room. He turned to Brodsky and said in English, "Quickly now, check every room—kitchen, toilets, bedrooms, closets."

Brodsky hesitated and touched his glasses. "*Was mich betrifft, ist der Idiot recht verstoert,*" he whispered.

Trosper glanced quickly at Nash. Brodsky was right, the young man's face was strange—twisted with fear, Trosper hoped, not rage.

Nash caught Trosper's eye. "What's happening?" he demanded. "I've got a right to know . . ." As Brodsky hurried out of the room, Nash stood and began to step closer to Trosper.

"Sit down and shut up," Trosper said. He did not want two people moving at the same time.

Trosper lowered the pistol and motioned Lukin to a straight chair beside the wall.

Lukin buttoned his jacket, and walked to the chair. He moved stiffly, his heavy, black shoes greasy with waterproofing. "You've reclaimed your little rabbit . . . and captured the fox who snatched him," Lukin said in Russian. "Why are you risking this confrontation with me?"

At close range, the sharp planes of Lukin's face were less impressive. Like an actor seen off stage, he was older and less forceful than at a distance. There were dark circles under his eyes and heavy lines down his cheeks. Gray hair, shaved in a tight arch above his ears, and trimmed high above his collar in the back, underscored the rough, military aspect of his bearing.

Before Trosper could speak, Brodsky interrupted from the doorway. "There's no one here," he said, his chest heaving slightly. "But there's a tape recorder in the bedroom closet, running . . ."

"All the comforts of home," Trosper muttered.

"I had to break the lock . . ."

"Take the tape. If there's another tape, put it on the machine and start it. If there's no tape, smash the machine." Trosper turned back to Lukin.

"You're making trouble for yourself, too much trouble for a shitty little affair like this." Lukin's Russian had a harsh, parade-ground edge, but it lacked the authority Trosper had expected.

"In the circumstances," said Trosper, "I'll have to be the judge of that . . ."

"You Americans are so quick with your guns," Lukin said. "All that business in Grenada, Libya—now it's a war because I got inside your Geneva office?" He glanced at Nash. "All for this . . . *zero,* as you people say?"

"Nash is yesterday," Trosper said.

The Russian remained motionless, his immobile face so perfect a mask it betrayed itself. Only his eyes, half covered by heavy lids, gave any clue to his intense concentration on Trosper.

"I've come for some information," Trosper said.

Lukin did not seem impressed.

"We can begin with Bondarev . . ."

Lukin's eyes opened wide. "You made this trouble to ask me about him? All these years, and the first time I meet a senior American, you want to talk about *Bondarev?*" For want of a better audience, Lukin turned to Brodsky to display his astonishment.

"That's right . . ."

"Three years ago, when I read the file, it was hard to believe your service could be so hungry as to go along with that stupid operation. Now, you come to Vienna with a gun in your hand and demand an explanation?" Lukin shrugged in disbelief.

"There are loose ends . . ." Trosper spoke quickly to hide his surprise at the Russian's response.

Lukin was motionless, his eyes fixed on Trosper. "You and I are professionals, nothing like the two you brought here. We each have a position, you in your Firm, me in Moscow. To use your folk saying, our services are"—he hesitated, seeking the words in English—"six of one and six of the same."

"You surprise me," Trosper said. "The notion that your service and mine, that you and I, are opposite sides of the same coin is a stupid joke, part of the crap floated by your propagandists. You've been around long enough to know better." The coin concept, so treasured by editorial moralists, had always infuriated Trosper, but it irritated him to have let his emotion show.

A flicker of amusement softened Lukin's expression. Then he glanced at Brodsky and Nash. "That fat Pole speaks Russian better than you do. I won't talk in front of traitors. Why don't you get them out of here?"

This was not the head-to-head conflict with a *Spetsburo* survivor that Trosper had braced himself for. There was an odd, resigned, and almost indulgent aspect to Lukin that did not square with Colonel Aksenov's remarks to Ida in East Hampton or the image created by Brodsky. But the Russian was talking freely and to only one purpose that Trosper could perceive.

Trosper turned to Brodsky. "You and Nash had better wait in the bedroom. Leave the door ajar, I'll call when I want you back."

"I'm staying here," Nash said, his hands twitching like a puppet whose strings were pulled too tight. "I'm not going anywhere with him."

"Get your ass out of here, right now," Trosper said.

Brodsky heaved himself to his feet, and steered Nash through the door and toward the bedroom.

"Make sure the chain is on the entrance door," Trosper called after Brodsky.

Lukin studied Trosper for a moment before saying, "You're just like all Americans, so smug, so sure that all the world envies your marvelous society, you don't even see other people. You're so pleased with yourselves, all any comrade has to do is smile at one of your *apparatchiks,* and you think you have a new spy—someone who will take you deep inside our system." The Russian raised his eyebrows slightly. "That's really all you need to learn from the Bondarev operation."

It was a valid observation, but Trosper was not interested in an exchange of operational wisdom. "As may be, but the fact remains that your operation went nowhere and was abruptly closed down."

Lukin was silent, as if at the point of a decision. Finally he said, "You've come so far, and will leave with so little, I can only feel sorry for you . . ." His mask twisted into a smirk. "Bondarev took you in completely—you sent two people to Geneva to handle what was really just the first step in some little deception involving your policy in Latin America. But what our young geniuses thought was Bondarev's brilliant acting was simply the truth, he was a spoiled child and hated us all. I examined the operation and told the Center that if Bondarev stayed much longer in the West, he really would go over to you people. Later, when I caused his recall, I did our counterintelligence people a favor and they know it. The only profit in the whole operation was that it brought Gandy and his assistant to Geneva." Lukin glanced around the room and at the door before saying, "You knew Gandy?"

Trosper shrugged, aware that Lukin had used the past tense, but still not sure why the Russian was talking.

"He was a fool to go along with the Bondarev case."

"Do you think your fiasco with Frost was better?"

Lukin shifted his weight in the straight chair and tugged at the sleeves of his jacket. For the first time Trosper sensed having penetrated the Russian's arrogance.

"Nash was my creature, not Frost," Lukin said. "And from the start, the Nash operation was developed correctly. I knew Nash's assignment to Geneva would end in a few months. At my direction, he was to ask for assignment in Washington. There, he could stay on with your Firm, or, with my guidance, possibly transfer to the Agency, perhaps the Pentagon—wherever the hunting was best. He is a mercenary, and it would have been a challenge to control his spending, and his leisure activity. But he could have reached the highest level."

Could it be only vanity, the interrogator's best friend, that fueled these disclosures? "But then you forgot Nash and got so greedy that you tried to force Frost's recruitment . . ."

"My operation with Nash was correct in every respect. It was the Second Chief Directorate that made the mistake. The counterintelligence people insisted on the recruitment of one of your officers before Nash left Geneva and while we could still read your cables there."

"Surely," Trosper said with a faint smile, "cipher work still has an absolute priority over all other activity?"

"The counterintelligence staff chose Gandy—a big cash payoff and ample payments for the next few years," Lukin said. "That's the one inducement your people understand."

The memory of Gate Cottage echoed in Trosper's mind, and he could feel Gandy's wasted hand as he answered the last question— "There's not a damn thing I can think of . . ." But here it was, straight from the horse's mouth—Peter Gandy, Moscow Center mercenary. For a moment, Trosper sickened. It was as if he had tripped over a bucket of rotting slops.

Lukin was still talking. ". . . so, I decided to do my counterintelligence friends a favor. I made a personal appeal to my chief. I recommended he approve the approach to Frost." For a moment his eyes closed. "It seems to have been a mistake . . ."

Trosper focused again on the Russian and listened for another moment before asking, "Then why was Gandy killed?"

Lukin thrust himself forward in the chair. "I've had enough of your stupid provocations."

"This is no provocation . . ."

"Be glad you've got a gun in your hand."

Now Trosper leaned forward, closer to Lukin. "You goddamn well listen . . ." When he realized he was waving the pistol for emphasis, Trosper eased the weapon onto his lap. "I came here for two reasons. One is to find out who killed Peter Gandy, the other is to blow you the hell out of your service. We're going to make a public issue of your murder of Gandy. My government will grant a warrant for your arrest and extradition for the murder of Gandy. We will serve it on your ambassador in Washington. The British will do the same in London. There will be immense publicity. We have all the details of the poison. We have pictures of you, and we will expel the entire rezidency in Washington. The British will do the same . . ."

"Nonsense," Lukin said, his face flushed with fury. "Shit and nonsense . . ."

"We scarcely expect Gorbachev to extradite you for trial, although he will surely discuss the prospect with your chief, Comrade Kryuchkov, and will have questions about Vladimir Aleksandrovich's lack of control over a clumsy operative . . ."

"Nonsense . . ." Lukin struggled to control his heavy breathing.

"Your story will be in every newspaper in the world. You'll never go abroad again, the Center won't even let you live in Moscow . . ."

Lukin took a deep breath and leaned back in the heavy chair. "Did you think I'd be fool enough to respond to your stupid suggestion and actually meet Jordan in his apartment? Or be primitive enough to come to this place *alone*?"

"You've been trying to recruit Jordan for a year," Trosper said. "You came here because it was to be the final step in the recruitment of Jordan . . ."

"Think again . . ." Lukin jammed his left hand into the side pocket of his jacket.

Trosper leveled the pistol.

With a reassuring gesture, Lukin pulled out what seemed to be a book of paper matches. Holding it in his fingertips to show it wasn't dangerous, he tossed it onto the table beside Trosper.

It was a half sheet of lined yellow paper torn from a pad and folded several times. With the pistol still on Lukin, Trosper unfolded the paper. He glanced at the carefully written message.

"Dear Colonel, I have been arrested. Don't believe a word Tolya Brodsky says. He is in on it. Please remember the promises to help me to escape. Sincerely, Terrence A. Nash." In parentheses beneath his signature, Nash had written his codename, Viktor.

"There's one son of a bitch who can't claim to be his own best friend," Trosper said in English.

"Viktor gave me that last night, when he said goodbye and shook hands," Lukin said. "He's more resourceful than I thought . . ."

39

VIENNA

Lukin was silent, savoring Trosper's surprise. "We have a lot to discuss. Let's settle down for a moment." He lighted a cigarette. "Was it Nash that bothered your service so much?"

"Operations are operations. Gandy's death is quite different."

Lukin took a deep drag on his cigarette. "The Viktor operation is classic, a sanitized version is already being used in our school," Lukin said slowly. "From the beginning, it attracted favorable comment and was good for my reputation."

"Considering that you had to work with Nash, it was well done," Trosper said. The praise did not come easily, but Trosper was cuddling. It was slang, kept alive at the Fort to describe the maneuvering of a case man to establish confidence by ostensibly moving closer to an adversary's views. But cuddling was a luxury, most useful when there was time for long development.

"There are more important things, and we have very little time . . ." Lukin had an irritating mannerism of interrupting his conversation by exhaling blasts of cigarette smoke at various objects. It was like target practice—the table lamp, the tip of his shoe, and then a blast that fell short of a framed poster, crooked on the wall.

"You said it was a mistake to have made the recommendation to your chief about the recruitment in Geneva . . ."

"Before that," Lukin said, "things had gone well for me. I could work on my own cases, mostly cipher procurement. I never reported to anyone in the field, only to my chief in Moscow." Lukin frowned. "It happens that some of our delicate young scientists in the Eleventh are wary of the counterintelligence people, so I also served as an informal liaison to the Second Chief Directorate. In a way I was more at home with the counterintelligence people, and sometimes did favors for old friends." Lukin dumped the nuts from a chromium-plated dish and ground out his cigarette. "Our peasants say that a man with two horses will travel farther."

"But only if he is smart enough to ride one horse at a time." A gratifying flash of irritation crossed Lukin's face.

"What recommendation was it that you made?"

"I suggested to my chief that it would not harm our cipher interests if he agreed to let counterintelligence make the approach to your man in Geneva." Lukin lighted another cigarette. "When the operation failed, the Center withdrew Bondarev and his case man. We even considered severing contact with Brodsky. We were worried that your investigation of the recruitment attempt would expose Nash. This was a problem because the operation had been mentioned to the Secretary General himself."

"Now you've got three problems—Brodsky, Nash, and Jordan?" Trosper managed a smile. "In my service that would be a catastrophe . . ."

Lukin twisted in the chair and fidgeted with his shirt cuff. "It was essential that we do nothing to upset the routine of your Geneva office. Any leak of our attempt on Frost could have been disaster. Your people would have investigated everyone in the office, as well as all the operations. Someone would have recognized that Nash was spending too much money, and that there was no serious operational activity in Geneva. But we knew from Nash that no security investigator had come to Geneva, that no one had been questioned. Nash continued to work as usual. After a few months, it seemed clear that Frost had not reported Brodsky's clumsy approach."

"But Gandy would have informed you if Frost had told him about Brodsky's approach?"

"Why Gandy?" Lukin appeared surprised.

"Why not Gandy? You had recruited him . . ."

Lukin shook his head.

"You told me, you recommended that your boss agree to let the counterintelligence people approach Gandy before Nash left Geneva . . ."

Lukin shook his head. "The counterintelligence people wanted

Gandy—an easy target. But in my opinion, Gandy was finished, just a drunk, soon to be retired. It was Frost I recommended, and it was Frost they chose. We had nothing to do with Gandy."

"Gandy was not recruited?"

Lukin shook his head.

"You are certain?"

Lukin scowled. "You're wasting time. Our study showed Frost was a dilettante and weak, but he had a good education, and had bragged to Nash about his personal relationship with your Controller, Bates. Frost had all the credentials for a future in your service." Lukin opened his eyes slightly wider. "Counterintelligence agreed and pressured me to convince my chief that an approach to Frost would not affect Nash's security." He shook his head slowly. "I should have insisted that my chief make his own decision but he was too weak. I was forced to make it—but it was my boss's mistake."

"Then, why was Gandy killed?"

The Russian shook his head. "There is no time for this. My man is outside, he'll be here soon . . ."

Trosper would not stop now. "Why was Gandy killed?"

Lukin grimaced with irritation. "When the recruitment failed, I was . . . disciplined." He took a deep breath of smoke and blew it to the ceiling. "After all my years of service—Order of the Red Banner for the Kube assassination, five combat decorations, many citations, and my positions of great responsibility in the service—I was censured and subjected to *administrative* discipline—imagine, *administrative* discipline." He opened his eyes wider and raised his heavy brows. "My activity was curtailed, I was told that Nash was my primary responsibility. I was to have no further contact with my friends in counterintelligence. Then, as soon as I reported on the possibility of recruiting Jordan in Vienna, I was directed to review the Nash and Brodsky case—obviously, we would not risk Nash unless we were sure of success with Jordan. I went through the Nash file thoroughly, including all of the Geneva cable traffic on the Bondarev case. It was clear from the outset that only two people could possibly know that we had inside data on your Geneva office—Gandy and Frost. Sooner or later, I knew that someone, maybe in your special operations staff, would begin to wonder why the Geneva office was unproductive—and suspicions would be raised. When that happened, an investigation would begin. There would be interrogations. In a forced interrogation Frost would have broken. Then it would not have taken you long to uncover Nash and Jordan."

Lukin's notion of a forced interrogation—with Frost being tortured in the cellar on Wisconsin Avenue—echoed back to Dzerzhinsky, Beria, and the Lubyanka.

"And you killed Gandy on that chance?"

Lukin frowned in irritation. "I found a small clue that proved Frost had spoken to Gandy about the Brodsky approach."

"What clue?"

Lukin was becoming nervous, he tapped his wristwatch. "We have almost no time—we must talk of other things . . ."

"What clue?" Trosper knew he had the advantage. For once time was on his side.

"It was a cable." Lukin glanced around the room and at the door leading to the hallway and bedrooms. "A brief cable through Gandy's private channel to your headquarters. It asked for background data on the activities of the German FAK units on the Eastern Front."

Trosper remembered the cable.

"It came after Brodsky's approach to Frost. Only Gandy could authorize messages through the closed Bondarev channel to your headquarters. There was no reason for Gandy to have sent that cable unless Frost had confessed the Brodsky incident to Gandy. Gandy was an old hand, he would have knowledge of the Nazi intelligence and the FAK. It was clear Gandy was trying to get information on Brodsky without raising suspicion in your headquarters."

"You took action on that scrap of information?"

"The security of the Nash operation was my responsibility. I had to certify that Nash was sound and that the approach to Jordan was in order. I had to be right—my professional life depended on it. I had no alternative but to close all possible leaks. Nash would have returned to Washington within a year—and once he was there I could have developed him into a great source. If I could have recruited Jordan as well, it would have been a triumph, a singular achievement."

"You had authority to kill Gandy and Frost?"

"My responsibility for Nash's security was authority enough. I drew the weapons on my own. They were old weapons, outdated and to have been destroyed. They were issued to me as a favor—a favor to a veteran fighter, a true Chekist. That was my authority. It is the authority I have earned. It was enough." Lukin tapped his watch again. "There is no time . . ."

Trosper looked at his watch. It had been thirty-five minutes since he had taken off his coat. "Then why are you here?"

Lukin jammed his cigarette into the metal dish. "Last night I took a decision." He looked sharply at Trosper. "With Nash gone, Brodsky defected, and Jordan lost, I must admit that I am finished. There will be nothing more for me in Moscow."

Trosper affected a look of concern.

There was a noise from the kitchen.

"I have ten good years left to work," Lukin said heavily. He inhaled deeply and blew a tower of smoke toward the ceiling. He watched it dissipate. Without looking at Trosper he said, "I propose that I come to your service. I will submit to interrogation on the written commitment that afterwards I will be given work, pay, and a position commensurate with what I am abandoning in Moscow."

Trosper pretended surprise.

"I will not work directly against my former comrades, but I am prepared to operate in Latin America or Africa. My assistant, Comrade Leditsa, will probably accompany me to your service. I will insist that he be given appropriate compensation and position."

There was another sound, a door opening. In the kitchen, Trosper guessed.

Lukin started, and stared toward the living room door.

"There's a chain lock," Trosper said confidently. "We will hear anyone who tries to come in from the outside." There was another sound. Trosper turned.

Golo Leditsa wore the same hat as in Florence. But this time he had a pistol in his right hand, and pointed at Trosper's chest.

Lukin barked a command in Russian. "No weapons. Everything is correct here." It was the Lukin of old, and fully in command.

Trosper's pistol was at his side. If he raised it, the Russian would fire. He decided to wait. As Lukin said, even the Russians had learned to wait.

40

VIENNA

"THERE'S no problem, Golo. Everything is in order, I've been expecting you, Golo." Lukin spoke in Russian, and softly, as if he were gentling a horse. "Sit down, Golo."

The big Russian ignored Lukin. "Give me the gun," he said to Trosper.

Trosper shook his head. Golo was taller than Trosper remembered. His face was rounder, his features flatter, and he spoke with a throaty Ukrainian accent.

"Give him the gun," Lukin said in English. It was an order.

"How did he get in here?" Trosper spoke in English.

"There's a door in the kitchen, in the old days for servants," Lukin said. "He has a key." He glanced at Golo, and turned to Trosper. "You must put the gun down right now. He will shoot . . ."

"Tell him to put his gun down . . ."

Lukin shook his head. "He's going to kill you . . ."

It had begun to seem like a reasonable observation. Trosper laid the Browning on a table behind the sofa.

"Take off your coat, Golo, we have a lot to talk about." Lukin gestured toward the sofa.

Golo motioned Trosper away from the table. Without taking his eyes off Trosper, he wriggled free of his raincoat. The coat was brown with an orange sheen, and lined with a flimsy, blue plaid fabric.

"I could hear what you were talking about, the proposition you were making." Golo's voice was highpitched for such a big man. "It was just what Borisov warned me about. I am ordered to prevent it." He tossed his hat onto the coat. It was flat topped, with a broad brim. It was a porkpie, and it reminded Trosper of the style fancied by Lester Young.

Trosper tried to keep his eyes on the automatic pistol, half hidden in Golo's thick fist.

"This is the only way," Lukin said. "Everything has changed, there's no place for us anymore."

"*Ty yebanty predatel*," he spat.

"We can go together, as always," Lukin said. "It will be a new life. We'll do nothing against our old comrades—the Americans have many other interests. But it will be the same game."

"*Ty gavino.*"

Trosper wondered how long Lukin would tolerate the stream of Russian obscenity.

"I can't just retire, and wait to die," Lukin said. "I've done too much, given up too much. I can't just stop all of this, it's my life."

"I protected you . . . twenty years."

"It will be the same game, but with more money, an easier life." Lukin's face was gray.

"Borisov came to me, right after I got back from Italy. It was official—he warned me, you've gone too far. The Second Directorate—your friends, you think—they know all about it. They know all about London. I told Borisov about Florence . . . I thought you were authorized, that everything was official. You said it was all done on orders. But there weren't any orders. Nobody knew . . ."

"I did what was right. I was protecting Viktor."

"You ruin everything you touch . . ."

Trosper heard a door open.

"Be calm, Golo," Lukin said.

"Traitor, defector—*Yyeb tvoyu mat.*"

"It's all arranged, you will come with me . . ." Lukin glanced at Trosper. "The American has fixed everything . . ."

"It's just as Borisov said. I have orders to stop you . . ."

"You will come with me, it's all arranged . . ." Lukin looked at Trosper, expecting support. He got none.

"I never believed what I heard about you in Minsk, on the Kube operation during the war. But Borisov swore to me—you really did betray your comrades . . ."

"I was half dead, but I got the explosives to the house in Minsk."

"You sold out to the SS, that's why you keep that shit of a Pole working . . ."

"Without me the assassination would have failed. Stalin personally approved my decoration . . ."

"You're a traitor," Golo shouted. "First the SS, now the Americans . . ." He raised the pistol until it was level with Lukin's chest.

Trosper shifted his weight, ready to dive out of the way. Over Golo's shoulder he saw Ida edge through the open kitchen door. She dabbed at her fogged glasses and dug in the heavy handbag hanging from her shoulder.

The pistol made a popping sound. Trosper would remember it made less noise than he would have expected.

Lukin's hands moved as if to fend off the bullet.

Golo fired three more times. Three more popping sounds.

Trosper saw wisps of smoke as the lead tore and burned through the thick fabric of Lukin's suit.

Lukin staggered a step forward, both hands tearing at the pain in his chest. His knees buckled and he fell backward. The impact blew the remaining air from his lungs. A spasm contorted his face and he belched a mass of blood.

The four rounds were perfectly grouped. Lukin could have covered them all with the palm of one hand.

Golo stepped closer, ready to fire again. Then, satisfied, he turned away from the corpse to face Trosper. He leveled the pistol. *"Ty pizoyuk,"* he bellowed. *"Ty khuy . . ."*

In the doorway, Ida crouched into the approved turret position, both hands holding the pistol. She fired. Brodsky loomed beside her.

Trosper threw himself to the floor, rolling toward the table and the Browning.

Ida fired again.

The pistol flew out of Golo's hand as the impact of the shot spun him around. With his left hand Golo grabbed at his right arm, and fell to his knees. Still clutching his shattered elbow, he hitched himself along the floor on his knees toward the pistol.

Brodsky rushed across the room, and kicked the pistol aside.

Trosper felt the thumper tapping discreetly against his wrist.

Golo toppled sideways. His thrashing legs began to spin him in a circle, as if he were struggling to crawl away from the pain. He keened in agony, trying not to scream.

Ida retched. Gun in hand, she braced herself against the back of the chair and retched again.

Trosper got to his feet and took the Browning.

Nash dashed through the door. He stopped short. Staring at Golo thrashing on the floor, he shouted, "You crazy bastards, now look what you've done. You've ruined everything."

Brodsky braced himself and smashed his right fist into Nash's face. Nash reeled back against the wall. He covered his face with both hands and began to weep.

Trosper bent over Lukin. A foul smell of warm blood and feces. Dead in spades. The left sleeve of his shirt and jacket had hiked up, away from his wrist. In the circumstances, the scars on his arm seemed less ugly.

Brodsky pried the gun from Ida's hand and led her to a chair.

Trosper went to Golo. He had stopped thrashing. His right arm, turned back to front, dangled at a grotesque angle. Blood seeped through the rough green tweed of his jacket. His chocolate brown trousers were wet with blood. Or urine. Trosper could not be sure. The Russian's eyelids fluttered, his face was drained of color and covered with cold sweat. Deep shock.

"How much noise, Tolya? How loud was it?" Trosper had no idea how much noise had been made.

"Maybe not too bad, but let's get the telly turned on . . ."

Trosper stepped to the television set.

Brodsky turned from Ida and walked over to Nash. "No noise." He slammed Nash's head back against the wall for emphasis, and pulled Nash's hands away from his face. "No more noise," he said softly. Blood ran from Nash's broken nose and dribbled down his chin as he tried to control his sobs.

"There must be something, some cognac for Ida . . ." Trosper talked aloud to himeslf as he opened the cabinet beneath the TV set. A liter of Russian commissary vodka, and a small bottle of

Cointreau. Trosper took the vodka and a glass to Ida.

As he bent to hold the glass for her, the doorbell chimed. "Damn, damn, damn," he said loudly to himself.

Brodsky grabbed the vodka bottle, picked up Golo's pistol and stuffed it into his pocket. As he hurried to the door, he loosened his tie, unbuttoned his shirt, and spilled vodka down his tie and chest. He unlocked the door and, vodka bottle in hand, pulled it open.

A fat Viennese, his face red with outrage, spewed a torrent of neighborly complaint.

Brodsky smiled, and began in pidgin German. *"Grosser Russiche Feiertag . . . gross wie Sovietische Neues Jahres . . ."* He tried English. "Big Russia holiday . . ." In Russian, he invited the neighbor into the apartment. He lapsed back into broken German. *"Vodka, viel Vodka, kommst Du hinein . . ."* He listened to the Austrian's complaints for a moment and then turned toward the living room where the television was blaring. He bellowed *"Ruhe, Ruhe,"* and for measure, shouted "Quiet."

Then, in a parody of a drunk, he took a swig of vodka from the bottle, wiped his hand over the top, and offered it to the Austrian. *"Wir muss' nachbarlich sein . . ."*

As the Austrian, still growling complaints, hurried away from the door, Brodsky added a final touch to his performance, and whispered, "Fasheest . . ."

Trosper lowered the television volume.

EVEN by safe-house standards the apartment was a mess.

Trosper checked his watch. It was 8:10. He had been in the apartment sixty-five minutes.

Brodsky, the combat veteran, bent over Golo, and with a kitchen knife, cut the sleeve from his jacket. He peeled back the shirt and studied the Russian's shattered elbow. "It's a mess, but the artery and veins are intact. Not too much bleeding. He's good for an hour, probably two, even without a doctor."

"A tourniquet?" Trosper asked.

"We didn't use them too much unless there was arterial bleeding," Brodsky said. "I'll put a wet towel compress and as much ice as we have on the arm. That's the best I can do now."

"We leave in five minutes," Trosper said. He collected Golo's and Lukin's guns and slipped his own Browning back into the shoulder holster. He turned to Ida. She hadn't moved since Brodsky had led her to the chair. "We'll have to walk out of here and around the corner quite a way to Riley in the car. Are you okay for that?"

Ida nodded. Still dazed, she looked around the apartment. "Should I try to clean up a little?"

Trosper shook his head. "It's their problem now."

Ida hesitated. "I'm sorry about everything. I tried to do it right. Nothing seemed to work. I activated the thumper the minute I saw the big Russian come into the building. I was afraid it wouldn't work, so I followed him in. When he got upstairs, he just walked right in through the kitchen door. I didn't know what you wanted me to do . . ."

Trosper put his arm around her shoulder. "You did superbly. Nobody could have done it better. The thumper didn't begin to work until you got into the apartment—it's probably just as well." Behind the heavy glasses, Ida's eyes were red-rimmed and swollen. Her makeup was streaked, and her hair was mussed.

"When I thought he was going to shoot you, I shot to kill him."

Tears streamed down Ida's cheeks. "If you hadn't brought the pistol, I'd be dead," Trosper said. "We've only got a few minutes before we leave. The bathroom is all yours—quickly now."

He watched as Brodsky adjusted the cold compress. "There was damned little ice, but this will have to do."

Golo stirred, but did not attempt to move from the floor as Brodsky adjusted the pillow under his head. "We need blankets now, something to keep him warm as the shock develops . . ." He looked at Nash, holding a wet towel to his face. "Get off your ass and fetch the blankets."

As he covered Golo, Brodsky leaned close and spoke in Russian. "We're leaving in a few minutes. Your friends from the rezidentura

will be here within a quarter-hour. You'll be all right. Stay perfectly
still."

The Russian's face was the color of lead, his teeth chattering.

"You want vodka?" Brodsky put the bottle in Golo's left hand.
"Not too much . . ."

Trosper handed the telephone to Brodsky. "Your Russian is
best, you'll have to make this call."

Trosper caught fragments as Brodsky spoke rapidly in Russian.
"Two of your people . . . shot . . . no police . . . seriously wounded . . . immediate help . . . at your place off the Strudlhofgasse . . .
your doctor at once . . . Colonel Lukin . . . Leditsa . . ." He put the
phone down. "They got the message."

"It's time," Trosper said. He turned to Ida. "You okay?"

She nodded. Brodsdky took her arm.

Nash started to get his coat.

Trosper shook his head. "You're not going anywhere."

"I'm coming with you." Nash's shirt and tie were spotted with
blood.

"No, you're not." Trosper pulled on his coat.

"What the hell do you mean? Of course I'm going, I can't stay
here, these crazy bastards will kill me . . ."

"You're their creature," Trosper said. "You've served them well.
You've even joined them twice—in Geneva, and again last night.
Not many of their mercenaries can say that."

"You're as crazy as they are . . . I'm coming."

Trosper thought for a moment. "I'll do you one favor. As soon as
I can make a copy of the tape that's been running in the back room,
I'll mail it to you, in care of the Soviet embassy in Washington. It
will tell the whole story."

"I won't stay." Nash's nose started to bleed again.

"You'll be better off here." Trosper pulled on his hat. "Don't get
any ideas after we leave. Moe Riley will be on the street until he
sees your friends come in. There's nothing he'd like better than to
dissuade you from leaving."

Brodsky and Ida were at the door.

"There's one more thing," Trosper said. "Before your friends get here, stop whining and clean yourself up a little. First impressions are always important."

Trosper swung the car door open. "Let's move right along."

Brodsky helped Ida into the back seat.

Mozart Riley turned the ignition key.

Trosper slipped into the seat beside Riley and picked up the hand mike. "We're shoving off." He repeated the code phrases. "Shoving off."

"Loud and clear," Fuller replied from the safe apartment. The reception was scratchy, but Trosper caught the excitement in Fuller's voice. Fuller and Hamel had thirty minutes to get the luggage from the two safe apartments to the Mahlerstrasse behind the Bristol Hotel on the Ring.

"I've got to go right past the Strudlhofgasse," Riley said. "With this snow, I can't use the back street . . ."

"That's okay," Trosper said.

With only the parking lights, the small sedan moved slowly away from the curb.

As Riley turned into the Liechtensteinstrasse, heading for the First District, a black Fiat swerved across the intersection, and skidded toward the apartment building.

"Diplomatic plates," Trosper muttered as he strained toward the license. "They really are in a hurry." He pulled a yellow pad from the shelf below the dash, jotted down the number, then began to write. "Urgent. Eiderdown/Teak. Controller Only. 2030 hours. Regret inform you that in meeting with contact team in Soviet safe apartment, Colonel Lukin shot dead by his security escort Golo Leditsa. Escort seriously wounded. Contact team not harmed, proceeding directly Daisy by car. ETD Vienna 2200 hours. Catpan has remained with Moscow reps and will presumably defect . . ." He paused to consider the propriety of the improvised pseudonym he had just assigned to Nash, and then continued to scribble as Riley drove slowly along the snow-banked streets.

In the back seat Brodsky attempted to distract Ida with random comments on the Viennese. ". . . and the one expression you hear every day—*'Nur net hudeln'*—is just a slangy way of saying 'Above all don't hurry.' It's more or less the Vienna *Sinnspruch,* a sort of motto . . ."

41

WASHINGTON, D.C.

"DOES that about wrap it up?" Duff Whyte peered across his desk at Trosper and Castle. "If so, I'd like to have a word with Miss Rowan."

"Sorry, Duff, but I left Ida in London with Emily," Trosper said. "She's still a little shaken, and they seemed to hit it off." He took a sip of the pale coffee. "Toward the end, Vienna got to be rather trying—what with our Soviet hosts looking so damn tacky." He pushed the coffee aside. "Ida deserves a little R and R, and she wants to go on a diet."

Castle stopped working on the jagged ink design and looked up at Trosper. "I'm glad she did so well—we'd have missed you, Alan."

"I'll be briefing the Director in an hour," Whyte said. "Is there anything more I should know about your, er, unilateral decision on Nash?" Whyte smiled, "Or Catpan, as we've learned to call him?"

"He'd told Moscow everything he knew long ago—by leaving him behind we avoid a messy trial. Besides, I like the idea of Moscow Center having to take care of him while he contemplates the verities for the next few years."

"He'll be back," Castle said. "Not one of those *plouks* ever makes a go of it."

"If he comes back, you can still prosecute—he typed and signed his own confession the first morning in Geneva." Trosper had a question for Castle, but it could wait.

"What about Brodsky?" Duff Whyte began the ceremony of lighting his long, slim pipe.

"He's a more serious fellow than I first thought, but he played straight and came through in the pinch," Trosper said. "Through the years, he probably could have wriggled free of Lukin. If he'd had one serious case man on our side in the early years, it could have been different. The trouble was, our people accepted him at face value, and never made any effort to find what made him tick. We were getting on pretty well toward the end, but it was Ida who brought out the best in him. Still, it wasn't until the last night that he trusted us enough to give me a peek at his past."

Castle spoke to Whyte. "I want the cache of old reports he deposited in the Swiss bank." He stopped talking to add another touch to his design. "And I recommend we resettle him here. After Brodsky's interrogation is sorted out, and I learn a bit more about Zotov, I might be able to use him."

Whyte nodded, and turned to Trosper. "What about you? You look as if you could use a night's sleep."

It was late afternoon, and Trosper had come directly to the office from the Air Force's London red-eye. His suit was wrinkled, his shirt dingy, he needed a haircut and had deep circles under his eyes. He glanced enviously at Whyte's gray flannel, as immaculate and unwrinkled as if it had just been taken off the hanger. He rubbed his eyes. "I have a question," he said.

Whyte nodded. Castle continued inking his design.

"About Angelica Church . . . ?"

Whyte glanced at Castle.

"I've not been able to get it straight why you thought to send Teddy Vermont back to Florence at the exact time Angelica Church spotted Leditsa's surveillance," Trosper said.

Castle held his design at arm's length and studied it.

"And, I'm still not sure why Gandy and Frost first came under suspicion . . ."

Whyte remained silent, contemplating his pipe.

Castle looked up from his pad. "Do you remember the lectures at the Fort on agent control?"

Trosper did not feel obliged to answer.

Castle addressed himself to Whyte. "The lectures are dead wrong. They define a controlled agent as one who 'obeys' his case man . . . an unsophisticated, even primitive notion."

Trosper strained to hear Castle's whispered comments.

"We must learn to think of 'control' in the French sense. The French verb *'contrôler,'* to control, has another aspect. It assumes an overview, perhaps a lateral view. But above all, it demands an independent view of an activity . . ."

Castle glanced at Trosper and then turned to Whyte. "What I'm talking about goes back to Sun Tzu . . ."

"Tommy, for God's sake," Whyte said. "That was twenty-five hundred years ago. Alan asked a very simple question."

"Sun Tzu said there were five types of agent . . ."

"I know, I know," Whyte exclaimed. "And so does Alan . . ."

"He said that when these five types of spy are working simultaneously, and none knows of the other, it is called 'The Divine Skein.' "

Whyte leaned forward, elbows on the desk, his hands supporting his head. "Can we get back to Angelica Church?"

Castle added a tangent to his design and tore the page from the pad. He held it to the light for a moment and stuffed it into his pocket. "Frankly this has not been one of my best efforts."

Trosper wondered whether Castle was talking about his sketch or Angelica.

Castle pulled himself to his feet. "As I told you, Duff, I have a late meeting . . ."

Trosper started to speak. Whyte motioned him to silence.

"It is also worth remembering that Sun Tzu referred to The Divine Skein as the 'treasure of a sovereign.' " Castle screwed the top onto his fountain pen and wedged it into his breast pocket. "I'd like to go into this in depth, but these discussions always come down to epistemology, and that would involve more time than we have today."

Castle moved slowly across the room. As he reached the door, he stopped for a moment and raised his hand in salutation. "It was a good show, Alan," he said, and pulled the door shut behind him. A moment later, the handle moved. From the outside, Castle had made sure the door was tightly shut.

Whyte turned to Trosper. "All clear?"